A great friend
will become a
greater enemy...

THE ALIENS OF
LUCASFILM'S
ALIEN
CHRONICLES™

THE VIIS . . . A race of seven-foot tall, beautifully reptilian creatures. Their physical attractiveness has convinced the Viis that they are the most important, godlike creatures in the universe. This has led to an underground race of the "uglies"— Viis that were cast off as unacceptable, worthless spawn . . .

THE AAROUN . . . The race of Ampris are powerful, golden-furred carnivores with sharp teeth. They have long been kept by the Viis as slaves, or as in the case of Ampris, pets.

THE KELTH . . . A submissive, doglike race with stiff, bristly coats and simian hands. Because they are so easily intimidated, Kelth are considered unreliable to handle important tasks. They are not to be trusted . . .

THE MYAL . . . Renowned for their insight and memories, Myal stand barely three feet tall and are usually poets, musicians, and historians. They control the archives of the Viis empire.

THE ZHRELI . . . They are filthy, noisy, foul-smelling, and socially repulsive creatures. Yet they are unequaled at maintaining and repairing quantum hardware (the only reason to tolerate them).

THE SKEK . . . Less than two feet high, furry, multilimbed, and quick, the Skek live like rats in the ducts and garbage of the Viis. It's a common slave belief that if you dropped one Skek in a barrel, the barrel would explode with Skek offspring within a day.

Continued . . .

THE TOTHS . . . Big, stupid and brutal, Toths roam the ghetto streets as thugs, but they are also used by their Viis masters as hired enforcers and brownshirts. Nearly as tall as the Viis, they have massive heads covered with thick mats of dirty, curly brown hair. Flies usually buzz around their long, floppy ears. Their faces are broad and flat, with wide nostrils, and their eyes are small and cruel.

THE GORLICANS . . . Merchants, shopkeepers, traders, the Gorlicans are a steady, hardworking, nonviolent race allied to the Viis. A heavy shell encases their torsos, rendering their balance sometimes precarious, and their arms and legs are covered with thick gray scales instead of skin. Their faces are ugly, with a prominent horned beak for an upper lip, and they have orange and yellow eyes. They must wear masks in public to avoid offending the Viis.

THE PHIVEANS . . . They are cephalopods and have thick, elongated bodies supported on four stout legs. Their tails are flat and spade-shaped. Smooth-skinned and entirely hairless, male Phiveans are olive-green in color. Females are a yellowish pink. They have numerous tentacles lining their bodies on either side. The two front tentacles are longer than the others and have pod-shaped tips of considerable dexterity. Their heads are bulbous, with two knobby, prominent eyes. Their mouth is a round opening lined with waving cilia. Phiveans are never completely still. Either their tentacles, eyes, or mouth cilia are constantly moving.

THE SAMPARESE . . . These creatures are tall with long, graceful bodies. Their heads are wedge-shaped with cold, cruel eyes, blunt muzzles with whiskers, and razor-sharp fangs. They have muscular, sinuous necks. Extremely graceful in motion, they are lithe, fluid fighters. Their fur is short and sleek, in the tawny range of colors. Their temperament is quite fierce. They are loners by nature. Intelligent but undomesticated, they are used only as gladiators by their Viis owners.

LUCASFILM'S ALIEN CHRONICLES

THE CRIMSON CLAW

Lucasfilm's Alien Chronicles™ *by Deborah Chester*

THE GOLDEN ONE
THE CRIMSON CLAW

LUCASFILM'S ALIEN CHRONICLES

THE CRIMSON CLAW

Deborah Chester

ACE BOOKS, NEW YORK

LUCASFILM'S ALIEN CHRONICLES™: THE CRIMSON CLAW

An Ace Book / published by arrangement with
Lucasfilm Ltd.

PRINTING HISTORY
Ace edition / October 1998

All rights reserved.
Trademark™ and Copyright © 1998 by Lucasfilm Ltd. Used under authorization.
This book may not be reproduced in whole
or in part, by mimeograph or any other means,
without permission. For information address:
The Berkley Publishing Group, a member of Penguin Putnam Inc.,
375 Hudson Street, New York, NY 10014.

The Penguin Putnam Inc. World Wide Web site address is
http://www.penguinputnam.com

Check out the Ace Science Fiction/Fantasy
newsletter, and much more, at Club PPI!

Visit the Alien Chronicles Web site at http://www.lucasaliens.com

ISBN: 0-441-00565-9

ACE®
Ace Books are published by The Berkley Publishing Group, a member
of Penguin Putnam Inc.,
375 Hudson Street, New York, NY 10014.
ACE and the "A" design are trademarks
belonging to Charter Communications, Inc.

PRINTED IN THE UNITED STATES OF AMERICA

10 9 8 7 6 5 4 3 2 1

CHAPTER ONE

The smell of blood, sweat, and aggression filled the arena—
a hot, primitive smell that made the fur bristle around Ampris's neck beneath her battle collar. Feeling anticipation
coil tighter in her belly, she growled low in her throat.
Soon, she promised herself as she watched the two Kelth
opponents circling each other with sly hesitation on the
kicked-up sand. A male and female, they were well-
matched in size. Both gray-furred with slim, long muzzles
and tall upright ears, they yipped insults at each other. The
female darted at the male, stabbing with her glaudoon, the
short sword of the gladiator games. The male yelped and
stumbled back. Blood splattered on the sand, and the trainees in the stands roared with excitement.

Ampris panted. Soon she would be out there, fighting.
She growled again, leaning forward inside her starting gate,
her gaze intent on the combat.

In the other cramped gate next to hers, her opponent-to-
be shifted restlessly, muttering and growling. Something
thudded against the scarred wooden door that closed the
back of her gate, and Ampris whirled around with a roar.

Rapid thumping and a yelp told her that more graduates
were being loaded into the chute that fed into her gate.
Ampris ignored the commotion and turned her attention
back to the fighting in the arena. Boos came now from the

crowd. The Kelths were still circling, neither willing to commit to close fighting unless victory was sure. A referrent strode up to them and cracked his whip across the male's back.

Yelping, the Kelth male dropped to his knees. The referrent, encased in body shielding and closed helmet, mercilessly whipped the female, hitting her hard enough to make her stagger. "Fight, damn you!" he shouted.

The Kelths attacked each other with new vigor that set the crowd cheering again.

Backing her ears, Ampris snarled to herself with renewed determination. She would need no whipping to make her fight.

A hand snaked through the slats of her gate and claws raked at her arm. Ampris whipped her head around with a snap of her teeth, but quick as thought, the hand vanished back into the adjoining gate. Laughter rumbled from behind the slats, then a pair of hostile yellow eyes appeared.

Ampris recognized Sheir, her bunk-mate but no friend. They had been paired together since their first day of training. Never, in all the intervening months of rigorous drill and practice, had Ampris been able to relax her guard completely, knowing Sheir was just waiting for the chance to pounce. They were both Aaroun females, and of similar age and size—yet they had nothing in common, nothing except the desire to survive this hellhole that was Bizsi Mo'ad.

Beige-furred with an even sprinkling of tiny brown spots and a brown streak that ran up her nose and over the top of her skull, Sheir was no beauty. She had nicks and old scars that marred her hide, and she was missing one toe. But her stamina never gave out. She was heavy-boned, with plenty of powerful muscle. Sheir's teeth were sharp; her claws were sharper. Quick and cunning, she never lost an opportunity to trip Ampris, to jostle her, to throw dust in her food, to mess up her bunk just before inspection.

In hand-to-hand fighting drills, she always volunteered to oppose Ampris. She was a dirty fighter, snapping at tender ears and trying to gouge eyes with her fingers. She never obeyed the *halt* command; the instructors always had to pull them apart. A ruthless cheat at everything, Sheir would probably enjoy a long, successful career as a gladiator.

Fighting outside the practice arena was forbidden, yet twice Ampris had gone to the whipping post for losing her temper and retaliating against Sheir's constant provocations. After a long day of relentless drills, punishments, screaming instructors, and harsh discipline, Ampris would stretch out on her bunk to rest her aching muscles. But always there was Sheir lying in the bunk above her, humming softly in her throat while she dangled one foot over the side. It was a constant temptation to lunge for it, to bite through her heel tendon and cripple her.

The punishment for such an attack was death, but sometimes as Ampris lay there, burning with dislike, she told herself it would almost be worth it. Every night they played the same contest of seeing who would be the first to drop into sleep. If Ampris could not battle her fatigue enough to outlast Sheir, she paid for it with a sharp nip to her ear or shoulder, a swift rake of claws that Ampris had to fend off before Sheir bounded back into her bunk. If Ampris was not the first to awaken at the dawning before the whistle sounded, the same thing happened.

No one in authority intervened, as long as Ampris and Sheir stayed within the rules. After all, the trainees weren't supposed to make friendships. Once graduation day came and their training ended at the Bizsi Mo'ad, they would be sold as professionals expected to kill each other in the arenas.

Now graduation day was finally here, and blood smell filled the air. Ampris inhaled it with a quiver of her nostrils. A month ago she had asked permission to be trained to stay here as an instructor. She did not want to spend the rest of her life killing others for the sport of her masters. She'd heard the grim tales of life in the arena circuit, how tough it was, how cruel.

High in the spectator seats today, buying agents were watching the graduation combats, making their own evaluations separate from those of the school's judge. Cams, marked with the crest or colors of their owners, floated above the arena, taping the competition for absentee bidders who would participate in the auction via linkup.

The only way around this fate was to be withdrawn from the auction for further training as a school instructor. As a life, it would not be much . . . years spent in this dreary compound, where there was no art, no music, no kindness. The Bizsi Mo'ad, once a training camp for officers at the apex of the Viis empire's conquest years, now trained warriors of entertainment owned by the gambling-mad Viis aristocracy. This facility knew nothing beautiful, or tender, or true. To live here meant years spent in the clang of practice weapons, in the shouting, in the harsh, unyielding discipline. Not much of a life at all, yet it would *be* a life.

Not the death sentence handed to each graduate that went into the auction, and thereafter into the ring.

Ampris loved to fight. Yes, she found it to be an addiction, that sweet yielding to the rage and savagery inside her. But as much as she loved to fight, she wanted to live more.

Nothing had come of her request. And now she stood in the starting gate, waiting to be decanted into the arena. She and Sheir would fight to the death unless the referents pulled them apart in time.

They weren't supposed to kill each other in the arena final, of course. Above all else, the Bizsi Mo'ad centered itself around profit. The more trained, healthy graduates it could put into its empire-famous auctions, the more money it made. Therefore, the combat referents prowled around the perimeter of the ring with nets and stun-sticks in hand, ready to intervene if today's combat turned deadly. But

Ampris knew she could not hold back, or Sheir would tear her apart.

Now, locked in her gate, Ampris glared into Sheir's yellow eyes and growled in warning.

Sheir curled her lips back from her teeth and laughed low in her throat. "Soon," she called. "My score will be the highest in the school. I will bring much money at auction, going to the Blues or the Greens. You will lie dead on the sand, and they will throw your bones to the carrion eaters."

"Boasts do not draw blood," Ampris replied softly, determination heavy in every word. "You won't beat me."

Sheir didn't listen. "I will sink my teeth into your soft throat before any referrent can stop me. I taste your blood already."

She was using the conditioning words, although she was unskilled and lacked the modulator device used by their trainers. Still, Ampris felt the savage element inside her stir in response. She flattened her ears to her skull and turned her gaze away, trying not to listen.

"Coward!" Sheir called. She stuck her hand through the slats and extended her strong claws. "I will feast on your heart—"

"You will bite air," Ampris retorted. "You cannot match my quickness."

"What's the matter, golden one?" Sheir asked, her voice like oil, yet mocking and bitter at the same time. "Do you fear me? Do you worry that I will slit that pretty hide of yours?"

Ampris bared her teeth. But she said nothing, knowing that Sheir would keep this pointless argument going on forever. Sheir hoped to appear so aggressive, so dangerous that she would be sold privately for a high price. According to the rumors, the more money a gladiator sold for, the better he or she was treated. Or maybe Sheir was building her battle courage with her boasting. Ampris, with one kill already in her past, knew such courage was false.

Out in the arena, a howl of agony filled the air.

Both Ampris and Sheir lunged at the front of their gates, crashing against them with twin roars of excitement. Ampris saw the male Kelth thrashing in agony on the sand while blood spurted from a gash in his side. The referrents closed in with nets and stun-sticks ready, but the victorious female was strutting back and forth, brandishing her blood-stained glaudoon high in the air. Throwing up her slim, pointed muzzle, she yipped shrilly.

The spectators up in the metal seats ringing the arena jumped to their feet, shouting and banging on the benches until the air rang with noise.

"Blood," Sheir said, panting heavily. She groaned from within her gate. "The smell of it . . . oh, the sweet smell."

Ampris backed her ears and forced her gaze away, even as she felt the trained savagery inside her awakening, coming more fully alive. She knew she must draw on all her strength, all her courage, and find the blood fury. It was always there, seething hot beneath the control she kept clamped on it.

Sheir was throwing herself against the gate, howling like something mad.

Medics came running to clear the mess.

The Viis mediator stood nearby, towering head and shoulders above the abiru workers. Green-skinned with blue markings on his throat that spread up to bracket his eyes, he puffed out his air sacs while he made his evaluation. He spoke his decision into his hand-link, and the score flashed across the board hanging over one end of the arena.

Ampris stared at it, watching the names and scores shift and waver until the new ranking had been established. Someone at the end of today would be school champion, and that someone would sell tomorrow to the highest bidder in the annual auction. The rest of them would then go on the block, with their scores affecting how the floor bids would be set.

When she first came here, cabled in restraints and panting

in terror, she had not believed she would survive. Only her anger had kept her going. The first practice drill had left her collapsed on the sand, her muscles cramping. The first kick to her ribs had brought her staggering upright with her vision blurred by tears, her heart thundering in her chest, her fur bristling around her neck. Terrified, she knew that if she didn't learn, didn't excel, didn't find her inner strength she wouldn't last the first week. She knew she couldn't give up. She couldn't let betrayal by those she had most loved and trusted destroy her.

And she hadn't. She was a survivor of the toughest training program in the empire.

The wounded Kelth was dragged out of the arena, while slaves raked the sand. Medics pushed his floating stretcher past the starting gates, arguing with each other as to how to best conceal the sutures so he could go into the open auction tomorrow afternoon—the sale for the failures, when the Bizsi Mo'ad cut its losses ruthlessly.

A warning bell rang overhead, and a handler came running along the catwalk above the starting gates. Ampris drew herself erect, flexing her muscles in readiness. She found it suddenly hard to breathe. Her heart was pounding.

"Ampris!" Sheir shouted. "It is time!"

Ampris said nothing. She closed her eyes and tried to master her ragged breathing. She tried not to listen to the anger drumming inside her heart. Oh, yes, she was ready to fight Sheir. She wanted to claw and rend and bite. She wanted to take a glaudoon and thrust it through Sheir's vitals, paying back every taunt, trick, and cruel act. But she knew she must remain in control of herself. She would fight with a bold heart and a cool head, remembering her training, using skill and knowledge. If she didn't, Sheir would maul her badly.

Not for the first time Ampris wished she knew the old religion of her people. What were the Aaroun prayers? Who were the Aaroun gods? She knew only the panoply of Viis deities, all unavailable to her.

The gate opened with a snap that startled her. Ampris ran out into the deep sand, stumbling slightly as it caught her feet. A handler seized her on one side and unfastened the buckles to her battle harness. Another released the catch on her battle collar.

Astonished, Ampris twisted in their hands. "What are you doing?"

It was forbidden to speak to a handler. One of them slapped her across the muzzle. "Silence!"

Pulling the harness and collar off her, they gave her a shove that sent her staggering on into the openness of the arena. Another handler ran after her and pressed a glaudoon into her hand.

Ampris took it absently, looking behind her. Despite her puzzlement, she knew the drill: Run from the gate into the center of the arena as fast as possible. Turn and get set to meet your opponent.

But she heard no bell, heard no second gate slam. She looked behind her again, and still Sheir's gate did not open.

Ampris backed her ears, trying to understand what was happening. Why had the handlers stripped her? Instead of switching on the modulator on her battle collar so that the conditioning words would activate her training, she was entirely on her own.

Anger flared inside her. This wasn't fair.

Then she realized she wouldn't have to battle the equipment for control of her emotions or her wits. She could keep her cool head. She could remember her own strategy instead of being driven artificially into bestial rage.

But where was Sheir? Ampris could hear the other Aaroun screaming and slamming herself around inside her gate. Why hadn't they turned her out?

"Run, you fool!" a handler shouted at her. "Get to the center and look like you know what you're doing. The judge is watching!"

Collecting her wits, Ampris turned and did as she was told.

She had confused impressions of sound—great tides of it washing over her as the crowd shouted. They weren't cheering for her, she knew. They were cheering for combat, for blood. She felt dwarfed by the arena, arching up high, high over her. The spectators themselves, a mixture of trainees, instructors, buyers, and the merely curious, were a blur surrounding her on all sides. The cams hovering overhead floated lower to record her.

She reached the center of the arena and stood awkwardly, feeling increasingly ill-at-ease and nervous.

The scoreboard changed colors, shimmering as names and scores were abruptly canceled. As they vanished and a blank red screen glowed in their place, Ampris stared up at it and backed her ears in alarm.

What did this mean? Why weren't her name and number on the board? Wasn't she going to be scored at all?

A fresh roar from the spectators made her look up swiftly, expecting to see Sheir coming at last. Instead, she saw the judge and referrents leaving the arena, the latter dragging their nets with them.

The blood drained from Ampris's head. She stared, unwilling to believe what their departure meant.

The loudspeaker boomed, bringing quiet to the stands.

"Scoring is halted," the announcement came. "Combat is challenge by trainee One-one-A to instructor. Open rules."

Cheers swelled up from the trainees in the stands. The announcement, however, had been made for the buying agents, some of whom were craning their necks and murmuring to each other. Some tossed down their refreshments and moved intently to the edge of their seats. Others spoke hurriedly into their hand-links.

Ampris stared with her mouth open, unable to believe her ears. Her request hadn't been denied after all. But which instructor was she to fight?

That mattered less than the fact that the combat was to be held under open rules. Suddenly she understood all too clearly what the red scoreboard and departing referrents meant. This was to be a real competition, a real battle, with no team of referrents to save her once she was pinned or struck down.

This was to be a fight to the death . . . and if fortune did not suddenly smile on her, it would be *her* death.

Ampris's courage deserted her. What insanity was this? In seeking to avoid dying in an arena, she had brought about that very situation. And even sooner than she might otherwise have had to face it.

Her heart froze in her chest. Her legs lost their strength, and she barely kept herself from sinking to the sand. She wanted to run, but all the gates were closed and guards stood everywhere.

From the holding pen came a ragged, savage cheer. "Ampris!" the graduates called her name. She saw several of them holding their fists aloft and snarling. *"Saa-vel harh!"*

Ampris swallowed hard. Saa-vel harh meant to draw first blood. It was both a war cry and a wish for victory. They were cheering for her, giving her their support.

Her heart started thumping again. She drew in a full breath. Never mind that her heart was beating too fast, or that her mind was racing, or that her grip felt awkward and slippery on her glaudoon. They had wished her victory, these comrades who were not supposed to be friends.

A sudden hush dropped over the crowd, warning her even as she saw the gate open that her wait had ended. Ampris backed her ears and held her breath, straining to see who it was.

The instructor who came striding out was Mobar, a male Aaroun of middle-years, at the peak of his physical prowess. He was the gruffest, most demanding, most short-tempered of the instructors, the perfectionist she could never satisfy. Heavy-shouldered and short-necked, he crossed the arena as though he owned it. Gray silvered his shoulders and chest, but his muscles were thick and strong, and his stride sure. For the first time, Ampris understood what it was like to face an arena veteran, to see the confidence, the economical movements, the dangerous intensity all radiating from an individual who intended to kill her.

As he drew near, his dark brown eyes glared at her intently, already sizing her up as prey. He swung his weapon in the air. To her horror, Ampris saw that it was a glevritar, longer than her utilitarian glaudoon, its blade curved, serrated, and gleaming bright under the artificial lights. Her courage sank inside her. She wanted to flee, to call out to the judge for mercy, to retract her stupid request. What had ever made her think she could take on an instructor?

But there was no more time to wonder, no more time to fear. Mobar was now holding his glevritar in attack grip. Crouching low, he shifted into a run, closing the final meters between them with a speed and agility she hadn't expected.

Swiftly Ampris pulled herself together, realizing that to stand there flat-footed and staring was the stupidest mistake she could possibly make. From the very first day of training she had been told to keep moving, to stay in constant motion, to never stand still.

But although she shifted her feet, it was only to retreat before his advance. She realized she was expecting him to stop and launch into one of his dry, terse lectures. Mobar's training sessions were filled with dull, repetitive moves. Over and over he forced trainees to work on footwork and correct swing techniques. He was capable of working them at a single move all day, while he screamed criticisms. Ruthless, bitter, and exacting, he had often put Ampris and others through hours of rigorous calisthenics until their tongues were lolling in distress and their muscles burned like fire.

Ampris retreated again, scrambling away from him and bringing jeers from the stands. Low score, she thought automatically, then grew angry at herself.

There was no score. There was only life or death. She

had to remember that, had to get herself together.

Furiously, she shifted her stance, settling her weight on her back foot, reminding herself yet again that Mobar wasn't going to stop. She met his eyes, and saw a stranger there—one calculating the swiftest, most efficient way to disembowel her.

He reached her, the glevritar swinging high in the air with a flash of light down its blade. Ampris willed her muscles to respond, to swing up her glaudoon and meet his attack.

Instead, a sheet of fear dropped through her. She panted, finding her lungs suddenly unable to draw enough air. Instead of parrying his weapon, she dodged the blow— ducked it like a coward before she could stop herself.

Boos and jeers came from the stands. But they were nothing compared with the scorn and contempt Ampris felt for herself. Backing her ears in raw humiliation, she shifted her feet again, darting in recklessly under his guard and slashing with all her might.

Her glaudoon cut him between ribs and hip, shocking Ampris but astounding Mobar more. With widened eyes, he roared in pain and knocked her weapon aside, giving himself time to spin out of reach.

Stumbling in the deep sand as he knocked her off balance, Ampris twisted around to face him and brought her glaudoon up in readiness as she'd been taught.

Her fear vanished, and suddenly she could think again. It was as though time slowed around her, and she understood his strategy perfectly. He had counted on her fear, had expected her to stand there frozen before his initial attack. He had intended to rush her, grab her, and finish her with one swift thrust. His attack had been swift and terrifying, but sloppy, as evidenced by his failure to guard his own flank. He hadn't expected her to attack him in return.

Luck had given her this chance to draw first blood. But as Ampris met his furious gaze, she knew she could not depend on luck again. She had to fight as she never had before. She could afford no more mistakes.

Up in the stands, the crowd was banging on the benches more loudly than ever, but that noise hardly came through the roaring in Ampris's ears. Her mind had shifted into another dimension. She was intently focused, weighing and discarding options rapidly. She realized that while blood now stained the blade of her glaudoon, she had not struck a killing blow. Failing to strike with lethal force was a mistake that opened the door to defeat. Oh, yes, she had heard that often enough. Now she knew that it was true. Too many mistakes had been made already, but she was learning fast.

In the distance she heard cheers and the words *"Saa-vel harh!"*

Ampris bared her teeth in satisfaction. First blood dripped from her sword, not his.

The momentary astonishment that had flared in Mobar's dark eyes was already gone. He roared and attacked again.

Ampris roared back and met him halfway, parrying his glevritar with her stout glaudoon. The weapons clanged loudly together, and Mobar bared his teeth as he tried to force her sword down with his own brute strength. Ampris resisted as long as she could, feeling her muscles strain with the effort, then she suddenly dropped her weapon, twisted it away from his, and tried to feint.

He knew the trick, of course. He had taught it to her. He met the feint with a swift parry that nearly knocked her weapon from her hand.

Ampris shifted back from his reach, aware that she couldn't last long against such a master in direct swordplay. Again she read his eyes, trying to come up with a strategy of her own.

She darted around him, forcing him to turn with her to protect his back. She knew she was faster than he, more agile. She was also younger, and she wasn't losing blood.

With calculation, she eyed the blood matting his fur and

trickling down his leg. She had caught him low, below the ribs, where every movement and flex of his body would pull at the wound, bringing him pain, bringing him more loss of blood.

The smell of it, hot and fresh, excited her. She inhaled, using it to awaken her courage. Then she ducked her head and somersaulted at his feet, slicing at his unprotected lower body as she came out of the roll. He leaped aside, evading her, but as he landed he staggered.

Ampris bared her teeth. She knew what to do now. Keep him moving. Keep him off center. Keep him bleeding. She could wear him down, until he grew too weak to fight.

But that was the easy way. Even if the scoreboard wasn't posting her points, she knew the instructors were all watching intently. The crowd might be fooled, but the instructors would know the difference. If she was to earn a place among their ranks, she knew, she must fight with skill and courage. She must bring Mobar down decisively.

Their weapons crossed again, clanging in a swift attack, counterattack rhythm that made her blood sing in her veins. For a moment they were perfectly matched. Nothing he did surprised her. He could not move faster than she. She met him for the first time as an equal. His blade and hers danced in exhilaration. She was his best pupil. He was her most respected instructor. She had mastered everything he taught her, and she displayed that skill now, feeling her arm muscles burn in a good way. It was a signal of fatigue, but she was not yet tired. She rode the wave of adrenaline and knew a flare of sheer joy that made her roar aloud.

Then Mobar attacked her in a three-part feint, feint, parry move that caught her by surprise. Unable to follow it and furious at him for using a trick he hadn't taught her, Ampris realized he had been only toying with her until now, tiring her arm in that lengthy exchange. Now he was leaving her behind with this dazzling trick. But Ampris refused to follow a second feint and came straight at him in an attack of her own that left her guard wide open.

Baring her teeth and roaring, she swarmed him, breaking under his guard and hitting his chest with her shoulder.

He fell beneath her, but rolled before she could pin him and grip his throat. His sword edge raked across her thigh, and she felt a sting of pain so fierce it robbed her of breath.

His blade smacked hers hard and twisted her glaudoon right out of her grip. The weapon went flying, to land out of reach on the sand.

Again the crowd jumped to its feet, shouting and cheering.

Desperate, Ampris flung herself toward her glaudoon, but Mobar held her back. They rolled over, grappling together in the sand, too close now for him to use his long glevritar. Had this been the professional arena, of course, they would have been carrying a multitude of weapons.

Ampris felt his fingers twist her ear, then gouge at her eye. She turned her head aside quickly enough that his blow jabbed harmlessly into her cheekbone, then she snapped savagely at his thumb.

Her teeth crunched on bone, tissue, and sinew. Mobar screamed and flailed beneath her. His fist, still wrapped around his sword hilt, crashed into her face, but Ampris did not let go. He rolled her over, pinning her beneath his heavy weight, and pressed his forearm across her throat to choke her.

Growling, she twisted her head, and tore off his thumb. Blood spurted across her jaw, and Mobar reeled back. In that moment, Ampris sat up and knocked him off her.

Sprawling in the sand, Mobar gathered himself in an instant. He surged up to meet her, slinging blood, his teeth bared, his eyes enraged.

Ampris jumped to her feet, staggered as the pain in her thigh threw her momentarily off balance, and barely managed to duck his whistling glevritar. Again she rolled in a somersault, and this time she kicked his feet out from under him.

He fell hard, with a muffled grunt. Ampris whirled to

get her glaudoon, still lying in the kicked-up sand, but Mobar managed to snag her ankle and pull her down. She landed awkwardly and painfully on her side and found herself being dragged toward his sword point.

Snarling, Ampris kicked him in the face, knocking him back. She got free and scrambled for her glaudoon. Behind her, Mobar reared up on his knees and swung his glevritar. Glimpsing this from the corner of her eye, Ampris launched herself desperately at her glaudoon. She expected him to cleave her in half, but her quickness saved her. She felt a glancing blow across the back of her ribs, but she twisted desperately and gripped her glaudoon. Rolling onto her back, she brought the weapon up and around desperately, just as Mobar roared in victory and flung himself at her.

Ampris rose partially to meet him, and her short, straight blade plunged deep into his chest.

His momentum carried him onto the blade, and his eyes flared wide in brief astonishment. Then he landed on top of her, and the jolt drove her glaudoon's point out through his back.

Pinned beneath him, with the breath crushed from her, Ampris lay there stunned a moment, wondering if she also had taken a mortal blow.

When Mobar did not move, she backed her ears and heaved him off.

He sprawled there, his blood thick and wet around the glaudoon haft protruding from his chest.

Panting hard, dizzy from lack of oxygen, Ampris realized the combat was over.

She staggered upright, nearly fell, and finally gained her feet.

Mobar lay still, canted awkwardly on his side with the glaudoon through him, her opponent no longer. Ampris stared down at him, seeing his eyes dulled and fading, seeing the thick blood smearing his fur. It covered her as well, his blood. She could smell it, was drowning in it.

For a moment the arena spun around her, then a hard grip on her arm brought her back to reality.

She blinked and focused, saw the harsh gaze of a handler on her. He buckled her collar back around her neck while a referrent ran up to them. The medics came hard on his heels.

"The blood on you," the handler was saying to her. "Yours or his?"

Only then did Ampris finally comprehend that she had won. She had actually defeated one of the best instructors of the Bizsi Mo'ad. She had drawn blood. She had spilled her opponent's blood—was spilling her own now.

Aching all over, she watched the judge stride out to make his evaluation. He barely looked at her, his Viis eyes cold and remote. "How much of the blood on you is yours?" he asked her.

Ampris pulled her shoulders back and lifted her head with pride. She was still panting from her exertions, but she had done what she set herself to do and nothing mattered except that. "I have a thigh cut," she said. "A scratch across my back. The rest is his."

Still, the judge insisted the medics prod her chest for evidence of wounds. They found none. Flicking out his tongue, the judge turned away from her.

Now, at last, she could hear the crowd cheering. Over and over they chanted her name: "Ampris! Ampris! Ampris!"

She panted, lifting her head to look at them. She could not see individual faces. They seemed both close and far away. She felt dizzy still, unable to get enough air in her lungs. Her muscles trembled and burned, but she was the victor.

As the handler took the glaudoon away from her, he gave her a tap on the shoulder.

"Claim your victory," he said.

Ampris lifted her arms to the crowd in the victory salute she had been taught.

They cheered her more. In the professional ring, the crowd would have showed her with coins, flowers, and torn-up betting tickets.

Today, this was good enough.

She felt numb, unsure of herself, almost detached from her surroundings. Although she watched the medics load Mobar's body onto a floating stretcher, she still found it hard to believe that he was dead.

Ampris touched the amulet hanging around her neck. It's over, she told herself, clinging to relief when she could find no other emotion. Finally, it was over. Now she could start a new life, filling Mobar's position here at the school.

Overhead, the cams floated even closer, hovering almost on top of her. At the far end of the arena, the scoreboard flashed to life. Suddenly her name and identification number were posted on it, along with the highest score of the day.

Pride filled Ampris. She was school champion. She had done the impossible. No one else who fought today after her would match this achievement.

"I did it," she whispered, grinning as she jogged out of the arena.

As she passed the starting gates, Sheir rattled the panels of hers violently. "It's not over!" she shouted. "I will meet you in combat yet!"

Ampris didn't even bother to look Sheir's way. She and Sheir now belonged to different worlds. She had a feeling that never again would their paths cross.

Leaving the arena, Ampris was hustled swiftly past the chute containing the waiting graduates. Their faces held awe and admiration.

"Ampris! Victory!" they cheered to her.

She smiled at them and waved, buoyed now with what could not be happiness, yet came close.

Ahead of her, the medics pushed Mobar's stretcher. As they all filed into the dank confines of the locker rooms, Ampris saw Mobar's body placed inside a room and left there. No one wailed in grief. No one would. It was the way of the Bizsi Mo'ad. One lived or one died. There was no middle ground.

Only now, as Ampris sagged onto a battered wooden bench and allowed herself to surrender to her aches, did she acknowledge inwardly that she had killed a fellow Aaroun, one of her own kind. She tried to crush the guilt that swelled through her. No matter how she wished Mobar had been a Viis—for she longed to kill them as the oppressors of her people—Mobar had only been a slave under the orders of his master, as was she.

Ampris felt regret, but she would not grieve. This was survival.

Mobar's death meant she would never have to kill again. Right then, sore and aching and weary to her bones, she knew it was worth the price.

The door to the locker room burst open, and Cosvik—head administrator of the school—came in with a medic.

Ampris swallowed and dragged herself respectfully to her feet.

Cosvik was Viis, very tall, very thin. Well into his lunadult cycle of life, meaning he could no longer fertilize eggs, he showed a gray tinge in the skin beneath his jaws and beneath his eyes. They were a bright, harsh shade of red, and his face had no variegated shadings of color. His rill was small, with blunted spines. Ampris suspected that Cosvik had barely escaped being classified as a Reject—those Viis deemed at birth to be too ugly for inclusion in normal society.

She had seen Cosvik only twice before, and never this close. He rarely inspected the lowly trainees. He never spoke to them, any of them. He stayed in his office as a rule, and was usually only glimpsed crossing the grounds of the school compound on his way to his quarters.

The fact that he had come to her now, here in the locker room, told Ampris that her reward was at hand. This was an incredible honor.

She drew herself erect, feeling new pride ease her soreness, and bowed to him with all the finesse and grace instilled in her during her years at the palace of the Kaa.

Cosvik flicked out his tongue but otherwise did not acknowledge her. He gestured to the medic accompanying him. "Examine her quickly. What injuries does she have?"

Ampris said eagerly, "Only a cut—"

"Silence!" the medic snapped at her, and Ampris fell quiet.

Inside she raged at herself for forgetting the rules yet again. It seemed she would never learn to hold her tongue. But from birth she was indulged as the pet and companion of the sri-Kaa, encouraged to speak Viis against all rules of society, allowed to voice her opinions, expected to participate intelligently in conversations. That old habit continued to be impossible to break, although she did try.

As an instructor here, she would have to remember. She could not afford to offend Cosvik from the very start.

Also Viis, the medic scanned her with his instruments. He constantly glanced at Cosvik, seemingly more concerned about his employer than his patient. But his long-fingered hands were deft and sure as he went about his business. When he applied a bandage to her thigh, the medicine inside it soothed her pain immediately. He sprayed something across her back, and she straightened with relief.

"No serious injuries to report," the medic said. "Very healthy, very well-conditioned young female Aaroun adult. I can assure you that her pelt will heal with minimal scarring." As he spoke, he stroked his hand down Ampris's arm, making her shift with annoyance. "Beautiful-quality fur."

Cosvik lifted his rill in satisfaction and flicked out his tongue. His red eyes gleamed at her. "Most satisfactory," he said.

Basking in his approval, Ampris puffed out her chest but did not quite dare smile.

"Clean her up. Seal her cuts. Make her look presentable,'' Cosvik said. "I'll initiate the paperwork for the private sale. This is going to be a splendid coup for us." He glanced again at Ampris, who was staring at him in open-mouthed dismay. "Well done, graduate. Today, you've more than repaid the cost of acquiring and training you. Even the cost of replacing a most adequate instructor. Well done."

With another flick of his tongue, he turned away.

Horrified, unable to believe what she'd just heard, Ampris took a step after him. "But—"

The medic shoved her down on the bench hard enough to make her teeth jolt together. "Silence!" he snapped, his voice harsh with outrage. "You fool, be quiet or I shall have the handlers beat you."

Ampris barely heard his threat. She couldn't believe it. All her hopes were crumbling around her.

"But I am to stay here as an instructor," she said. "I was told—"

"Forget what you were told," the medic said without sympathy. "Anyone who fights as well as you *has* to be sold. You're going for a fortune, young Aaroun. Galard Stables is buying you. The Blues, the best privately owned gladiators in the empire. You should be proud of yourself."

But Ampris felt no pride at all. Her hopes, her dreams, her strategy had shattered yet again. She had killed Mobar for nothing. It would have been far better if she had defeated Sheir, and paid that braggart back for countless humiliations. Staring at her hands, Ampris clenched them slowly. When would she learn to stop trying? When would she ever give up and finally accept defeat? She had no will of her own in this life. She would never belong to herself. She would never be the master of her own fate. Again and again, the Viis plucked her from her path and threw her aside. And now she was going into the very thing she had most dreaded, had tried so hard to avoid.

Ampris sat there, while the medic finished his work, and battled to hold back her tears of defeat and bitterness.

CHAPTER TWO

Forty-seven days of spaceship travel, locked in a passenger cubicle since she was now too valuable to ride in a cargo pod, another seventeen days of quarantine to survive her inoculations and to pass customs, then a final transferal of deed and title on the shipping dock of a strange port city on a strange world called Fariance.

Ampris stood patiently in her restraint cables, ignoring the Bizsi Mo'ad handler who was finishing the last items of business with the Galard representative. Nothing they said or did was of interest to her. She stared at the odd sky overhead, noting that it was pale lavender with fluffy white clouds tinged a smoky blue shade underneath. A dim, hazy sun hung low in the afternoon sky.

The air was cool and crisp, like autumn descending into winter. Ampris shivered lightly beneath her fur, missing the hot sunshine of Viisymel already.

A tap on her shoulder pulled her from her thoughts.

"Pay attention," the Viis from Galard Stables said to her. He spoke the abiru patois rapidly.

Ampris glanced around and saw that the handler from Bizsi Mo'ad was gone. Not caring, she backed her ears. The school was behind her now. She must look ahead and adapt to this newest life.

"You are called Ampris," the Viis said. He did not inflect it as a question, yet he waited as though expecting an answer.

"Yes," Ampris replied. She kept her voice low and submissive, because she wore a restraint collar. He carried the transmitter on his belt now, she noticed.

"What is your age?"

Impatience jabbed her. Hadn't he examined her paperwork? All her statistics should be on the invoice in his hands, but she knew better than to say so. This interrogation was a test of some kind. The Viis always loved to play games with their slaves.

Swallowing a sigh, Ampris said, "I am seventeen in Aaroun years, fully adult in weight and height. I am vi-adult in Viis—"

He pressed the transmitter, and her collar jolted a quick burst of energy to her vocal cords, silencing her.

"Don't do that again," he said.

Ampris bowed her head at once in submission, although inside she battled feelings of rebellion. Why was it wrong for any member of the abiru folk to display intelligence? Why was it so forbidden to make comparisons between abiru and Viis? It wasn't as though any of the abiru races had much in common with their Viis masters. The Viis controlled everyone and everything. Why, then, were the Viis always so touchy, so defensive?

Were they afraid?

With sudden insight, she flicked up her gaze to study the Viis male before her.

He was not as tall as most males, but he had the fashionable proportions and gracefulness of movement considered so pleasing in the Viis. His rill folds lay thick and luxuriant over a tall collar of engraved brass. His pebble-textured skin was shaded in attractive hues of gold, bronze, and green. Large, intelligent yellow eyes stared at Ampris now without betraying emotion, still evaluating her, still measuring her.

He did not look afraid. He looked assured and competent.

Ampris told herself to forget her fanciful thoughts. This was no time to philosophize. She had to pay attention.

He flicked out his tongue. "At Galard, you will do as you are told. You will be respectful of your superiors at all times. You will train hard. You will fight successfully. Those are your duties. If you complete them well, you will be rewarded well. If you are lazy, insolent, or cause trouble, you will be punished. If you lose repeatedly in competition, you will be sold. Is this understood?"

He spoke clearly, yet without disdain. There seemed to be no arrogance in him; he addressed her as a rational being, not as a slave kept only to do his bidding. Ampris found herself liking him, although she immediately crushed such a feeling. Perhaps he was as decent as he seemed. Perhaps he would be a good master, but she did not know that yet.

"Yes," she answered. "I understand my duties."

"Good. You seem to be an intelligent Aaroun. That is in your favor. Are you willing to learn, Ampris?"

She backed her ears. "I know my drills—"

Seeing his eyes narrow, she stopped in mid-sentence.

Unsure how she had erred, she dared say nothing more. He stared at her in a silence that grew uncomfortable, and when next he spoke his tone was colder: "I have watched your training vids as well as your graduation combat at Bizsi Mo'ad. It was my suggestion to the school that you fight an instructor, and without the assistance of your conditioning modulator. You passed that test well enough."

Astonished, Ampris stared at him. Did he have that much influence? So much that he had only to make a request, and the school modified its combat evaluations to suit him?

But then, he did work with the famous Blues, the most successful gladiator team in the games.

"You show considerable promise," he said to her now. "But your training is only beginning. There is much still for you to learn."

Ampris met his eyes. "What I learn, I do not forget."

"Come then." He turned and lifted his hand in a wave. Ampris heard the engine of a transport start up in the distance.

Moments later, the craft rumbled up to them and halted, hovering above the ground. It was heavy and utilitarian, larger than the city transports she was used to seeing in Vir and Malraaket. Dark brown dust coated its undercarriage, partially obscuring the crest of its owner. She did not recognize the coat of arms and knew then that Lord Galard's estates and title were entirely colonial. He was not a member of the Twelve Houses. That meant his lineage would not be considered distinguished by Viisymel standards, and he would not be received at the imperial court. But with his obvious wealth, perhaps he did not care.

Ampris told herself she had no business judging her newest owner, whom she would probably never meet or see.

The Viis trainer now looked at Ampris again, as though weighing something. Then he said, "I am Halehl, chief trainer to Galard Stables."

Awed that she had been collected by someone so important, Ampris told herself she should have been more respectful. She bowed in silence.

He seemed pleased by her gesture of respect. "You have been trained in court manners, I see."

"Yes, Master Halehl."

"Very attractive. You were once the pet of the sri-Kaa, were you not?"

Ampris suddenly had to struggle to keep from snarling. "Yes."

"I thought so. Your provenance is muddled, but I recognized you from old newsvids. Well, pretty manners will not help you in the arena. You will have to be quick, well-trained, and savage. Is this understood?"

"Yes, Master Halehl."

He opened the cargo doors at the back of the transport. "Climb inside."

Ampris obeyed, her restraint cables making her clumsy,

and Halehl shut the doors behind her. She heard the security bolts engage with swift thuds, and her heart sank. At last she was here, ready to begin her new life as a killer. Halehl's decency only seemed to make things worse.

As soon as he climbed aboard, he spoke a soft, quick command to the Gorlican driver, and the transport lurched forward.

They were slow to clear the dock traffic and congestion, but once they finally headed down the streets of this city, very little traffic could be seen.

The avenues were broad and free of pollution, lined with stately villas spaced well apart. Shops stood clustered in their own separate districts. Tall trees with spindly trunks and strange puffs of foliage at their tops swayed lightly in the cold breeze. The air smelled metallic and clean—very foreign to her nostrils. She found herself missing the heat of Viisymel's arid plains, the bright sunshine, the slow turgid rivers that smelled of reeds and fish.

The transport crossed one canal flowing straight, narrow, and green between a row of tall buildings, but Ampris saw no other water. Buildings spread farther apart as they reached the outskirts, then they were heading into rural countryside. For nearly an hour the transport flew past rolling meadows bordered by thickets of undergrowth and tall trees. Ampris found it strange that they met no other traffic on the road. Saw no dwellings, passed no village clusters. This was an empty world, Ampris thought. From her old lessons, she knew that not all the colony worlds were heavily populated. Sometimes, the Viis established only a central port, with a governor, a military station, and little else to hold their claim on a planet. Ampris wondered what the native folk of Fariance were like. She had seen none yet. Perhaps there were none on this cold world with its muted colors and dim sun. Perhaps the Viis had long ago killed them all or deported them to work elsewhere in the empire.

To Ampris, this world seemed an unimportant place for

the most popular gladiator stable to be based.

The sun was sinking to the horizon by the time the transport passed through gates that were paneled with tall iron spears. Carved beasts of snarling fangs and extended claws stood atop the gateposts. Then they were winding along a lane bordered on both sides by heavy woods. The ground rose in a long sloping hill, and halfway up the woods stopped. Ampris saw a villa stretching across the crest of the hill.

In the murky remnants of sunshine, the building stood gray, square, and solid—its architectural lines unfamiliar to her. Towers flanked it, and at the rear she glimpsed a tall, solid wall enclosing a compound of some kind.

At the front, the house was aproned by elaborate gardens of low, clipped hedges planted in intricate patterns of knot and curlicue. Stone-paved walkways curled among the tiny hedges in pleasing patterns. But there were no flowers of any kind, no fragrance beyond that of tilled soil, shrubbery, and trees. Ampris sniffed, and found the garden a peculiar and unappealing vista.

The transport made its way around to the rear of the massive house—much larger up close than it had seemed from a distance—and lurched through a gate into an enclosed courtyard.

Once it parked on hover and Ampris was let out of the cargo hold, she stood quietly while her restraints were unlocked. Then she stretched fully, taking pleasure in unrestricted freedom of movement for the first time in too long.

From an upstairs window overlooking the courtyard, she saw movement and a glimmer of a face watching her. Then the watcher was gone, and Ampris wondered if she'd imagined it.

Halehl pointed at the upstairs windows rowed at regular intervals around the courtyard. "The fighters' quarters," he said. "Yours are at the end, over there." He pointed at a window, and Ampris found herself suddenly astonished.

"No barracks?" she blurted out before she could stop herself.

Halehl flicked out his tongue, and overlooked her transgression. "You are a professional now," he said, sounding amused. "Ah, Ruar," he said to someone approaching from behind her. "Come and get Ampris settled. We'll start her training tomorrow, but let her adjust to the climate and gravity for the rest of today. Take her around the training grounds. Let her sniff and look all she wants."

Ruar proved to be an elderly Myal with silvered fur and extremely short bowed legs. His mane was so sparse only a few strands floated around his face. His eyes were dark and rheumy, and he bowed to Halehl with a type of habitual anxiety not often seen in his kind.

"As the master says," he replied, bowing again. "And the evening meal?"

"No," Halehl said, puffing out his air sacs thoughtfully. "I think not just yet. Keep her isolated from the others. They'll meet her soon enough. I want to watch her train alone for a few days. Then we'll integrate her with the team."

Ruar glanced at Ampris as though she had just made his life harder. "They will want to see her," he objected, wringing his thin, bony hands. His prehensile tail was coiled tightly around one of his legs. "Master knows how Ylea is."

"Ylea will have to wait, just like the others," Halehl said firmly. "I don't want any turf fights. Is that understood? They will keep their distance until I allow the integration."

"As the master says," Ruar said with another bow.

Halehl flicked his fingers in dismissal, and Ruar gestured at Ampris.

"Come, come," he said.

She followed him beneath an arched overhang leading to a flight of stairs, but before they could climb them, a door slammed from above and footsteps came thudding down the stairs toward them.

An enormous female Aaroun, spotted in shades of brown and fawn, blocked their path. Garbed in loose, quilted trousers and a sleeveless vest, she was the biggest female Ampris had ever seen, with exaggerated muscle development that rippled beneath her glossy fur. Her neck and shoulders were massive, adding to the impression of sheer physical power. Despite that, her face was feminine, almost dainty, with long-lashed eyes tilted ever so slightly. Her ears were rounded and fringed with cream-colored fur on the tips. She flicked them back now, setting the ownership cartouche in her ear jingling.

Ampris noticed she wore much additional jewelry as well. Multiple necklaces hung around her neck. Rings glittered on every finger. Her claws were painted carmine, and she wore matching wrist cuffs of heavy gold.

Ampris could not help but stare at this creature. She had never seen a slave wear so much adornment before.

"Ruar," the Aaroun said in a silky, dangerous voice, "what kind of *ruvt* you bringing to our quarters?"

The word she spoke was an insult, very dirty. The fur bristled around Ampris's neck, and her lips curled back from her teeth.

Ruar glanced between them nervously, coiling and uncoiling his long tail as he did so. "Now, Ylea," he said in a placating voice, "don't cause trouble. The master says to stay away from this one for a while. You know the rules."

Ylea gripped Ruar's scrawny shoulder with her red-tipped fingers and moved him aside. Then she stepped right up in Ampris's face and sniffed the air.

This additional insult was worse than the word she'd called Ampris. Angered, Ampris fought to keep still, to keep from snarling openly. But now the hair was standing erect along her spine. She narrowed her eyes to slits and growled a low warning in her throat.

"Stop it. Stop it," Ruar said in alarm. He fumbled for

the transmitter at his belt and pushed it, sending a jolt into Ampris's throat.

She coughed and took an involuntary step back, furious with him for overreacting. This giantess wore a restraint collar too. Why wasn't he punishing *her*?

Ylea advanced on Ampris, crowding her again, giving her little pushes back into the courtyard. "You think you can just come here like princess, one of us from day first? You think you so golden, so pretty, we like you? You think you any kind of match for our team? Hah! You half our size, puny *ruvt*. You like weed, get snapped in half, in first combat."

Ampris felt dwarfed by Ylea's muscular bulk, but also sized her up in seconds and realized she was slow, almost ponderous, in the way she moved. Ampris could run rings around this behemoth, but she wasn't ready to betray that yet.

"I've already drawn my first blood," Ampris said proudly, refusing to back up again. She stood with Ylea towering over her, and held her ground. "I haven't been snapped in half yet."

Ylea's tilted eyes closed to slits. "First blood?" she repeated, then roared out a laugh. "*First?* One combat and you dare speak to me? Be silent—"

As she spoke, she raked her claws at Ampris's face, but Ampris moved in swift reflex to grip Ylea's wrist and hold it.

Surprise darted through Ylea's eyes before her face contorted with fury. She bared her teeth, roaring a challenge, and yanked her wrist free.

Ruar darted up and stepped between them. "Ylea, stop it!"

Ylea slapped him aside, sending him tumbling to the pavement, and leaped at Ampris in a body tackle that took her down.

It was like being landed on by a boulder. Ylea's weight drove most of the air from Ampris's lungs. She grappled desperately, trying to keep Ylea's snapping jaws from her throat.

A fang grazed her shoulder, and Ylea's claws dug in like spikes. But when a whipcrack sounded overhead, Ylea jerked back with a snarl.

"Get up!" It was Halehl's voice, deep with anger. He cracked the whip across Ylea's broad shoulders a second time, cutting a gash in her vest. "Get up and form ranks. *Now!*"

Ylea scrambled to obey him, and quickly stood with her shoulders hunched and her eyes sullen.

With his rill crimson and at full extension behind his head, Halehl paced in a circle around Ylea. His eyes were blazing, and even his heavy tail was switching back and forth beneath the long skirt of his coat. Without warning, he lashed her with his whip a third time.

Ylea flinched but made no sound. One of her necklaces, broken by the lash, fell in a glittering heap at her feet.

"Stand there," he told her. "Do not move."

Ylea slitted her eyes and opened her mouth.

"Silence!" Halehl shouted.

Flattening her ears to her skull, she bowed her head in obedience.

Halehl turned to Ampris, who was still sprawled on the ground. "Get up."

She scrambled to her feet quickly, brushing dust off her coveralls, and felt both rumpled and humiliated. So much for being the bright new gladiator of the team, she thought.

"Did she bite you?" Halehl demanded.

Ampris shook her head.

He glared at her as though he blamed her for this, then snapped his head around at the old Myal limping over to them. "Ruar, you fool! I gave you strict orders not to let this happen."

"He tried to carry out your orders," Ampris said instantly in Ruar's defense.

If possible, Halehl's rill turned an even darker hue of

crimson. "Hold your tongue, you impudent cub! Already you forget your orders. Already! Within a quarter hour of your arrival, you have disrupted and disobeyed. One more infraction, and it will be the whipping post for you."

Ampris dropped her gaze and said nothing more. Her eyes were burning, and she kept her jaw clamped tightly together.

"Ruar," Halehl said, turning on the Myal once again while the short male cringed visibly and coiled his tail around one leg, "get Ampris to her quarters *now*. See that she stays there."

"As the master says." The Myal snapped his bony fingers at Ampris and gestured urgently.

She stepped around Halehl and the glowering Ylea in immediate obedience. Ylea turned her head to follow Ampris's movements. Her lips skimmed back from her large, yellow teeth, and she growled.

Ampris hurried past her and followed Ruar up the stairs.

Behind her, although she dared not glance back, she heard Halehl's furious voice continue, although now his words were spoken too low for her to understand. She also heard the lash land again and again on Ylea.

Ampris sighed to herself. If she knew Ylea's type, Ylea would blame her for the punishment and hate her more than ever.

Ruar was limping along fast on his short, bowed legs. He shook his head. "Not good. Not good," he said. "Already you cause trouble."

"It wasn't my fault," Ampris said in annoyance. "Ylea started it."

"Your being here started it," Ruar insisted. "You."

Reaching a door at the end of the corridor, he unlocked it and flung it open. "Your quarters," he said. "You stay inside until I come back tomorrow."

"But—"

"Inside! Inside!" he said, almost frantically, glancing over his shoulder as though he expected Halehl to come after him next with the whip. "Now. There can be no more trouble today. Enough has been done already."

"She started it," Ampris said. It was important that he acknowledge the truth. She knew that trouble and blame could ripple out from this incident unfairly, keeping her from being accepted by anyone on the team. "I did nothing to her."

"You came here," Ruar said, refusing to meet her eyes. "That is enough for Ylea."

"Then she'll have to get over the problem."

Ruar sighed. "No," he said softly. "You will."

He pointed again at the door and Ampris stepped through it. But she paused on the threshold and turned back to him. "Is she the team leader?"

"Of course."

"Then how do I appeal to her good side?" Ampris asked. "I will not apologize, but how can I make friends with her?"

Ruar stared at her as though his eyes would pop from his skull. "Friends?" he squeaked at last. "Friends? There are no friends in the arena."

"But we're teammates, not competitors," Ampris said. "We're supposed to work together."

Ruar shook his head vehemently. "No friends. You stay quiet. Cause me no more trouble. Food will come soon, then you be very quiet."

"But, Ruar—"

He gave her a shove, hard enough to push her over the threshold, and swiftly slammed the door.

Annoyed, Ampris gave the door a kick, and in response the locks engaged.

She fumed a moment, glaring at the door, then recovered her temper and swung around to see her latest cell.

It was beautiful. It was spacious. It appeared to be filled with every luxury.

Astonished, Ampris forgot all about her anger. At first, she could do nothing but stare. She kept thinking this had to be a mistake. She was a slave. She'd come here to be an expendable gladiator, useful until she made a fatal mistake or met her match in combat.

But to be given such a room . . . it reminded her almost of Israi's sumptuous apartments in the palace, and for a moment Ampris's eyes stung with tears of remembrance.

Dusk closed her window now with shadow, but a trio of lamps burned softly around the room. It was furnished as a sitting room, with hangings of lavender and mauve silk, soft chairs filled with cushions, a slightly worn but handsome rug, and an assortment of small tables, one of which supported a geometric sculpture of Igthia crystal.

Ampris drew in a breath of wonder and went to examine the sculpture more closely. As soon as she touched it, she discovered it to be fake, merely a reproduction, but still . . . to have artwork of her own . . . she wondered if she had stepped into a dream.

After the plain, unadorned, utilitarian barracks of Bizsi Mo'ad, this was divine.

Delight spread through her. Ampris grinned, then rushed to explore further.

She found a curtained doorway off to one side that contained a tiny bedchamber barely large enough to hold a bed—a real bed and not just a hard bunk—plus a side table with lamp and a vid control, a vid cabinet, and a chest with pegs and drawers for clothing.

Beyond the bedchamber, Ampris found an equally small bathing room, with a sunken pool fitted with hydroponic jets, a steam cabinet, a massage table that unfolded from the wall, and a washing sink of reproduction crystal surmounted by a mirror that activated to shimmering, reflective life at her approach. In the ceiling, a tiny window showed her the first twinkles of alien stars.

Overcome, Ampris sank to her knees beside the pool and pressed her palms against the smooth coldness of the floor. All this was hers and hers alone.

Never, not even when she was a privileged cub inside

the Imperial Palace, had she enjoyed private quarters of her very own.

She could not believe it.

Oh, much of the magnificence in these quarters was surface only. But Ampris did not mind if the rugs were old or if the materials were synthetic. She had never believed she would live this way, especially after she was cast out of the palace.

And now, unexpectedly, so much was hers.

After the harshness at Bizsi Mo'ad, where there was no grace, no comfort, nothing civilized, it was like being given breath again. Hope bloomed inside her for the first time in a long, long while. She could not believe this gift, this kindness, this generosity of her new owner. And to think that she had struggled to remain at Bizsi Mo'ad, completely unaware of the better life awaiting her in Galard Stables.

"Oh, thank you," she whispered.

Then tears filled her eyes. Flinging herself facedown on the floor, she wept long and hard.

She wept until all her tears were gone, and she was left empty and somehow comforted. Yet still she lay there with her cheek pressed to the floor. The air grew chilly, but she did not care. Exhaustion pressed her bones into lead. She could not move, did not wish to move. Oh, if only she could stay in here, surrounded by this gift, for a year of days.

A soft tapping interrupted her thoughts.

Startled, she jerked up her head, then sat swiftly at the sight of a shadowy figure standing in the doorway. Who was this intruder whom she had not even heard enter?

"Pardon," said a soft voice with the unmistakable shrill singsong tones of a Kelth. A very ill-at-ease Kelth. "I brought your grub—uh—your dinner. When you want it served, you tell me."

Ampris tried to fluff up the tear-matted fur on her face. "Thank you."

"Yeah. I'll activate the heaters now. Should have been

on already. The nights here get cold enough to freeze your—uh, really cold. I just got assigned to your quarters, so things aren't as ready as they should be. Don't worry, though. It won't take me long to get this place whipped into shape.''

No lamp burned inside the bathing chamber. She could not see the Kelth clearly, yet something about him seemed familiar.

She rose to her feet, feeling embarrassed by having been caught lying on the floor. ''My rooms were locked. How did you get in?''

The Kelth bowed in the shadows. ''I'm your servant, see? The locks ain't much, more for your protection than—''

''Protection from whom?'' Ampris demanded. ''Ylea?''

The Kelth yipped softly in amusement. ''Ylea could come through the wall if she decided to. She's built like a Mobile Forces Tanker.''

''I've met her,'' Ampris said.

He yipped again. ''Yeah, you did. And she sat on you. Got herself whipped for it. Got herself assigned extra laps in the morning. She don't like you much.''

Ampris sighed. ''I'll have to make peace—''

''Don't go crawling to her!'' he said in alarm, handing out advice as though she'd asked for it. ''That's no way to handle her.''

As a servant, he was impertinent and far too familiar for his position, but at least he talked to her freely. Ampris tilted her head. ''For some reason Ylea is threatened by me—''

He snorted rudely. ''Threatened? By what? Her quarters are twice the size of yours. She's team leader. She gets the top rewards, most of which she strings around her fat neck.''

Ampris thought about having apartments better even than these. She was too grateful for what she had to feel envious. ''So why is she mad at me? Why does she hate me?''

"Ylea hates everybody. She's supposed to. She's a pro gladiator, see? No sweetness and good manners in her. That's why she's team leader. It takes fierceness to make it in this business."

Ampris snarled ferociously, and the Kelth jumped backward with a yelp.

Ampris laughed at him, enjoying her joke. She walked past him while he cringed back, staring at her through the shadows. Ampris could smell the faint aroma of meat coming from the sitting room. It was cooked in savory sauce with many spices, not all of which were recognizable. Her stomach rumbled, and her mouth filled with saliva.

The Kelth followed her at a safe distance, and Ampris laughed to herself again. No one had told her she would have a servant of her own. She felt unreal, almost free, except for the collar around her throat and the locks on the door.

It had been a long time since she'd last been served. She remembered when she took such luxuries for granted, believing her golden, magical life in the Imperial Palace would go on forever. She had once been the beloved pet of Israi, the sri-Kaa. Now she was afraid to believe in anything good, because the good things always got taken away.

The sitting room glowed with lamplight, enchanted and beautiful with its treasures. A small round table had been pulled into the open center of the room. A serving place was laid, with an empty platter and forks carved of ival—a fragrant, dense wood impervious to liquid. Covered dishes stood around the platter, arranged in order of size. In a glance, Ampris took note of the arrangement's composition and was amazed by it. Everything, from the dish placement to the alignment of the forks to the glowing touch of a single orange-colored flower laid diagonally across the center of the platter, told a poetic story. Indeed, she was being treated like aristocracy.

The Kelth servant had also pulled up a low reclining couch for her to eat in the Viis manner.

Seeing it, much of Ampris's pleasure crashed down. She backed her ears. "Take that away," she ordered without glancing at the Kelth behind her. "I will eat like an Aaroun, upright."

"Sure," the Kelth said without apology. He scurried past her to shove the couch back in its original place.

As he selected a hassock instead and maneuvered it over to the table, the lamplight fell across his face and shoulders, illuminating him clearly for the first time.

He was leggy and tall for a Kelth, thinner than he should have been. When he straightened and turned around, something about the twitching of his pointed, upright ears, something about the shape of his slim muzzle, something in his quick, sidelong glance made him look like someone she should know.

Ampris stared at him, trying to grasp the memory without success. "What is your name?" she asked him.

He glanced at her again, with that familiar darting, sideways cast of his eyes. "Don't you remember me, Goldie? Don't you remember the auction? You've come a long ways since then, you have."

The old nickname clicked everything into place for her. Recognition flooded her, and she gasped. "Elrabin!"

His lips peeled back from his pointed teeth in a grin, and his eyes filled with a look of glinting mischief that she well recalled. "That's me," he said. "I was hoping you wouldn't forget me."

Delighted, she rushed to him, ignoring his cautious flinch back, and slapped him on both shoulders. "Of course I remember you. How good it is to see you. I did not think we would meet again."

"No," he said, glancing down shyly. "I didn't think so either."

"But how do you come to be here?" she asked him. "Tell me your story. I thought you were sold to the gladiators. You should have been in the ring—"

"I'd be dead by now, wouldn't I?" he said. "Gladiator bait's all I'm good for."

"Don't say that. You're quick and agile. You—"

"Look, Goldie," he said in a voice that stopped her. "I ain't got the knack for fighting. Never did. But I got a head for details, and my talents work fine at this. Serving. It's a relief to me, not to have my hide tacked on some gladiator's door like a trophy."

She didn't know what to say to that, so she smiled at him again. "I am so amazed that you are here, that we are here together. To see you again, after all this time—it's astonishing. I feel that Fate must have brought us back together."

Elrabin's ears twitched. Swiftly he clenched his fist, tapped it, and blew on it in a quick, superstitious motion that amused her. "Maybe it did."

She touched the Eye of Clarity hanging around her throat, wondering a little.

Elrabin bent over the table and whipped the covers off the dishes with a little flourish. "So eat your grub before it gets cold. It's good stuff, but you don't get seconds."

Ampris needed no more persuasion. Ravenous, she seated herself at the table and dug in.

Elrabin hovered over her, attentive and silent while she ate. He kept her cup replenished constantly from a carafe of the metallic-tasting, icy cold water.

"No wine?" she asked, licking sauce from her mouth. "No mead? No imported ales?"

Elrabin swiveled his ears back and blinked in visible consternation. "Uh, you're in training now. No—"

"Stop it," she said playfully.

"I think I can find a way into the kitchens after hours, but they count all the supplies, everything, twice a day. It could be hard to conceal a missing—"

She realized he was seriously considering breaking into the kitchen stores to supply her request. She gripped his sleeve. "Elrabin, no. I was joking. I don't drink wine. It makes my head too heavy."

Relief flooded his gaze and his thin shoulders straightened. "Well, I could do it, all right."

"Don't," she said, having visions of Elrabin being caught and chained for punishment. "It was a joke."

He nodded, but he didn't seem sure. "You just let me know what you want, anytime you want it. I'll find a way—"

"Elrabin, I don't expect you to get into trouble on my account."

"My job is to take care of you outside the ring," he said. "Keep you fed, keep you warm, keep you happy. Whatever it takes—"

"You're my friend, not my slave," she said sharply.

He tilted his head to one side and stared at her hard. "No."

"Yes."

"*No.* You gotta be tough here, or you won't last. You gotta play the games, learn the rules."

Ampris smiled slightly. "I *am* tough. I understand the games. I'm not the naive cub you met before."

"Maybe," he said, but he didn't sound convinced.

Now her smile did widen. "No maybe about it. Don't worry about me."

"The Blues ain't easy," Elrabin said. "There's things you don't know yet, don't understand yet."

She met his light brown eyes and ignored what he was trying to tell her. "You're still my friend. That, I understand. I want you to understand it too. Now, sit with me. Eat some of this feast, and we'll talk."

Elrabin smiled for a moment, then his ears swiveled back and he dropped his gaze from hers. "You've got a golden heart, haven't you? Golden through and through. I'm glad you haven't lost that."

It was her turn to be embarrassed and look away.

"Thank you for saying what you did, Goldie," he continued quietly. "It means a lot. But for my sake, you don't let on that we're friends or that we ever knew each other in the past life."

Her gaze snapped up, and they stared at each other in fresh understanding.

"Does it have to be like that?" she asked. She glanced at her surroundings. "This is so pleasant, so private, like a dream."

"No dreams around here," he said sharply. "You'll see. They treat you like this"—he gestured at the luxurious room—"to make up for what you go through the rest of the time. The one I served before you, the last one to live here, she used to come in and wrap herself up in that bed and cry for hours, afterward. The arena is horrible, Goldie. Don't you ever think different."

His warning was well-intentioned, but she didn't need it.

"I know what it's like," she said. The rest of what she could have said tangled inside her throat, and could not be uttered. She sighed. "I know."

Elrabin cleared his throat and busied himself stacking the emptied dishes. "You know about the training ring," he said. "You ain't seen the pros at work yet. It only gets worse. You—"

"Elrabin," she interrupted. "Stop. This is a good place for me."

"You don't know about the surveillance, the—"

"No," she said sharply. "Don't spoil it. Not tonight. I need to know that sometimes life can still be good."

He snorted. "Call yourself tough. You ain't any tougher now than you were that night you wouldn't eat in the auction pen."

She drew in a breath to argue, but then stopped herself.

Maybe tomorrow she'd find out about the bad things he kept hinting at. Maybe tomorrow she'd be moved to the real training barracks to be fed hardtack and cold gruel before being hosed down with chemical sprays to keep off body vermin and sent forth for a long day of exercise and drills.

She knew he wanted to lecture her against still believing in hopes, dreams, and goodness, against still being young and naive, against still wanting the impossible.

There was a knot just at the base of her throat, jammed beneath the circle of her restraint collar. A knot of fear she couldn't cope with, a knot she had to deny was there at all.

And if Elrabin untied the knot, and let all her fears go spilling forth, she didn't know what she would do.

He picked up a piece of globular fruit and handed it to her. "Eat dessert while I fill the pool and heat your bath."

She laid the fruit on the table. "Elrabin," she began, but he gave her a quick warning shake of his head and rolled his eyes toward the ceiling.

Understanding his warning, Ampris knew better than to glance up in search of the surveillance device which must have been activated. She wondered how he knew. He would have to show her how to tell also.

Backing her ears, she said, "A bath sounds wonderful. Prepare it at once."

An appreciative gleam entered Elrabin's eyes. Bowing to hide his smirk, he did as he was told. Seconds later, she heard the rushing sound of water coming from the bathing chamber.

Ampris ate her fruit, smacking her lips over its ripe, exotic taste. She couldn't remember when she had eaten this well, yet the meal had not been heavy. She would sleep well tonight, and the good rest would help prepare her for whatever she had to face tomorrow.

While she wandered around the sitting room, opening table drawers and exploring, Elrabin returned to clear the remnants of her dinner.

She watched him work. His slender hands were deft and quick. He made almost no noise. Every movement was economical and efficient.

"What will I do tomorrow?" she asked. "I was supposed to see the grounds today, but Ylea put a stop to that. Will you show me around?''

Elrabin kept working, sweeping the cloth off the table with an expert flick, then folding it into a small bundle. ''Me? No. Ain't allowed on the training grounds,'' he said. ''Probably you'll hit the outside ring, show off what you can do. The next day you'll do weights and endurance in the gym. Then tumbling. By the end of the week, maybe the master will let you meet the others.''

''Are they all like Ylea?''

Elrabin kept his head down and his expression hidden, reminding her that they were still under observation. ''The Blues are a good team,'' he replied in a neutral voice. ''The best. You'll see.''

She hated being spied on, hated the feeling of violation, of having her privacy stripped away. Of course they would spy on her, watch her to see how she behaved in private. They would want to know if she complained or plotted or sought escape when she thought herself alone. It took effort for her not to back her ears, but she kept them erect and forward.

''It's a big honor to fight with the Blues,'' Elrabin said.

He glanced up then, met her eyes, and rolled his.

Ampris had to cough to conceal a laugh. Unable to mouth such platitudes in return, she changed the subject. ''So what's in the vid cabinet? When will I be allowed to leave my quarters? I'd like to take a walk, stretch my legs. I've been cooped up too long. I need to move.''

''Tomorrow you'll get to move plenty,'' Elrabin told her. ''There's a couple of vids in the cabinet. You let me know what you like, and I'll see that you get it. The better you fight, the more rewards you get.''

Picking up the heavy tray of dishes, he pulled out a transmitter and unlocked the door.

Watching, Ampris wondered if he would give her that transmitter if she decided to escape.

"Elrabin," she said, then stopped, not knowing what she wanted to ask.

He glanced over his shoulder and gave her one of his sidelong grins. "You'll get used to it, Goldie," he said softly. "Now, bathe and get some sleep. You need to be fit, in case you run into Ylea in the morning and she decides to sit on you again."

So that was to be a standing joke. Good enough. Grinning back, Ampris watched him go through the doorway, quick as smoke. Her amusement lasted until she heard the locks snap on. Then her grin changed to a silent snarl.

She paced around the sitting room, restless and far from sleepy. She intended to do what she was told. For now, she would be a good gladiator, a quiet gladiator. She would perform her practice drills. She would obey her orders. She would stay fit and sleek.

But there had to be a way out of this luxurious prison. Someday, hopefully soon, she would find it.

CHAPTER THREE

An insistent tapping roused Ampris from deep, dreamless sleep.

She rolled over, refusing to open her eyes, and burrowed deeper beneath the coverlet.

"Ampris!" said a voice. A hand gripped her shoulder and shook her hard. "Hey, Goldie, wake up!"

Startled, Ampris sat bolt upright and looked around wildly. For an instant she did not recognize where she was. "Where's the bell? How long till inspection?" she mumbled, rubbing her face.

"What inspection?" Elrabin countered. "Flash those big browns around and figure out where you are."

But by this time Ampris already had. She lifted her arms and stretched deep and long until her joints creaked. The smell of food tickled her nostrils, and she sneezed in anticipation.

"Is it morning?" she asked, looking toward the small window and seeing only darkness.

Elrabin flung open the doors of the chest and rummaged through drawers. Pulling something out, he rolled it into a ball and threw it at her.

Ampris caught the clothing just before it hit her in the face. "What kind of service is this?"

"Hurried. Get moving," he said, pulling out a training

harness. He turned with it jingling in his hands and bared his teeth at her. "It's daybreak. You have to be on the training grounds by the time the suns top the horizon. If you're late, I get the beating. So move your fur, will you?"

But Ampris was used to having less time to roll out, throw icy water in her face to smooth down her fur, and bolt down cold, unappetizing food before heading at a run for practice.

Here, she didn't have to worry about making her bunk. She didn't have to wait in line for the hygiene closet. Her breakfast was served hot and delicious on a spotless platter.

Garbed in the unfamiliar coverall that Elrabin had given her, Ampris found it clung too tightly to her body, making her fur itch underneath. It was made of a strange, stretchy fabric, web-thin, yet incredibly tough and resilient.

She plucked at her sleeve. "What is this?"

Elrabin crossed the sitting room with her training harness in his hands. "What do you think?"

"Sensor web?" she guessed.

He nodded, intent on adjusting her harness to fit her better.

She'd heard of sensor suits on vidcasts, chiefly because of controversy over whether they should be allowed in arena competition, but there'd been none at Bizsi Mo'ad. "Does it work?"

Elrabin finished with the last buckle and held the harness up against her to see if he had the size right. "No, you have to wear it because the master likes the color. Of course it works! Everything here is state of the art, see? At least when it comes to you fighters."

Nodding, she went back to her breakfast, swallowing the last flavorful morsel and letting the taste linger on her tongue. "This is so good. I haven't eaten this well since—" She broke off abruptly and stood up, making her amulet swing around her neck.

"Better tuck that piece of fancy inside the web," Elrabin advised her. "Especially if it's your good luck. You don't want to lose it in training. And don't let Ylea try to take it from you.''

Ampris narrowed her eyes. ''No one will take it from me,'' she said grimly. ''It's an Eye of Clarity, and it—''

Elrabin grimaced suddenly and tilted his head away from her as though listening to something.

Puzzled, Ampris stared at him. She heard nothing, but perhaps his ears were keener. ''What is it?''

But he was already straightening and turning to face her. He stood erect, with his thin shoulders pulled back. His eyes grew veiled.

''Time's up,'' he said. He held up the harness and helped her shrug it on.

Realizing that the surveillance of her quarters must have been switched on, Ampris found herself dying to ask him how he knew it, but she dared say nothing that might get him in trouble.

Elrabin finished buckling the harness for her. It fit too snugly over the sensor web, and she backed her ears in annoyance, not liking it. She slid her fingers under the straps, tugging.

''Too stiff,'' she said. ''Too tight.''

''It's new. You'll break it in soon enough,'' he replied without sympathy and gestured toward the door.

As she headed to it, he pulled out the transmitter from his pocket and disengaged the locks.

''Good training today,'' he said formally, bowing as she stepped across the threshold.

Ampris glanced back at him. As he started to close the door behind her, he stepped close and whispered in her ear, ''Watch your back. Ylea's blaming you for her whipping.''

''I knew it—''

''Hush!'' He lowered his voice even more. ''She won't get to you today, but Ruar's on her side.''

''He—''

''Don't trust the old *odger,* see? Now forget him. He's nothing as long as you keep an eye on him.''

"Thanks," she said, feeling nervous about what lay ahead of her.

"Yeah. And watch your step with Halehl. He's meaner than you think."

She drew breath to ask him questions, but his expression changed and he straightened away from her.

"Hey, Ruar," he said. "Good daybreak to you."

Hastening up with a long leather strap coiled in his knobby hands, Ruar scowled and grunted a response.

"Hello, Ruar," Ampris said.

Shaking back his scraggly mane, he ignored her and clipped one end of the leather strap to her harness.

Affronted, she stiffened in protest. "I don't have to be led. Take this off at once."

As she spoke she reached for the snap, but a tiny spark jumped from it and bit her fingers.

Wincing in more surprise than pain, she glared at him and shook her smarting fingers.

Ruar curled his broad lips back from his teeth and held up a transmitter. "I control your restraint collar too, so no bad talk from you today, no trouble."

Fuming, she opened her mouth to tell him what he could do with his transmitters and collars, but Ruar waved the transmitter at her in warning, and she remained silent.

Her temper, however, was boiling. There was no need to leash her and restrain her like some wild animal.

"Today, I take you where to go," Ruar said, leading her away.

Ampris glanced back over her shoulder, certain Elrabin was watching her humiliation, but he had already vanished inside her quarters with a firm snap of the door.

"Tomorrow, you will know," Ruar went on, tugging at her to quicken her steps. "Tomorrow you will go by yourself. Nowhere else will you go. You will be trusted, and you will cause no trouble."

He glanced at her as though to make sure she understood. She hated it that they all seemed to think she lacked intelligence. "Yes," Ampris said impatiently. "I understand."

They went down the steps into the courtyard where she had met Ylea yesterday. Unconsciously Ampris tensed herself, but the bulky Aaroun was not lying in wait to ambush her again.

They crossed the courtyard quickly in the chilly, gray dawn air. Inside her web sensor suit Ampris felt perfectly warm. But her ears quickly grew cold, and the damp air stung her eyes, making them water. She lengthened her stride, crowding close on Ruar's heels and making him strike an irritated trot in order to stay ahead of her.

To her right lay the entrance gate and the long road they had flown along in the transport yesterday. Ampris looked that way, considering how hard it might be to get past that gate.

A floating vidcam hovered just on the other side of it, flashing at her. Ampris backed her ears. "Is that a newscam?" she asked.

Ruar didn't even bother to look. "Maybe," he said, his voice sour and impatient. The light was growing rosy and clearer, and ahead she could see streaks of muted gold beginning to spread across the dusky sky. "Maybe news. Maybe spy. Maybe thief, wanting to steal high-priced gladiator. Always someone there. Always trying to get past shields."

He glanced up at her and curled back his lip. His rheumy old eyes held a momentary glimmer of amusement. "Nothing can record past your sensor web. Waste of spy money, trying to see what goes on in here. No news on the Blues till they *win*. Hah!"

They went through another gate, and Ampris saw a huge compound stretching out before her. Several utilitarian, rectangular buildings were on the left. According to Ruar, they contained the gyms, indoor arena, and pool. To the right, she saw a spacious open-air arena, ringed with slat-rail fencing of indigenous wood. Instead of sand, the ground was covered with some kind of wood shavings, fragrant and soft, packed down slightly underfoot by the cold dew sparkling on everything.

Halehl stood waiting at the center of this arena, clad in a hooded web sensor suit of his own that fit him like a second skin and glimmered wetly with every movement. A deep, square box hovered off the ground beside him.

On the opposite side of the ring, a group of Aarouns clustered near the fence. Her heart sinking with dismay, Ampris glanced at them and wished she didn't have her new teammates for an audience. She was nervous enough, and anxious to do well. She knew that she must learn to fight in their style, not her own. She must work hard to integrate herself into the team. None of them looked as young as she. They had that scarred, bored, well-seasoned slouch to their muscular bodies, and she felt increasingly self-conscious.

Then she noticed that each of them was tethered to the fence by a leash similar to hers. Somehow, that failed to make her feel better. Were they tied like animals to keep them from attacking her as Ylea had done yesterday? Or was it a game of humiliation, designed to shame them and remind them of their place? Either way, the sight of these intelligent adults standing tied up like beasts of burden depressed her.

She did not let herself look at them again, not even when the criticism and jeers started.

"Look at her!"

"Let her walk the walk. Prance, golden cub. Strut your stuff!"

"Did they buy her for her looks or for her muscle?"

"Muscle?" Ylea's voice rose above the rest. "She puny, a weakling."

"She walks like her arms and legs have been tied together. Wait till she gets to Ceunth Siltr and hits *that* gravity."

"She's hopeless. There isn't enough time."

"Pretty, though."

"You think any female in fur is pretty."

"Want to wager there're stripes under that sensor suit?"

"You're on!"

"She won't fight," Ylea said caustically. "She's a freezer. She'll freeze in the ring. I'll bet on it."

"What odds?"

A sharp command from Halehl put an end to the talk. Handlers appeared, mostly Myals like Ruar, who came to untie the Aarouns and lead them away. Ampris watched them stride into the distance, realizing that they'd already had their workout. She could smell the musky odors of sweat lingering in their wake. They walked away as though they owned the world, and she found herself admiring their pride and confidence. All Aarouns should carry themselves that way, she thought, even when led by leashes, with slavery rings in their ears.

With the other Aarouns gone, tension vanished from Ruar's shoulders. He slouched a bit and relaxed his grip on Ampris's leash.

She glanced around freely now, her nostrils quivering at the foreign scents on the cold air—scents of wood and Viis, scents of the forest beyond the walls of the compound, scents of growing things, and tiny animals burrowing for food in the fallen leaves. *Prey.* She swallowed and slowed down, looking into the distance with her head high and her gaze intent.

Ruar jerked on her leash impatiently. "You cannot run away," he said, his voice low and grouchy. "Climb the wall at any point, and the transponders of the shields will activate your restraint collar at twice the normal intensity. If you ever speak again, you will be lucky."

Ampris looked at him, this bowed, stumpy, elderly creature, with his too-intelligent eyes and the constant stink of fear on him. Only then did she notice that he wore a restraint collar too, a very narrow, very unobtrusive one mostly concealed in the hair around his throat. "What has made you so unhappy?'' she asked him softly. ''What has made you so afraid?''

Ruar's eyes widened. For a moment he stared at her in astonishment, then anger flashed across his face and he jerked on her leash again. ''You come. Hurry!''

He led her into the ring almost at a run, halting in front of Halehl and bowing low. ''The new one is brought, master.''

Halehl's yellow eyes took them both in, as though he believed they had been somewhere they shouldn't have, talking about things they shouldn't have. ''You are late.''

Ampris glanced at the horizon, where the sky was now lit in shades of turquoise, lavender, and gold. But the sun had not yet appeared. If Elrabin had spoken the truth, they were *not* late.

She backed her ears, but she knew to say nothing.

Ruar bowed even lower this time. ''As the master says. Forgive me.''

''It is a poor start to your first day, Ampris,'' Halehl said, his tone as courteous and gentle as always. ''You will have to work twice as hard.''

She kept her gaze down. ''Yes, Master Halehl.''

Ruar struck her with his end of the leash. ''That is no way to address the master! You are not Viis, to address him by name or—''

''Ruar!'' Halehl said sharply, making him freeze in midsentence. ''Enough. Go and check the security shields. Make sure we're not under outside surveillance. The security scans have been showing blips since midnight. I want to be certain our countermeasures are working.''

Bowing, Ruar started to unsnap Ampris's leash, but Halehl gave him an impatient wave.

''Go,'' he said. ''I'll deal with her.''

The old Myal bowed and shuffled away, mumbling to himself.

''Ruar!'' Halehl called after him. Now Ampris could

hear a note of exasperation in his melodic voice. "You have forgotten something."

Ruar wheeled around and returned to him, holding out the transmitter that controlled Ampris's restraint collar. Cringing as though he expected to be beaten, he handed it to Halehl without a word, then scuttled away.

Halehl pocketed the transmitter and unsnapped Ampris's leash. His gaze watched her constantly. "Is the gravity a problem?"

She shrugged. "I feel heavy."

"Good. That's the point of training on Fariance. You are moving differently today. The suit?"

Ampris flexed her arms, hating the tight constriction of the suit. "It's binding my arms and legs too much. It makes my fur itch."

Halehl flicked out his tongue. "Most satisfactory. You will learn to move in the suit as though it is a second skin."

"But it will hamper—"

"You will overcome that. Do one lap to warm up, then start your leaps."

She could not continue the argument. Sighing to herself and feeling already that this was going to be a long day, Ampris headed at a slow jog around the large ring. Normally she would have run, for she loved to dig in and push herself, but she'd been confined too long in spaceflight—a journey spent mostly waiting, docked in line for the few working jump gates. Her muscles were tight and needed a good workout. She knew it was prudent to take things slow until her body adjusted to these new conditions. There was no point in pulling a muscle.

But even at a slow jog, she soon began to feel the effects of the heavier gravity. Before she'd made an entire circuit, her tongue was hanging out. Panting heavily, she finished the lap and doubled over for a moment to catch her wind.

"Ampris!" Halehl called. "Leaps. Once across. Once back."

Swallowing a groan, she forced herself upright and began

making long running jumps as though leaping over imaginary hurdles. Her legs felt like lead. Her body had not been so clumsy, so slow since the first horrible days at Bizsi Mo'ad. It was like starting over, and she didn't like it.

While she was staggering her way across, with each leap lower and shorter than the previous one, Halehl busied himself emptying the box floating at his side. Bright blue balls hovered around him, then he tossed them to various points about the ring and used a control device in his hand to move them into position. There they hovered, spinning brightly about waist height above the ground.

Ampris finished her leaps, gasping for air, and sagged against the fence. Her fur was matted under the sensor suit, sweat-soaked now and doubly unpleasant. She longed to rip it off and be free. Instead, she started her stretches, loosening her muscles even more after the warm-up.

Halehl activated her suit without warning, sending shock waves of energy coursing all across her body. With a yelp, Ampris leaped away from the fence and barely kept herself from rolling on the ground like something gone mad.

He had it set too high. She could feel the waves coursing through her skin and upper muscle layers like an abrasive. Yet when she looked at him in appeal, Halehl gestured at her.

"Time to begin. You have much to learn before the season starts in three weeks."

The energy from the suit crawled over her like an infestation. She couldn't concentrate, could hardly think.

Halehl pointed at the obstacle course he'd set up, marked by the spinning blue balls. "Do you know this pattern?"

"Yes, Master Halehl," she said through gritted teeth. He wasn't going to turn down the setting. She knew she could not ask him to, yet she wasn't sure how long she could bear this. "It is X pattern. Tag each position, then cross over before doubling back."

"Correct. Only tag the positions by leaping over the balls. Use a body roll if necessary. I'll time you."

Intent on his equipment, he turned away from her. Ampris tried to pull her wits together and concentrate. She had to do well, she reminded herself. She had to show him what she could do.

X pattern was deceptively simple, yet its variations could become very complex. Ampris started at a jog, but when she reached the first position and started to hurl herself over it, a jolt of energy through the suit boosted her over with more force than she'd intended. Losing her balance, she fell on landing, swore beneath her breath, and scrambled upright to go on.

Sometimes he boosted the energy in her suit. Sometimes he raised the balls just as she reached them. Sometimes he lowered them or made them zigzag away from her.

Ampris was used to limited equipment and stationary positions. She realized what Halehl was trying to teach her about the unpredictability of an opponent, but that didn't help her second-guess which way to move next.

In addition, her usual quickness and speed were gone. She felt as though her body had been switched with another's during the night. She could not seem to time herself right or master her aching muscles. Still, she knew that, given time and much hard work, she could adjust to the gravity difference. It would strengthen her muscles, and perhaps she would even grow eventually to look like Ylea.

She was still smiling to herself at that last thought when she reached the far end of the ring. Without warning, the balls suddenly shifted positions around her. Confused, Ampris stumbled to a halt, but Halehl's voice—broken by static—came to her. She realized there must be a speaker hidden in her restraint collar, and remembered Elrabin's warnings. They were spied on not only by concealed cams in their quarters, but also via their bugged collars.

Now she understood why Ruar was so nervous and afraid, why Elrabin shifted behavior and speech patterns so rapidly. He did so according to when surveillance was on and when it wasn't.

A memory flashed through her mind of vidcasts of competitions, where the famous Blues entered the ring wearing blue capes and blue collars.

She grinned to herself in grudging admiration for the sheer audacity of it. The Blues cheated. They could be coached in competition via their collars. She imagined Halehl sitting high in the stands, issuing instructions softly into his transmitters. No wonder the Blues were so successful.

"Ampris," came Halehl's voice over the static. "Pay attention to me. I have shifted to wing variation. Do you know it?"

"Yes, Master Halehl."

"Don't speak," he said. "It interferes with my signal. Raise your left hand for no and your right hand for yes."

Ampris raised her right hand.

The balls shifted position again, floating past her.

"Do you know this variation?"

Ampris raised her right hand.

The balls shifted a third time. Before he could ask the question, Ampris lifted her right hand.

"Run it," Halehl said.

She did, with the blood pounding in her head, her skin on fire, her legs like lead beneath her. Panting hard, she longed for water but dared not ask for it.

This time, Halehl gave her directions as she ran, telling her to leap or dodge a certain way in anticipation of how the ball was going to move. After initial fumbling, she found herself beginning to respond to his voice quicker and more smoothly.

She didn't like being directed, though. It made her dependent on him instead of her own wits.

Halehl ran her through the pattern again, then shifted the balls to a pattern she did not know. She stumbled through it, trying to move fast while listening to his directions. After an hour or more of this, she was entirely disoriented and reeling with exhaustion.

Finally Halehl called a halt.

Gasping and trying not to be sick, Ampris sagged to her knees, panting so hard her sides were heaving. Her sensor suit was switched off, and she cried out in sheer relief. Ruar appeared with a canteen of water. She drank it thirstily and found the water tasted flat and distilled. Right then, however, the taste did not matter. It was very cold, and she drank it all in swift gulps, only to be immediately sick. Ruar gave her more water, and this time she swallowed it more slowly, rinsing out her mouth a few times and spitting.

Pulling back the hood of his sensor suit, Halehl came to stand over her. He stared down at her, his expression grim with displeasure. Flicking out his tongue, he said, "You are not worth the fortune we paid for you. Get on your feet."

Swallowing a groan, Ampris obeyed. She stood there at attention, her gaze straight ahead, while he circled her. She expected a beating for whatever she'd done, or failed to do.

"It isn't enough to do the drills, Ampris," he said to her in a voice that cut. "It isn't enough to follow orders. You won't last five minutes in the arena. You haven't got enough beast in you."

Ampris's gaze flickered to his face, then shifted hastily away again.

But he saw, and stepped up close to her, so close she could see the fine pebble graining of his skin. His rill was extending out from his neck. "You dare disagree with my assessment?"

"No, Master Halehl," she said softly.

"You disagree," he said harshly. "You want to tell me that you are not a beast. You are not an animal. No, Ampris, you are a civilized person, refined and able to appreciate aesthetic things like art and music."

She held herself stiffly, barely daring to breathe while he stood so close. His rill had turned red, betraying genuine anger.

He struck her without warning across the muzzle, making pain shoot up into her eyes.

She blinked hard, and held herself steady, knowing better than to move or even cry out. He was no different from any of the others, she knew now. He had seemed to be kind, but he was not. Elrabin's warning had been true.

"I don't want a civilized Aaroun in this stable!" Halehl told her. "I want a savage, barbarous warrior. I want a blood-crazed, out-of-control fiend. You, Ampris, are too eager to please. You haven't the heart for this. The first competition will see you mauled."

Again, protests rose to her mouth. Again, she restrained them.

He turned away from her, only to swing back and strike her again.

As she'd been taught, Ampris held herself under control, refusing to react. She took the punishment stoically.

His rill turned a darker shade of red. It flared out at full extension now behind his head. "Pretty *and* useless. You might as well be in manual labor, for all the good you are."

He struck her again, and again, rocking her back on her feet now with the force of his blows.

"I don't want placid!" he screamed at her. "I want—"

Ampris's temper finally snapped. She roared at him, in full volume, drowning out his sentence. Before he could react, she was already on him, driving him backward with a body block that pinned him hard against the rail fence.

He was reaching for the transmitter of her restraint collar, but Ampris knocked it from his hand, sending the yellow disk spinning across the ground. Roaring again, she blocked his struggles with her own bulk and gripped his throat in her teeth.

Halehl froze against her, his body going absolutely still. She could smell his fear, sour and pungent. Ampris went no further. She simply held him, letting him know that his life lay in her jaws. With one twist of her head she could rip out his throat.

An eternity passed between them, but Ampris was counting the seconds in her head. She held him the legal time required in the arena, then she released him and backed away fast. Her gaze stayed on him warily, and her heart was pounding.

He could order her killed on the spot for what she'd just done. Or maybe, she hoped, he was intelligent enough to get her message.

Backing to a safe distance out of his immediate reach, she met his blazing eyes without showing her fear. "I understand, Master Halehl," she said. "But I do know the difference between practice and real competition."

Ruar, who had fled halfway across the ring when she attacked, now ventured back to them. He scuttled over and picked up the transmitter, handing it to Halehl with a cringing bow.

Halehl grabbed it from him without a glance. But he didn't activate it, didn't punish Ampris.

She waited, holding her breath, not sure yet what he would do. But every passing second meant that he was thinking, which meant she had a better chance of surviving. Inside, she wanted to throw back her head and laugh. The expression in his eyes when she'd first grabbed him had been priceless.

For a few moments, he had feared her. She had seen his terror, his certainty that she meant to tear him to pieces. If he let her live, he would never feel completely at ease with her again. And that suited her fine.

"You will not do that again," he said, and his voice still sounded breathless. His tongue flickered in and out rapidly.

Ampris swallowed her smile and kept her face expressionless. "No, Master Halehl," she said meekly.

His gaze snapped to Ruar. "Tomorrow she will train in a muzzle."

"As the master says."

Ampris scowled and backed her ears. She hated muzzles.

Halehl was still giving orders to Ruar, his voice harsh and flat. "And make sure she spends the rest of the day on the track. I want her exhausted by the time you lead her back to her quarters. Is that understood?''

''As the master says.''

Halehl turned away from the bowing Myal and spoke into his hand-link. ''I want two slaves in the outdoor ring immediately. Rake it and put away the equipment. Yes, and have the team ready for drills. Indoors, yes. Out.''

Snapping off the link, he strode away without glancing back at Ampris.

She watched him go, knowing that today she had won. Satisfied, she let herself grin at his departing back. But she did not gloat long, for she knew that tomorrow she might be far less lucky.

CHAPTER FOUR

Ruar opened a pack and gave her a cold meal of grains and fruit, while her muscles stiffened in the cold air, then she spent the rest of the day walking around the long oval track at the rear of the compound. No running, just walking. Endless laps, around and around, until her hips ached and her leg muscles burned.

She saw no one the rest of the day, not a single individual except for Ruar and the slaves who came to put up the blue balls left in the outdoor ring by Halehl. The team never reappeared. No other staff members came to watch her.

In the places where the track paralleled the compound wall, she looked up at how it towered above her. It was solidly constructed of fired dirt bricks, taller than she could jump. Ampris could hear birdsong in the forest beyond. Now and then she heard a strange buzzing sound as though the shields were repelling something. The smells which came to her nostrils were of damp soil, leaf mold, fungus, and rodent scent—interesting, primitive smells that she used to distract herself from her physical misery as she walked lap after boring lap.

She was allowed to stop at dusk. By then she did not think she could make the long walk across the compound to her quarters, much less climb the steps. Yet Ruar kept muttering at her and jerking the leash. Damp, cold, and numb, she staggered at last into her sitting room, where Elrabin was waiting with the heaters on and lamplight glowing warm.

He unbuckled her harness without a word and peeled the sensor suit off her. Beneath it, her fur clung dark and wet to her skin. She shivered and moaned softly.

"I know," Elrabin said. His hands were gentle as he led her to the bathing chamber. Fragrant, steaming water filled the pool. He laced the water with additional oils and unfolded the massage table.

"Dunk yourself," he said to her. "When you're clean and dry, get on the table. I'll let Okal in."

Ampris pulled out of her exhausted haze for a moment. "Okal?"

"The masseur."

Delight filled her. "I have my own masseur?"

Elrabin grinned at her and closed the door quietly, leaving her in privacy.

Except for the collar. Ampris gave it a tug, wishing it could come off too, and wondered if it could read her thoughts as well as overhear everything she said. No, she must not become paranoid. It was only a piece of equipment, and like most items of Viis manufacture, it would break down sooner or later and cease to function as it was supposed to.

She soaked in the warm, fragrant water until she fell asleep. Only Elrabin's tapping at the door awakened her.

Once she was dry and dressed in a long robe of soft, loosely woven material, Okal came in.

He was a Phivean, a cephalopod with a thick, elongated body that ended in a flat, spade-shaped tail and was supported on four stout legs. He was smooth-skinned and entirely hairless, and his olive-green color proclaimed him male, as opposed to the yellowish-pink hue of female Phiveans. He had five waving tentacles lining his body on either side, the front two tentacles being longer and stronger than the rest, with pod-shaped tips that curled and uncurled with obvious dexterity. His head was bulbous, encircled with a prominent brow ridge beneath which two knobby, bulging eyes protruded, rolling in all directions and never seeming to focus on or gaze at anything in particular. The upper portion of his mouth formed a sharp, cartilage beak above a round opening lined with waving cilia. There was no part or portion of the Phivean ever completely still. Ampris's entire impression was of constant movement, rippling and waving.

While she had seen vids of Phiveans, she had never actually met one before. Phiveans were one of the many Abiru species not permitted in the Imperial Court. Nor had there been any at Bizsi Mo'ad.

Okal went directly to her. With both of his front tentacles, he pointed at the massage table.

Ampris looked at him without moving. "I am Ampris," she said with courtesy. "To be massaged by the expert touch of a Phivean is an honor I have never enjoyed before. Thank you."

Okal's eyes rolled in all directions, and half of his tentacles lifted into the air. He approached her on his stout, slow-moving legs, then one of his long front tentacles reached out and ever so gently touched the Eye of Clarity suspended around her neck.

"Do you recognize it?" Ampris asked softly. As she spoke, she glanced at Elrabin to see if it was safe to speak freely.

As though he understood her unspoken question, he gave her a nod. "No surveillance cams in the bathing chambers," he said with a grin. "The steam makes 'em malfunction."

"The Eye of Clarity is a symbol of abiru unity," Ampris said to Okal. "It is very old, from a time before the Viis became our masters. I wear it now in hope of our future, when we may again someday be free."

Okal explored the surface of the amulet tenderly, with reverence, the tip of his front tentacle moving with extreme gentleness to curl around it and hold it for a long moment. His bulging eyes closed, and he stood there swaying slightly from side to side.

Ampris stared at him in astonishment, wondering if he recognized it from some legends of his own past culture, wondering if he simply accepted what she had said. Or perhaps the Eye of Clarity communicated with this individual in some way that she could not understand. After all, her old teacher Bish had told her the Eye of Clarity had considerable powers, if she could only learn how to unlock them. So far, she never had.

"Does it speak to you?" she asked. It wasn't glowing with light like it had once done for her, but Okal seemed to be communing with it in some way. "What is it like, to feel what it says?"

Okal opened his eyes. His tentacle uncurled, releasing the Eye of Clarity, and slid away. Backing up from her, he lowered his head respectfully until the end of his bulbous skull nearly touched the floor.

"I've never seen him bow to anyone but Halehl before," Elrabin said. "You're a big hit, Goldie."

She shot Elrabin a look of impatience. "I just wear the thing, that's all."

"Thing of beauty," Okal said. His voice was thin and soft, barely audible, a hissing, sibilant sound filled with air. It made her think of reeds whistling together as the river waves shifted them against the bank. "So many beauty," Okal whispered. "Eye of Slarities. Many precious. Symbols we see from times before."

"Yes," Ampris said eagerly. "So you know what it is."

"Yes. Symbols we see from times before."

"That's what Bish told me," she said to Elrabin, ignoring his look of puzzlement. "My old teacher. He said that all the abiru races knew these and used them, long ago."

Elrabin shrugged. "Never heard of 'em, myself." He came over and peered at the pendant with the appraising squint of a thief. "That stone's not a precious jewel. Some kind of natural crystal, maybe. But so many occlusions inside it will bring down the value.''

"Its value has to do with its history,'' Ampris said impatiently, pulling away from his scrutiny. "It's old, a relic of the past.''

"Yeah, and how did you get it, bright eyes?'' he asked.

"It was given to me.''

"By who?''

Annoyed, she looked away from Elrabin's bright curiosity and Okal's reverent attention. She didn't want the conversation going in this direction. "It doesn't matter now. That's all in the past, anyway. I wear it for luck.''

Okal took the hint and moved away, unrolling towels across the massage table and patting them deftly into place.

But Elrabin went on staring at Ampris. "It came from her, didn't it?'' he asked. Suddenly his light brown eyes knew too much, saw too much. "She gave it to you.''

Ampris backed her ears and didn't answer.

"Why do you wear something given to you by a Viis?'' he asked. "Do you still think she's grand?''

"No,'' Ampris said, her voice very low. She stared into the distance, seeing nothing.

Elrabin touched her arm. "Yes, you do. You're still hoping, see? Gods, Goldie, ain't you learned nothing?''

She whirled on him in fury. "I've learned a lot! I don't hope for anything. And I don't need your opinions. No one asked you, anyway.''

"Who?'' Okal asked, his question like a breath.

Ampris glared at him, but Elrabin answered. "The sri-Kaa gave her the necklace,'' he said with scorn. "It's old, cheap, and worth nothing, but she thinks it's just grand. Ampris, if you want to be tortured, why don't you just stick your hand in Ylea's mouth and let her chew?''

"Necklace symbols from times before,'' Okal said before Ampris could retort. "Comes from hands of sri-Kaa?''

He sounded impressed, and his eyes rolled about more than ever.

Ampris sighed impatiently. "Now look what you've done," she said to Elrabin. "No one is supposed to know that. Halehl will order it taken away if he thinks it's worth something."

"Oh, no, don't take it away," Elrabin said, his scorn raking her. "Don't lose a gift from your precious Israi. Didn't she betray you? Didn't she sell you? Ain't you here, now, because of her?"

"I hate her!" Ampris said, goaded too far. She growled at Elrabin, baring her teeth. "With every whipping I've taken. With every set of blisters worn on my hands. With every cold meal I've choked down. I wear her gift so I won't forget her, so I won't stop hating her, so I won't forget my vow to get out of this, somehow, someday."

Her voice rang out in the bathing chamber, loud and bitter. She fell silent then, breathing hard as she struggled to master her emotions, to keep them hidden and controlled and festering deep inside her.

Okal dropped his towels and simply stood in place, tentacles fluttering aimlessly in distress.

Elrabin swiveled his ears back and dropped his gaze from hers. "Sorry," he said. "Guess I went too far."

Ampris swallowed another growl. She turned away from him, gathering the folds of her robe around her. "I guess you did."

Elrabin said nothing more, but Okal seemed agitated.

He rolled his eyes and the tiny cilia around his mouth worked frantically. "You sent to palace?" he asked. "You see Kaa?"

Ampris battled her rising exasperation. Now the rumors would fly, and every slave in the compound would know about her past and hate her for it. She had no idea how her teammates would react to the news that she used to live in the palace and play with the sri-Kaa when she was a cub, but she could guess. It was bad enough that Halehl had recognized her.

"You see Kaa?" Okal asked again, sounding more excited than ever.

Although she was furious with Elrabin, she couldn't take it out on Okal. "Yes," she said as evenly as she could, "I have seen the Kaa."

Elrabin yipped softly to himself. "That's an understatement. She used to live in the palace, Okal. She was the pretty playmate of the little sri-Kaa. They went everywhere together. Goldie here used to live the high life, didn't know how to be anything but a Viis aristocrat herself."

Ampris flexed her claws, wanting him to shut up. "That's past. It's over. You don't have to keep talking about it."

As though he finally heard the anger in her voice, Elrabin blinked and snapped his jaws shut.

Okal patted Ampris's shoulder with one of his tentacles. "Slinging many hatings is to be sorry. Send kindness and clarity between you as the Eye teaches."

Astonished, Ampris turned to stare at the Phivean. Okal's eyes darted between her and Elrabin, his short tentacles upraised and swaying.

Ampris realized she had no business losing her temper with Elrabin, even if he was being a pest. Why he had to start bragging tonight, she had no idea. But there was no point in overreacting.

"Okal is right," she said in apology. "The old teachings about the Eyes of Clarity were about harmony and peace, about different races working together. We should have only one enemy, the—"

"Shut up!" Elrabin said so sharply he startled her. "Just shut up, *now*."

Her eyes widened as her breath caught in her throat. "The collars—surveillance—is it on?"

A faint whine came from Elrabin's throat. He circled the bathing chamber as though he could not be still. She could see his fur bristling around his neck, and within it gleamed a narrow, metal restraint collar, no wider than a filament.

Chilled suddenly, she wondered if they—if she—had gone too far. "Is it on?" she asked again.

Elrabin was still pacing and muttering to himself, rubbing his muzzle with both hands. Growling, he gave her an exasperated nod and strode out.

Ampris stared after him with her ears flat to her skull. She tugged at her own collar, wishing she could rip it off. Elrabin had not yet explained how he knew when the bugs in their collars came on. She had felt nothing, sensed nothing. How much, if any, of their conversation had been recorded? Would they be punished for anything they had said? It had been harmless talk, but when did anyone know which remark or question would offend a Viis? Elrabin's display of fear worried her.

Sighing, she lifted her gaze and found the Phivean pointing at the massage table. Ampris climbed onto it, and the masseur set to work, finding all her sore and stiff spots. Moaning as he kneaded her muscles back into pliancy, Ampris sank into the luxury of his care.

After a while, Okal said, "Soothe yourself, Ampris." His soft voice hissed to her, reassuring and calm as he applied pressure to a sore spot until the tightness melted away. "Your path is certain and sure. You see what others do not see. Clarity is yours."

"I don't feel much clarity," Ampris said, her voice muffled as she spoke, facedown, into the towel. "I feel confused and afraid."

"Many precious is the Eye," Okal said. "This is truth you see?"

"Yes."

"Trust the Eye, Ampris," he said, working down her back. "Trust the Eye."

She twisted her head to look at him. "What do you know? Please tell me. There is so much I would like to learn."

Okal went on massaging without reply.

A wave of exhaustion washed over her, making it hard to think.

"I had the chance once to learn and I threw it away," she said drowsily, thinking of the sivo data crystal the archivist Bish had given her long ago, a crystal she had not bothered to read completely. The knowledge it contained had been forbidden, and her possession of it had led to her expulsion from the palace. "What were you taught about the Eye, Okal? Who taught you? You knew immediately what it was. Most abiru don't even recognize it. The Viis certainly don't."

"Viis do not see beyond what is Viis," Okal said so softly she could barely hear him. "This is not a way of lasting."

"Okal—"

"Session is finished."

She lifted her head, but the Phivean was already leaving. "Okal!" she called after him, but he did not stop.

Slowly she sat up and gathered the loose folds of her robe around her. Her eyes were heavy. She wanted to sink down and sleep forever.

Yawning, she wandered into her bedchamber and found the coverlet turned back in readiness for her. She stumbled toward the bed, then heard a faint noise elsewhere and walked into the sitting room instead.

Elrabin crouched on the floor, sorting a stack of vids into separate piles. Even through her haze of fatigue, she could see his hands were shaking. Again, she wondered if they would be punished.

"I'm sorry," she said.

Startled, he jerked and the stacks of vids tumbled together. Rising to his feet and turning to face her, Elrabin's eyes were stony. "Grab the winks," he said. "Tomorrow will be harder."

She held out her hand in appeal. "Are we in trouble?"

"We are not permitted to discuss our betters," Elrabin said, his voice stiff and cold.

Ampris understood he was speaking for the benefit of the activated surveillance. "I was wrong to forget that," she said. "I won't repeat my mistake."

"You need sleep," he said, his voice almost a growl. "I'll go if there's nothing else you require."

He turned away as he spoke, but Ampris tapped his shoulder to stop him. "Wait," she said, thinking quickly. She had too many questions to let him go just yet. "I—I want another bath. Fill the pool for me."

Elrabin stared at her a moment, then blinked several times as though he understood. "Another bath? But—"

Ampris growled. "Do you question my request? Do it!"

"At once."

Without further protest, he headed back into the bathing chamber. Ampris followed him, and stood watching while he turned on the water in the pool, the sink, and even the hygiene closet. With the noise of the water rushing around them, Elrabin turned around to face her.

"Are we safe here?" she mouthed.

He gave her a wary nod.

She wanted to be sure and tapped her collar. "Even with these?"

"Yeah," he said. "Transmission quality ain't never too good. The noise of water really messes it up."

"Good," Ampris said in relief. "Now we can talk."

"There's been too much talking already," he said. "When I give you a warning, Goldie, you gotta pay attention to me *at once*. Get that?"

She growled. "I hate these restrictions! Oh, to be free to say what I want when I want!"

His gaze held no sympathy. "Might as well wish to be Kaa. You ain't going to get nowhere thinking like that."

"Someday I will be free, Elrabin."

"Sure you will," he said with a smirk of pity. "Keep talking that way, and you'll get the rod."

"How do you know when surveillance is on?" she asked. "Your collar is different than mine. How do you—"

He held up his hand. "Secret, Goldie. I ain't sharing that with no one, not even you."

"But—"

"Forget it. Cost me plenty already to have my collar tampered with, but it's worth it, see? Saved my hide several times." He snarled at her in sudden hostility. "You say one word about this, and I'll make sure you get stolen by the competitors."

Ampris backed her ears. "You don't have to threaten me," she assured him. "I would never betray you."

"Heard that one before," he said bleakly.

She met his gaze. "It's true," she said. "I keep my word. You can trust me. After all, I trust you."

"Drop it, okay?" he said, glancing away. He looked distinctly uncomfortable. "When folk start talking about trust, I know what's coming."

She looked at him, saw the ghosts of old hurts and betrayals swirling in his eyes. Pity filled her, but she stopped giving him the assurances he was afraid to believe in.

"Besides, Goldie," he went on. "You ain't going to be around long."

"What do you mean?"

"You take stupid risks, unnecessary risks."

She drew in a breath. "Ah, so you heard about what happened today."

"I did. We all did."

She heard criticism in his voice, and she didn't like it. "That was a necessary risk."

"Someone says you killed a Viis before. That's why you got sent to the gladiators."

Ampris sighed. That terrible day was going to follow her the rest of her life.

Elrabin watched her intently, panting a little. "You're not denying it," he said.

Still she said nothing. She wasn't proud of what she'd done in the city of Malraaket. While a lowly household slave, she'd killed her owner's steward in self-defense, and that did not justify pride.

"Now you've attacked the master here," Elrabin said, shaking his head. "If you're not careful, you'll end up a rogue."

"I was proving a point."

He yipped caustically. "You're lucky he didn't have you flayed alive. Your hide could be a rug on his floor tonight."

Grimly she said, "He got the message."

"Maybe. You better not try that again."

"I'm not stupid," she said, annoyed.

"Then don't do it again."

Ampris lifted her head proudly. "Is the lecture over?"

"Yeah. Get some winks. I'm going."

"Wait," she said. "I have something else to discuss with you."

"Getting late, Goldie," he said.

"This won't take long," she replied, thinking of the stack of vids he'd left on the sitting room floor. "Do I have a real vid link that feeds off the main signal, or do I just have a player for those vids you were handling in the other room?"

Elrabin snarled something beneath his breath, and looked at her in suspicion. "It's a real link. Why?"

"Can I link to data archives?" she asked in excitement. "Can I retrieve information from—"

"Stop!" he said, holding up his hands. "What're you up to?"

"Freedom!" she said, panting eagerly. "Knowledge is the first step. The more information I know, the more truth I learn, and the better I can begin to—"

"No," he said sharply, swiveling back his ears. "That's it. I ain't getting into this."

"Listen to me," Ampris said, moving to block his exit. She smiled into his hostile eyes, eager to convince him of all the possibilities just waiting for the two of them. "We can make a difference, Elrabin. I know we can. Opportunities are waiting to be grasped. The abiru folk need a leader, someone to give them a vision of hope.''

"Hope." He spoke the word with flat contempt. "Don't be stupid."

"It's not stupid to have a dream, a vision."

"I don't want to hear any treason jabber," he said. "My, my, Goldie. Not only do you take risks with the master that'd make my fur turn white, but now you've turned out to be a crusader. Here you stand, making speeches, talking like an activator, a rebel, a traitor."

"Like a Progressionist," Ampris said softly. Then she lifted her head with pride. "You didn't think I had it in me, did you?"

"Going to get yourself killed," he said flatly.

"No, I won't. My beliefs are true—"

"Stop it," he said angrily. "Truth . . . beliefs . . . bah! Are you crazy in the lid? You start preaching treason, Goldie, and the Viis will cut off your head and hang it on the gate for the birds to peck."

Ampris thought of the trophy room in the Kaa's mountain lodge and shuddered.

"Yeah," Elrabin went on, "you think about that. Good and hard. Treason ain't for the likes of you. It ain't worth the risk."

"Because of our collars?"

Exasperation flashed in his eyes. "Nah. They ain't always on. But you trust folk too quick for your own good, Goldie. You got to be more careful."

"I will."

Elrabin rubbed his muzzle and snorted to himself. "I'm just trying to keep your head on your neck. I told you this place ain't all it seems. The master *likes* to punish us, see? He speaks soft to you, and you think he's decent, but you ain't seen the cruelty yet."

Ampris remembered how Halehl had whipped and berated Ylea for attacking her upon her arrival. That was nothing more than normal Viis punishment. She herself had received worse for her own transgressions.

"Don't give me that look," Elrabin was muttering. "You don't want to believe me? Fine. So what you planning to do next? Go out and teach old Aaroun harvest songs to your teammates, just because they're Aarouns and their genetics should make 'em trustworthy? You going to make your first converts to the cause with that bunch?"

"I do want to talk to them," Ampris said, ignoring his sarcasm. "I've never been around my own kind much. I want to learn the Aaroun ways."

"See?" he said, too shrilly. "No sense. Let me tell you about Aaroun ways. Ylea will slit your throat if she gets a chance. Not up here in the private quarters, because you're guarded. But in the arena, she'll turn on you and make it look like your opponent cut you down."

"They can't all be like her."

"Why not?" he asked her in open exasperation. "*Why not?* Why look for the good in folk? Why waste your time? Why take the risk?"

Ampris let the silence spin out a moment beneath the rush of water around them, then she said in a quiet voice, "I don't know yet what I'm supposed to be doing in this life, but I'm beginning to get an idea. Living in the palace got me a fine education. I can read and write and do higher mathematics. I know some history—both the real as well as the falsified versions. I understand music and art. I can read a basic star map and figure out where I am. I know how to survive court intrigues. I know protocol and I can speak Viis fluently. So what does that make me, Elrabin? A freak, or someone who sees what all abiru folk can be like if given the chance and opportunities?"

"No one gets a chance," Elrabin said resentfully.

"There has to be a way to make chances," Ampris said. "I was lucky enough to be in the right place at the right time, but we have to find a way to get around luck. We have to make our own opportunities, and show others how to do the same.''

"Save the speeches, Goldie,'' Elrabin said with a jaw-cracking yawn. ''There's no one to hear.''

Hurt, Ampris backed her ears and swung away. Elrabin was so typical, so closed-minded and afraid to venture out, just like nearly all the others. He had many gifts and talents. He could be so much more than he was, if he would just believe in himself.

But then a voice rose up in the back of her mind, jeering at her. What did she expect Elrabin to be? He was a slave. He could not do as he pleased, go where he pleased, no more than she could. And besides, what was all her fine education for, except to make her aware of all the possibilities denied to her?

"The way I see it,'' Elrabin said, startling her from her thoughts, ''is we got to find us some rules here, Goldie.''

"What kind of rules?''

"Rules between me and you.''

She looked at him, trying to read his eyes and failing. ''Explain.''

"I can't trust you if I think you're going to risk our necks by jabbering this junk at everyone you meet. So maybe we should just call it quits. You ask for another servant. Leave me out of this disaster you're planning.''

Dismay filled her throat. ''I thought we were friends.''

He wouldn't meet her gaze. He was panting, and his fists were clenched. ''Friends,'' he muttered. ''Yeah. Trouble is, you want to be friends with everyone. I hang with you, and you get your hide in trouble. Then I'm in trouble, too. You want to trust folk just 'cause they're abiru, but there's plenty of the abiru here who will run to turn in anything they overhear. Ruar is the biggest squealer in the place. And Okal—''

"You *know* Okal can be trusted,'' she said quickly.

"Maybe. Yeah. He's no squealer,'' Elrabin admitted.

"But who can tell with a Phivean? You know how weird they are."

"Okal believes in the Eye," Ampris said, touching the pendant around her neck. "That's why I trust him."

Elrabin backed his ears. "Don't go asking me to judge folk that way! What kind of stupid idea is that?"

"Call it foolish if you want," she said wearily. "I can't explain it to you." She sighed, feeling herself sag. "I'm sorry. I shouldn't have expected you to get involved. But I have to try, and I will try until someone stops me."

"Then you're doomed," he said with pity.

Disappointment spread through her, but she accepted his decision. She couldn't expect him to take risks with her if he didn't want to. "Can I ask you one last favor before you go?" she asked.

He rubbed his muzzle, whining in the back of his throat again. "What?" he asked reluctantly.

"I still intend to access the data archives, if I can," she said. "Will you tell me how to do it? Then that's all. I won't get you involved beyond that."

Elrabin stared at her a long moment, then finally tipped back his head and laughed. "You just don't give up, do you, Goldie?"

She didn't like being laughed at, but she smiled anyway. "Why should I give up? I haven't started yet."

He sighed. "Maybe you can link into the central library—"

"Not *that,*" she said in quick scorn. "It's laced with Viis lies."

"That's the best—"

"No," she said. "I want to get into the data archives beneath the old Imperial Palace, the ones the Kaa ordered restored. Can I link to them?"

Elrabin drew back from her and paced a small circuit around the bathing chamber. "Don't ask for much, do you, Goldie?" he said softly. "Just the impossible."

Her hopes crashed down again. "Is it? Really? I was hoping—"

"What? You think a place like that's going to be available to just everybody?"

"No, but that doesn't mean it's impossible to access it."

"Even if you get into the data files, you won't be able to read them."

"I can read Viis," she said. "I told you I'm fluent."

He stared at her in disbelief. "You're lying."

She backed her ears. "I *can.* Israi insisted I learn."

"Everybody knows how to speak a few words of Viis," he said, his ears twitching back and forth. "Can't help but pick it up. But no one can read it."

Ampris met his skeptical gaze steadily, proudly.

"It's forbidden," he said.

Ampris shrugged. "The law doesn't apply to the sri-Kaa. Listen, no one knows this except you. I've trusted you with my secret. If I'm ever caught committing treason, you can condemn me further to the master in exchange for clemency for yourself. Fair enough?"

He said nothing.

"Okay," she said, accepting defeat where he was concerned. "It was just an idea. I'll figure out another way."

"Not here, you won't," he said. "You got to keep your mind on fighting, remember? If you don't, you'll be cut off at the knees in the first competition."

She rolled her eyes at him impatiently. "I know how to fight."

"Yeah, in practice maybe. I'm talking about the pros."

Ampris turned away from him. "All right. Forget it."

He gripped her shoulder to keep her from walking away. "Wait. Maybe I can mess around with the signal. But no promises, see? I got to make sure no one in security catches the signal divergence and gets nervous." He rubbed his muzzle worriedly. "The master is paranoid about someone stealing one of you, or breaking in to get at his strategy secrets so the betting odds can be rigged. That's why security is so tight.''

Ampris grinned at him. ''Then you'll do it? For me? Oh, Elrabin!''

''I said I'll try,'' he said gruffly, tugging at his coat while looking stern and disapproving. ''I don't like it, but if that's what you want—''

''Oh, yes! I want it very much.'' She tugged at one of his ears affectionately. ''Thank you.''

''Slow down. Don't thank me yet,'' he said. ''We're making a deal here.''

She blinked, slightly taken aback. ''Yes, of course. What kind of deal do you want?''

''If you're set on starting some kind of rebellion, you got to be careful. You follow me?''

''Yes. But you've already stressed that.''

''So I'm saying it again. Being careful means you don't make friends,'' he said, his voice fierce and cold.

''But I must if I'm to form a network.''

Elrabin choked. *''What?''*

''I thought you understood. The Viis civilization is crumbling. We can—''

''No.'' He stepped back from her, shaking his head. ''No. You're crazy. It can't happen. The Viis are too strong.''

''They are weak,'' she insisted. ''I know. They can't do anything for themselves. Won't do anything for themselves. They're lazy, conceited, and arrogant. It's the abiru folk who do the real work. We run businesses and households. We do the manual labor. We work in the space stations. We operate the jump gates—most of which don't work anymore. Almost nothing works the way it should. You know that.''

''If they'd shell out credits to maintain their equipment—''

''But no one knows how to do the maintenance,'' Ampris said. ''No one . . . except abiru workers. If we could ever unite, join forces, and trust each other, we could over-throw the Viis yoke. I know we could."

For a moment the possibilities radiated like stars in his eyes, then that light dimmed, and Elrabin shook his head. "Pretty dreams you got, Goldie. But it ain't happening."

"It could, if we—"

"We're slaves," he said harshly. "Born slaves. We'll die slaves. They *own* us. We got no say, got no chance to get together."

"Why can't we try?" she shot back at him. "Because it looks impossible, we're just supposed to give up? How do we know what we can or can't accomplish until we try?"

He shifted under her scornful gaze, refusing to meet her eyes.

"I'd rather be called crazy," she said softly, not quite able to mask her scorn, "than a coward."

His head snapped up, and he bared his teeth. "Yeah, Elrabin the Coward, that's me. But it keeps me alive."

"Do you love your Viis masters so much?" she asked him. "When the master whips you, don't you long to do something to get back at him?"

Hatred gleamed in Elrabin's eyes, but he shook his head. "You're into major treason, Goldie."

"What have I got to lose?" she asked, exasperated. "My head?"

"Yeah."

"But I'm already condemned to the arena, Elrabin," she said softly. "Don't you see? I can't be safe, no matter what."

He swung away from her, whining low in his throat.

She could see his fear, his worry. "I guess it's no deal after all," she said after a moment. "If you'll tell me how to adjust the link signal feed, I'll do it myself. Then they can't blame you if I get caught."

"Can't they?" he echoed.

"All right, then. I'll—"

"Besides, you're no good at this," he went on as though

she hadn't spoken. "Everything you think is right out on your face. You learn not to trust everyone at first sight. You keep your secrets. Yeah, and don't say everything you know. Hold back some, Goldie."

She nodded. "That's the way things were at Bizsi Mo'ad. Spies and tattles, everyone wanting to betray everyone else in hopes of currying favor. I hoped it would be different here."

Elrabin laughed. "Here, everything is *exactly* the same as Bizsi Mo'ad. Don't let these fancy quarters and all the toys fool you. No matter how it looks, the purpose is the same. You remember that, Goldie. Have you noticed that little plaque outside your door? It's to display your number of victories this season. They keep you up in style so you can kill in the competitions that Lord Galard bets on. That's all you're good for. You haven't faced it yet, the horror, but you will. And that's when you're going to need to be strong, inside yourself. No one can help you face that. You'll face it alone."

She shivered, refusing to deal with what he was talking about. Why did he feel he had to prepare her for what lay ahead? She dreaded it too much already. "Are you with me, then?" she asked.

He met her eyes, and his own were clear and steady. "Me? I'll watch your back, Goldie. I'll warn you when I can if Ylea is planning to get at you in the ring. I'll guard your quarters and your gear. I'll help you survive and live a long time with the Blues, so we can both prosper."

Tears came to her, stinging the backs of her eyes while she struggled to hold them in. "That's a long answer," she whispered. "But it says nothing."

"It says all I can say," he told her.

"Elrabin—"

"You think you got nothing to lose, Goldie, but I got plenty," he said. "This is a pretty good place, see? If you win enough, you stay here, get the good treatment. If you win big, you can become team leader. Then we get the biggest quarters, and I have a room for myself. You can stockpile a fortune, if you let me place your bets for you. Maybe, one day, you can escape with your winnings and lose yourself in a backwater where the bounty hunters won't find you.''

She stared at him in dismay, beginning finally to comprehend.

''It's that chance you were talking about,'' he said eagerly. ''Making your own opportunity. See, I don't know yet how you are in the arena, but the Blues paid top credits for you. A lot more than they paid for Ylea years ago. Why do you think she's so mad at you?''

Ampris's head was spinning at his change of subject. ''No,'' she said. ''You don't understand—''

''I do,'' he said, gripping her hand hard. ''Believe me, Goldie, I do. They paid so much for you that Halehl didn't punish you for that stunt you pulled today. You could have killed him, and old Ruar's getting drunk on sour beer tonight wishing it had happened. So the Blues think you're great. But that won't last long if you spoil everything you got going for you now. You got to reach for what you have a real chance of getting, see?''

Weariness washed over her. Whatever he might promise, she realized he didn't really believe anything she'd said tonight. ''I want that link, Elrabin,'' she said with determination.

He sighed and tilted his head to one side. ''I don't know, Goldie. It still don't seem worth it. Why don't you go to bed and think it over another day?''

''Don't you care?'' she whispered. ''Don't you care at all?''

''I care,'' he replied, his voice flat and unsympathetic. ''I care about saving my hide. If we can strike a deal where we help each other . . . then I guess I care about saving your hide too. I can't get more honest than that.''

She could no longer hold back her disappointment. Fresh tears welled up in her eyes.

Elrabin glared at her, then flattened his ears. "Hush now," he said. "Don't do that. Don't cry."

Angrily she wiped her face. "I don't want to. I'm not doing it to get your sympathy."

A slow cynical grin parted his jaws. "Yeah? Okay. Come on, then. You go to bed and rest. You're too tired, and we got no business plotting this stuff tonight."

"Plotting?" she said, a little hysterically, wanting to laugh but finding herself crying instead. "Is that what we're doing? Talking to you is like trying to catch windblown sand."

"Yeah, it's kind of bred in me," he said with pride. "Never mind, Goldie. You forget about half of what I said, see?"

"Which half?"

He yipped, his eyes gleaming. "You let me check folks out first, see? Then if I think it's okay, you can talk treason to them. Fair enough?"

She caught her breath and wiped her eyes, hoping again. She tried to read his eyes for sincerity. "Is that a promise?"

"Here's the rest of the deal," he said, squirming a bit before he squared his shoulders and finally looked her in the eye. "I'll help you like you want, within reason, see? And in exchange you make something of yourself in the arena."

Ampris backed her ears. "What?"

"Don't just get by. You become the star, take the team leader spot. Yeah, you do that."

She stared at him in astonishment. "Just like that," she said sarcastically.

"Come on. You're a big, healthy Aaroun. You're supposed to be good. Halehl don't blunder when it comes to picking out fighters. And you had him on the rails today."

"But that was just catching him by surprise—"

Elrabin pointed his finger at her and said fiercely, "No, Goldie. No buts. You take top spot away from Ylea, and you hold it. No slacking. No just getting by. No bottom spot on the team, or our deal's off.''

Her astonishment was spreading, along with irritation. "You're serious about making money, betting on me."

"Sure," he said with a shrug. "You've told me your dream tonight. So now I'm telling you mine. You want to save the universe. I want to afford a bolt hole where no bounty hunter can get me. See, I got it all planned. All I needed was the right fighter to come along. You're the one. You help me, and I'll help you."

"But—"

"That's the way it works," he said flatly. "Or it don't work at all. You decide."

"But, Elrabin, can't we—"

"Sleep on it," he said, shutting off the running water. "You let me know when you're ready."

She wanted to protest further, but with the water shut off there was nothing to mask their conversation from the surveillance devices. Elrabin left the bathing chamber to put away the vids in the sitting room. By the time she got there, he was at the door.

"Get your rest," he said. "If there's nothing else, I'm gone."

His eyes met hers, sharp and merciless. Ampris opened her mouth, then closed it again. This wasn't how she'd planned things. But somehow Elrabin had managed to outmaneuver her.

The door clicked, and she heard the locks engage. Glancing up, she realized he was gone—as elusive and hard to pin down as smoke.

Ampris sighed to herself, her heart heavy with disillusionment. Yes, she saw how the abiru races could eventually free themselves, but how did she carry her ideal to others when no one—not even her one friend, Elrabin—wanted to believe in it?

One step at a time, she told herself. Back when she still lived in the palace and asked Bish to teach her the true history of her people, he had told her she must learn patience. It seemed she had many other lessons to learn as well.

So she would begin with compromise. If Elrabin had to be paid with winnings for his help, then she would give him winnings. After all, if she had to be a fighter, she might as well be the best one in the arena. And if she became the best, then her name would be famous, so famous even Israi in her shining palace would hear it spoken.

Israi might have thrown her away, but Ampris was not going to let herself be forgotten.

"I am the splinter in your foot," Ampris whispered, making it a vow. "I will fester in your heel until you cry out. Somehow, someday, I will shake the foundation of your empire."

She clutched the Eye of Clarity and shut her eyes. "This, I swear."

CHAPTER FIVE

Across the empire, on the Viis homeworld Viisymel, the palace of the Kaa drowsed through the warm afternoon siesta. Only the servants were stirring, putting the finishing touches on preparations for the coming Festival. In the wives' court, however, all was not entirely quiet.

Israi, sri-Kaa and Daughter of the Empire, languished on her couch beneath slowly revolving fans only until the door shut behind her ancient Kelth nursemaid Subi. Then she arose from her couch, scattering tapestry cushions onto the floor, paused a moment to find her balance, and slipped on her jeweled sandals.

She tiptoed silently across the polished stone floor. Halfway to the door, a strange sensation passed through the swollen egg sacs in her sides. She paused, clutching herself, feeling breathless and a little dizzy.

For a moment she felt too unwell to continue, but she was determined not to let her carefully laid plans be spoiled by mere physical weakness. After all, she was the Imperial Daughter. What she willed came to pass. Even her own body had to obey.

The sensation left her, and she shuddered with cold chills. Then those also passed, and Israi was able to straighten and become fully erect.

She walked forward to the door, moving more slowly

than ever. She realized she must take care, for she was very near her time. Tonight the bells would ring to mark the commencement of Sahvrazaa Festival. Tonight she would dine in the company of the Kaa and his favorite wives at the banquet feast. Then she would be expected to retire early in preparation for the call.

Already she could hear it thrumming in her blood, a restless, primitive need to be alone, to prepare her nesting place, to utter the melodic cries that would bring fertile males to her freshly laid eggs.

Israi flicked out her tongue, feeling thirsty and tired. This was her first laying, marking her true passage into full adulthood. Many gifts already filled the antechamber to her private apartments. The banquet tonight was supposed to feature special festivities to honor her.

But Israi wasn't thinking about tonight. She was thinking about now, and whether she could get out of here without being seen.

Well, she was expert at slipping away from her attendants. She had been doing it all her life, first to play pranks when she was a little chune, then to meet vi-adult friends who did not meet with the approval of her attendants, and now to seize her future with both hands.

She listened at her door and heard no sound in the room beyond where her attendants were napping or doing embroidery. Those not affected by egg laying were chatting to each other in soft voices pitched low to avoid disturbing Israi's rest.

Israi flicked out her tongue in satisfaction and turned away from the door to slip out through the secret passages. Servants used these, in order to come and go unobtrusively. Israi knew every centimeter of them.

She met no one in the dark dusty corridors hidden within the walls. She had timed herself to slip through here when the servants would be occupied with tasks elsewhere. Unless one had received a summons, none of them would be in the passages now.

Finally, she emerged into a loggia running parallel to the back garden where flowers were cut for arrangements inside the banqueting hall.

She slapped dust from the hem of her loose silk gown, finding it a struggle to bend over. She had to lean a moment against a column to fight off another wave of dizziness, then she walked on.

How heavy her body felt, how peculiar and clumsy. She had never in her life experienced such bloat, such a feeling of pressure. She wished now that she had arranged this meeting closer to her apartments, but that would have meant too great a risk of being seen. Anyhow, she hadn't much farther to go.

The sound of footsteps made Israi freeze a moment, listening. In the distance she heard shouting, but it was only someone berating a slave for a mistake. When no other sound reached her ear canals, Israi went on, making her way slowly up a flight of stairs. The effort caused that odd sensation to ripple through her sides again. She paused, breathing heavily, feeling her senses float and spin. Swallowing a moan, she pressed the side of her face against the cool surface of the wall, refusing to surrender to her weakness. Finally she walked on.

The door she sought was located at the end of the passage, tucked into a corner. When she reached it, she knocked in the prearranged pattern.

The door opened at once. She stepped over the threshold, and swayed.

Strong male arms encircled her, helping her to a chair, while commotion broke out around her.

"She's unwell."

"She's going to lay her eggs now."

"Hush, both of you! Get her refreshment."

A cup of cold, thick fruit juice was pressed into her hand. Israi opened her eyes and managed to focus on the three concerned faces hovering above her. She sipped the juice a moment, feeling it revive her.

"Shut the door," she said.

One of the males hastened to obey her. "How stupid of me," he said, puffing out his air sacs in embarrassment. "I keep forgetting I have no servant to close it for me."

Israi leaned back in her chair and smiled up at Baneen, the tallest and oldest of her three chosen ones. He had been fully adult for two years, while the others had entered that life cycle only recently. In him the urge to go on the migration was strongest. She had to plead long, cajole much, offer him many promises to get him to stay here, concealed inside the palace. Baneen with his dusky red skin shaded with darkest blue at his throat and wrists, Baneen so handsome in his uniform of the Palace Guards, Baneen so strong and glorious in looks, yet no more than average in intelligence . . . he was her favorite, her most loyal supporter. The others did what he said without question, and Baneen served her, body and soul. She had many plans for him, plans she had been formulating since the day at parade inspection when she first saw him and knew him to be ideal for her purposes.

Baneen was here to fertilize her eggs, along with these other two selected males. He would help her create offspring that were gorgeous, but not more intelligent than she. Thus would she be able to easily control and manipulate them as they grew up. Israi had watched her father sort through and manage his numerous offspring over the years. She knew he had selected her mother from among his favorites, isolating her eggs from the others. When Israi was chosen as the Kaa's successor, it was a paramount honor for Israi's mother. So great an honor, in fact, that the lady had been put away in a country villa far from court, living her days pampered and separate, never again to see the Kaa. Each year during Sahvrazaa Festival, her eggs were collected by hatchery attendants and destroyed privately so that no possible rival to Israi could be born.

Now it was Israi's turn to follow her father's example and create her own successor.

But Israi liked to spread the odds, and so although she had chosen Baneen, she selected these two other young officers as well. All three were besotted with her, enough to do whatever she commanded, no matter how great the risk.

Someday, she told herself, gazing up at them, she would make Baneen her Commander General. The others she would deploy offworld, as governors of colonies, far from her so that their ambitions could not become a problem.

Catching her breath at last, she held out her hand to Baneen, and when he stepped forward to take it in his strong one, she looked around.

The room was small and plain, clearly servant quarters not in use. The males had made some effort to improve it. Hangings concealed the plain plaster walls. Rugs covered the floor. The furniture was of pleasing line and quality. Over in one corner stood a screen. Behind it, she knew, must be the birthing stone.

An involuntary shiver passed through her. For the first time she considered the risk she was taking and grew afraid. Then she shut it away, refusing to pay heed. Fear had no place in her character.

"Is everything ready?" she asked.

"Yes, highness," Baneen said. "We have the birthing stone there." He pointed at the screen. "We have the candles ready to be lit, the incense ready to burn, the swaddlings waiting in those baskets. We have purified ourselves. We will do what you require."

Baneen made his obeisance. She admired his lithe, masculine form and knew she had chosen well. On the day she finally ascended to the throne, she might even take him as consort, for when he held her in his arms and stroked her jaws in the places of pleasure, her body sang in ways that astonished her.

"Forgive me, highness," said Nulalan. The youngest of the three, he was pale yellow in color, with bold green streaks shading the underside of his rill. His green eyes looked troubled, and she wondered if his courage was failing him in these final moments. "Are you certain this is safe? For you? I fear for your welfare."

Baneen puffed out his air sacs and moved toward Nulalan, but Israi chose to be charmed rather than annoyed by his remarks.

"Your concern is pleasing," she said loftily. "Would I not be here in private, trusting myself to your care alone without my attendants, if I had fears?"

Outside a bell rang the hour, and Israi jumped.

The males shifted uneasily, and Baneen came to her side. "It is time, if you intend to do this. Are you sure—"

"Have courage, all of you," she said fiercely and drew forth from her pocket two vials.

The one banded with red she handed to Baneen. "Keep this safe and give it to me in liquid when I have finished. It will revive me quickly and give me strength enough to return to my apartments."

"I think Nulalan should escort you—"

"No!" she said furiously, glaring at Baneen. "I forbid it. Not one of you is to leave my eggs unguarded. Not one! Is that clear?"

She glared at each of them, until one by one they bowed to her.

"Yes, highness," Baneen said, all protest banished from his voice. "We will guard them with our lives, for part of our lives shall be with them."

"Well said." Nodding, Israi held up the second vial and poured it into her cup. She swirled the contents together, mixing the drug into the fruit juice with a sudden surge of anticipation.

For three days she had been taking the drug in secret, preparing her body to lay its eggs early. This final potion would be the trigger that induced birth.

As she raised the cup to her mouth, Israi hesitated, feeling a qualm of doubt. She wanted Subi to be with her, holding her hands and pressing cold, scented cloths to her brow during the birthing. This was her first time, and she was not sure exactly what to expect. Some females said it was painful. Others claimed the experience to be exalting.

Israi only knew that if anything went wrong, the males would not know what to do.

Still, she had asked her father for permission to lay her eggs here at the palace, and he had refused her request. Worse, he had refused to answer her in person. Instead he sent Chancellor Temondahl to relay the message. Temondahl, a pompous replacement for the ancient Chancellor Gaveid, had further taken it on himself to remind the Imperial Daughter that until she claimed the throne on her succession she must go to the Public Hatchery during Festival like any other commoner. Israi's eggs would pass into public hands, adopted by unknown Viis families.

The idea was unsupportable. Israi could not believe her father gave this no second thought. Did he not realize that if she were special, so must her offspring be special?

Since the Kaa did not relent to a subsequent request, Israi had decided to take matters into her own hands. And now it was time.

She took the first small swallow, dreading the bitter taste of the drug, and was about to take another when the door to the room burst open, crashing against the wall.

Startled, Israi dropped her cup, sending the potion splashing across the floor. Baneen and the others whirled around, their hands reaching automatically for the ceremonial weapons at their sides.

A tall, thin Viis male stood framed in the doorway. His rill lay in artfully arranged folds atop his tall collar of worked gold. His coat was cut from bronze-colored silk, shimmering beautifully as the sunlight slanted over his shoulder and pooled at Israi's feet. His eyes were narrowed in slits of suspicion as he looked at each of the conspirators in turn.

"What is transpiring here?" he asked, his voice loud with accusation.

Fury swept Israi, a fury so intense she nearly blacked out. She wanted to jump to her feet and attack him, but her swollen body would not move. Instead, she sat there, helpless and seething, with her fists clenched hard in her lap.

"Oviel," she said to her despised egg-brother, hating him to the very tip of her tail. "Get out."

But Oviel stepped over the threshold instead, making Baneen stiffen and the other two males move to flank her. Oviel, however, looked at them in contempt and continued to advance. He had grown into a sour, scheming adult driven by his jealousy of her. Why he thought he should be the heir to the throne when he was so clearly inferior to Israi, she did not understand. Now she could add spy to his list of faults. Disgusting, loathsome spy. He had no right to interrupt her like this.

Oviel's gaze dropped to the floor, to the spilled cup lying there beside the vial she had also let fall.

"Israi," he said, his voice very soft but holding a note of sheer glee, "what are you up to?"

"Nothing that concerns you," she said. "Get out."

Oviel tilted his head at her. "No, I think this concerns me very much. I think you have been naughty, Israi."

Her hands clenched hard on the arms of her chair.

Nulalan took a step forward. "Shall I remove this person from the presence of the sri-Kaa?"

Baneen flicked out his tongue. "Be quiet, you fool," he said in warning. "That's Lord Oviel. You must not touch him."

Oviel cast a benign smile in Baneen's direction. "Very wise," he said with a slight inclination of his head. Then his smile faded. "All of you, step away from her."

"No!" Israi said, but the males obeyed Oviel instead of her.

She knew he held a courtesy officer's ranking in the Palace Guards that put him in command of them, but her will was supposed to govern them all. That the males now ignored her made her entrails twist. She felt as though she had swallowed hot coals. Fury roared in her blood. She wanted to scream at them, to throw things at them. She wanted to kick and scratch and destroy. How dare they bow to Oviel? How dare they obey him? He was nothing, a mere hanger-on at court, scheming for a future place in the Kaa's government. Well, she would continue to block his advancement with every wile at her disposal. He had no abilities, no sense, no loyalty to anyone but himself. The Kaa did not like him; Israi had seen to that. And if Oviel thought he was going to be rewarded for his interference today, he could—

An odd pang struck her, low in her left side. She gasped, and bent over.

Oviel rushed to her immediately. "In the name of the gods, Israi, what have you done?" he demanded.

Even through the pain she resented his tone, and refused to answer. "My business," she said, curling her tongue inside her mouth as another stab of agony hit her. "Oh!"

Oviel bent and scooped up the vial. Pocketing it, he spoke into his hand-link: "Security, this is an emergency. The sri-Kaa has fallen ill. Send a physician to—"

Israi reached up, clawing through the pain, and gripped his sleeve with all her strength. "Stop it!" she gasped out. "No! Take me to my apartments. I will not be seen here. You will not make a scandal of this. You—" She broke off, gasping again.

Oviel bent over her in visible exasperation. "What did you take? An abortive?"

Horror swept her, giving her new strength. She glanced up and almost spat in his face.

"How much did you take?" he asked her. "How much?"

She shook her head, sinking into the pain again. A terrible contraction squeezed her body, locking her muscles in a spasm so intense she thought she might scream.

Baneen tried to intervene. "She took one sip only," he said gravely. "It was not an abort—"

"Silence," Oviel snapped. "You will be dealt with later."

"Baneen!" Israi cried, struggling to hold back a scream. She was frightened now. It wasn't supposed to be like this. She knew she must have help, and quickly. These stupid males had to stop arguing now. "Baneen, take me to Subi—"

A whirlpool seemed to fling her around the room. She could hear Baneen and Oviel arguing, both of them so stupid. Finally a pair of strong arms scooped her up. Opening her eyes through the swirling vertigo, Israi saw that it was Nulalan who carried her away. Gratitude filled her. She tried to speak to him, but darkness came over her, cold and frightening, and she fainted.

When she awakened, it was to find night at her windows and lamps burning at her bedside. Outside, fireworks burst open the night sky, raining down fire of many colors into the river. Israi felt cold, small, and weak. Yet her dizziness was gone.

For a moment she caught her breath. Had she given birth? Were her eggs being guarded now in the palace hatchery? What a relief to have it over. If such agony was a normal part of laying eggs, she never wanted to experience it again.

Meanwhile, Festival had begun. She could hear the distant strains of music and revelry. If she recovered quickly, then perhaps tomorrow or the next day she might join the festivities.

Shifting position, she swept her hand down her side and felt the swollen sacs that still burdened her.

Israi groaned aloud. None of it was over.

Only then did she notice the sound of voices murmuring nearby. Israi tried to turn her head, and found the movement difficult.

A voice said clearly, "She is awake."

This announcement brought a flurry of activity. Israi

drifted a moment, but when she next opened her eyes she found the lamps shining a little brighter and five of her attendants crowding behind the physician, who was running a scanner over her slowly. His gaze never left the readout on his instrumentation, but his other hand encircled her wrist, and the air sacs in his throat puffed in and out with the same timing as her pulse.

"Am I dying?" Israi asked.

The physician's gaze shifted to her face momentarily. "No, highness," he said, his voice calm and soothing. "The Imperial Daughter is making excellent recovery."

While he was placing a white tablet beneath her tongue, the doors opened and a small Kelth herald said, "Heads up! The Imperial Father is coming."

Moments later, the Kaa swept into Israi's bedchamber with Chancellor of State Temondahl in his wake.

Towering above everyone else in the room, the Kaa was breathtakingly magnificent as always. Garbed in a long-skirted coat of silver cloth studded with clear jewels that winked and flashed glittering fire with his slightest movement, he wore a tall, elaborate collar covered with the same jewels. More jewels hung from his rill spines, so that as he came in he seemed all radiance from head to foot. Yet his bronze skin looked slightly ashen tonight, and his brilliant blue eyes were clouded with visible worry.

Ignoring formality and protocol, he went straight to her side, oblivious to everyone else as they bowed deeply to him. Temondahl gestured, and the room cleared of people, leaving the Kaa and Israi alone.

"Our beloved daughter," he whispered, taking her slender, cold hand and squeezing it. "We are thankful you have been spared."

Israi curled her tongue around the tablet, then swallowed it to be rid of it. She wished she had had time to prepare for his visit. She could have donned a fresh sleeping robe of heavy silk. She could have had her skin oiled and perfumed to mask the scent of medicines. She could have been propped higher on her cushions, with her rill arranged above a pretty collar, instead of lying limp upon her shoulders.

"I think I am well, Father," she said. "The physician says the attack has not harmed me. My eggs are well."

The Kaa closed his eyes. "The gods be thanked," he said. He sounded old tonight, not himself. His obvious concern touched her, and she smiled at him in love.

"Truly I am blessed to have a father who adores me so much."

The Kaa bowed his head and sank wearily onto a stool next to her bedside. He still gripped her hand, as though he would never let it go. "You are infinitely precious to us," he said. "Always, from the moment of your hatching, we knew you were more special, more dear to us than our own heart. Please, Israi, never frighten us this way again."

The tablet she had swallowed must be working, she reflected as the last traces of her nausea vanished. She felt stronger, and suddenly impatient. "Then you do want me to be happy?" she asked.

"Always."

Israi smiled in satisfaction. "Thank you, Father! To hear you say you have relented makes my heart sing with joy. I will lay my eggs here in the palace and—"

The Kaa released her hand. He rose to his feet. "No, Israi."

She stared at him, not certain she had heard correctly. "But, Father, you just said—"

"We just said we were relieved and thankful for your swift recovery," he told her as his rill began to redden. "We did not say you could take our imperial privileges from us!"

Aware that she'd made a mistake, Israi sat up and pulled a cushion impatiently out from beneath her tail. "Please don't be angry," she said, tilting her head in a way that she knew enhanced her beauty. "I'm not sure what you've been told, but I—"

"Oviel explained what he found. He submitted the drug you took for examination." The Kaa's voice grew steadily louder and angrier. He flicked out his tongue. "You were going to lay your eggs early, in direct violation of all that is sacred. You were going to lay them in an unsanctified place, for fertilization by males of your own choosing. And then what did you propose to do, Daughter? How did you intend to explain the presence of your blasphemous hatchlings?"

Israi flinched. He was seldom furious with her, but she knew now that she must act swiftly to make amends. She had offended him deeply, and she was in trouble.

"Father, please don't be angry with me," she said, pleading with all the charm she had. "And please don't believe everything Oviel tells you."

"Oviel has proof. We have seen with our own eyes the squalid room where you meant to work your misdeeds."

"But, Father—"

"Silence," he said with a curt gesture. His blue eyes glared at her. "You have committed a grave transgression."

"Nothing happened."

"Be thankful it did not. That is all that has thus far saved those three officers from having their necks broken in execution."

She gasped, well aware that when angry the Kaa was more than capable of putting people to death. Worried for Baneen's safety, she said, "Oh, please do not kill them. Baneen is a fine officer—"

"He is stupid and a fool."

"He did only what I commanded," she said, determined to save him. "He—"

"Yes, he followed your orders," the Kaa said with disgust. "Despite knowing that what you ordered was wrong."

Israi smiled with smug satisfaction and plumped a cushion between her hands. "That is the mark of a loyal officer."

"The mark of an idiot unfit for the rank he holds!" The Kaa flicked out his tongue. "It is wrong, Israi, very wrong to turn an officer against his known duty. It is wrong to put someone in that position, having to choose between serving an imperial request and obeying the laws."

"The throne is law," Israi said with a shrug. "There is no difference and no conflict."

The Kaa glared at her. "You do not have the throne yet, Daughter."

His voice was low and very, very cold.

Israi looked at him, and for a moment her heart nearly stopped. She met his blazing eyes, and dared not even breathe until he swung away to pace over to the window. She blinked. "Please, Father," she said. "You know I don't mean to disobey you or make you angry. You know how much I admire and adore you. I want to be so much like you that sometimes I really do forget it's not allowed."

"You know exactly what is permitted you," he said sternly, returning to her. "There is a line you may not cross. Only the Kaa has the privilege of a private hatching. Only the Kaa!"

His shout brought someone to the door, but the attendant retreated hastily after one swift look inside. The Kaa bowed his head, breathing heavily, and seemed to be struggling to control himself.

Israi hesitated, then reached out to grip his sleeve. The jewels scratched her fingers, but she did not release him. "I'm sorry," she said. "It was not my intention to offend. But all my life you have praised me and admired me. How could I not expect my first eggs to be as special as I am? How could I not wish, with the strongest instincts of a new mother, to preserve them? Is this not the imperial drive of my heritage, to keep what is mine?"

"Israi—"

"Oh, Father. Will you please forgive me?"

He puffed out his air sacs, and she leaned closer, pressing her face to his hand. "Please?"

"Israi, stop this," he said, uneasily pulling away. "It is unbecoming in a member of the imperial family to beg."

"But how else am I to obtain your forgiveness?"

He looked into her eyes, and she saw his anger melt away. He sighed, flicking out his tongue. "Of course you are forgiven."

She beamed at him, clasping her hands together in relief, and dared not press her luck by asking for his mercy toward Baneen and the others. "Thank you for your kindness. You are the best father, truly the most understanding and benevolent—"

"Hush, now," he said, interrupting her. "You must lie down and rest. We have talked too long. It is time for us to leave you."

She refused to lie down. She wasn't finished yet. "At dawn I will enter the sacred passage of giving life. I am afraid."

He came back to her side, as she had known he would. "Little one," he said, using his old pet name for her. "There is nothing to fear. You are adult now, with adult responsibilities. At dawn you will enter a new understanding of what it means to be Viis and a mother within your race. When you go to the hatchery with the others, you will have fulfilled your most sacred duty to our subjects. You will be one of them, one with them for the first time in your life. This will—"

"One of them!" Israi cried, pulling away. She tossed a cushion at the wall. "I don't want to be one of them! I am not a commoner. Why should I have to go among strangers and people of low station?"

"All Viis females of high and low birth will be there," he said. "It is not a time of position."

She flicked out her tongue, pouting. "This is Oviel's doing. He hates me, Father. He is jealous of me."

"Oviel did not create our world or the laws of nature,"

the Kaa said patiently. "Do not blame him for what is—"

"I won't do it," she said. "It will be dirty and—and common. I cannot bear it. I will not do it."

His eyes grew cloudy and impatient again. "You will. When the call comes upon you, you will follow it with the others. You will do what is natural and right, and then you will return to take your place in the festivities."

"But, Father—"

"No, Israi," he said, and there was no relenting in his voice. "Be glad you have our forgiveness for your serious transgression. But do not expect us to go beyond that. We will not grant your request. Do not ask it again of us."

Israi glared at the coverlet, furious with him. Why did he always have to think of himself? Why did he have to always come first? She was his successor. Why couldn't he share more of his privileges with her? It was ridiculous to make her wait, to make her ask, to deny her what she wanted. She felt as though she were tied with chains, unable to act or to live life freely. And her impatience was like something raging inside her, driving her to challenge him, forcing her to reach past him at every opportunity. She hated it that he would deny her anything. After all, she had apologized prettily. Why could he not now relent?

"Father—," she tried one last time.

But the Kaa left her in silence, without a backward glance, striding out as rapidly as he had entered.

Startled by his abrupt departure, by the very rudeness of it, Israi stared after him openmouthed. Then her anger came boiling up anew. She seized another cushion and hurled it at the door. Then another, and another, until all her cushions lay scattered across the floor.

Wearied by her tantrum, she lay down again, curling on her side although it was uncomfortable now to lie in her favorite position with her egg sacs full. She thumped her bedding restlessly, still seething with resentment.

The Kaa was unfair, with no sense of justice. If she had to lay her eggs in the Public Hatchery, then she wanted no part of them. She wished she'd aborted them. She would have been in deep disgrace, but she wouldn't have had to enter a public facility among commoners, *as* a commoner. To be reduced in rank for even a day was degrading and humiliating. Every female present would be permitted to stare at her. Everyone would see her inexperience. She would never recover from the shame of it, especially from the idea of some stranger from another city fertilizing her eggs. He might be anyone, of any occupation. Her imperial progeny squandered in this way . . . she loathed the whole idea.

Well, so be it. If her father was so shortsighted that he couldn't see the advantages of allowing her superior offspring to live in the palace, then let him mourn the fewer and fewer hatchlings born every year. Why should she care, when he was determined to be not only a hypocrite but a fool?

How many hours until dawn? She felt restless. She could feel the hour approaching in the very thrum of her blood. She would go, because she would be forced to, and she would leave as swiftly as she could. She would not say her prayers, and she would not bless her eggs before she departed. Though she carried them, they were not hers, would never be hers. Therefore, they had no importance. They were like her body's natural wastes, to be disposed of and left. She would not waste her thoughts or her feelings on them again.

But neither would she forget her father's cruelty. Neither would she forgive, down deep in the secret places of her heart.

CHAPTER SIX

Ampris dodged Ylea's thrusting spardan point, stumbled in the deep sand of the indoor practice arena, and went with the fall, hitting the ground and rolling rapidly to avoid another jab of the spardan that narrowly missed her eye. Grunting with the effort, she jumped to her feet in an acrobatic kip and swung around on her heels with a whistling slice of her glaudoon.

The edge smacked hard against Ylea's armored side and bounced off harmlessly. Ylea roared in fury and attacked, but the whistle was blowing.

"Halt!" Halehl's amplified voice called down to them from the stands.

Ampris obeyed at once, stepping back at attention. But Ylea continued her charge. Still roaring, she plowed into Ampris and knocked her flat, pounding her with both fists before a charge jolted through her restraint collar.

Her roar rose several octaves to a shriek. Flailing, she fell over while Ampris scrambled free. Ylea's muscles locked up and went into spasms, making her jolt against the ground with her eyes rolled back in her head for several seconds before she was released.

Ampris watched her warily, knowing the jolts couldn't be as harmless as everyone said. Ylea got too many of them, too often. It was making her crazier than ever, and harder to evade.

Bruised by her hard fall in the tackle, Ampris resisted the urge to rub her aching hip, and stood at attention again while Ylea snorted and moaned into the sand. Finally the older Aaroun staggered upright and shook herself with a grunt.

Glaring at Ampris, she stood a short distance away and pulled herself to attention also.

Silence fell over the arena.

"Well done, Ampris," Halehl's voice came down to them. "Ylea, go cool off and get some water. Teinth, your turn."

Teinth came trotting over to Ampris. After Ylea, he was the second most seasoned gladiator on the team. Never one to say much, never one to get himself in trouble with Halehl or the subtrainers, he was blocky and sleek, with pale beige fur marked with light brown stripes. A distinctive streak of brown marked his nose, and his eyes gleamed at Ampris in open appreciation. He was the one who had called her pretty on her first day. He was the one who always managed to sit beside her during their shared midday meal. He was the one who mumbled distracting chatter in her ear during their training vids unless one of the subtrainers caught him and made him sit elsewhere.

Ampris, unused to being courted, had learned that among Aarouns it was the female who initiated the mating rituals. Teinth was just making himself attractive and available. But she had no desire for him. There was too much to do, too much to learn, and only a week left until the season opened. Ampris was still scrambling to learn how to fight with the team, in the famous Galard style. She had adapted to the gravity. She was learning to cope within the tight constraints of the sensor suit. But as the days went by, zooming up to her first professional competition, her nervousness was increasing.

"Teinth," Halehl's voice called down to them, "show Ampris the Wind as Air trick."

Teinth lifted his right hand in acknowledgment of the order and turned to Ampris. "This is the best one got by us," he said, his voice hoarse and ruined from an old blow that had once crushed his throat. "Can only use it once. Only if you outmatched."

"That'll be the first day," Ylea said from near the wall, where she was helping herself from the drinking pail.

Ampris backed her ears, but Teinth ignored the interruption. The other team members stood out of the way, silent and watching. There were four males on the team and two females, herself and Ylea. The males had begun to accept her, although they continued to tease and talk about past seasons in a way that left her out. Ylea hated her more than ever, and constantly tried to trick her, hurt her, or get her in trouble with Halehl. But at the Bizsi Mo'ad, fellow trainee Sheir's constant persecution had taught Ampris how to avoid dirty tricks during practice drills. She'd never thought she would be grateful for Sheir—until she met Ylea. As for getting her into trouble with Halehl, Ylea's methods were crude and pathetically obvious. Usually they backfired on her, making her hate Ampris more than ever.

"Ampris," Teinth said loudly, snapping her attention back to him. "Listen close."

"Sorry," she said, embarrassed, and focused on what he was trying to show her.

"First, show you how to take trick," he said. He gripped her shoulder and kicked at her feet. "It comes at you, you fall straight back, see?" He arched his back, demonstrating without actually falling over. "Fall back, clean and fast. No tumble. No roll like do most times."

Ampris backed her ears, not understanding. "But then you're exposed—"

"Listen close. Want to fall fast. Get to ground fast. Get back parallel to ground. Tuck legs this way." He stretched himself out on the ground and drew up his legs tight against his middle, drawing one arm around them. "Momentum pull you down and under opponent. Like leap, only you fall. Must be fast, like wind sweeping under." He motioned with his hand, then scrambled up and pulled her around to face him, kicking her feet apart until her stance suited him.

"Attack. You drop back. Use attack force to help. Drop back, fall fast, tuck legs, go under."

Ampris nodded. "Then I cut from underneath."

"No! No cut. No slash. Stab, straight up into vitals."

Revulsion shivered through her. Quickly she looked away, to hide it, but Teinth had seen.

With a growl, he gripped the front of her training harness and pulled her close. He glared into her eyes. "No mercy in arena," he said, his ruined voice rasping at her with more hostility than she'd ever seen in him. For the first time she glimpsed how he would be in the ring, facing down his opponent. The appreciative flirtation had vanished from his eyes, and only implacable purpose bored into her.

"No mercy!" he repeated. "Stab to kill. You down where you can't get up. No kill opponent, opponent surely kill you."

Swallowing hard, Ampris nodded.

He glared at her a moment longer, as though to make sure she got the point, then he gave her a quick rub between her ears and pushed her away.

"Try now," he said, pointing at the ground. "Fall and tuck."

Ampris hated this part, especially when Halehl boosted the energy field in her sensor suit, making her suddenly twitch all over. Trying to ignore it, she flung herself on her back and pulled up her legs as Teinth had directed.

She hit hard, making her teeth snap together, and knew even before Ylea's raucous laugh drowned out the snickers of the others that she'd done it wrong.

Teinth was shaking his head. He gave her a hand to pull her up. "Pretty one, listen close," he said. "Don't drop like supply sack falling off transport. Angle of momentum all wrong. Not straight down. *Under.* Try again.''

Ampris thought a moment, visualizing the move in her mind. She realized she had to put all the momentum into her hips, leading with them. That meant she must spring up at an angle that would then turn her into a falling projectile.

She leaped into the air, flinging herself back, and tucked. When she landed, the air came out of her with a grunt.

Once she could focus again, Teinth was standing over her, shaking his big head. "Too high," he said while she scrambled upright. "Throw your pretty self on my sword point that way. Not good to be here." He held his hand at chest height, then moved it down below his hips. "Stay out of target zone. Do again. Not so high, and faster."

She pulled her ears down flat against her skull, determined to get it right.

This time he lunged at her, and in startlement, she jumped too fast and got it all wrong.

The next time she did it perfectly, finding herself skidding beneath him. He jumped aside, although she wasn't holding a weapon, and grinned at her toothily.

"Better," he said, and she warmed to the praise.

"Now, show you how to attack," he said. "Trick go two ways. Someone come at you with this, drop under and stab up. Good. But maybe you go at someone too big, arms too long. You can't get in close enough to reach."

"Yeah!" Ylea called, pounding on her chest. "Someone like me!"

Teinth rolled his eyes. "Wish could be so," he muttered, and Ampris had to battle back a laugh.

"Wind as air," he went on, regaining her attention. "Wind hold you up, and you dive at opponent. No drop on back this time. Instead, leap forward. Must go up high now, not low. Go high, over guard of blade, in arc." He motioned with his hand, and she nodded, visualizing it. "Tuck in elbows close to sides, this way. Weapon part of you, part of arc. Again, you stab, but not with arm, with whole body."

"Like this?" she asked, tucking her arm close to her side, then driving it forward. "My momentum puts the force behind the blade?"

"No. Arm not move. Hold tight to body. Hold hard. Blade in hand will be taller than head when held this way." He drew his glaudoon and demonstrated.

Ampris saw how the tip of the blade extended maybe a hand's length above his head.

"Stab with whole body, with force of whole body hurled at opponent. No move arm."

Ampris backed her ears uneasily. "But the opponent's blade can draw back and slash me—"

"Wind as air," he said. "Too high. Too fast. Up over blade. Drive whole force into opponent's chest, or throat. Throat is best if you get that high. Follow through completely. When you get high and fast enough, opponent no get you first."

She didn't like it, but Teinth pulled his sword arm tight against his side, and leaped in demonstration. Not until he nearly hit the ground did he break the arc of his body and fold swiftly to roll upon his shoulder.

Bouncing upright, he faced her breathlessly and said, "Will take opponent down. Hold blade till opponent hit ground, then break fall in roll. Timing must be good, otherwise, good way to break arm."

Sheathing his glaudoon, he took a stance and held his arms in front of him. "You try. Without weapon."

Ampris backed up several steps, taking short, quick breaths in preparation. She pulled her elbows to her sides, tucking her arms tight, then launched herself. As she leaped, the sensor suit boosted its energy wave, making her yell as though scalded. She jumped too high and too hard, hurtling nearly over Teinth's head and landing in a rough, jolting tangle of arms and legs.

Stunned, she lay there a moment until Teinth dragged

her up and gave her a shake. "Okay, pretty one?" he asked in hoarse concern. "Okay?"

The world was still spinning a little. She blinked at him, trying to focus, and gave an unsteady little nod.

Teinth snarled and turned to glare up into the stands. "The master must stop!" he called. "She don't need the boost."

A subtrainer ran over to them. "Quiet," he said. "You know better than to question Master Halehl's methods."

"They're wrong for her," Teinth insisted, while Ampris dizzily put her hands to her skull. "Work on Ylea. Work on Sanvath good. Not for Ampris. Mess up her talent. Make her—"

A jolt went through his restraint collar, silencing him abruptly. Teinth dropped his hold on her and staggered sideways, gasping with his hands at his throat.

The subtrainer glared at Teinth, then at Ampris. "Get back to work," he said coldly and strode back to his place.

Ampris gazed up into the stands, where Halehl sat in the shadows, but Halehl said nothing.

When Teinth stopped gasping and choking, he slowly came back to her and resumed his stance. "Again," he said to her in a strangled whisper.

She gathered herself, putting her anger aside in order to concentrate. Again she ran at him and leaped. This time, however, Halehl did not zap her through the sensor suit. She went up and over Teinth's outstretched arm, making the arc of her body like he'd told her, and crashed headfirst into his chest just below the base of his throat.

He fell like a sack beneath her, but not before something flashed in his eyes. Even as they landed together, she knew that this was how his throat had been crushed.

She scrambled to her feet, offering him a hand up, while she thought about Halehl's cruelty in making Teinth show her the move that had probably nearly cost him his life. But at the same time, she knew there could be no fear in the arena, no hesitation.

Teinth met her sympathetic gaze with eyes clear and reflective. He didn't want her pity, and she knew better than to offer it.

"Better," he said and cast a defiant look in Halehl's direction.

They tried the move a few more times, with Ampris improving steadily, then they tried both moves with weapons.

"Before leap, don't tuck arms so far ahead," he told her. "Too much warning to opponent. Last minute."

She had to practice it again and again and again before he was satisfied. Not until her fur was soaked beneath the sensor suit and her lungs burned for air did Halehl finally call a halt.

Sanvath and Omtat were put through drills after that. Ampris rested on a bench and watched, learning and refining her skills. Then Teinth and Nink were harnessed together at the waist before working out against machines rolled into the arena.

Ampris enjoyed watching them. They worked well together as team fighters, their footwork always in unison, their bladework complementing each other.

Then Sanvath and Omtat were harnessed together and faced the machines. And finally it was Ylea and Ampris's turn. Ylea's huge size made her an awkward teammate, especially when she and Ampris were yoked together. She tended to sling them around without warning, pulling Ampris off her feet. If Ampris lost her balance, Ylea would turn on her with a snarl of blame, forcing the subtrainers to intervene.

"Ylea, you're on the same side," Halehl said, his voice less patient than usual. "It's not Ampris you're trying to kill. Remember that."

Ylea flicked her ears back hard enough to set her fancy cartouche jingling. "As the master says," she replied reluctantly.

The practice went on, with Ampris jerked and yanked about mercilessly. She stumbled, missed sword strokes that she shouldn't have, and felt like a fool. This was the one way that Ylea could make her look stupid, and by the time they halted for midday break, Ampris was boiling.

In the messroom, located to one side of the indoor arena, Ampris grabbed her filled tray from the Kelth worker who served her and marched over to smack it down on the table beside Teinth's. She sat heavily next to him and bit into her meatroll with a snap of her teeth.

As team leader, Ylea took her reserved place at the head of the table. She wore only two necklaces today and a number of bracelets that bulged beneath the tight webbing of her sensor suit. Her claws were painted green instead of carmine.

"Two days from now we ship out," she announced, her beady eyes glowering at each of them. "It's a fast jump gate to round one this year."

Teinth was eating steadily, ignoring her, but Sanvath looked up from his food. "Rentaur?" he asked.

Ylea flicked her ears. She was still rearranging her food on her tray. It was a ritual with her. Fruit had to be on the top left corner. Meat had to be in the right bottom corner. Grains had to be in the middle. The cup had to be in the top right corner, turned so that her name, which was inscribed on it, faced her. Vitamin and mineral supplement pellets had to be off her tray and rowed up on the table along the top center of her tray. She wouldn't eat a bite until everything was in its place.

Ampris tried not to watch her. She knew Ylea was crazy. So did everyone else.

"Ylea?" Sanvath asked around another mouthful of food. "I asked if we're starting at Rentaur."

Ylea finished her arrangement and took a dainty bite of her meatroll. She would finish it and then begin on the next item, moving in a clockwise direction. Her eyes flashed at Sanvath. "Yes, Rentaur."

Sanvath tipped back his head with a mock roar and chuckled. Omtat leaned forward. "Sure?" he asked.

Ampris knew then that they had a bet laid on the answer.

Ylea finished her fruit and started on her grain. "I be sure," she said, almost growling. "Got it from the master, when he give me strategy. We'll go through that tonight, plus we got training vids on our opponents."

"But—"

Ylea's eyes shifted to Ampris. "You speaking to me?"

They all stopped eating and stared at Ampris. Disconcerted, she wished she'd kept quiet. But now she had to answer. "I thought our opponents would be chosen by lot, from the entrants."

The males laughed, and Ylea snarled in scorn before resuming her meal.

It was Teinth, finishing the last morsel on his tray ahead of everyone else, who explained. "Chosen, sure. By bribe, not lot."

"Oh." Ampris looked down at her food, while Omtat snickered. She didn't know why her ignorance gave them so much amusement. After all, she couldn't learn everything just by watching. Sometimes she had to ask questions.

But Omtat forgot her a moment later as Sanvath pounded him on the shoulder. "Owe me," he said, holding out his hand.

They started a low-pitched argument, and Ampris glanced up to find Teinth staring at her.

She bottled up what she wanted to say until Ylea finished with her tray and left. Sanvath and Omtat followed her out, still arguing over the bet. That left Nink scratching his jaw and Teinth still staring.

"How am I going to fight with her in the paired events?" Ampris demanded. "You two are so good together. You make pair fighting an art. But we're terrible. Any suggestions?"

Teinth smiled, slow and lazy, and gazed deep into her eyes.

Finally Nink answered, "She won't work with you."

Ampris wanted to choke both of them. Thoroughly exasperated, she rose to her feet. "We're supposed to be a team. Don't you think we'd be better if we all tried to get along, tried to be a success?"

"Blues already a success," Nink said without concern. He studied his claw tip, then scratched his shoulder.

"Ylea and I aren't going to be," Ampris said. "If we don't improve, we'll be killed in the opening round."

Nink grinned. "*You* will. Ylea will let you take the blow. She's practicing already."

Ampris's mouth fell open. It made sense, the way Ylea kept her off balance, the way Ylea jerked her suddenly off her feet and whirled her around. "You're right," she said slowly, while fresh anger began to burn inside her. "So she is practicing to swing me around into a blow. That—"

She broke off with a growl and started to rush out.

"Hold," Teinth said hoarsely, grabbing her arm.

Ampris tried to twist free of his grip. She was going to take Ylea down here and now. "Let go," she said and kicked him.

He grunted, but didn't release her. "Listen close," he said, giving her a shake. "Take her on now, and the master will have you whipped. Got to outsmart her. Got to *think*. Ain't no getting out of it."

"But we can't work together if she won't cooperate," Ampris cried in frustration.

Teinth looked at her. "You work with her. She won't work with you."

Letting go of her, he jerked his head at Nink. The two of them went out together, leaving Ampris standing by the table. A moment later Ruar came stumping inside, bowlegged and sour-faced as usual. He coiled his tail at the sight of her. "Come now!" he ordered. "Lazy one. Hurry!"

Ampris rushed back to the arena to join her teammates. Halehl had them sit around and rest until their meal was digested. He talked to them about the upcoming competition, explained who their opponents were, and showed them the illegally obtained vids of their foes in action. While he droned on about strategy, Ampris was thinking over a plan of her own.

Nink and Teinth were right; she was sure of it. That meant she had to find a way to keep Ylea from getting her killed. That Ylea was more clever than she appeared. She could fling Ampris onto an opponent's blade, then attack in retaliation. At the end, Ampris would be dead and Ylea would look braver than ever. Extending her claws, Ampris stared at the back of Ylea's head and snarled silently to herself.

When they resumed practice, Ampris let herself be harnessed to Ylea without hesitation. As soon as the subtrainer walked away out of earshot, Ampris met Ylea's hostile eyes.

"I know what you're doing," she said clearly. "It won't work."

Ylea snarled, not even bothering to pretend she didn't know what Ampris was talking about. "Works fine," she said.

"Ampris! Ylea!" Halehl called to them as the machines were positioned in place. "Maneuvers five and six. Start with five until I give you the voice signal through your collars, then shift to six. I want the shift to be as smooth as possible."

Chained together at the hip, they walked over to their starting place and got ready. Their practice was as jerky and as awkward as before. But this time, whenever Ylea jerked Ampris around, Ampris leaped with the motion, using the momentum of Ylea's strength to hurl herself around. Her glaudoon whacked into the shield of the machine with a crash that shattered the blade.

Smoke curled up from the machine, and a grinding whir could be heard from inside it. From over to one side, the males cheered.

"Enough," Halehl said, halting the practice.

The subtrainers shook their heads over the broken machine, and even Halehl came down from the stands to examine it. Ampris stood quietly next to Ylea, expecting to be reprimanded for breaking it. She still clutched her shattered glaudoon in her hand, which was tingling from the shock of impact. Well, she had tried her best. Now she would probably be whipped for it.

Halehl ordered the machine taken out, then he came over to Ampris and Ylea. His rill stood at full extension behind his head, but it had not turned red. "Well done, Ampris," he said. "I am pleased to see such enthusiasm. If you attack with that much force in your opening round, you will intimidate everyone exactly the way I like." His tongue flickered out. "Ylea, you were wise to think up this new move. When you refine it, we will let you give it a name. Together, the two of you are becoming a formidable pair. Let's see more work like this. Start again."

As he walked away, calling for Sanvath and Omtat to be harnessed quickly to oppose the female team, Ampris and Ylea looked at each other.

"Can we make a truce now?" Ampris asked, looking up at the taller female. "It's clearly to our advantage to work together. I'd like to be part of the most formidable fighting pair. Wouldn't you?"

Ylea snarled at her. "Don't push me, *ruvt.*"

But as the practice went on, she no longer crossed Ampris's footwork, and instead of trying to impale her on an opponent's blade, she positioned Ampris and herself where they could fight the most effectively.

By the end of the day, Ampris sank exhausted into her bath with every muscle aching and the feeling of having done well. At last she was beginning to fit in. At last she had found neutral ground with Ylea.

"I'm making progress," she boasted to Elrabin as she seated herself in her evening robe at her tiny table.

He filled her platter with steaming, aromatic ragout, making her mouth water in anticipation. His tall ears swiveled with alert twitches while she told him of the day's events.

"We will never be friends, but I think she's beginning

to respect me now. Halehl was very diplomatic with her, and that helped also.''

Ampris finished, only then growing aware of how silent Elrabin was. Swallowing a bite of hot food, she glanced up at him and saw his expression.

''What's wrong?''

''You.''

Ampris backed her ears and reached for her cup of cold water. ''Speak up, then. I'm too tired for mysteries tonight.''

''You're too quick to trust her, see? She ain't making friends with you.''

''Well, she stopped trying to get me killed.''

Elrabin yipped in exasperation. ''For now, maybe. She'll have to think up new tactics, that's all. Don't trust her. You ain't made progress. All you've done is get her to back off some.''

''That's progress,'' Ampris said stubbornly, reaching for her fruit and wishing she could have some civa cakes. But sweets were a violation of training. Elrabin had already let her know he wouldn't steal any from the Viis larder for her. The mandatory medical scan prior to competition would betray her if she'd eaten refined sweets, and Elrabin wouldn't go to the whipping post just because she couldn't control a craving for dessert. ''If Ylea leaves me alone, then I've accomplished a lot,'' Ampris said.

''She'll try something in the arena,'' Elrabin insisted. ''You watch her close.''

Ampris sighed and tilted her head to look up at him. ''You really are a pessimist.''

''Yeah, and I expect the worst too,'' he said. ''You watch yourself.''

''I will,'' Ampris said, swallowing the last of her fruit. ''Any luck on my vid?''

Elrabin shot her a stern look and shook his head. ''Not yet. Maybe after season is over. I got a lot to do now, packing your gear.''

Ampris didn't believe him. "That's quite an excuse. What is there to pack? My glaudoon? The armory takes care of that. My harness? Oh, that will take a very long time to fit inside a duffel."

"Don't get so smart," he shot back and beckoned. "You come here."

She followed him into her bedchamber and watched while he pulled a shallow storage chest from beneath the bed. Opening it with a flourish, he pulled out a vibrant blue cape made of a lightweight synthetic fabric that billowed and flowed with the fluidity of silk. He held it up before her a moment, while her eyes widened and she reached out a hand to stroke the shimmering folds. Then he spread it across the bed.

"It's beautiful," she said, touching it again. "Much brighter than what I've seen on the vidcasts."

"There's more," Elrabin said. He bent over the chest and pulled out a fighting harness fashioned of supple leather, very lightweight but incredibly strong. The oiled leather was adorned with tracings of worked gold, like stylized tongues of flames.

Ampris ran her fingers across it. "Real gold," she said in amazement.

"Of course. You're one of the Blues," Elrabin said proudly. He pulled out a wide blue collar of stiffer leather.

Ampris grimaced at it, refusing to admire it.

"Required for all entrants," Elrabin said, then he turned it over and showed her the delicate wiring beneath the leather lining. "The communications wire is hidden inside the restraint circuitry. Pretty slick, see? Ain't been detected yet."

He held it up again, then dropped it on the bed. "You'll like these better."

Leather wrist protectors, also adorned with the flames of gold. Greaves for her lower legs. A belt of fine workmanship, studded with blue semiprecious stones in gold settings. And finally, a dagger and a pair of swords in ornate sheaths that Elrabin held out to her with a proud gleam in his eyes.

Ampris felt stunned. For a moment she could not touch them. She stared, unable to believe that she actually had her own weapons.

"For show or use?" she asked, thinking of how they had to parade around the arena in the precompetition show. If they survived, they went on the vidcast, standing behind their trainer, who granted a short interview.

"For use, of course," Elrabin said quickly. He swiveled his ears. "Don't you want to look at them?"

He held them out to her again. This time Ampris grasped the hilt of the glaudoon and drew it from its scabbard.

The weight and balance of the weapon were exactly right, as though it had been made for her alone.

"It was," Elrabin said as though he could read her mind. "Remember all those medical scans and measurements you went through when you first came here?" He gestured at the finery on the bed. "Everything tailor-made. Only the best for the Blues."

Ampris could not find words. She hefted the glaudoon again, then sighted critically down the blade. Although the weapon had a fancy, wire-wrapped hilt with an elaborate guard of engraved metal, the blade was simple and strong. It remained a serviceable, working weapon. She tested the edge with her thumb, and found it honed to razor sharpness.

In silence, she sheathed it and drew out the other weapon. It was a glevritar, curved and serrated, a deadly piece intended only for destruction. How it shone in the lamplight as she turned it over in her hands. Only yesterday Halehl had mentioned to her that he wanted her to become proficient with swords showier than the simple glaudoon. It appeared he had meant what he said.

By the time she sheathed it, Elrabin was opening a long, slender case. Inside it lay a spardan, as tall as Ampris herself, the wood polished and smooth against the curve of her palms. She lifted it above her shoulder and hefted it, knowing already that if she threw it, it would fly true. If she stabbed with it, its haft would not break.

She put it back in its case, and Elrabin grunted as he lifted another. Inside this one lay a parvalleh, a heavy brutal weapon that was half hammer and half ax. She had never used one, but she had seen demonstrations. Both hands were required to throw it, and it was necessary to spin around and around in a circle to get up enough momentum to hurl the thing at its intended target. It was an ancient weapon, impractical in close combat, but the Viis audiences for some reason always cheered when the parvalleh was brought out.

"Ylea can use these single-handed," Elrabin said.

Ampris backed her ears, understanding his warning, and lifted the parvalleh from its case. Although she had expected it to be heavy, its actual weight still surprised her. She nearly dropped it, then fitted its carved wooden handle properly into her grip. She swung it back and forth experimentally. There was a rhythm to the handling of it. At once she understood on some instinctive level that to swing it two-handedly was wrong.

She lifted it in one hand, and Elrabin took a step back. His eyes shone a moment, reflecting the lamplight, and she felt something primitive and ancient go through her. She growled deep in her throat.

"You know how to use that?" Elrabin asked. His voice sounded shrill and oddly breathless.

"It's a parvalleh," she answered dreamily, holding the Eye of Clarity unconsciously in her free hand while she swung the hammer back and forth. "A weapon of war."

"I—I looked it up," Elrabin said nervously. "It's not Viis. It's Aaroun, some kind of old, ceremonial weapon."

Ampris nodded, accepting the information which he offered like a gift. Instinctively she knew he was right. "The Viis do not know how it should be handled," she said. "This way."

And again she swung it aloft with one hand.

Elrabin backed up until he stood with his back to the wall. "Be careful with that thing."

But Ampris was thinking, flexing her muscles and feeling the quiver in them that told her she needed to double her strengthening exercises. The parvalleh should feel light-weight in her grip, not heavy. It should be thrown in an underhanded swing, with the wrist not snapping but instead held like an extension of the haft. Then the release—

"Be careful!" Elrabin said with a yip of warning.

Ampris blinked back to the here and now and found her-self clutching the Eye and growling loudly while she swung the parvalleh back and forth.

She stopped immediately and put the weapon in its case. For an instant she imagined the Eye to be warm inside her hand, but when she looked at the clear stone, it was not glowing. She must be imagining things, she thought. The only warmth here lay in her blood, which still thudded through her ears.

Ampris closed the lid of the case and left her fingertips pressed against its top. She drew in several deep breaths, trying to still her raging instincts.

"This is the proper Aaroun weapon," she said, and her voice sounded deep and foreign to her ears. "It had another name, once."

"I—I don't know it," Elrabin said cautiously. He stayed by the wall. "You, uh, like it, don't you, Goldie?"

She forced herself to stop staring at the case and glanced over at him. "Yes. It feels right to hold it. Natural."

"Yeah, Ylea likes it too."

Something about the way he said that made her attention suddenly snap and focus. She stared at him in suspicion. "Does Halehl know it was originally an Aaroun weapon?"

Elrabin looked everywhere but at her. "Don't know. Maybe. Uh, what difference does it make?"

"He knows." She drew in a sharp breath and turned away, thinking hard.

Elrabin crept up to her. "Why do you care, Goldie? It's just a weapon—"

"No it's not," she said sharply. "Do the males have these? Or just Ylea and me?"

"Just you two females. He said something one day about it looking flashy for the—"

"Flashy," she said in contempt. She snarled and left the bedchamber.

Elrabin trotted after her. "What's wrong? I thought you'd like to see your new gear, Goldie. Thought you'd be proud of it."

She turned on him so fast he yelped and jumped back. "Halehl is manipulating us," she said.

"Sure. That's what trainers do," Elrabin said uncertainly. "Make you fight."

"What kind of ceremony was it originally used for?" she asked, feeling the fur starting to bristle around her neck.

"How should I know? Just a ceremony, see? Don't matter."

"Yes, it does matter. You find out."

He panted, looking rebellious. "What for? Why you getting all stirred up like this?"

"It's a war weapon," she said in excitement. "Not for combat. For something bigger. I have to know all about it."

"Maybe when I get the signal switched in your vid—"

"Are you going with me to Rentaur?" she demanded.

"Sure. All the successful fighters take their servants. The more prestigious the team, the bigger the retinue."

"Then you can ask around."

"Ask what?"

"Ask about the parvallehs—where they came from, what their original purpose was."

He rubbed his muzzle, looking more skeptical than ever. "No one's going to know stuff like that. It's too old."

"Someone knows," she said. "Halehl knows. He's realized that just my holding it will make me want to fight.

He's out to get me to turn savage, the way he turned Ylea savage.''

"Born that way, she was," Elrabin said.

"No," Ampris retorted. "She's Aaroun. We aren't born like that, not crazy and vicious. Never. I may not know much about my people or their ways, but I know that much. I remember the birth memories, and they are good.''

"Hey, Goldie, you were lucky," he said. "Maybe Ylea's mother wasn't as wonderful as yours. Maybe when she was a cub, things weren't sweet like you had it.''

Ampris turned on him with a snarl. "I was stolen from my mother before I could walk. I was starved and mishandled, then sold in a shop by a Gorlican scoundrel out to make all he could off black market wares. What do you know about sweet beginnings? What do you know about how things were when I was a cub?''

Elrabin lowered his head submissively and backed up. "Sorry. Guess I got that wrong.''

"Don't make assumptions about me," she said, still in a huff. "And don't make assumptions about Ylea. She may be crazy now, but she was all right once. Aarouns don't go bad unless they're driven to it. I won't let Halehl do that to me. I won't.''

Elrabin watched her, pity in his eyes. "Gotta be bad in the arena, Goldie. Gotta learn to be so bad you can't stand yourself the rest of the time. That's why Halehl uses the conditioning words, and your instincts, and the sensor suit. He's trying to make you crazy, see? Crazy like the others.''

"Only Ylea is insane—"

"Nope," Elrabin told her. "They're all crazy. Some more than others. You ain't seen them go for blood yet. But get ready, Goldie, 'cause it ain't going to be pretty and it ain't going to be nice. The more you hack and slash, the better they like it. The more blood and gore you smear, the more they'll cheer your name. Gotta play to the crowd, see?''

She faced him with her head held high. "Halehl isn't

going to make an animal of me. I had his throat in my teeth, but I let him go. As long as I have a rational mind, and can make my own decisions, I know they haven't turned me into a beast. They won't do that to me.''

''I hope not, Goldie,'' Elrabin said. ''But I ain't going to bet on it.''

CHAPTER SEVEN

The Kaa stood at the tall windows of his throne room, gazing out at the broad expanse of the parade ground below. It was barely daybreak, with the sky a grayness still glittering with dimming stars. The cold air of dawn made him shiver beneath his heavy robes, but he did not leave the window.

Around him the palace still slumbered, except for the furtive comings and goings of the servants. No one, however, disturbed him here. He was alone, a rarity in his life of ceremony and endless responsibility. The guards outside the door had orders to let no one disturb him prior to the meeting scheduled with his council this morning.

Outside, on the parade ground, he could see tiny figures moving about in the center of the vast field. A shuttle waited there, to take the prisoners away.

The Kaa sighed and turned from the sight. His daughter's lovers were to be banished, exiled for life. Although he had been tempted to order them executed, in the end he had realized that such an action would disgrace the males' families and create an ever-widening pool of scandal. Better to dispatch the matter swiftly and quietly, with a drop of mercy sufficient to avoid future trouble.

Fatigue pulled at him. He ached all over in his joints, and his eyes felt gritty from lack of sleep. Still, he could not rest. Even if he curled up among his bed cushions, there would still be no sleep and no rest from the endless thoughts circling through his weary brain.

Slowly he walked over to his throne and sank into it with a soft groan. If only he could find his old energy and drive, but both seemed to have vanished recently. Normally he enjoyed Sahvrazaa Festival and looked forward to it as a respite from his usual obligations. But this Festival had seemed flat, below par. The amusements and evening banquets had barely held his interest. No doubt much of it was Israi's fault. How could a father enjoy festivities when his beloved daughter sulked and pouted, casting sour looks over the company the few times she deigned to appear at all? While her body might have reached maturity, she continued to exhibit the self-centeredness of a ta-chune.

The Kaa sighed. He craved rest and solitude, neither of which were possible. If only he could recover his old decisiveness, his former assurance. But so many things seemed to be going wrong lately.

The Progressionist Party continued to foment unrest and discord across his empire. Many long-standing treaties were expiring, requiring innumerable diplomatic summits and new, tedious negotiations. His treasury was depleted at present, bringing a complete halt to his beloved project, the restoration of the old palace. The ground radiation problem on the western continent here on Viisymel was spreading again, threatening to contaminate the primary water sources. There were so many demands, so many petitions. Galactic border nine—long a trouble spot—had rebelled in open warfare, and prompt action needed to be taken.

He was tired. He felt a thousand years old.

Only yesterday Festival had ended. Only yesterday he had been informed by the trembling Master of the Imperial Hatchery that of all the imperial eggs laid and fertilized this spring, only four hatchlings were strong enough or suitable enough in appearance for acceptance. Seven Rejects and four hatchlings . . . a dismal result, especially in consideration of years past, when he'd accepted at least double that number. Even now, thinking of yesterday, when the salutes had fired only four times and the crowds had waited in disbelieving silence for a long, long moment before raising a ragged cheer, the Kaa's heart swelled with grief.

He wanted to shut himself away and mourn the hatchlings he would never know. He could barely bring himself to visit the wives' court, where the nursery was almost empty and his ladies wandered aimlessly about with vacant, unhappy eyes.

But he knew he could not withdraw from his duties, his endless obligations. He must tell his heart to be strong. He must lock away his grief. He must ignore the hollow silences in all but one corner of the nursery. He must go on, for he was Kaa, the Imperial Father, the Supreme Being who held his troubled empire together by sheer strength of will.

Worst of all, there still remained the problem of Israi. How to solve it? The chancellors were outraged. The whole court was whispering, shocked and titillated by rumors which flew in all directions. If not curbed soon, this situation she had created would be blown out of all proportion. Israi's own tantrums and sulks were not helping.

He sighed. Israi could not have chosen a worse time to cause trouble. So young, yet growing up . . . more beautiful, more impatient, and more demanding with every passing day. Oh, he was proud of her, greatly proud. He had trained her well, prepared her well to rule. One day—many years from now—she would take the throne for her own, and her radiance would shine glory across the empire.

But it was not yet her time. He would not give her everything she asked for. He would not let her exceed her place.

A chime sounded at the door, interrupting his thoughts. The council was here, and he had come to no decisions. Pulling his robe more tightly around him against the cool spring air, he closed his eyes a moment to summon all his inner forces.

"Come," he said.

The doors at the end of the throne room swung open, and the chancellors entered in single file by order of rank. Carrying their staffs of office, their chains gleaming across their chests, they marched in silently and rowed themselves before the semicircle of chairs arranged facing his.

Temondahl walked to the feet of the Kaa and bowed low. The other chancellors also bowed.

"Welcome," the Kaa said formally. "Let the proceedings begin."

Temondahl straightened and tapped his staff of office once on the polished stone floor.

The others seated themselves. Temondahl glanced around, saw the open window, and gestured for a lackey to close it. As soon as the servant disappeared, he took his seat in the center of the group and faced the Kaa with a grave expression.

Temondahl's lineage descended from the Fifth House, with its distinguished reputation for public service. Temondahl, with his pale blue skin and lack of variegated shadings, even around his blue eyes, seemed at first glance to be a dull bureaucrat. But slowly, in the time since he had taken office, he had made his intelligent mind and calm, rational approach to difficult decisions useful to the Kaa. He was not Gaveid, with the old chancellor's brilliance or insight, but he was a solid adviser, and the Kaa respected him.

Now, the Kaa lifted his hand wearily, allowing Temondahl to proceed.

The chancellor of state opened a small data case. "Our agenda this morning is quite long. This is usual following the close of Festival. Also, we should discuss preparations for the Imperial Father's annual visit to Malraaket, which is coming up during the summer. There are the mining agreements with various colony worlds to review, and a number of petitions from the usual sources, including a new funding request from Ehssk, director of the Vess Vaas Research Laboratory.''

The Kaa sighed and rested his head against the back of his tall throne. "Give Vess Vaas what it has requested."

Temondahl sputtered. "But surely we should first review the itemized—"

"No," the Kaa said, sweeping these details aside impatiently. "Ehssk's work is vital to the future of our race. If he can find a cure for the Dancing Death, then he is a hero. Settle this and continue with the next item."

Puffing out his air sacs, Temondahl complied.

Outside, the shuttle carrying the exiled officers took off with a muted roar, and the Kaa's gaze shifted to the window. He glimpsed a momentary flash of silver metal, burnished as it reflected the early morning sunlight, and felt his heart settle colder inside him.

"Israi," he said aloud without realizing it, then blinked as Temondahl's droning report faltered to a halt. The Kaa pulled himself together and met their stares. "Let us deal with the matter of the sri-Kaa now."

Temondahl exchanged a swift glance with some of the other chancellors and puffed out his air sacs. He lowered his agenda to his knee. "As the Imperial Father requests. First, the chain of evidence and the confessions of the three officers involved."

The Kaa gestured this material aside. "We have seen the room. We have seen the chemist's report of the drug taken. We have considered the confessions. Let us not go over old ground."

His haste and impatience clearly disconcerted them. The oldest member of the group, an amber-skinned southerner named Malvnhad, leaned forward. Malvnhad had flat, merciless eyes like burnished stones. His rill spread above his collar, luxuriant and wide with ruffled edges rimmed in green.

"Her actions smack of treason," he said bluntly, no apology in his voice. "She has tried to divide members of the Palace Guard, the Imperial Father's own elite protectors, against him. She has attempted to break the laws of the birthright. She has made efforts to usurp imperial privileges from the very hand of the Kaa. These transgressions must not be ignored."

A tremor of annoyance passed through the Kaa's rill. He said nothing, however, letting them talk now that Malvnhad's words had broken the dam of courteous silence on the subject.

Temondahl leaned forward to address Malvnhad at the end of the line. "Lord Malvnhad is correct," he said smoothly. "However, the sri-Kaa has not actually divided the guards. She did not break the laws of birthright. She usurped no privileges."

"Only because she was stopped in time," Malvnhad muttered.

"But she explained her actions and motivations," Temondahl continued. "The Kaa has forgiven her misdeeds."

"The Kaa's mercy is great," Malvnhad said harshly. "But perhaps the Kaa's mercy has been hasty."

"The sri-Kaa did not commit actual treason," Temondahl said, keeping an eye on the Kaa as he spoke. "This fact must remain clear."

"She came very close," Malvnhad argued.

"But she did not commit it," Temondahl said. "And we must not confuse the impetuous actions of a youthful Imperial Daughter facing her first—"

"What is forbidden, is forbidden!" Malvnhad said, crashing his fist down upon his knee. "Youth and impetuosity do not excuse the act. Further, let us consider the ramifications of this disobedience. If she rebels against what should be an obedient, meditative, gentle time in the cycle of the female, what else will she do?"

Temondahl hesitated, still watching the Kaa for his reaction. The Kaa said nothing, allowed no flicker of expression to appear. Looking like one of the carved stone edifices of his ancestors, he sat stolidly on his throne and listened in silence.

"May I speak?" piped up another chancellor. Lord Huthaldraril was no taller than a female, willowy and green-skinned, with eyes bright and eager. He was the youngest member of the council, newly elected and self-conscious of his position. Like most of his generation, he was over-indulged by his family, overeducated, and underexperienced.

Temondahl narrowed his eyes and nodded permission.

Huthaldraril moved eagerly to the edge of his seat. "I believe what Lord Malvnhad really wishes to say is that were the sri-Kaa a male, her actions would be seen as a direct threat to the throne. Historically, such rebellions indicate that next an attempt to subvert the loyalties of the army will be—"

"Enough," the Kaa said with a sweeping gesture.

Huthaldraril fell silent, his rill turning bright red. He scooted to the back of his chair and hunched down.

"It is unnecessary for the council to overreact," the Kaa said. "There is no need for hysteria. The sri-Kaa has made her apology. She has received correction. She is forgiven."

"And when the next incident happens?" Malvnhad asked.

The Kaa's rill extended in ire. He flicked out his tongue. "There will be none."

"Can the Imperial Father be sure?"

Now Temondahl's rill rose behind his head. He answered for the Kaa, "Lord Malvnhad, your concerns are noteworthy, but do not take them too far. The Imperial Daughter's actions may have been unfortunate, but she is not a subject for criticism."

"Until she ascends to the throne, she is subject to the laws," Malvnhad said, refusing to back down. "It is time she learned this."

"What would you do?" Temondahl retorted. "Punish her?"

"There will be no punishment," the Kaa said sharply, and both chancellors fell silent.

"She is most high-spirited," ventured Lord Curmn timidly. "This appears to be perhaps a more adult version of the pranks she used to play as a ta-chune."

A general consensus was murmured among them.

Pleased by this interpretation, the Kaa flicked out his tongue and sat less stiffly. "Agreed," he said. "Israi is young and healthy. Naturally she is active and favored with much energy. It is time we assigned her more imperial duties, both to acknowledge that she is now an adult and to occupy her abilities in a positive way."

Again they nodded and murmured approval, with the exception of Malvnhad, who sat and glared in silence.

Temondahl lowered his rill as much as his collar would allow. "An assignment of duties is an excellent suggestion made by the Imperial Father. I can have a roster of possibilities drawn up by the next—"

"Yes," the Kaa said, interrupting. "That is acceptable. But we will go further and send her to Malraaket this year to represent our glory."

A babble of voices broke out, mostly in consternation. More than one chancellor rose involuntarily to his feet, and it required much banging of Temondahl's staff on the floor to restore order.

"My lords, please," he said in disapproval, glaring at them until they were quiet and seated once again. "Such breaks in decorum simply will not do."

"But the Imperial Father always goes to Malraaket," said Curmn. He pulled out a handkerchief from his sleeve pocket and fanned himself. "The tradition is one of long standing. What would such a change convey to the officials and citizens of that city? What would it say to them?"

"It would say to them that we wish them to meet the sri-Kaa at last," Malvnhad replied impatiently. "More to the purpose, what would it say to the sri-Kaa herself?"

The chancellors blinked.

Malvnhad leaned forward. "It would say that she is to be rewarded for her actions. That she can do exactly as she pleases without consequences."

"Why shouldn't she have such a splendid duty?" Temondahl asked loyally, glancing at the Kaa as he spoke. "What is there against this plan of our Imperial Father's?"

"Nothing, if her highness could be trusted," Malvnhad replied, with more boldness than ever.

The Kaa smacked his palm hard against the arm of his throne, and Malvnhad faltered momentarily.

His stony eyes met those of the Kaa's, and the old chancellor bowed his head. "If my speech is too strong, then I beg the Imperial Father's pardon."

"You accuse her of treason," Huthaldraril said, his voice high-pitched with alarm. "Such a charge is serious indeed. According to the historical precedent, we must—"

"Nonsense," Malvnhad broke in with a glare his way. He puffed out his air sacs and returned his gaze to the Kaa's. "Can she be trusted to behave according to imperial protocol? Can she be trusted to remember the official speeches she will be asked to make? Will she carry out the onerous duties assigned to her? The trip involves a lengthy visit, a strenuous round of meetings and functions, and diplomatic finesse. As the Imperial Father knows well."

The Kaa curled his tongue inside his mouth. Yes, he knew very well. He hated the annual visit to hot Malraaket, major spaceport of the Viis homeworld. The people were provincial, their conversations tiresome and unsophisticated. This year he'd been dreading the prospect of visiting their manufacturing plants and distribution centers more than usual. The very idea of it exhausted him.

That was why he felt sending Israi was the perfect answer. The anticipation of the trip would keep her occupied and out of trouble until summer. While there, she would bask in the adulation they would pour over her. She would enjoy every moment of their attention. When she returned, she would be happy and satisfied for a while, still basking in the afterglow of a successful adventure. He should have thought of this solution sooner. Israi, with her boundless energy, constant demands, and craving for excitement, needed to be kept busy.

"It is decided," he said, breaking into the continued discussion of the council. "She will go as our representative. It is time the people met her. Let this be recorded. Let this be done."

The meeting went on to other matters, lasting far beyond his patience. But when at last the chancellors filed out and the Kaa rose to return to his chambers for his first official dressing ceremony of the day, Temondahl approached him with a bow.

"If I may have a word in private, Imperial Father?"

The Kaa paused with a graciousness he was far from feeling. His head buzzed with exhaustion. He wanted only to crawl into bed, but he knew if he did, the palace would erupt with gossip and rumors, and his physicians would be sent for to determine what was wrong. The Kaa wanted no one fussing over him. It would only make things worse.

"Yes, Temondahl?" he asked, keeping his voice courteous. How he missed Gaveid, with his sly wit, his shrewdness, his perfect understanding of minds and motivations. But Gaveid had gone into his otal life cycle, too old for service, his health failing him at last. He had died during the winter, and the Kaa mourned him still. Temondahl was a capable, hardworking individual, but utterly boring company.

He approached the Kaa now, bowing respectfully with a formality he never surrendered, even in private.

"I hope Lord Malvnhad's blunt remarks were not too offensive to the Imperial Father?"

Impatience consumed the Kaa. Was that all he wanted, to apologize for another chancellor's behavior? What a crashing bore Temondahl was.

The Kaa raked his chief adviser with a glare. "They were not."

Temondahl blinked as though he had not expected that answer. "Very well. I hope that—"

"The matter is closed to further discussion," the Kaa said in warning.

Temondahl flinched and bowed low. "Ah, yes. I understand. Sire, there are two private reports that I wish to share. They are just in, and very serious."

The Kaa's depression darkened. Private reports deemed unsuitable for the ears of the council meant extremely bad news. For a moment he was tempted to flee, to refuse to cope with any of it, but that he could not do.

"Speak," he said and braced himself.

"Our colony world in the Tescearu system has fallen to rebels. The government is overthrown. I lack complete confirmation, but there is a chance the governor has been killed."

The Kaa's anger came swiftly. He did not hesitate. "Subdue the rebellion. Send orders to the Commander General to dispatch appropriate military forces without delay."

"It shall be done."

"The rebel leaders are to be rounded up and executed. Make sure this trouble does not spread," the Kaa ordered. "We cannot have the Tescearu mines endangered."

"The Imperial Father is wise."

"What else?" the Kaa demanded.

"The Mynchepop Bank of the Empire is on the verge of failing," Temondahl said in a hushed voice. His eyes looked grave indeed. "The director sent me word by encrypted linkup only minutes before the meeting started. He reports he can hold things together long enough for the imperial treasury to be moved, but that is all. Unless they are warned, many noble families will be wiped out."

Stunned by this catastrophic news, the Kaa could only stare.

"It will be necessary for the Imperial Father to authorize an immediate transfer to the Bank of Solein Global on Fariance. May I have the imperial seal to—"

"No!" the Kaa said, unable to draw enough breath to make the word as forceful as he wanted. He thought of Mynchepop, that delightful planet, as breathtaking as a jewel. Its climate was perfect. Its scenery too lovely for description. He loved its beaches of lavender and pink sand, the seas that were so clear and unpolluted, the soft sigh of fenankath trees in the wind. It was the favorite vacation world of the empire. He had known only happiness in his all too rare visits there.

"No," he repeated. "This is impossible. Mynchepop bankrupt? How?"

"The primary jump gate to Mynchepop failed several months ago," Temondahl said tonelessly. "Perhaps the Imperial Father has forgotten. Zrheli quantum engineers were pulled off the repair project on Shrazhak Ohr and dispatched to help as soon as it happened, but thus far it has not been reactivated. Only the secondary gate is operational. This has cut down on travel and tourist visits by sixty percent. The bank is overextended, having based its empire-wide lending policies on a projection of full income. It cannot recover."

The Kaa turned away. He needed wine. He needed to sit down and think. It was impossible to assimilate such devastating news, much less cope with it.

"There is not much time to act," Temondahl said quietly but urgently. "I believe that if we promise assistance to Mynchepop, the economy there can be stabilized. Perhaps industry could diversify its economic base and—"

"No," the Kaa said in horror. "No industry can be established there. We will not permit the planet's beauty to be polluted."

Temondahl bowed diplomatically. "That matter can be discussed by the council at large. More important is the issue now before us. The imperial treasury must be saved."

"But must it go to Fariance?" the Kaa asked in dismay. His limbs felt frozen. He could not seem to think. "Lord Galard owns the Bank of Solein Global. We will be putting our money, the very heart of the empire, into his hands. No, this is not prudent. We cannot agree to this."

"Galard does not own the bank outright," Temondahl said. "He is only a director, on a board of many—"

"We cannot do this," the Kaa said, shaking his head. "Put our treasure into the hands of one not even born into one of the Twelve Houses? This upstart is a gambler, a scoundrel, with a paltry colonial title inherited through his mother's line."

"The bank, however, is sound," Temondahl argued. "I have the assurance of the management that—"

"No," the Kaa said in a tone of finality. "The imperial treasury belongs on Viisymel, here within the palace vaults. It should never have been taken offworld."

Temondahl stared at him, opening and closing his mouth several times. His rill lay limp on his shoulders. "The— the Imperial Father cannot mean this."

"Yes, of course we mean it," the Kaa said in irritation. "Why should it not be here, at the center of the empire? Why not?"

"But in the palace vaults it can earn no interest," Temondahl finally said. His voice was hoarse, and he continued to stare. "It cannot be used to secure lines of credit. How will we finance the—"

"Do not trouble us with these minor details," the Kaa said, turning away. "Our decision is made. Here, the treasury will be safe. Here, it shall return."

"But, sire—"

The Kaa whirled on him and extended his rill fully. "Will you argue with us, chancellor?"

Temondahl gulped and seemed to swallow his tongue. Coughing, he sputtered and shook his head, sinking into a low bow.

The Kaa eyed him with open displeasure. "As for our personal fortune, where is that?"

"In—in the same bank as the—"

"Bring it here also," the Kaa said.

"But—"

"Come to us later for the seal, when you have the transfers prepared," the Kaa commanded and walked out.

CHAPTER EIGHT

The crowd stood on its feet, stamping in unison and yelling Ampris's name. With a fine spray of indigo-colored blood drying on her golden fur and her blue cape billowing and swirling around her, Ampris walked her victory lap around the small, intensely hot arena while medics dragged out her fallen opponent. Every twenty steps, she paused and lifted her gore-stained glevritar aloft with a flourish that made the crowd cheer again.

Trailing after her came a score of vidcams, recording her every move. The scoreboard was flashing her name in huge letters, with zooming starbursts of laser-guided fireworks. High in the commentators' box at the top of the stands she could hear their staccato report being recorded in voice-overs for this evening's vidcast that would go out over sports link feeds across the empire.

"Yet another victory in the rising career of the Blues' newest young warrior. All season Ampris—the Crimson Claw—has improved her skills and dazzled crowd after crowd with her agility and lightning swordplay. Let's cut now to the chief trainer of the Galard Stables—"

Ampris turned toward the gate, where handlers were gesturing impatiently for her to come in. She ignored them, paused once more, and swung back to salute the crowd a final time with the glevritar.

"Crimson Claw! Crimson Claw!" the crowd shouted in a tremendous roar that crashed and thundered in the enclosed space, echoing off the rafters of the arena in this nameless place on this nameless day.

No, she realized, blinking against the dazzle of lights, this day had a name. It was the final competition of her first season. She had one more event to go, and then she could finally rest.

Spinning around so that her cloak swirled out in the flashy manner Halehl insisted on, Ampris walked out of the arena, through the gate, and down into the dark tunnel leading to the locker rooms.

Elrabin pushed his way through the bystanders crowding the tunnel, all wearing bright orange pass cards slung around their necks. He reached her side and gripped her arm through the folds of her cloak. "You okay?"

"Here." She handed him the glevritar, knowing he would clean, polish, and oil the blade with exacting care. Sanvath's servant might send him into the arena with rust spots on his blades, but Elrabin had high standards. Her gear was always clean, always shining, always ready.

One of the vidcams floated in after her, getting past the barrier. Elrabin glanced back and spotted it at the same time as one of Halehl's guards did.

"Hey!" the guard shouted. He drew his side arm and fired a neutralizing field at the cam, which spat, whirred, and crashed to the floor.

One of the bystanders stepped on it, crunching a fin, and laughed.

Elrabin hustled Ampris through her assigned door, slamming it shut, and the guards positioned themselves in front of it.

Wearily, her brain numb, Ampris untwisted the catch at her throat and let her cloak fall from her shoulders. Elrabin caught it before it landed on the floor and bustled past, tossing a stack of fresh towels to Okal, who was waiting to massage her.

Climbing on the table, Ampris let the Phivean work on her rapidly stiffening muscles, wishing he could massage away the ache in her brain. "How long till my next bout?" she asked.

"Maybe an hour," Elrabin replied, crossing the narrow room again. He laid out a fresh cloak, clean and unstained, but made no move to unbuckle her blood-splattered harness or wrist guards. "Okal, all the blood on her belong to some-one else?"

"Yes," Okal answered in his breathy, hissing voice. His tentacles worked gently, rubbing out the kinks. "She is without hurts. Is easy to see when wrong color."

"Okay," Elrabin said in satisfaction. He went over to the wall and activated the linkup recessed there. It was a text feed only, very unsophisticated, but Ampris saw his tall ears swivel in satisfaction. "Doing good, Goldie," he said after a moment, panting happily. "Look, the odds on you are changing about every ten seconds. That means the rumors are working."

Halehl had probably mentioned something in his inter-view about her shoulder sprain, which was still nagging her two weeks after she'd injured it in a fierce battle with one of the Aarouns of the Kavmahlcd Stables. He might even have let drop that it was getting worse, or that she'd rein-jured it in the combat she'd just finished. Now the rumors would be flying, making the odds shift back and forth on the tote. At the first competition of the season it had aston-ished Ampris to hear on vidcasts that Omtat had nearly lost his arm from a sword cut when the big Aaroun was sitting unharmed in the lounge, idly rolling chance stones in his hands. Elrabin had explained the ferocious lying and spying that went on all during season in an effort to rig the betting odds. Now Ampris ignored most of it, if she could.

Yipping happily to himself, Elrabin dashed over to the crude bath, which was basically a stone trough beneath a wall spigot, and turned it on full force. Rust-colored water, unheated, thundered out, making up in plenitude what it lacked in purity.

Smelling it, Ampris wrinkled her nostrils and turned her face away. Okal prodded a sore spot, and she winced.

"Is some pulled," he announced and reached his long front tentacle over to his treatment box while his shorter tentacles continued to work on her. A moment later he applied a patch to her shoulder, and the pain vanished. He prodded her gingerly. "Tendons still sore?"

"I can't tell," Ampris replied. "Your stuff is still working."

Okal had a strong interest in healing. Being both a slave and a Phivean, he had been denied any official medical training, but he had taught himself a great deal over the years. He was always experimenting with salves and healing patches, modifying the ones he was given by the medics, plus inventing his own methods of massage and therapy to quicken healing or to prevent injury.

He pushed on a spot in the web of her shoulder. "Sore?"

"No."

He moved over a fraction and pushed again. "Sore?"

"No. Ow!"

"Ah, yes," Okal hissed to himself. He applied another patch and tapped her. "Sit."

Ampris sat up and rotated her shoulders experimentally. She gave him a nod, and the Phivean's bulging eyes rolled and darted in pleasure.

Elrabin joined her, his light brown eyes gleaming wickedly. Under the sound of running water, he said rapidly, "We're doing okay today, Goldie. Now, as you know, betting on the Crimson Claw isn't bringing us much return on account of you being too good."

Ampris nodded, not paying much attention. She rubbed her face, feeling a buzz of weariness in her head, and wished she could crawl into the darkness somewhere and not come out.

He nipped her ear lightly to get her attention, then

pressed a cup into her hand. "Drink up. You're fading on me."

She was thirsty, but she sniffed the contents first.

"Just water, from home," he said impatiently. "I won't give you the boost till it's time to go back in."

She hated the stimulant Halehl gave them to keep them fighting past the point of exhaustion. She hated what it did to her afterward. How many times had she fought today already? One more to go, then the season was over. She clung to that, with a desperation she didn't want to acknowledge.

Gulping down the water, she listened while Elrabin chattered on, "You know how I've been working on getting that network in place for spreading our bets? It's working great. No way they can trace anything back to us."

"Is unwise to risk bets on selves," Okal said in disapproval.

Elrabin barely shot him a glance. "Yeah, yeah, the voice of doom over here. Shut up, see? If you won't bet, then you got nothing to say."

Ampris put out her hand and squeezed Elrabin's shoulder. "Don't be so harsh," she said, interceding between the two of them as she always did.

"Slaves should not place bets," Okal said, hissing his words more than usual. His shorter tentacles fluttered in distress. "Against—"

"Just shut up," Elrabin snapped, and Okal stared at everything in the room with his mouth cilia waving agitatedly before he turned his back to them.

Ampris sighed, wishing the two of them could get along. "Now you've offended him."

"Nah, you can't offend a Phivean," Elrabin said. "Now listen. I got the code to the bookies' main link. With that, I can call in and they don't know me from Halehl, see?"

"Be careful," she warned him.

"Yeah, I'm careful. My name is careful," he said impatiently. "Look, Goldie, I know how to do this. Now with the code I can place the bets, but I don't. No, 'cause then there might be a security trace run back and catch me that way. These bookies got no trust, these days.''

Ampris smiled into her cup as she finished her water. "Maybe they have reason."

Elrabin brushed the front of his coat. It was new, a gift from her. She'd learned how much he loved finery. This one, with its embroidery on cuffs and collar, had for once rendered him speechless. He was still preening in it at every chance.

"No reason from me," he said, not catching her teasing. "Now there's this Myal I got a tip on, that for a hefty percentage of the take she'll reroute a bet through a carrier line to clean it so it can't be traced, then tap it back in.''

Okal closed his treatment box with a snap. "You speaks of such things as make no sense.''

Elrabin glared at him, but went on talking. "The Myal is like this central processor, right at the hub of her own network of trace lines and reroutes. She's an informational genius, knows everything about how to tap into all kinds of links and data retrieval lines.''

Ampris slowly looked up and met his eyes. Only now did she realize what he was actually telling her. She drew in a sharp breath, and her whole body came alive again.

"Elrabin!" she said.

He glanced over his shoulder at the running water still thundering into the trough and gestured for her to keep her voice down.

Ampris reached out and gripped the fancy front of his coat. "What have you done?"

He tipped back his head proudly, letting mirth dance in his eyes. "That's right," he said. "I found you a network, just like you been asking for. We're tapped in. All you do is ask for something, and my contact will track it down.''

She felt as though she'd already swallowed the boost. Jumping off the massage table, she said, "Can she get into the palace archives?"

"I've got a request in," he said. "It takes time. She's good but she's slow. Too many precautions maybe, but if she gets caught she gets burned big time."

"I can wait," Ampris said, excited. "This is perfect. If she's Myal, then she'll have access to all kinds of knowledge—even the—"

"Now slack yourself, you," Elrabin said. "I just said she's slow. I don't talk to her direct, see? We gotta keep this simple and clear, 'cause the messages get passed along through a lot of checkpoints. We can't trace straight to her, and she can't trace straight to us."

Ampris didn't care. Her hope was bouncing high, right along with her spirits. "She must contact Bish, and—"

"It don't work that way," Elrabin said, twitching his ears in exasperation. "It ain't that quick, and it ain't direct. I told you, it's complicated."

"But it's there, and we can find out things now."

"If you're patient," he said. "*If* you don't expect too much. I thought you'd be happy, yeah, but not go over the ceiling."

She pounded him on the shoulder. "It's a start," she said happily. "I feel like finally we're getting somewhere. Good work!"

"Don't expect too much," he warned her.

A thud on the door made them all freeze in place. "Time!" the guard on the other side called. "Fifteen-minute warning."

Elrabin was the first to react. Darting over to the trough, he shut off the water, picked up a sponge, and rushed back to Ampris to start cleaning the blood-splattered fur on her arms. The vidcasters preferred they not spiff up until the final interviews, but Ampris liked to enter the arena clean. Besides, she knew it justified their having run so much water. Sometimes the handlers got suspicious and put meters on the spigots to monitor the water usage.

The door opened without warning, making her start. Elrabin gripped her arm tighter than ever and went on scrubbing the dried indigo blood away.

"Must have been a fast slaughter out there," he muttered, finishing her left arm and starting on her right. "Shouldn't be done this soon."

Ampris was looking at the door and didn't reply. Halehl stood there, cloaked in Galard blue striped with black chevrons. Behind him, hubbub raged in the tunnel as handlers and subtrainers led gladiators back and forth on leashes, struggling to keep fighters apart as they roared and clashed with each other.

Halehl stepped inside, and the guards shut the door behind him, thrusting back a scrawny Kelth slave who was trying to jump high enough to see into the room past Halehl's shoulder.

Readjusting his cloak, which had been pulled slightly awry, Halehl swept his cold Viis eyes over them, taking note of the water cup in Ampris's hand, the clean cloak folded and ready on the stool, the bundled towels on the massage table, the wet sponge in Elrabin's hand, the dark streaks of moisture on Ampris's fur, the water droplets glistening still in the bottom of the trough.

"How is the shoulder?" Halehl asked, speaking abiru in his precise, almost courteous way.

Elrabin released Ampris and backed away with his head lowered respectfully. He went to stand beside Okal, who was fluttering his tentacles and rolling his eyes with his bulbous head pointed at the floor in obeisance.

Ampris answered the trainer's question. "I've pulled it again. Nothing serious. Okal's patches are helping."

Halehl pulled off one of the patches and sniffed it with a quick flicker of his tongue. "This is not a standard drug." His rill reddened and rose behind his head as he glared at Okal. "You fool! She could be disqualified for this."

"Simples," Okal replied, his voice barely audible. "Simples as the natural remedies always best. Is my—"

"I haven't authorized any of your natural remedies."

Halehl pulled off the other patch and flung it on the floor. Lifting his hand-link, he spoke into it rapidly, "Send me Fuvein, now. Don't make a fuss about it. Never mind Omtat's gash. His slave can stop the bleeding. I want Fuvein, and tell him to be discreet."

Ampris opened her mouth to protest, to assure Halehl that she didn't need the team's official physician. Okal's methods suited her far better than Viis medications, which sometimes had side effects that clashed with her Aaroun physiology. But Halehl's glaring eyes and stiff rill warned her to be silent. Her well-being was his business, not her own. She knew she had no say in the matter.

Halehl turned in a circle and began to pace. He flicked his fingers at Elrabin. "Resume your work. You," he said, pointing at Okal, "get out."

The Phivean gathered his things with several tentacles and left as fast as his awkward, stumpy legs would take him. As he passed Ampris, his beaked mouth opened as though he would speak, but he said nothing.

Distressed, Ampris watched him go, wondering if he would be punished, wondering if he would be taken from her little retinue. She liked Okal, who was gentle and harmless. He only wanted to help. He did not deserve to be hurt.

Halehl was still pacing, nervous and increasingly impatient when the physician did not instantly appear. "Abiru potions. Abiru quackery," he muttered in Viis, fuming. He glared at Ampris. "You know better than to allow this. I ought to have all of you whipped for it."

Her eyes widened. Perhaps he didn't realize that he was still speaking to her in Viis. She understood him perfectly, but she realized that she must not show it. When angered, the Viis could be so touchy about unimportant things. Why did they care so much if a slave knew their language? Why were they always so insulted?

They obsessed over stupid, meaningless details, and let their machinery and systems fall apart around them. How long did they expect the glorious Viis empire to continue like this?

The door opened, and Fuvein hurried inside. A chime from the still-active wall link showed new text running across the screen. Ampris glanced at it, and her heart sank in dismay. They should not have left that on.

Halehl noticed it and swore in Viis at Fuvein. "The odds have changed again. How many people saw you come in here?"

"Everyone with eyes," Fuvein replied. He was a green-skinned Viis in his lun-adult cycle, no longer fertile but still active and alert. Ampris knew him to be skilled at his work, but impersonal and detached from his abiru patients. He met Halehl's gaze now, his own calm and unruffled. "The tunnel is nearly blocked with a crowd. I almost didn't get through."

"Look at that," Halehl said in Viis, pointing furiously at the patches on the floor.

Fuvein bent slightly to stare at them, but he didn't pick them up. Elrabin darted forward and handed them to the physician, who still would not touch them.

Fuvein's tongue flickered out. "The Phivean's handiwork, I see."

"Illegal!" Halehl spit out. "If she is disqualified for this, *now,* in the final round, Galard will lose a fortune."

Good, Ampris thought in the depths of her heart. *Such a loss will be good for our lord master and owner.*

The two Viis went on talking as though neither Ampris nor Elrabin were in the room.

"You are going to burst a vein if you do not calm yourself," Fuvein said calmly. "It is you who needs treatment, not the Aaroun."

Halehl puffed out his air sacs, his rill stiffer and redder than ever. "Do a test on her, quickly. See if you can mask it."

"There isn't much time."

"Then hurry."

When Fuvein unsnapped his scanner and approached her, Ampris backed up.

Fuvein's eyes dilated in irritation. "Now, Ampris, don't be difficult," he said, speaking the basic abiru patois. "Don't show your teeth to me. This won't hurt."

She stood still, because she had been whipped once for trying to bite him. The whipping had been brutal enough to keep her out of two competitions. She had not forgotten the pain, or the lesson taught her: Halehl might pamper her to keep her in good fighting condition, but no matter how her popularity swelled with the public, she had to obey the rules. And the supreme rule of all was that no abiru slave ever attacked a Viis, for any reason, under any provocation.

The scanner hummed over her, pausing a long while at her shoulder. "The muscle tear is healing," Fuvein reported. "The inflammation is down. She makes good progress."

"What about the patch? How large a dosage went into her system?"

Fuvein made a little humming sound of his own and shut off his scanner. "Topical application only, maybe a few millimeters. It's a very rudimentary—"

"But will it disqualify her?" Halehl insisted.

Fuvein did not answer. Instead he pulled out a small, tube-shaped device no larger than an Aaroun finger, and pressed it against her shoulder where one of the patches had been. A zinging sensation hit her skin.

She flinched, and Fuvein moved the device to where the second patch had been. It zapped her a second time. Ampris didn't flinch this time, but she had to struggle to swallow a growl.

Fuvein stepped back and turned to Halehl with a smile. "I've freeze-burned away the affected skin layers."

Halehl approached Ampris to examine her for himself. The spots were beginning to burn like fire.

"Don't rub her fur," Fuvein said in warning as Halehl reached toward her. "It will fall out."

Halehl swore and gestured at Elrabin. "Glue it, quickly! She's got to be harnessed and ready to go."

Elrabin scurried to obey him while Ampris glared at both Viis. "The freeze mark will show when I'm scanned," she said, struggling to keep her exasperation from her voice.

Fuvein turned away from her, ignoring her remark. He and Halehl conferred a moment longer with their heads together.

Elrabin returned to spray her shoulder with the glue. The smell made her sneeze, and Elrabin swore at her.

"Hold still," he whispered, spraying again, then blowing gently on her fur to dry the glue in a way that looked natural. "Freeze burns wear off in a few minutes. Fuvein knows what he's doing. He's been slipping illegal stuff past the qualifier for years."

"You," Halehl said loudly.

Elrabin spun away from Ampris like he'd been shot. "Yes, master?"

"Put the harness on her. Get her weapons. Daggers and parvallehs. This will be a finale no one will forget."

Elrabin bowed low and turned away, leaving Ampris standing there wide-eyed. The parvalleh was indeed the ancient Aaroun weapon of war, evolving gradually through history into ceremonial usage. In primitive times, it had been used to crack open the skulls of sacrificial victims. In peaceful times, it had been used to crush the grain sheaves at harvest ceremonies. Now it was used to entertain the Viis masses.

Once Fuvein had left the room and slipped past the guards who held back the jostling crowd outside, Halehl approached Ampris. "You and Ylea are both able to swing the parvallehs with one hand. No one has ever seen the hammers fought with in this way before, not in public competition. It will be exciting for the crowd. It will make a newsworthy spectacle. It will please Lord Galard, who is in the audience today. I've already spoken to Ylea. She knows what to do. You work with her, Ampris. Follow her lead.''

Ampris's heart sank. She knew what that meant. Ylea would take her out there and tell her nothing. But there was no point in protesting. "Yes, Master Halehl," she said.

He met her gaze, his own boring in hard and cold, right to the core of her. "Do well, Ampris. Much depends on you today. Do not fail me.''

She said nothing at all, only nodded. At last he swung away and left, glancing at Elrabin one last time.

"Hurry," he said. "Get her ready.''

As soon as he was gone, Ampris let out a roar of pent-up anger and kicked the stool across the room. "That—''

"Hush, Goldie," Elrabin said in warning. He rushed to pull out the hip harness and chains, tossing them on the floor while he rummaged for the designated weapons. "Don't waste your temper in here. Save it for the arena.''

"Why does he do that? Why?" Ampris fumed. "He always tells her the strategy, never me. Why does he think she will share any instructions with me?''

"She's team leader," Elrabin said, fitting the harness around her and buckling it tight into place. "But you're making good progress on taking that spot. You just keep at it, see?''

Ampris growled as she picked up her dagger and fitted it into her belt.

Elrabin checked her wrist guards, muttered about one, and replaced it. Lacing it tight, he said, "You know why Halehl's acting like his tail's been twisted, don't you?''

She didn't answer, busy as she was pulling on her glove with her teeth, but Elrabin kept on talking, "Because Galard's got two or three hundred thousand credits riding on the finale.''

Ampris dropped the glove and stared at him in disbelief. "What?''

Elrabin tried to act nonchalant, but his ears were twitching. "You heard me.''

"Three hundred *thousand*? But that's a fortune. That's—"
She stopped, unable to compare it to anything. She knew
that it cost aristocrats that much a year to live at court, but
the idea of someone's putting that much stake on one bet
boggled her mind.

"Once he bet a million *ducats,* at four-to-one odds, and
won," Elrabin said. "He's one of the biggest gamblers in
the empire. And he has great luck. Now you see why Halehl's rill is upside down? He's put you and Ylea together
as a pair, talked you up on the vidcasts, and old Galard has
plunked down a fortune."

"He is a foolish male indeed," Ampris said, thinking of
all that could go wrong. "What if—"

"Hey. Don't get your fur in a twist," Elrabin said, giving
her a soothing pat. "It ain't your problem if he wins or
loses."

"But if I fail—after all, Ylea and I have never fought
with the parvallehs in a paired fight before." She drew in
a nervous breath, her ears flattening to her skull. "Why
does he want to try something new and unpracticed at such
a time?"

"It's called gambling," Elrabin said, flinging her cloak
around her shoulders and twisting the catch. "You don't
risk on the tried and true. You risk on the *risk,* see?"

"No, I do not see."

"It ain't your problem." Elrabin stepped back from her
and looked her over with approval. "If you win, our owner
and trainer both get fat pockets. If you lose, they don't.
Why should you care? You still get fed, either way."

"I could lose my head if I fail," she muttered, wishing
Elrabin hadn't told her about this. "Halehl told me the first
day he would sell me if I don't win. Now, with so much
at stake—"

"Goldie, Goldie, don't you ever learn?" Elrabin came
over and gave her an affectionate rub between her ears.
"He bet half a million credits on you for your very first
fight. At three-to-one odds. He tripled his money the first

day of the season. You've already paid for his expenses on the whole team.''

''Oh.''

She digested that, her head spinning at the amounts El-rabin was throwing around. Truly the Viis were mad, all of them.

The guards threw open the door and looked in. ''Time.''

Her heart started racing and she forgot about the bet. Elrabin struggled to pick up the case containing her par-valleh.

Behind them on the wall, the vid chimed an announcement. Ampris glanced at the screen and saw that all betting had been closed on her fight. She took a deep breath, trying to rally her courage and calm her nerves. It was time to concentrate on her business, on the fight to come, on *surviving* it.

''Good victory, Goldie,'' Elrabin whispered, following the ritual he always did.

Ampris touched the clear stone of her Eye of Clarity and made her own swift prayers. Then, with head high and gaze straight ahead, she strode out through the crowd that surged to get at her past the guards struggling to hold them back. Like a queen she walked through the jostling, the yelling, and the blazing lights of the vidcams.

CHAPTER NINE

In the starting gate, Ampris and Elrabin found Ylea and Ruar already waiting for them.

Ylea, towering massively over everyone else, was pacing back and forth, snarling and clanking the stout chain that hung from her harness.

Halehl appeared, distinctive in his blue and black striped cloak, his rill standing stiff behind his head. With his own hands he chained them together, Ylea on the left and Ampris on the right, testing every link until he appeared satisfied, then shortening the length by half.

Ylea pulled away, snarling in protest. Her eyes blazed with madness. Foam dripped from the corners of her mouth. "No," she said gutturally, pulling on the chain. "No!"

"We can't maneuver this close," Ampris said, bracing herself against Ylea's tugs. Ylea was normally hyped for combat, but right now she looked completely out of her mind. Seeing her like this, Ampris felt a finger of fear slide up her spine.

"Please, Master Halehl," Ampris said. "We need enough room to swing properly."

"You will attack first," Halehl said to them. "No matter what it takes, whether you are set to go or not. You *must* attack first. A secondary bet is riding on that. Do you understand?"

Ylea growled and snorted, flecks of spittle flying.

Ampris nodded in resignation. "Yes, Master Halehl."

"Your opponents are Samparese—"

Ylea leaned back on the chain, snapping it taut, and roared loudly enough to shake the gate panels. The handlers perching on top of the fence drew up their dangling legs in sudden caution.

Ampris filed the information away. Samparese—a race used only in the arena—were tough opponents, nearly as big as Ylea, lithe, fluid, quick, utterly fearless, and nearly impossible to kill. Long-bodied with wedge-shaped heads atop muscular, sinuous necks, they had blunt, bewhiskered muzzles and razor-sharp fangs. But they did not work together well when paired, and that had to be an important advantage.

Unless, Ampris thought with a shiver, that advantage was balanced against the fact that she and Ylea did not work well when paired either.

When Ruar bent to open the battered case containing Ylea's parvalleh, she knocked him sprawling and bent to grab it up herself. Brandishing it in her left hand, she roared and struck the gate panel with it, sending splinters flying.

"Ylea," Halehl said in warning. "Save yourself for the arena. You will go in soon."

Ylea roared again, but she stopped swinging the parvalleh.

Watching her act like this, Ampris felt her heart plummet to her feet. She did not think Ylea was going to be able to focus.

A beeping noise from overhead made them all look up. A wide disk-shaped qualifier scanner was floating above them, a red light flashing on its undercarriage.

Elrabin scuttled to one side and flattened himself against the gate panels in an unobtrusive corner. Ruar did the same on the other side. Halehl remained where he was, one hand resting lightly on the taut chain stretched between Ampris and Ylea. None of them moved until the scan was finished.

A yellow light flashed on, replacing the red, and the scanner hummed away.

Halehl flicked out his tongue and glanced at Ampris in visible relief. "Excellent. Now, both of you, listen to me."

He was finishing his instructions when Elrabin darted up beside Ampris. While Halehl went on talking, smoothly stepping between Ampris and the surveillance cam mounted over the gate, Elrabin popped a boost globe into Ampris's mouth.

For a moment the oily, slick surface of the globe slid across her tongue, then she bit it, and its sweetly sour contents splashed through her mouth in an intense burst of flavor.

A second later, her head grew marvelously clear and her senses heightened. She seemed to grow taller and stronger. All of her reflexes speeded up, and she seemed to notice everything at once with the greatest clarity.

Elrabin whisked her cloak from her shoulders and stepped away. Halehl's eyes flashed at him in approval.

Ylea was slipped her boost globe, and soon her eyes were clear and surprisingly rational again. She stopped tugging on the chain like something demented and wiped the foam from her mouth with the back of her hand.

"Let's go kill," she said.

Ampris gave her a wary nod, hoping that in Ylea's case the boost lasted. Sometimes it wore off too soon.

In the arena, the crowd was stamping on the benches, cheering and yelling in a swell of noise that drowned everything else out. At first it was just a roar, but then Ampris could hear a single word chanted over and over: "Ampris! Crimson Claw! Ampris!"

Ylea heard it too, and her ears went flat to her skull. Her eyes met those of Ampris, and sheer meanness raged in their depths.

The gate opened, but as they started out, Elrabin darted past Halehl and gripped Ampris by her harness. "Watch her," he said breathlessly, his eyes wide with concern. "She's going to turn on you."

There was no time to react. Ampris kept going, matching Ylea's eager stride, and Elrabin was dragged back and shut behind the closing gate.

They jogged through the shimmering barrier field that enclosed the interior of the arena. It blocked the signals to their restraint collars, or was supposed to. The arena officials kept trying to stop trainers from cheating, and the trainers kept thinking up ways around them.

Ylea's steady growling swelled into a roar. Ampris's own instincts fired up as well. She roared with Ylea, and the fearsome sound of two female Aarouns in battle cry reached above the cheering and silenced the crowd.

Ampris and Ylea broke into a run toward the center of the arena. As they came into view of the entire crowd, fresh cheering broke out, swelling as the spectators saw their weapons.

The Samparese females were not allowed to enter the arena until Ampris and Ylea reached the center.

"Go," Ylea grunted, her gaze locked on their opponents.

Instead of stopping in the center of the arena and waiting for the Samparese to come to them, they kept running forward, straight at the other pair.

After a moment, the Samparese seemed to realize what was happening. One tried to bound forward. The other seemed to want to circle. Snarling and spitting at each other in argument, they drew their glaudoons and faced Ampris and Ylea.

Ampris snarled in joy. Somewhere in the back of her mind, she was aware of Halehl's soft voice murmuring to her from her collar. She knew then that while her restraint might be blocked, the secret communication feed still operated. Halehl was speaking the conditioning words, firing her blood, arousing her battle instincts, making her lust for blood.

Holding her parvalleh in her left hand, Ylea drew her

dagger and gripped it in her right fist. They were running full tilt now. Ampris kept the pace easily, but knew that if Ylea did not slow down soon she would be spent before the battle started.

Then they met, the Aarouns' greater momentum crashing them into the Samparese.

In well-trained unison, Ampris and Ylea swung their parvallehs back and forward. The lights reflected off the broad heads of the war hammers, making them glint and shine.

First blood for her weapon, Ampris thought. *"Saa-vel harh!"* she screamed, uttering the war cry she had learned at Bizsi Mo'ad.

Glaudoon steel crashed upon parvalleh iron, sending up an echoing clang that made the crowd gasp and rise. The Samparese, neither set nor braced for such a swift attack, stumbled back. One of them skidded off balance and nearly fell.

Ylea screamed and swarmed over her, pulling Ampris aside before she could finish a blow that would have crushed her opponent's skull.

Furious, Ampris twisted in midair, gripping the chain that hampered her. She barely kept herself from landing on a Samparese dagger, and parried it with the broad side of her parvalleh.

Ylea was yelling curses as she was driven back, dragging Ampris with her. Drawing her dagger and finding both Samparese females close and furious now, Ampris went to work in feverish hand-to-hand fighting.

Blood splattered. Ampris, parrying and striking for all she was worth, had no idea who it belonged to; for all she knew, it might have been hers. Jabbing with the dagger in her left hand, she spun on her inside heel and swung the parvalleh around.

The Samparese opposite her, white-furred with beautiful patterns of black stripes, snarled something, blocking the swing of the parvalleh with her glaudoon.

Ylea twisted and jumped to one side, pulling Ampris off

balance again. A Samparese dagger whistled a bare centimeter past Ampris's arm. Furious, she snarled at Ylea, but Ylea only glanced at her and laughed.

The madness had returned to the big Aaroun's eyes, and Ampris knew then that Elrabin's warning was right. It was the last fight of the season, and Ylea meant to get rid of Ampris here and now.

Ampris told herself that there had to be a way to get through to Ylea, to convince her they were on the same side. They were both Aarouns; they should not be enemies. Perhaps during off-season, when they weren't under constant training pressure, she and Ylea could talk, could maybe find some common ground.

But in the meantime, if she didn't watch both Ylea and the Samparese, between them she was going to be dead meat.

Ampris ducked low beneath her chain, spinning around and this time yanking Ylea off balance. Yelling her battle cry, Ampris swung her parvalleh low and straight, clipping her Samparese in the legs.

She heard the snap of bones, and the Samparese's scream. Blood spurted in a high, crimson arc, and the Samparese went down in a crashing fall that pulled her partner down with her.

Ampris surged to her feet, pulling Ylea back into position with her. Now it was Ylea's turn, the remaining opponent sprawling awkwardly with her glaudoon flailing as she tried to right herself. Ampris had served Ylea with an easy kill, like an offering of peace, the best gift she could think of for the veteran Aaroun.

Ylea roared and cracked open the wedge-shaped skull of the Samparese with her parvalleh. Lifting her war hammer aloft, she roared again.

It was over. Breathless, panting hard, Ampris sheathed her dagger and stood there next to her partner over their fallen opponents while she lifted her voice to roar in victory with Ylea.

Together they lifted their parvallehs, handling the heavy weapons as though they weighed nothing. The crowd threw coins and flowers at them, screaming accolades. Lights flashed across the top of the arena, filling the upper stands with dazzling arrays of color. Banners of blue waved here and there among the spectators. Some were leaping in the air, clutching their betting tickets like creatures gone mad.

"Crimson Claw! Crimson Claw!" the chant began, with the spectators stamping on their benches in unison.

Still panting hard, alight with triumph, Ampris stood side by side with Ylea and grinned at her. "It's over," she said. "We did it. We're going to—"

Ylea's eyes narrowed to slits. Twisting her large bulk with more agility than Ampris could have expected, she leaned close and plunged her dagger deep into Ampris's side.

The pain took away Ampris's breath. She could not move, could not cry out, could not even gasp. Her whole existence seemed frozen, held suspended on the blade of that dagger driven into her body. It felt immense, larger than anything she could imagine. The shock of it drove everything from her mind. She could not think, could not feel. Everything within her became the dagger in her side. She heard the thud of her parvalleh's landing beside her feet, and only then realized she had dropped it.

Snarling, Ylea parted her jaws. "Yeah, it be over *now*," she said. "Fancy hide, fancy moves. You got too fancy with Samparese, and Samparese dagger got you. So will I say when the master questions me."

Little dots began to dance in Ampris's vision. She heard what Ylea was saying, but her ears were roaring. With all her remaining will, she struggled not to pass out.

The crowd was still cheering, and now the vidcams came flying toward them. It was as though the cams had been caught unawares by the quickness of the combat and only now were coming this way. But maybe, Ampris thought hazily, maybe time was standing still while she was quickly—much too quickly—living out what was left of her life.

She gulped for air, feeling the strength fading from her legs.

Ylea released the dagger and lifted both hands to salute the crowd. Ampris gripped the haft with her hand, and for a strange, surreal instant she wondered how she came to be holding a dagger in her own side.

Then her thoughts stopped spinning dizzily, and she could think again, in short bursts of coherence.

Ylea reached for the dagger. "They coming now. Time to take what is mine."

But her fingers curled around Ampris's hand instead of the dagger hilt. Their eyes met and locked.

Ylea snarled. "You fool. You be finished."

Ampris bared her teeth and lunged at Ylea's face, snapping so fiercely Ylea leaned back. In that moment Ampris withdrew the dagger.

The sensation was horrible, indescribable. It felt as though she were pulling out her entire life force with it. Then the blade was finally clear, dripping blood. At the same time Ampris smelled it, hot and fresh, air hit her wound.

Pain ripped through her like fire, but it also cleared away the fog.

At such close quarters, Ylea could not use her parvalleh. She dropped it on the ground and reached for the dagger sheathed at Ampris's side.

Ampris, however, struck fast and hard, gashing Ylea's arm. Ylea screamed and yanked it back. Ampris lunged at her, plunging the dagger down through the harness buckled around Ylea's hips. The blade sliced through the heavy leather, and chain and harness swung free, dangling from Ampris's hip now.

Ylea roared and darted around her like something gone mad. She grabbed up a glaudoon from the dead hand of a Samparese and turned on Ampris.

In that small moment of opportunity, Ampris should have thrown the dagger into her throat, but a wave of dizziness made her hesitate, and the moment was lost.

From the corner of her eye, Ampris saw handlers racing toward them. She heard Halehl's agitated voice coming from her collar, giving her instructions she could not hear.

Some individuals in the crowd were screaming. Others went on cheering. A siren blared warnings, and the vidcams hovered closer overhead.

Ampris braced herself, but Ylea hit her at full charge, toppling her over like straw and driving her to the ground. The pain flashed white in Ampris's mind, obliterating everything, and yet Ampris knew she could not surrender to it. She rolled, by instinct alone, and by the time she got her vision and senses back, she found Ylea pinning her legs and swinging the glaudoon.

As long as they were inside the arena, there was no way Halehl could use his restraint mechanism in their collars. There was no way he could pull Ylea off. Ampris was on her own.

She raised her dagger and parried Ylea's glaudoon, although the impact jolted the bones in her wrist and hand. With steel grinding against steel, they strained against each other, snarling ferociously. Ampris held on, refusing to give way to Ylea's strength, feeling blood still leaking from her side, weakening her more with every passing second. She groped with her other hand, her fingers digging into the sand. Then she threw a handful of the stuff in Ylea's eyes.

Screaming, Ylea reeled back, clawing at her eyes and slinging her head from side to side. Had she been sane, such a trick would not have rattled her. But Ylea was past all control or sanity now. Still screaming with her eyes clenched shut, she hacked blindly with the glaudoon.

Rolling free of that dangerous blade, Ampris struggled to get her feet under her. From behind her she heard shouts, but she wasn't going to stop.

This was what she knew. This was what she had been trained to do.

She staggered up, took one step toward Ylea, nearly fell, and barely caught herself.

Ylea spun around on her knees, blinking open her streaming eyes. Finding Ampris, she uttered a feral cry that made the hair stand up on Ampris's spine, then drove her blade at Ampris's midsection.

Wind as air . . . Teinth's instructions came back to her from that day early in training. All season Ampris had had no occasion to use the move. But now, in the moment of Ylea's lunge, Ampris knew it was the only maneuver that could save her.

Without further thought, she tucked her arms to her side, holding the dagger tight, and did not let herself think that it was too short for her purposes. She leaped, twisting her body up and over Ylea's blade a split second before it could hit her. For a moment she hung suspended, in time and in space, seeing the lights reflected on Ylea's glaudoon, seeing the blood-splattered fur beneath Ylea's crazed eyes, seeing the pretty gold cartouche of Lord Galard's name swinging from Ylea's ear. Only Ylea wore the cartouche, marking her as team leader. Everyone else, Ampris included, wore a plain iron ring with Galard's name stamped inside it.

That was the last detail Ampris noticed before time shifted into normal speed again. Before she was ready, before she realized she must thrust her arm forward, she crashed headfirst into Ylea's throat, knocking the bigger Aaroun down.

Ylea heaved once beneath her weight, nearly throwing Ampris off, then lay still.

Ampris, stunned by the tackle, lay there as well, unable to find her wits, unable to catch her breath. The black spots were dancing around her again, clouding her vision. She told herself she had to get up, had to move if she wanted to live.

With a groan, she pulled herself upright just as the handlers reached her.

One of them carried a long pole with a noose on the end. Seeing it in a confused blur as they surrounded her, Ampris flung wide her hands in surrender and did not move.

Only then did she see her dagger, buried haft-deep, in Ylea's throat. Ylea's eyes stared at the ceiling of the arena, sightless and already dull with the film of death. They were crazed no more.

"Get back from her!" one of the handlers shouted. "Get back!"

They crowded closer with whips and the noose, and behind them hurried another figure, tall and Viis-thin. It was Halehl, actually running, with his subtrainers at his heels.

"Get back from the body," a handler said to her, shaking his whip in readiness to lash her with it.

Ampris did not obey. She did not move at all. Tipping back her head, she sucked in air greedily, but it did not seem to be enough to keep the black spots away.

Then there was darkness around her.

Then there was nothing.

CHAPTER TEN

In the summer, when heat baked the skin and the air lay still and thick, Israi's imperial river barge came sailing into the harbor of Malraaket. Capital of the southern continent, the city dated from ancient days, when it had been a spice and trading center, an exporter and importer of exotic goods. Today, it was a modern port city, with a crescent of receiving docks and warehouses curving into the wilderness away from the ancient, seaward side, where old buildings of stone arches and spires stood clad with age and history. According to Lord Huthaldraril, who had accompanied her on this journey, Malraaket today served as the principal port of call for all Viisymel. Malraaket was the true center of commerce for the homeworld, just as Vir served as the center of government.

Lord Huthaldraril droned on, but Israi tuned him out, refusing to listen to his lectures. The pedant was far from old in terms of his actual life cycle, but he had a soul dried to dust by his love of history.

Besides, her barge was coming into harbor under escort from dozens of smaller craft as well as five sleek military cruisers. All flags flying, the barge gleamed in the sunshine, with her splendid fittings of gold and brass polished to shining brightness. Skimmers and shuttles zoomed by overhead, darting here and there so their occupants could catch a closer glimpse of Israi.

Conscious of all the attention, Israi stood on the bridge deck, gripping the railing and waving merrily. Her scarves whipped in the wind, and her heart thudded fast from all the excitement.

She had never been so happy.

No longer did she remember her impatience on the slow, stately journey, dying of boredom with nothing to do but lounge on the deck with her retinue of attendants, courtiers, advisers, and Palace Guards—each and every one of whom was too old for her taste. Worst of all, her egg-brother Oviel had been included in the entourage. He called himself her companion, but she considered him a spy and would never forgive him for having betrayed her during Festival. She ignored him as much as possible, seeking every opportunity to slight him in public.

Besides Lord Huthaldraril, she was encumbered with Lord Brax, Minister of Finance, and Lord Manhaliz, Minister of Industry. They each came with their own retinues of attendants and servants. Daily they met her with agendas, reports, and boring lists of statistics to memorize. Israi yawned through these sessions, but at least they were less boring than watching the muddy banks of the river slide by. The scenery was usually uninspiring—mostly reedy marshland, sometimes forests that came down to the very banks, sometimes small villages perched beside its meandering course, sometimes factories pouring waste into the water and creating a stink of dead fish and evil-smelling foam.

Israi could have flown here in three hours aboard a shuttle. It was a much more efficient, more comfortable way to travel. However, her father maintained the imperial river barge as an important tradition. Never mind how slow it was, or how cramped and awkward belowdecks. Her stateroom, although considered spacious by everyone else aboard, was the smallest room she'd ever occupied in her life. She took no delight in tours of the antiquated craft, conducted by the captain himself in his stiff uniform and rows of medals. She felt as though she'd been confined to a relic—one out of date and embarrassing.

But this morning, as they sailed at last into the broad mouth of the river, where the waters of the Cuna Da'r flowed into the sea harbor, Israi finally understood what the barge was good for.

Clad in finery and broiling in the sun, she stood on the bridge deck and was brought into port with a slow stateliness that gave her ample time to drink in the adulation pouring at her from the darting skimmers, the sailing craft bobbing on the choppy harbor waters, and the cheering crowds massed on shore.

She smiled and waved, loving every moment of the pomp and pageantry. The officers of the barge lined up on the foredeck beneath her, standing at rigid attention, and saluted as cannon salvos roared over the harbor.

Slowly and smoothly the barge docked at last. A cluster of Malraaket officials and aristocrats stood waiting on the wharf to greet her. As the automated gangway projected itself from the barge to shore, Lord Huthaldraril puffed out his air sacs and made a low sound in his throat to catch her attention.

"Is the Imperial Daughter ready to go ashore?"

Israi gathered her scarves around her and turned to step into the shade of the open bridge. Complicated machinery surrounded her. The bridge crew stood at attention to one side, and saluted her as she turned to them. The captain himself bowed low.

Israi had already been coached. She knew exactly what to do.

"Captain," she said formally, her melodic voice charming everyone present as it had been trained to do, "it has been the very great pleasure of the Imperial Daughter to sail on this vessel under your command. Thank you."

The captain bowed again, his rill flushing with gratification.

Israi walked off the bridge deck and climbed carefully, with great dignity, down the narrow spiral of steps onto the main deck below. Here, her entire entourage waited for her.

Oviel stepped forward and bowed. He wore a coat of green and white stripes, the sleeves very wide in the latest style. His rill stood high above an engraved collar studded with a single small Gaza stone. His eyes met hers as he straightened, and he flicked out his tongue.

"Everything is arranged," he announced. "I have been selected to escort the Imperial Daughter if it is her pleasure to grant me this honor."

Incensed by his brazenness, Israi opened her mouth to protest, but Oviel pushed rudely past Lord Huthaldraril and stepped very close to her. He said softly so that only she could hear, "Take care. You know you must behave yourself on this trip. You are being watched, Israi. Do you want to make another mistake like you did during Festival?"

Her temper flared hot, but the warning in his words held her in check. She glared at him, hating his smug, mocking tone, but although her rill went rigid and dark blue behind her head, she flicked out her tongue in a pretense of meekness.

"Very well," she said.

Oviel waited, as though he expected her to say more, but when she let the silence stretch awkwardly between them, he bowed and took his place at her side.

Israi whirled on him fast, hissing in displeasure. "Behind me!" she snapped, pointing.

Oviel pretended to be contrite. "My error. An oversight on my part, in all this excitement. Forgive me for having provoked the imperial temper."

He stepped back a pace in the correct position while Israi watched him through narrowed eyes. Lord Huthaldraril took him by the arm and murmured to him. Turning her back on them both, Israi lowered her rill. She loathed him to the very tip of her tail, but she knew she must never allow her temper to make her underestimate him again. Oviel was sly and ambitious. He circled her constantly, like a naavsk watching the egg nest of a waterfowl, always searching for her weaknesses. He had said she was being watched. Yes, by him. He wanted her to start doubting herself. He wanted her to feel pressured and unsure.

Israi lifted her head even higher. Oviel was no match for her.

At the moment she had too much to do to concern herself long with her pesky, overly ambitious egg-sibling. Ahead of her, members of the Palace Guard formed a double line on either side of the imperial red carpet stretching down the gangway. On shore, another double row of soldiers in the sleek, crimson uniforms of the professional army spread out into a large circle surrounding a clear area with a dais. The city officials—arrayed in finery—waited there.

At the sight of them, Israi realized she would have to endure a speech. She sighed.

But before she could pout about it, the soldiers saluted in unison and musicians struck up rousing music.

In the background, vidcams floated above the heads of the cheering, waving crowd, recording everything for the public vidcasts that would be aired across the city and planet later that day.

One of her ladies in waiting joined her side and hastily rearranged the folds of her disheveled scarves, then tucked down the hem of her gown. Israi was wearing raw silk woven with threads of actual gold. The strands kept catching the sunlight as she moved, so that to the onlookers she seemed to be radiating light itself. Her rill collar was also of gold filigree, as befitted her station, and tiny Gaza stones on golden wires dangled daintily from her rill spines. She had matured into a tall, slender, and infinitely graceful female. The tilt of her large eyes, the arch of her throat, the perfection of her long arms all combined to take the spectators' breath away. With her golden, flawless skin and flashing emerald eyes, she was in person far more magnificent and beautiful than any vidcast had ever shown her to be.

As she stepped onto the gangway, coming into full sight for the first time, the crowd gave a collective aah and surged against the protective clear barricades behind the soldiers. Even the officials drew quicker and shorter breaths than before, and their smiles broadened into ones of genuine welcome.

She walked slowly and gracefully down the incline of the gangway, knowing she was radiant in the hot sunlight, knowing she dazzled them all. Everywhere she looked she saw open mouths and faces filled with awe, astonishment, and adoration. It appeared the whole city had turned out just to greet her.

Tremendous satisfaction filled Israi. At that moment she knew her life to be perfect. She forgot about Oviel walking at her heels. She forgot about the recent months of intrigue, failure, and humiliation. Her father had forgiven her transgressions, and sent her here in his place, representing the glory of the Kaa. Malraaket, far from acting disappointed in having been sent a substitute this year, seemed to be overwhelmed with excitement. Israi smiled, basking in the adulation. This was what she had been born for. This was all that she craved.

Partway down the gangway, at the point where the row of Palace Guards ended and the soldiers stationed here in Malraaket began, Israi paused with a showman's sure knowledge of how to please a crowd, and waved to the spectators on both sides.

Their cheering roared forth, even louder than before, and drowned out the music.

The officials of the city bowed low and moved forward to greet Israi. Lord Huthaldraril adroitly murmured in her ear, identifying each official in turn. Israi beamed graciously and called each one by name.

Inside, she was laughing at their provincial ways, at how

they swelled with pride and puffed their throats to make themselves look more important.

"Welcome to our humble city, your imperial highness," the governor said with another low bow. He launched into his speech, his words echoing over the roar of the crowd, barely heard:

". . . later tomorrow the procession . . . unveiling of the statue dedicated to the glory of your imperial highness . . . banquets and a tour of the . . ."

"Thank you, Lord Unstuleid," she replied graciously. "On behalf of the Imperial Father, Sahmrahd Kaa, the Imperial Daughter is pleased to be received by you, your officials, and the citizens of Malraaket."

A tiny Viis chune, no more than a year or two out of the egg, came pattering forward with a bouquet of exquisite flowers.

Israi exclaimed with delight and bent to caress her.

Fresh cheers went up, and the vidcams zoomed closer to record a charming moment that would be aired across the empire. Israi smiled to herself as the chune raced back to her mother.

Governor Unstuleid eyed Oviel with momentary uncertainty when no one introduced him, but then he adroitly moved to Israi's right and gestured at the enclosed litter waiting in hoverpark at the opposite end of the wharf. Slowly they walked that way, with Oviel trailing awkwardly behind her. Lords Huthaldraril, Brax, and Manhaliz clustered behind Oviel. They walked past the honor guard while the governor's young adjutant trailed the other Malraaket officials. Israi's entourage had not yet disembarked from the barge. They would be transported to the governor's palace later and were not to be part of the official procession.

The litters were adorned with festoons and streamers of ribbons in the gaudy Malraaket colors. The governor's hovered at the head of the line, its doors opened wide to reveal an interior of plush crimson.

The crowd began to chant, "Israi! Israi! Israi!"

People surged against the barricades, and Israi's smile widened. She stopped and waved to them again while Huthaldraril, Brax, and Manhaliz boarded the second litter.

Governor Unstuleid paused, his smile pinned in place while he waited to assist her in. Oviel puffed out his air sacs and started toward the litter, only to suddenly veer off and circle back to Israi as though he realized he could not board without her.

More vidcams clustered about Israi, recording her as she stood there, so young, vibrant, and beautiful in the sunshine.

Some of the soldiers waved the cams off, and while their attention was directed that way, a chune broke through and came running with another bouquet of flowers.

Oviel touched Israi's arm lightly to get her attention. "How charming," he said. "Another little one bearing tribute. It will make a delightful tableau for the vidcasts. You've planned this very well. My commendations to your publicity staff."

Israi glared at him. "This was not planned," she said, wishing he would go away.

She turned to face the chune, but by then the governor had stepped between the little one and Israi.

"I'm afraid not," he said impatiently. "You are not authorized to bring those wilted blooms near the—"

"Stand aside, Lord Unstuleid," Israi said imperiously, annoyed that he should take it upon himself to interfere. She bent down to the chune and accepted this second bouquet. Unlike the first, these flowers had not been professionally prepared and were not pleasing by Israi's usual standards. But such spontaneity from one of her youngest subjects delighted her. Aware that she must charm these citizens if she was to begin weaning their adoration away from her father to herself, Israi received the tribute from the chune's trembling hand and smiled.

Suddenly there was a shout, and more onlookers poured

through, pushing the barricades aside like flotsam. They came surging at Israi and the others, engulfing them before anyone could act.

Israi found herself surrounded by strangers, all of them eager to touch her, to handle her skin, her clothing. Alarmed, she looked around and realized she was cut off from her guards by an ever-widening sea of people.

"Stand back," the governor said, gesturing to the crowd, which buffeted him and ignored him. "Good citizens, please stand back."

The guards were coming. Trying to keep calm until they reached her, Israi turned around and reached out to Oviel for his help. But Oviel met her eyes and grimly retreated, pressing himself back from the onrush of the crowd.

"Oviel!" she shouted.

But he did not answer as he continued to move away from her.

Infuriated by his cowardice, she wanted to throw something at him. How dare he desert her like this. He was her official escort, bound by protocol to protect her. She would see that he paid dearly for abandoning her.

People surrounded her on all sides now, milling against her, touching her hands and skirts while they asked for her blessing. Israi had never been touched by common citizens before. She had never been cut off or engulfed by strangers like this. Horror rose inside her. She gasped and tried to draw away from them. But the crush and jostling grew worse, as more and more people pressed forward.

Someone lunged at her, shouting her name as though crazed, and yanked off one of her scarves. He ran away with it streaming in his hand, and others reached for her scarves as well. Spun about and grabbed from all sides, Israi found them now reaching for her jewels, her clothing. They pulled her this way and that, suddenly shouting and fighting over her. Someone nearly knocked her off her feet, only the crowd surging against her from the opposite side keeping her from falling to the ground.

Realizing she could be trampled to death in this mob, Israi was suddenly terrified. She cried out, pleading with them to release her, then commanding them. But in the yelling and shouting, her voice could not be heard. Jerked back and forth, she heard a loud rip of fabric, and now a group of ragged, dreadful creatures swarmed around her. Clad in hooded jerkins and tattered cloaks, they elbowed the citizens aside, fighting their way closer, ripping and grabbing at her gown.

"It's got gold woven in it," one shouted.

"Get the cloth! Get the cloth!" another yelled.

Grappling with one of these thieves, Israi knocked back her assailant's hood and found herself staring into a Viis face, yet one such as she had never seen in her life. His skin was pale green, almost colorless, and mottled with ugly red splotches as though he suffered from some disease. His rill was practically nonexistent, with only a vestigial fold of skin along the back of his skull. The fingers that gripped her arms were too long to be normal.

Horror swelled through her. Israi was frozen for what seemed like an eternity, her mind unable to cope with the sight of this monster. Then he raised a crudely made knife and slashed it at the bodice of her gown. Arching back, Israi screamed.

Her cry carried piercingly over the din. In the next second, there came the cough of a side arm, and the Reject staggered back from Israi with a smoking hole in his chest. Without a sound, he crumpled at her feet.

The crowd panicked around her, and now people were pushing and shoving in all directions in an effort to get away from the advancing guards. Screams broke out, and the sizzle of stun-sticks could be heard as a path was cleared through the mob. The guards were shoving people aside bodily, striking and pummeling anyone in their way.

Israi staggered as she was shoved. She nearly fell headlong over the body of the dead Reject. Screaming again, she tried to get away from the corpse, but something hit her in the small of her back, right above the base of her tail, and knocked her down.

Jolted by the impact of hitting the ground, Israi tried to roll herself to safety away from the trampling feet, but she was stepped on and kicked before someone grabbed her.

Thinking it was rescue at last, Israi found herself instead in the clutches of another hooded Reject who ripped and hacked at her torn gown. She kicked him with all her might, knocking him away from her, then the guards reached her at last.

They shot the Reject and anyone else in Israi's immediate vicinity, even those who were trying to flee. The stench of charred flesh filled the air, and the groans of the dying mingled with the screams of those running away.

A pair of strong arms scooped Israi up and carried her rapidly out of the riot. Two guards pushed ahead of the one carrying her, clearing a path to the governor's litter with kicks and blows. Sobbing and unable to catch her breath, Israi had only confused glimpses of the frenzy and panic surrounding her. She saw the scarlet-clad soldiers still firing into the crowd, mowing people down. Others were surrounding the area, hemming the frantic citizens in as they tried to get away.

The governor's litter had been turned on its side. Its bright ribbons and festoons had been ripped away, and the interior was slashed and looted. The next litter in line, however, remained intact, with soldiers grimly guarding the nobles who occupied it.

Israi was shoved bodily into this litter, where the anxious hands of the other occupants dragged her the rest of the way to safety. The doors slammed shut, and the litter took off immediately with an acceleration that rocked her against the cushions.

Gasping and shuddering, Israi righted herself with the assistance of a horrified Lord Huthaldraril.

"Is the Imperial Daughter well?" he asked, over and over, as though unaware of what he was saying.

The other ministers of state stared at her, looking stunned and shocked. Governor Unstuleid sat among them. The litter was too crowded with so many passengers. It flew sluggishly, straining its accelerators, and was escorted on either side by military skimmers with blaring sirens.

The governor's fine coat had been torn, and dirt smeared his face. He was puffing rapidly, and he reached out an unsteady hand to Israi, who shrank back from him.

Lord Huthaldraril intervened, pulling the governor back. "To touch her is not permitted," he said fiercely, then he turned again to Israi. "Do not fear, highness. All is well," he said soothingly, yet his voice held a quaver of shock. "All is now well."

Israi could not speak, could not recover her composure or her wits. Sobbing and rocking herself from side to side, she tried to hold her torn gown together while the litter sped along.

Lord Manhaliz removed his coat and placed it around her while she cringed from him. Gently he finished covering her and backed away.

"She will not speak," Lord Huthaldraril said in despair to the others.

"She cannot speak," Lord Brax said gruffly. "Gods, you fool, the Imperial Daughter is in shock. Don't keep chattering. Don't pester her. Leave her be until we can get her to safety."

Israi choked and shuddered, realizing at last that she was in the air, away from the mob, safely away. She made a muffled noise, and Huthaldraril bent close to her with concern.

"Yes, your highness? What did you say?" he asked.

"He left me!" she screamed. "I reached out to him, and he left me!"

"Who?" Huthaldraril asked worriedly. "Who?"

But the plush, crimson interior of the litter began to spin around her. Thinking they were crashing, Israi screamed again and flung herself back against her seat.

Huthaldraril and Manhaliz both tried to calm her, but their efforts only terrified her more.

"No!" she screamed. "No!"

Then the spinning became a blur, and a whiteness around her. Through a haze she faintly heard their voices, rough with growing alarm as they tried to assure her she was safe.

Israi did not believe them. She knew the litter was crashing. She could feel her heart being crushed as the craft plummeted from the sky. Clutching at one of the tiny ports, she tried to claw her way closer to the window.

"Highness, please. You are safe. You are safe."

The litter slowed down, dropping altitude as it crossed a major intersection. Blinking back her vertigo, Israi peered out at gawking pedestrians and stalled traffic. The city looked foreign and dangerous. Panic flooded her throat with sour bile. "Kill them," Israi said, her voice suddenly returning to her, shrill and loud. "Kill them all! They are barbarians. I want them punished for this—all of them!"

"She is hysterical," Lord Brax said. "Driver, call ahead for a physician. Warn him that a sedative is needed."

Israi wanted to swear at the old fool, but her head was becoming cold and detached from her body. Her ears were roaring. She could not breathe.

And then, for her, there was nothing.

That night and all the next day Malraaket remained locked in the grip of disaster. The governor stormed about his palace, screaming at his underlings. The city had been placed under martial law, and citizens were ordered by blaring announcers floating up and down the streets to stay indoors. No one was allowed outside on pain of arrest.

Israi had been placed in strict seclusion, with only the governor's personal physician and her ladies in waiting admitted into her presence. Rumors abounded that the sri-Kaa had been killed, that the sri-Kaa had been gravely injured, that she was suffering a nervous breakdown, that she was furious and calling for everyone in the city to be executed.

Governor Unstuleid himself believed he had entered a waking nightmare. This fabulous visit which was to be the crowning achievement of his political career had turned into a disaster. His internal organs felt as though they were being squeezed in a vise. He wanted to take to his bed and seclude himself to recover his nerves, but he dared not. Every few minutes it seemed he was called forth to the linkup to take another call from the Imperial Palace. The interrogations went on forever, repetitious yet terrifying. He spoke to generals. He spoke to Chancellor Temondahl, an awe-provoking individual who squinted at the linkup screen as though he believed nothing the governor said. He spoke to an unidentified individual he was certain must work in the dreaded Bureau of Security. If he was not on the linkup then he was summoned by one of the visiting ministers of state for additional questions. They all wanted answers he could not give.

Thus far, however, he had not heard anything from the Kaa himself. Unstuleid lived in constant fear that at any moment his adjutant would bring him word that the Kaa had landed in Malraaket and was coming here.

Gods, how had such complete ruin fallen upon him so quickly? The Kaa would blame him for this. The Kaa would demand his head. He wondered whether his private shuttle could get him to the spaceport in time to escape the Kaa's wrath. No, no, he could not flee. The palace itself was under guard. He was under guard. Surveillance monitored his comings and goings. No one could enter the palace without passing stringent security checks. No one was allowed to leave. The Palace Guards had taken over. Anyone who did not obey their orders was shot on sight. One of the storerooms held the corpses of several courtiers and servants who had not learned that lesson quickly enough.

Unstuleid felt a fresh tremor pass through him. He'd had no sleep. His brain could not seem to work. Horror and despair kept overwhelming him, rendering him mute and shaken at unexpected intervals.

His adjutant entered the governor's office with an abruptness that startled Unstuleid. "My lord," Xuvar said breathlessly, his tongue flicking in and out rapidly. His rill stood at full extension. "The Kaa wishes to speak to you via linkup."

At last the dreaded call had come. The governor's heart quailed inside him. He felt his rill droop around its collar while his hands grew damp and cold. Struggling to breathe normally, Unstuleid attempted to compose himself, then activated his wall screen with a shaking hand.

The Kaa's resplendent features shimmered into life upon the large screen, filling the room as though a god had entered it. His crimson-stained rill framed his head, and his vivid blue eyes held the coldness of stone.

Gulping, the governor rose to his feet and bowed deeply.

"Unstuleid," the Kaa said without preamble, using the governor's name without title or courtesy, "what is your personal report?"

Although what he really wanted to do was crawl beneath his desk, the governor forced himself upright from his deep bow. He struggled to meet the Kaa's stern gaze. His bowels were water; his tail hung behind him like a leaden weight. Yet he had to stand there and exhibit Viis courage.

"May the Imperial Father have mercy upon us," the governor began. His voice came out shaky and weak. "We have—"

"Never mind your speeches," the Kaa interrupted. "What is your report?"

"The Imperial Daughter is unharmed," Unstuleid said, repeating what he had assured every other official who had called him hour after hour. "She is shaken by this most unfortunate incident, naturally, but I have seen her—um, briefly—and much of her natural force and vigor are entirely returned." He did not say that when he had ventured into the sri-Kaa's guest apartments of state, she had screamed at him like a creature gone mad and hurled expensive vases at his head. "My physician assures me that she will make a swift and full recovery."

The Kaa's rill lowered slightly, and he closed his eyes a moment. "The gods be thanked."

"Indeed, sire. We are all most thankful."

The Kaa's stern gaze bored into him again, interrupted only by a band of static that quickly cleared. "Where were your precautions? What are your excuses? How do you explain this assault upon the Imperial Daughter?"

"The crowd was not hostile, sire," the governor said, trying to keep his voice steady. Again, he repeated the same assurances that he had made to all the others, to the Bureau of Security, to various members of the council, to Chancellor Temondahl, and now to the august visage of Sahmrahd Kaa himself. "We are a loyal people. We revere the Imperial Father and the Imperial Daughter. Never would we harm—"

"Harm was done," the Kaa snapped while crimson streaks darkened across his rill. "Violence was done."

"No violent assault was intended, I do assure the Imperial Father. Only excessive zeal and emotion are to blame. The citizens of Malraaket adore the Imperial Daughter. In a spirit of adoration only did they approach her. Their zeal, unfortunately, overcame their—"

"Enough," the Kaa said. "We have heard this."

Unstuleid's tongue tangled within his mouth. Hastily he uncurled it and tried again. "I—I assure the Imperial Father that we took excellent precautions. A squadron of able-bodied soldiers was present. Crowd barricades stood in place. A chune was let through, sire, a small chune carrying flowers to honor the sri-Kaa. We only wanted to honor her. We meant no harm."

He realized he was babbling like a slave caught in a transgression. Flushed and trembling from head to foot, the governor forced himself to stop talking. He stood there, silent and wilted, fearing the worst.

The Kaa also said nothing. His pupils contracted to tiny

black dots, and his gaze remained flat and merciless.

Breathing hard, the governor beat his brain, trying to decide what to add. He dared not lie. The vidcams had recorded everything as it happened. Even if he'd had the chance to have the recordings edited to show something different, there were too many witnesses, too many horrified members of the court present.

"We had hoped, on the basis of old friendships, that you would give us more than these pathetic excuses," the Kaa said at last. "We expected you to do better."

Unstuleid found his composure crumbling. "I'm sorry," he whispered. "I'm sorry. It was an accident—"

"The sri-Kaa will return to Vir as soon as she is well enough to travel," the Kaa said. "Our imperial shuttle should be reaching Malraaket at any moment. You will admit it with full security clearance."

"Consider it done, sire," the governor said, struggling to hold his voice steady. "Shall I expect the Imperial Father's presence?"

"No," the Kaa snapped. "We no longer consider Malraaket to be friendly to our personage."

"Oh, but, sire—"

"See that all is prepared for our daughter's return."

"Yes, sire."

"You may also expect the arrival of the Commander General and an investigative staff."

"Yes, sire."

"You will cooperate fully with that investigation."

Unstuleid had no desire to meet the Commander General. Lord Belz's reputation was not amenable. Yet he had no choice but to incline his head again. "Yes, sire."

"We are not yet satisfied as to the truth of this incident," the Kaa said stonily. "We are not yet mollified."

"Sire, I will do anything—"

"We are not yet assured of the safety of the sri-Kaa."

"Please, sire. I swear that the sri-Kaa is very safe," the governor said with rising alarm. "She is—"

"You were careless," the Kaa broke in sharply, anger cutting through every word. "We shall not forget the behavior of Malraaket toward the Imperial Daughter. We shall not soon forgive."

The governor opened his mouth to reply, but the screen went blank.

Flicking out his tongue, the governor tugged at his constricting rill collar and dropped weakly into his chair. He was still trembling. He found himself without the strength to even summon his adjutant, but Xuvar entered anyway.

"It went well?" he asked hopefully. "The Kaa has always been fond of you. Did you assure him that—"

"I managed to assure the Kaa of nothing," Unstuleid said in despair. He stared at his adjutant blankly, seeing disaster all around him. "He is furious. He blames us. We—I think we are in grave trouble."

"But surely the Kaa understands—"

"No," the governor said softly, lifting his hand for silence. "I have spoken now to them all. They all ask the same questions, and nothing I say satisfies them. Nothing!"

"But, my lord—"

"No, Xuvar, go now," Unstuleid said wearily, sinking into despair. "Leave me in peace. I—I need a few moments alone."

Across the planet in his palace, standing in the communications center, the Kaa paused a moment with his hand still on the switch of the linkup. It was unheard of for the Kaa to touch the controls himself. From across the room, the Zrhel technician blinked at him fearfully, dropping feathers where she stood. Flanking her were his green-cloaked guards, weapons hanging in full sight on their belts as they impassively awaited his next move or command.

The Kaa ignored all of them and stood there with his eyes closed as he tried to regain his imperial composure. But fury continued to boil in his blood, hammering through his skull, throbbing in his stiffly extended rill. His body shook with the very pressure of his rage. It had taken all his willpower not to scream curses at the stupid face of Governor Unstuleid. It was taking all his willpower now not to order Malraaket blasted into radioactive dust.

Israi is still there, spoke an icy inner voice to the seething cauldron of his brain. *Not until she is safely away.*

His Israi, as precious to him as his own heart. Israi, the future of the empire. Israi, an extension of his majesty— carrying his blood, his genetic stamp, his imperial heritage. Israi, with her breathtaking beauty, fiery spirit, and nimble intelligence. How could these *fools* in Malraaket have let her be mobbed by a common crowd? The very notion of it was inconceivable, yet it had happened.

A hiss broke from him and he whirled around, striking his forearm against the giant screen of the linkup. The glass surface cracked with a loud pop, and pale blue gas began escaping into the air, bringing with it a noxious odor. On screen, the imperial seal logo slid down and began to distort, as though melting.

The Zrhel technician squawked and raced to hit an alarm.

Instantly a siren blared, and a fine whitish dust sprayed from the ceiling, physically pushing the escaping blue gas to the floor.

Shouts of consternation came from outside the encryption room. The guards rushed forward, beckoning for the Kaa to leave for his own safety.

The Kaa hissed again, then let his throat boom as his rage engulfed him. The guards jumped back, their eyes suddenly wary, and pulled themselves to attention, while the white dust coated their cloaks.

Sahmrahd Kaa glared around at all of them—from the cringing technician covering her beaked mouth while she coughed in the dust and gas, to the rigid guards, to the additional technicians peering inside with alarmed curiosity.

''The Imperial Father must come out!'' one of the technicians said, looking in horror at the damaged screen. "It's not safe to breathe the containment dust."

The Kaa hissed again, but he strode from the encryption chamber, moving so quickly his guards had to jump out of his way.

His matched Kelth heralds jumped up and ran to get ahead of him, crying their official warning. "Heads up! The Kaa is coming! The Kaa!"

The chief communications technician bowed low as the Kaa strode past him. "The Imperial Father has honored us greatly—"

The Kaa swept on without pause. His visage was thunderous. His air sacs kept filling with an almost painful rapidity. He did not allow his throat to boom again, for that was a primitive sound of attack, yet he wanted to tear something apart. His long legs carried him rapidly past the staring operators and technicians standing respectfully at their stations.

Exiting the communications center, he strode down a passage into the main part of the palace. Hastily his retinue hurried after him while his guards trotted grimly on either side.

He walked through the vast audience hall as the heralds' cries cleared a path. Courtiers hastily stopped their conversations in mid-sentence and bowed to him with murmurs of respect, but the Kaa looked neither left nor right. He acknowledged no one. He registered not a single face. Their countenances seemed to be only blurs as he passed them.

With every rapid stride, his rage pounded even more strongly through his body.

That anyone could dare to strike at Israi . . . that anyone could even dare think of harming her . . . his vital forces churned and boiled. He felt shaken to his very bones. What madness had seized the city of Malraaket, making it launch a treasonous rebellion against the sri-Kaa? He felt as though he personally had been attacked, and by his own people. Was he not the Imperial Father? Were they not the children of his empire, these subjects who had turned against his majesty with a violence both shocking and unjustified?

Suppliants were lounging outside his apartments as usual, hoping for a private audience. The Kaa's guards of escort called ahead on their hand-links, and by the time the Kaa reached his quarters, those waiting to see him had been shooed away by the sentries at his door.

The Kaa passed through the tall doors of embossed gold that swung open for him. Making a sharp turn to the left, he entered his study. Only here, in this chamber of reflection and sanctuary, did he come to a halt and stand still, breathing hard, his mind wild, his tongue flickering in and out rapidly.

The study's tall ceiling was painted in scenes from ancient Viis mythology. Its walls were paneled in expensive wood imported from offworld and carved by master craftsmen whose bones were long since dust. A massive desk, numerous chairs and stools, racks that held antique scrolls in elaborate cases made of ivern and gold, cabinets concealing modern data crystals provided by the archives, a tiny linkup with its own encoding lines for security, and a perpetually spinning model of the many planets and solar systems contained within the empire all served to furnish the room. Costly rugs woven on distant worlds covered the floor. The study was both a place in which to conduct the affairs of the empire and a refuge, where the empire could be shut out.

He had come straight here without thinking, without planning. Now, he stood in the center of the room, stunned by his own exertion, and had no idea of what to do.

Finally he strode over to a table which held a tray of wine cups with a matching ewer. The Kaa pointed to this, and a slave hurried forward to fill a gold and jewel encrusted cup with his favorite wine. The Kaa drank, gulping the exquisite liquid without tasting it. He tried to pull his wits together without success. All he could register was the burning anger inside him. His body had ceased to be made of flesh and bone. No, he was fashioned of wire, stretched taut and humming.

Only when he turned around did he see Temondahl bowing low to him. The chancellor—silent and unobtrusive until now—wore a coat of red flax cloth very finely crosswoven. He held his staff of office at exactly the correct angle to indicate his respect. With dignity the chancellor approached the Kaa and made a second, deeper obeisance. His motions were graceful and well-executed, but at that moment the Kaa looked at Temondahl without appreciation.

"If my presence displeases the Imperial Father," Temondahl said, "I will leave at once."

"No," the Kaa replied, pointing to the wine table again. The same slave hurried forward to pour a cup for the chancellor, who took it politely.

Then the slave refilled the Kaa's gold-encrusted cup and placed it in the Kaa's outstretched hand. He drank, but still tasted none of it. Slamming down the cup, he turned and glared at Temondahl.

"Speak," he commanded.

Temondahl inclined his head respectfully. "I was waiting to hear from the Imperial Father's own mouth what the governor of Malraaket had to say. Was he more truthful with you, sire?"

"The same lies and excuses."

"What does the Imperial Father intend to do?"

The Kaa glared at him. "How long until Lord Belz lands in the city?"

"I believe he has yet an hour of transit time."

The Kaa curled his tongue inside his mouth. Nothing he heard pleased him. "These fomenters of rebellion in Malraaket have committed a grave error against us," he said stormily.

Temondahl, ever calm, regarded him without blinking. "The Imperial Father must weigh all sides of the situation—"

"All sides!" the Kaa broke in with fresh fury, filling his air sacs until the skin on his throat stretched painfully. "How many turns of the lie must we weigh before we perceive the untruth? We're uninterested in delicate negotiations, or diplomatic care. We are injured by this. We have been deeply insulted, and we shall not forgive."

"Sire, naturally the Imperial Father has been most concerned over the sri-Kaa's well-being, but I have received another assurance from Lord Brax and Lord Manhaliz that the sri-Kaa is in good health. She is recovering quickly from this experience."

"Experience!" the Kaa exclaimed. He pointed at his cup again, and again the slave refilled it. His fingers curled tightly around the jeweled sides of the golden goblet and for a moment he was tempted to hurl the thing, contents and all, at Temondahl's pale blue head. "Experience! Our daughter mobbed in a riot. Our daughter attacked in open rebellion. The city should be razed to the ground."

"Sire, please!" Temondahl said, beginning to sound concerned. "Do not judge in haste. The riot was not treachery planned and executed."

"Now you sound like Unstuleid. That whining, shivering fool. He has bowed and cringed to us, but no truth of this matter comes forth. Is the Imperial Father considered stupid? Naive? Is the Imperial Father expected to believe this nonsense of emotional crowds, of excessive zeal and adoration? Bah!"

"The sri-Kaa is stunning," Temondahl said carefully. "It is possible her presence overwhelmed the good sense of the crowd."

"We shall not hear this nonsense," the Kaa declared with a sweeping motion of his hand. "Had this occurred on a barbarous planet on the frontier side of the empire, perhaps we might believe such a feeble explanation. But this is homeworld, the very cradle of our civilization! These citizens were incited to rise up and smite the Imperial Daughter. Someone organized them. We shall know who."

"The Bureau of Security is conducting its investigation with all due haste," Temondahl assured him.

The Kaa paced back and forth, his tail swinging beneath the long hem of his coat. "The Bureau had better discover the truth of this plot quickly."

"All preliminary investigations still point to a happenstance, sire. Suppose there was no treason. Suppose there was no plotting involved."

The Kaa waved this statement aside, refusing to discuss such stupidity. "Are you asking us to ignore this event?"

Temondahl's rill darkened. "Not at all, sire. I merely wish to point out the need for mercy. People have been killed—"

"Good."

"Sire, consider. The guards have killed many, over a hundred citizens at the last accounting. Is that not sufficient punishment?"

The Kaa stared at him in disbelief. Was Temondahl actually advocating forgiveness? Was he mad? "We have not even begun to consider the appropriate punishment."

"Hasty decisions can lead to unwise acts," Temondahl said as though tutoring a young ta-chune. "Until the Commander General has assessed the situation and received a more accurate picture, let us not speak of destroying such an important city."

"Malraaket is no longer our friend," the Kaa said. "Planned or not, treason was done. They must be punished."

"Sire, please have patience," Temondahl said again, his pupils dilating in visible alarm. "There are other answers to be found. I realize Governor Unstuleid is a fool, yes, and blame must be assigned, but to destroy the entire city! Its importance to the entire homeworld . . . its contribution to our trade, our economy—"

"We do not wish to hear these assurances," the Kaa said raggedly. His breathing was coming with difficulty. Again he puffed out his air sacs, but it did not seem to help. He felt as though a band were constricting his body. For a moment he felt quite dizzy. He could not seem to focus or comprehend what Temondahl said. Then he managed to draw breath again. He wished with all his heart for the sage counsel of old Gaveid. Temondahl—possessing the mind of a minor bureaucrat—had no understanding of the warrior heart.

"You speak of patience," the Kaa said, his voice hoarse. "You speak of waiting. You ask us to stay our hand until more is learned. But hear this. Already we know enough to make up our mind. Malraaket has much to answer for."

"But, sire—"

"Silence!" The Kaa's voice seemed to echo loudly in his own ear canals. His heart was thundering inside his torso. He opened his mouth to pronounce the judgment, but the band was back, tightening around him. He felt a sharp pain stab all the way to the vital part of him. Gasping, he dropped his cup. It bounced with a clang on the floor. Wine splashed across the Kaa's slipper.

"Sire?" Temondahl said. "Is something amiss? Is the Imperial Father unwell?"

The Kaa could not speak. The world was spinning around him. It grew dark, as though the lamps had been extinguished by invisible slaves. He could see Temondahl's worried eyes staring at him. The chancellor leaned forward, yet was too timid to come closer.

"Sire? Can you speak?"

The Kaa was swaying on his feet. The band of pain around him tightened even more until he felt as though it would squeeze him in half. Fear touched him for the first time. He could not answer. With all his will he tried not to fall, not to give way to whatever illness had suddenly struck him.

Temondahl exclaimed something the Kaa did not understand and hurried past him to the door. "Guards!" he said sharply. "Send for—"

"No!" the Kaa rasped out, somehow by sheer will managing to speak the protest.

No matter how feeble, it was enough to stop Temondahl immediately. The chancellor spun around, staring at the Kaa with wide eyes. "But, sire, you are unwell."

"Don't," the Kaa gritted out. His rill was standing up furiously behind his head. With the last of his strength he gestured at a chair.

Temondahl quickly beckoned to a slave, who pushed the chair over just as the Kaa's legs failed him. He dropped heavily into the chair and felt the blackness come nearer. Again he fought it off, refusing to give way. His blood was thudding inside him. The pain grew, encompassing his consciousness.

Although he could hear Temondahl shrilly giving orders to the personal slave in attendance, the Kaa seemed to be far away. He clutched the arms of his chair harder than ever, feeling the carved wood crush ever so slightly in his grip. Meanwhile, the slave hurried out, then returned moments later with others. They bustled around, competent and well-trained. After peeling off his beautifully tailored coat, they loosened his clothing to give him comfort. One brought him a cup of chilled water, sweetened with the juice of ripe plubiots. The cup was held to the Kaa's mouth. He sipped weakly, gasping for breath. Another slave brought a cloth dampened with fragrance, which was pressed against the Kaa's fevered skin. A third swept a fan back and forth, while the first propped a stool beneath his feet. Eased by these ministrations, the Kaa closed his eyes and sighed.

Temondahl hovered nearby. "Sire," he said, "in the name of the gods, allow me to summon your physician."

The Kaa gestured, and when Temondahl ventured closer, leaning down, the Kaa reached out and gripped the chancellor's sleeve. "No," he croaked while inside his rage flailed like something bound within the pain. Temondahl was indeed a fool among fools. Could he not see that no one at this moment—*no one*—could know that the Kaa was ill? Not when the entire planet was galvanized by the news of the treasonous attack on the sri-Kaa. Not when the whole empire was waiting and watching, some with fear, some with eagerness to find any weakness. There were always enemies, always those anxious to seize the throne. The Kaa had to be strong, had to remain glorious, a figure larger than life to all his subjects, or there was no majesty. For without majesty there was no respect. And without respect, finally, there could be no throne.

The Kaa held on to Temondahl's sleeve, refusing to let the chancellor go. He had not the strength or the patience to explain this most basic pretext to his fool of an adviser. No matter what path of bureaucracy and public service Temondahl had taken to get to this position, he did not truly understand imperial politics.

Finally, after what seemed like forever but was really less than an hour, the band of pain weakened, allowing the Kaa to draw full, deep breaths again. Sighing with relief, he closed his eyes and let his head lean back against his chair. His fingers loosened on the chancellor's sleeve, but Temondahl did not move, as though he dared take no initiative action on his own.

Again, deep in his heart, the Kaa cursed his adviser and wished for someone better to guide him at this moment. But there was no one. Temondahl was the best of the available chancellors. The Kaa sighed, weary now to his very bones. In this newest crisis of his rule, he needed help and guidance, but he knew he must make his decisions alone, depending on his own judgment first and foremost.

A soft tapping sounded at the door. One of the guards stuck in his head. Temondahl hurried to him and stood in a way that blocked the guard's view of the Kaa. There was a murmured exchange, then the door closed and Temondahl returned.

"Sire," he said, his voice anxious and hushed. He crept

up to the Kaa as though afraid the Imperial Father might collapse completely.

The Kaa opened his eyes and gazed at the chancellor in silent acknowledgment.

Temondahl bowed. "Word has come that the Commander General has landed in Malraaket."

The Kaa forced himself to sit erect. He felt weak, but at least he now had breath enough to speak. "Let us know as soon as he makes his report."

"Indeed, I shall, sire," Temondahl promised him. "The technicians are working now, with all haste, to install a new link in the communications center."

If there was a note of censure or rebuke in Temondahl's voice, the Kaa did not wish to hear it. He closed his eyes again, aware that his private linkup here in his study was powered directly from the communications center. "Let them hurry," he said. "Notify us when the sri-Kaa leaves Malraaket."

Temondahl bowed deeply and went away, leaving the Kaa to rest. When he returned, sometime later, the Kaa was startled from the doze he had fallen into.

"Forgive me, sire, for waking you."

The Kaa glared at the chancellor. "Stop apologizing," he said sharply. "Our illness has passed from us. Now speak. What news do you bring?"

Temondahl looked at him and flicked out his tongue. "Fresh communiqués have arrived. The sri-Kaa is en route. She should be arriving at the palace shortly after dinner. All has been prepared for her. Attendants are waiting to conduct her to—"

"See that she is taken directly to her apartments," the Kaa ordered. "Let none of the courtiers wait on her. She is to be seen by no one in the court. She must have her privacy at this time, if she is to make a swift recovery."

"She is reported to be well, and the courtiers are most concerned for her."

The Kaa's tongue flicked out in annoyance. "She is to

be cloistered in her apartments, with only her servants to attend her. She must make a complete recovery, with nothing to distress her. Let there be no visitors, except for the physician.''

"Yes, sire.''

"We shall go to her as soon as she is settled. In the morning would be best,'' the Kaa said. "See that she is informed of this and prepared for our visit.''

"As the Imperial Father commands.''

"We shall see for ourself what damage has been done.'' As he spoke, he felt a tremor of fresh anger, like heat, building inside him. Swiftly he controlled it, not wanting to reexperience that terrible pain.

A chime sounded on the small linkup, indicating an incoming message.

The Kaa gestured for it to be activated. Temondahl himself touched the controls.

The blank screen formed an image of the distinctive argent and azure seal of the Commander General; then that faded and the fierce visage of Lord Belz shimmered into place. Wearing his uniform of bright green, his medals winking and glittering with every breath, the Commander General blinked as though trying to focus, then inclined his head low enough for the Kaa to see the old battle scar that puckered the skin at the back of his skull. Normally such a scar would have been removed surgically, but Lord Belz wore the reminders of his war wounds with pride and honor. No one at court dared avert their gaze from the ugliness of his scars. Seeing Belz now reminded the Kaa of his general's many years of service, as well as his utter loyalty.

The Kaa forced himself to sit very straight and regally in his chair, displaying none of his recent infirmity.

"Greetings of Belz, Commander General, and all due respect submitted to Sahmrahd Kaa,'' the Commander General said formally, his voice gruff and terse.

The Kaa inclined his head every so slightly. "What

news?'' he asked, dispensing with the normal courtesies.

Belz did not even blink. He stood at attention on the screen, his gaze direct and his rill semierect behind his head. ''Evidence of premeditated treason or rebellion against the throne is sketchy. The plotters were clever and kept things simple. Whether the attack was organized locally or from elsewhere has not yet been determined.''

''Find out,'' the Kaa said grimly.

''Interrogations are proceeding,'' Belz answered. ''At this stage, the Bureau of Security believes the riot was designed to mask an assassination attempt carried out by Rejects.''

Shocked, the Kaa hissed loudly. His pain returned, and it took him a moment of struggle to master it. ''Who has been caught?''

''Most of those involved were shot during the rescue of the sri-Kaa. A lone survivor of the gang claims he was only trying to steal the gold cloth she was wearing.''

''Sacrilege,'' the Kaa breathed, unable to conceive of such infamy.

''He will be executed as soon as his interrogation is finished. The Bureau of Security is determined to discover who paid him for the attack.''

''Unstuleid?'' the Kaa guessed.

''No, sire,'' Belz said without hesitation. ''No such connection has been found. The governor appears to be guilty of nothing more than inefficiency and poor preparation for the imperial visit. The crowd turned into a mob from intense public desire to see and touch the sri-Kaa. The assassins seized the chance provided.''

''It is forbidden to touch the imperial person without special permission,'' the Kaa said in outrage.

Belz nodded. ''Exactly so. But the Imperial Daughter allowed two chunes this privilege, and the crowd forgot everything but the desire to be closer to her. We have reviewed the recordings of the incident. There has been no evidence of tampering with these recordings.''

The Kaa sat there in stony silence, absorbing the information he'd been given. His anger pulsed steadily inside him, stabbing him with pain.

"Continue," he said at last.

The Commander General's gaze did not waver. "We have established true martial law over the city, by our imperial forces, supplanting Governor Unstuleid's attempts to control the population. Strict curfews are now in place. Citizens are not allowed to leave their homes. All shops and businesses have been closed. The spaceport has been closed. The army is now in possession of the shuttle takeoff codes. No cargo can be loaded or unloaded. We are surveilling all comings and goings at the docks. All land routes to and from the city have been placed under checkpoints. The harbor itself has been closed, and ships have been seized by authorities. We will continue to search for the traitors until they are found. The city itself will remain locked down until the will of the Imperial Father is made known to us. Are there any further orders at this time, sire?"

"Where is the sri-Kaa?"

Temondahl stirred at this question, as though to remind the Kaa that Israi was en route. The Kaa shot him a glare, and Temondahl said nothing.

Belz was already replying. "The sri-Kaa is flying under military escort. Her transit time has been shortened and she should be arriving at the Imperial Palace in Vir in less than an hour. She is under the full protection of my personal staff, and will be returned to her Imperial Father shortly."

"Excellent," the Kaa said in approval. He had always liked Belz, one of the rare highborn Viis who got things done in a very short amount of time. A member of the First House, Belz came from a long line of warriors who had all distinguished themselves in service to the throne. The Kaa leaned forward. "You will of course investigate the guards assigned to her service on this trip."

"That investigation is already in place. Interrogations are

proceeding,'' Belz said. ''Loss of civilian life is totaled at one hundred twenty-four. I have no accurate figures on the number of injuries. Numerous arrests have been made. Those under arrest will be questioned at length. It would seem the guards were lax in depending on the local security arrangements. However, none of the early evidence points toward a coup on their part.''

''We are relieved to hear it,'' the Kaa said. ''Well done, Lord Belz.''

The Commander General flicked out his tongue. ''I wish to add on the guards' behalf that they acted swiftly to separate the sri-Kaa from the crowd. They got her out of the area, and contained the riot. While a reprimand is in order, court-martials would cause more harm to morale than is necessary.''

The Kaa said nothing. He knew that Belz always put the welfare of his forces first. He would naturally protect the guards involved. This kind of leniency the Kaa could accept.

Temondahl rubbed his hands together and flicked out his tongue. ''Lord Belz has delivered excellent news. As always, the Commander General is most efficient in the performance of his duties. It is a considerable relief to hear that the government of Malraaket has not rebelled. I am sure that the situation can be smoothed over now quickly and without further delay. No doubt Malraaket will wish to tender its apologies on behalf of all involved citizens and—''

The Kaa lifted his hand for silence.

Temondahl's voice faltered to a halt. He stared at the Kaa, his rill raised inquiringly.

The Kaa sat erect as though carved from wood. His gaze remained on the screened image of the Commander General. The anger went on pulsing inside him, stabbing him. Had he possessed a sword at that moment, he would have sliced off Temondahl's head.

''This incident will not be smoothed over and it will not

be forgiven. This we have said. This will be so."

Temondahl turned to the Kaa in dismay. "But sire," he said. "Malraaket and Vir have been on excellent terms for centuries. This is our sister city, the second capital of the homeworld. We—we depend on Malraaket for our—"

"Malraaket must be punished," the Kaa said implacably. His voice was hard and without mercy.

"Surely the Imperial Father is not going to blame the entire city for the actions of a few—"

"Malraaket is responsible for the actions of its citizens. And its vagrants. Where was the intelligence force? Why were these Rejects not being watched more closely to avoid trouble? Why was security not tightened when word came that the sri-Kaa was to visit?"

The Commander General was nodding on the screen. "I agree with the Kaa's assessment. No mob should have been allowed to form behind the barricades, much less find a way to break through. No riot should have taken place. The forces stationed in Malraaket are lax and undisciplined. They were not prepared. This could have been avoided with proper precautions."

Looking annoyed, Temondahl opened his mouth, then closed it without speaking.

The Kaa glanced at Lord Belz. "What should be done to the city, to teach it a lesson it will never forget?"

Temondahl sputtered protests, his staff tapping on the floor in his agitation. "Please, sire! Please, my lord general. This is a matter of diplomacy, not force. Malraaket is too important to—"

Again the Kaa cut him off. "What is your recommendation, Lord Belz?"

The Commander General did not hesitate. "My recommendation is that the city remain under martial law. This is the first step in teaching them that they must not harm the imperial presence."

The Kaa's rill lifted behind his head, spreading itself to its full extent. He said, "That is not enough."

Again Temondahl sputtered, but no one paid any attention to him.

Belz regarded the Kaa. His gaze was clear and direct. "Does the Imperial Father order the destruction of Malraaket?"

"No," Temondahl said. "By all mercy and justice, no!"

The Kaa ignored him. "No city on our homeworld will be destroyed," he said coldly.

Temondahl loosed an enormous sigh. "At last, the wisdom of the Kaa is seen."

The Kaa kept his gaze on Lord Belz's screened image. "We wish harsh sanctions leveled upon the city. There will be no trade to Malraaket. All imperial franchises will be canceled. It will be a crime to deliver anything other than food and the most basic necessities there. Malraaket's warehouses are to be confiscated and emptied; the contents now belong to the crown. Malraaket will not be permitted to export its goods or manufacture. Its factories may operate to supply its own needs, and nothing more. The city will exist in isolation under armed barricades. No individual may visit it. No individual may leave it, not even for Festival migrations. This is our imperial will."

A silence fell over the room, as though no one dared breathe. The Kaa's words seemed to echo in the study.

The Commander General bowed to him from the screen. "As the Imperial Father commands. I will report our progress tomorrow morning. Belz out."

The screen went blank, displaying once again the Commander General's silver and blue seal before fading to black.

The Kaa drew a deep breath, satisfied at last, and only then turned to look at his agitated chancellor.

Temondahl's eyes held dismay. He opened his mouth, but the Kaa spoke swiftly to cut him off.

"We will not hear protests, chancellor," he said coldly and formally. "We have made our decision. No more will be said."

Temondahl drew a deep breath and shuddered visibly. "May the Imperial Father forgive me," he said in a quiet voice of despair. "Does the Imperial Father realize that he has doomed Malraaket to economic ruin, and all of Viisymel with it?"

"Nonsense," the Kaa said sharply. "Malraaket is swollen with riches. It has enjoyed protected trade for three centuries. It can live off its own fat until the sanctions are lifted."

"May I ask the Imperial Father how long such sanctions will be in place?" Temondahl asked softly.

The Kaa glared at him, wanting no censure, no criticism in either tone or implication. "You may not ask," he said, his voice sharp as a whipcrack. It pleased him to see the chancellor flinch. "We will not relent until we are satisfied that Malraaket has learned its lesson. This audience is ended, and you are dismissed, chancellor."

There was no more Temondahl could say without risking death. He made a deep obeisance, then gathered his staff of office close to his side and walked to the door with his shoulders slumped and his head low.

Alone at last, the Kaa sat in his chair while a slave brought him a full wine cup. He sipped slowly, his heart cold and stony inside his torso. Despite his illness, he felt like a warrior for the first time in too many years. Sometimes it was good to cast the diplomats aside and slip the tight leash off the army.

He knew, as Belz and Temondahl both knew, that tonight and in the nights to come the military forces would loot Malraaket. It was Viis tradition that whenever the army occupied a city it could take what it wanted.

In the Kaa's long memory, he could not recall a moment in history when the army had looted a Viis city on the homeworld.

For a second, a chilly sliver of concern touched him. Was he doing the right thing? Or had he been too harsh?

The Kaa held out his cup for more wine. He turned the

questions over and over in his mind like polished stones in the hands of a juggler.

Sahmrahd Kaa knew his own reputation. Most of the time he dispensed justice tempered with mercy and leniency. But some actions he did not condone or forgive. He would not forgive Malraaket, no matter what Temondahl said. And although he might have led the chancellor to think his orders regarding the city were temporary, inside his own mind the Kaa's decision was firm: While he lived, Malraaket would remain cut off from the rest of the empire, a prisoner exiled within its own walls, forever.

Across the empire, his enemies and critics alike would see the strength and harshness of the Kaa. He would be feared, as was proper.

No matter how much Temondahl might moan, the Kaa knew he had done the right thing. Malraaket, city of old history, city of merchants with provincial ways, was indeed doomed—as it deserved to be for allowing Israi to get hurt. And as the citizens of Malraaket fell tonight into the hands of the army, which would loot, burn, and destroy anything it wanted, let them be thankful, he thought, that they had been spared at all.

CHAPTERELEVEN

Ampris awakened in a strange place of sterile gray, a place of indistinct light and muted sounds. A steady humming from equipment surrounded her. She tried to lift her head, but it weighed too much. Weakly she let it fall back.

Someone came to her, a shadowy figure draped in a gray smock. Not until it leaned over her to adjust placement of the monitor clip in her ear did Ampris see that her attendant was a female Aaroun with pale beige-colored fur and a V of dark brown shading her throat.

"Awake?" the female whispered, her voice so low and soft Ampris could barely hear it. "Any pain?"

Ampris stirred, restless and groggy. "Not much."

"You are healing quickly," the Aaroun told her with a gentle smile. She rubbed Ampris between her ears, and the caress was comforting. "The medics are pleased with your progress."

Ampris tried to remember what had happened, but couldn't. "What is this place? Who—"

"Hush. You must stay quiet and rest. You will heal better if you allow the machines to do their work. If you cause trouble, the guards will return and you will have to wear your restraint collar."

Ampris tilted her head just enough to look at the rectangular block of metal fastened across her midsection. It was the source of the humming she'd heard. And now she could feel a strange sensation crawling through her stomach, not unpleasant but odd.

"What happened?"

The Aaroun nurse smiled. "You won a great victory," she said. "In the season finale of the gladiatorial games. People have been yelling your name in the streets. Many made fortunes on you."

Ampris smiled back drowsily. "Did you?"

The Aaroun's long-lashed eyes dropped modestly. "I am of the abiru. I am not permitted to place bets."

"But you did," Ampris said astutely.

The Aaroun's eyes flashed up, gleaming, then lowered again. She said nothing, but satisfaction radiated from her while she retucked the blankets over Ampris's feet. "I have three cubs," she said with pride, her gaze flicking to the far side of the ward where a cluster of medics stood talking. "Now all will have enough food this winter. All will have warm clothing. My mate will not have to work the dangerous third shift the rest of this year."

Memory returned to Ampris. She backed her ears in sudden distress, making something beep above her head.

"Hush," the nurse said soothingly, bending over her again. "Hush. You are safe. You are healing well."

"I killed my teammate," Ampris said. Tears filled her eyes, blurring her vision, but she could not lift her hands to wipe them away. Puzzled, she tugged harder, and this time saw the restraint cables fastening her wrists to the sides of her bed.

She growled.

"Hush," the nurse said, again glancing over at the medics. "They'll sedate and collar you if you cause trouble. That's why you're so groggy now. They've pumped you full of chemicals to keep you unconscious."

Ampris had her emotions back under control now. She met the concerned eyes of the nurse and saw no hostility there, only kind concern and decency.

"Thank you," she whispered. "I'm thirsty."

The nurse nodded and vanished for a time. When she returned, the medics had left the ward. All was quiet and still except for the moaning of another patient several beds away.

"Here," the nurse said, lifting her head so that she could drink. "Very small sips."

The water was tepid, with a harsh chemical taste, but Ampris drank all she was allowed. When the nurse eased her down, Ampris gazed up at her and forced her voice to stay steady.

"Have I been sold?"

The nurse's eyes widened. "No, of course not. You're famous now. You should see the tributes that have been sent here for you. Packages of all kinds, torn-up wager tickets, fruit offerings, flowers, and oh, I cannot remember half of it. None of those things are allowed in here, but your servant comes every day to collect them."

"Am I back on Fariance?" Ampris asked in confusion.

"No. You haven't been cleared for travel yet. When you are dismissed from this facility, you will be collected by your trainer and taken back to where you belong."

"I want to see Elrabin," Ampris said. She was beginning to feel better, more alert. "Is he here?"

The nurse smiled and shook her head. "That one. He's a sly fellow, isn't he? The things he will say. He isn't allowed to visit you, but he hangs around the nurses' station and flirts with everyone. He comes only in the mornings. Of course, the medics won't let him stay here long. They send him away as soon as they know he's in the facility, but he comes back again the next day."

Ampris felt confused. "He's allowed to come by himself? Where are the guards? Where is Master Halehl?"

"You're getting tired. You'd better rest," the nurse said.

"Is it morning now? Will he come soon?"

"It's late afternoon. The medic on call will be making his rounds soon. If you pretend to be asleep, I'll reset your vital signs on the scanner to match. Then he won't order another sedative for you that you don't really need. As long as you're not in pain, there's no need for you to be kept unconscious.''

Gratefully, Ampris said, ''You're very kind. Why are you helping me?''

''Told you. You helped me by winning in a big way. It's the least I can do. Besides . . .'' The nurse paused, staring down at Ampris. ''We Aarouns should help each other. You're of the Heva clan, aren't you?''

''I—'' Ampris hesitated, not sure what to say. Embarrassment flooded her, but at last she spoke the truth. ''I don't know. I was taken too young from my mother.''

''I think you are,'' the nurse said with sympathy, tilting her head as she scrutinized Ampris. ''It's in the shape of your eyes and that golden tint to your fur. And of course you're beautifully proportioned. All the Heva are quite handsome.''

Modesty made Ampris unsure of what to say to such compliments, but at the same time she smiled eagerly at the nurse. ''Are you of the Heva clan?''

''No. I have the blood in me, from my father's side, but I am descended from the Firze clan. We carry our ancestry through our mothers, we Aarouns do.''

Ampris could not believe her luck. At long last, after a lifetime of searching, she had found someone who could answer her questions. ''What is your name?''

''Fula.''

Ampris's smile widened. ''I am pleased to make friends with you, Fula. Your kindness means a great deal to me.''

''Kindness is our responsibility toward all strangers,'' Fula said softly, but she looked pleased. ''It is the Aaroun way.''

Ampris didn't explain that Fula was the first Aaroun she'd ever met who'd said so. Dozens of questions crowded her brain. ''There is so much about our race that I want to know.''

Fula chuckled. "Why, all Aarouns know—"

"I don't. I don't know anything except a few names of our legendary leaders and—"

"We can't talk about them," Fula said, flattening her ears warily. She looked around the ward to make sure no one was listening. "That is forbidden."

"But you know them," Ampris said, refusing in her delight to heed caution. "You know their names."

"Of course. But you have to rest now. You're getting too excited, and the medic will know."

"Zimbarl," Ampris whispered, her voice very soft.

Fula nodded, pretending to look exasperated. "And Nith-lived," she said, equally softly. "Satisfied?"

"Will you tell me the old stories?" Ampris asked eagerly. "Will you teach me the songs that mothers are supposed to teach their daughters?"

Fula's eyes softened. For a moment Ampris thought she saw pity glisten in them. Again Fula's hand rubbed her between her ears.

"You poor *erizana*," she whispered.

"*Erizana?*" Ampris asked eagerly. "What does that mean?"

"It means beloved girl-cub and last of litter." Fula backed her ears, struggling for a clear translation. "The last born. When a female Aaroun knows she will bear no more cubs, she turns a special affection on the one born to her last of all. It is not the same affection shown to the firstborn of all her cubs. We have different words for all these things."

"How do you know so much?" Ampris asked her, drinking in every word. "Who taught you? Your mother?"

"Yes. She lives here still, in the same tenement as my mate and I. She has the healing arts, which she taught me. Now she teaches them to my *erizana*, my last-born daughter."

"I wish I could meet her," Ampris said wistfully, feeling a longing for all that she had lost when she was taken from her mother at birth. "I wish I could meet all your family."

"So do I, Ampris," Fula said with kindness. "But that is impossible. You belong to the Blues. You are not permitted the freedom we common workers know. Even your Elrabin comes and goes wearing a surveillance strap on his arm. It is a shame for you to live this way."

Ampris backed her ears. She did not want to be pitied. "Someday, all the abiru folk will be able to come and go as we please," she said.

"Is that your dream?" Fula asked. "It is a good dream, Ampris. Freedom is something to be cherished. But it will not come for you and me."

Ampris didn't want to hear such pessimism in Fula's voice. "It might," she said stubbornly.

"Perhaps. My dream is for my daughter to become a medic. Such aspirations are not allowed now. But perhaps by the time she is grown, the regulations will be loosened. That is my dream," Fula said. "Small steps taken over long years."

She bent down and briefly allowed her fingers to skim across the surface of Ampris's Eye of Clarity. "I have told my mother of this necklace you wear. She says you are blessed to have it."

"Yes," Ampris said quietly. "I think I am."

"Now you will rest. I can hear the medic coming."

Because of the restraint cables, Ampris could not reach out to grip Fula's hand. She lifted her head instead. "Will you come again tomorrow? Will you talk to me some more about the ways of our people?"

"Better than that," Fula said. Again she glanced about warily, then stepped closer. "If you promise to be very, very careful with it, I will record a data crystal for you. With the old tellings and perhaps with some of the prayer songs of my clan."

Gratitude swelled inside Ampris. Her eyes widened, and she thought she might burst with joy. "Oh, Fula—"

"Hush now. Hush. Say no more of it, for it is forbidden."

"I understand," Ampris said quickly, knowing the risks involved.

"You will not betray us, for you are one of the good in this life," Fula said. "But take care."

"I will. I promise no one will ever trace it back to you."

"Then it will be arranged," Fula said. "If your servant is trustworthy, I will give it to him. Here in the ward, you have no place of concealment."

"Perfect," Ampris said. She could not believe her luck.

Fula gave her a brisk nod and turned away.

"Thank you," Ampris called after her.

But the medic was coming in, a tall Viis male in a smock embroidered with his family crest. Following him came an abiru attendant who would do the actual procedures on any abiru patients who needed them.

Fula flicked her ears, showing that she heard, but she hurried away from Ampris without looking back.

In the following days, Ampris rarely saw Fula. Or if she did, there never seemed to be an opportunity to speak privately. When Ampris was released from the clinic, one of the subtrainers came to collect her, along with several burly Toth bodyguards and Elrabin. Bustled swiftly into the closed cargo hold of a transport to avoid the hovering newscams, Ampris had no chance to tell the Aaroun nurse goodbye.

They went straight to the spaceport, shuttled up to a ship, and departed for Fariance.

Ampris was shut away in a cargo cabin under tight security, with the smelly, brutish Toths on constant guard for her protection. She noticed that the ship's crew came by frequently on various pretexts. Sometimes other passengers wandered past her cabin. All were sent away, but Ampris could hear their voices outside her door.

"A big celebrity you be now," Elrabin told her proudly.

Grinning, he used his hands to slick back his ears, then blew on his fingers in admiration.

"Stop it," Ampris said, uncomfortable with her new status. "I ruined our team—"

"No, you stop it," he broke in sharply. "None of that, Goldie. Ylea went rogue, and you did what you had to do. Master Halehl ain't blaming you. No one's blaming you. So don't waste time blaming yourself."

She told herself he was right, but she still felt guilty. "Ylea was driven to it," she said. "Will I go mad, like her, eventually?"

Elrabin rubbed his muzzle. "Don't think so. It was all the conditioning they did on her that got to her. You know, the collar—"

"I know," Ampris said, fingering her own.

"Hey," Elrabin said, tugging at one of her ears. "You're wearing Lord Galard's cartouche now. Pretty, ain't it?"

She backed her ears. "I'm team leader."

"It's a sweet spot to be," he said eagerly. "Wait till you see your new quarters. Word is, they're being redone just for you. Ylea's tastes were bizarre, see? Nothing you'd like."

Ampris was glad the quarters were being changed. She wanted no reminders of her dead teammate.

"Hey," he said again, to get her attention. "I'll tell you something about old Ylea that you don't know. She wouldn't fight when she first became a Blue. They bought her for her size, see? But she didn't have it in her. Omtat says she'd been brought up free—"

"Free!" Ampris said in astonishment. "Impossible. All Aarouns are born slaves."

"Ain't so, Goldie," Elrabin told her. He tilted his head to one side. "You born in the cities, sure. You born outside, out in the wild places, who finds you? Who puts a registration implant in your arm? You think the Viis are going to round up every stray that's out there?"

Her eyes went wide. She turned the idea over and over

in her mind, astonished by it. Exhilaration began to build inside her. "I never knew this. You never mentioned it before."

"Thought you knew. For someone who used to hang in the palace, Goldie, you can sure be ignorant at times."

"It's called being sheltered," Ampris replied icily. "We didn't grow up watching public vids."

"Shame," Elrabin said, her sarcasm going right past him. "Anyway, I hear there's whole villages on the homeworld—on Viisymel—where abiru folk live free. They move around a lot like—like, uh . . ."

"Nomads," Ampris supplied.

Elrabin yipped. "Yeah, like nomads. Gotta keep ahead of Viis patrol sweeps. But that ain't hard. Anyway, Ylea was raised that way. Free, see? Her folks were rebels, the rumor goes, tried to start an uprising and got caught. Folks got killed, and Ylea went into the auction. She got bought by the Blues, but she wouldn't fight."

Compassion touched Ampris. She felt more guilty than ever, and stared at her hands. "Oh."

"Yeah. They conditioned her, turned her mean, made her crazy. Ain't nothing you could have done about it."

"I could have talked to her—"

"No," he said sharply. "Don't go down that road, Goldie. She was gone before you ever came along."

"Why didn't you tell me this sooner?" Ampris asked. "When she was still alive. I wouldn't have treated her the way I did."

"No, you'd have tried to be her friend, and she would have killed you." Elrabin swiveled his tall ears. "Now that's done. You go forward and don't think about her, see? You got a good first season on your belt. You going far now. Far."

Ampris didn't want to think about resuming training or preparing for another season in the arena. Changing the subject, she said, "I met someone in the clinic. She told me—"

"Yeah, I know," he broke in, warning her with his eyes to be cautious.

She tapped her collar questioningly, and he shook his head. But Ampris still understood that it was better to name no names whenever possible.

Elrabin took her hand and pressed something small into it.

Ampris looked down at the data crystal and smiled in delight. "She kept her promise," she said excitedly.

"Yeah, I guess she did. Made a big deal of it being important. Told me the ghosts of my people would haunt me if I lost it." Elrabin shrugged. "Like I believe in any of those old tales."

Ampris curled her fingers around the crystal. This time, she promised herself, she wasn't going to run through only part of it and then hide it away. This time she understood what a priceless gift knowledge actually was. She meant to study every bit of what was contained in the small, cylindrical crystal.

Elrabin hummed to himself and opened a small cabinet to reveal a player.

Ampris gasped in delight, then turned to him in amazement. "How did you get that?" she asked. "You're not allowed to— "

"I told you when you first joined the Blucs," he said, pretending indifference while his eyes gleamed. "You do good, and you get rewards. I put in the requisition, and the master authorized it."

"But what did you tell him I would use it for?" she asked. "Not the truth!"

"Why not? The master don't care what you do in your own time, as long as you don't break training. You gotta stop thinking that any Viis really cares what goes on inside your head. As long as you obey orders and do what's expected, you can get along on your own business with little interference. Part of the game, Goldie. You see?"

"I see perfectly," she said, grinning. She handed him the crystal. "Let's play it."

"Now?"

Ampris nodded, eager to resume her education. "Now."

During the slow flight back to Fariance, Ampris filled her imagination with Fula's songs and stories. Over and over she played the crystal, teaching herself bits and pieces of her historical language, teaching herself to imitate the ritual gestures performed by Fula's mother during the prayer-songs. Slowly she learned the lore held inside the crystal.

In her new quarters at Galard Stables, Ampris found the off-season break a perfect opportunity to study. As she learned to speak Aaroun, finding the language far more complex and sophisticated than the abiru patois, Ampris spent many of her free hours devising a code for the freedom network she wanted to establish.

Elrabin was able to wheedle the second-season fighting schedule out of one of the subtrainers. Ampris took the schedule and together she and Elrabin mapped out the circuit route on her vid's galactic schematic. After that, it was a matter of Elrabin's stealing data crystals from Master Halehl's library and playing the information on each world or station. Grumbling and grousing, Elrabin would then slip the crystals back where they belonged. He was an excellent thief, never getting caught. Ampris paid no attention to his complaints. She knew he took great pride in showing off his talents.

By the time she began her second season of fighting, she was ready. She had memorized key information on each arena locale. She had a short list of simple objectives for each place: Make contact with the local abiru staff working at the arena or brought in for day labor. Spread the word about the freedom network. Offer further information if the contact wanted it.

Most were afraid at first.

But by the time Ampris entered her third season as a

gladiator, her fame was growing both in the arena and out of it. The Viis spectators knew her as a tough and wily fighter, the best of the best, as shrewd as she was strong. She never failed to delight the crowd with her swordplay and acrobatic skills. She grew renowned for always having a superb trick in her repertoire, something new or rarely seen before. The crowd never knew when she would use it or if she would use it at all. But somewhere, sometime, she executed a maneuver that dazzled everyone. The suspense made good box office.

She was Ampris, the Crimson Claw of the Blues. Holocubes featuring her trademark moves were sold as souvenirs at every arena on the circuit. Sometimes she saw vidcasts of Viis chunes wearing toy glaudoons and headdresses with her features on them. Her likeness, daubed with fake blood that dripped from her claws, blazed on arena marquees across the empire.

Among the arena staff, the abiru slaves who scrubbed, fetched, carried, delivered, and toiled, Ampris had another reputation. It was slow to take hold at first. Few wanted to listen to her ideas. Fewer trusted her. In those first years she was tempted often to give up. But she kept on mentioning the ideas of abiru freedom. She dropped hints, offered information from the slowly growing stockpile of history and legend that she and Elrabin gleaned together from vidcasts, archives, and any data crystals they could obtain. Gradually, the slaves began to trust her.

She asked for nothing in return but information and consideration of the ideal she held before them. She invented code phrases from the Aaroun language. Then she began teaching herself Kelth in order to better win the trust of Elrabin's sly, nervous, distrustful race. At every available opportunity she tried to convince the slaves that there was hope, if not for them, then for their offspring. The Viis empire was crumbling. Everyone could see that. Technology continued to fail. Older folk grumbled constantly about how well things used to work, whereas now equipment was cheap and easily broken. "Viis-made" was a label that inspired contempt. Yet the Viis went on ignoring the problems around them. The aristocrats seemed to live in denial, to a degree that amazed Ampris and her network. The middle-class Viis went on trying to pay escalating taxes and starving their slaves to save money.

With each passing season, more jump gates failed. The arena circuit lost two distant locations as a result, because it became too difficult to reach them in a reasonable amount of time. Vidcasts relayed news of increasing trouble on the empire borders. More rebellions flared up along the rim worlds, requiring additional military campaigns and extra taxation on colony planets. Prosperity reached fewer hands, and many aristocratic households—now bankrupted—cast out their abiru slaves to fend for themselves, or starve, in the streets. Toth gangs grew bolder, preying on everyone in the ghettos and sometimes even venturing past the security barriers to attack Viis citizens in their homes or skimmers. Patrollers seemed unable to cope with the rising crime. Often imperial soldiers marched through streets.

Ampris herself was seldom personally inconvenienced by the growing disintegration of the empire. She lived a protected existence in many ways, her only true risks coming in the arenas. But even there, conflict was direct and simple. She fought, and she won. Outside the arena, she lived a pampered life by any standard short of that of the Imperial Palace. Sometimes a shipment was delivered to the stables on Fariance that held only multiple cartons of a single item instead of the luxuries expected by the team. Sometimes Ampris overheard the cooks complaining in the kitchen about shortages and misrouted supplies. Sometimes she saw the subtrainers arguing among themselves. But most of the time, the stables ran smoothly along a familiar routine.

For Ampris, the troubles of the empire remained a beacon of hope that her dreams of freedom could someday come to pass. The constant travel of the gladiatorial life was exactly suited to her purpose of spreading secret rebellion among the slaves. Although she had little respect for her occupation, she found solace in her greater purpose and thus kept her sanity.

Going into Ampris's seventh season, the Blues still held the team championship. When Ampris was called into Master Halehl's office to be told the strategy for the first competition, he instead informed her that Lord Galard had just received an offer of a million ducats for her alone.

She stood in his office next to the indoor training arena, puffing lightly from the workout she'd just finished. Astonished by his announcement, Ampris thought she heard a peculiar note in his voice. She grew very still inside.

"Did his lordship accept?" she asked, her voice small.

Halehl shifted his gaze away from Ampris. "It is a handsome sum, especially in these times."

Ampris backed her ears, wondering who could afford to buy her at such a price, and in actual coin, not credits. So many aristocrats now lived on illusions of past grandeur, their fortunes stripped from them.

"Very handsome," Halehl said thoughtfully.

Why didn't he just say she'd been sold and get it over with? Annoyed, Ampris glared at the floor. She didn't want to go to another stable. She had made a home for herself here. She had worked hard for the Blues, had brought them more fame than they'd ever had before. A dozen fears and questions filled her mind. Would she have to give up Elrabin and Okal? Would she be allowed to bid farewell to her teammates? Which of her possessions could she take with her? Would there be time to empty her hidden cache of seditious materials and data crystals? Who had bought her? When would she be delivered?

She wanted to protest, to plead, but she knew better than to try. Because she was a champion, plus intelligent and well-mannered, Halehl allowed her certain liberties, including these conversations in his office. But Ampris was always aware of the lines she could not cross.

"Such an offer is of course government-backed. Few individuals can now command such resources." Halehl raised his rill in disgust. "That Ehssk and his genetic experiments. He always wants the very best of our abiru slaves. He's never satisfied to work his abominations on ghetto dregs."

Ehssk . . . Ampris recognized that name. It belonged to a prominent—some would say notorious—scientist on Viisymel. Ampris's dismay tightened into fear. She stared at Halehl with her eyes frozen wide. Oh, yes, she knew about the controversial Ehssk, who recombined DNA in an effort to find a cure for the Dancing Death, a plague that periodically wiped out entire generations of the Viis population. It was a disease they had never been able to defeat. Ampris did not know of any Viis who was not terrified of the plague. In her lifetime, the Dancing Death had struck twice on colony worlds. She'd seen vidcasts of the grim death statistics, had listened to the fear shaking through the commentators' voices. It seemed to come without warning, without apparent cause, and nothing Viis physicians could do stopped its swath of destruction. The disease took the old, the young, the weak, and the strong. Quarantines and other decontamination precautions seldom proved effective. It had even reached Viisymel, before Ampris was born, and she had often overheard the courtiers at the palace still lamenting the untimely deaths of relatives or loved ones.

Before this century the Viis had believed the plague was transmitted by abiru slaves, although none of the slave races were susceptible to it. Accordingly, It had been customary to run slaves through chemical dips so caustic that fur and sometimes patches of skin were burned off. If a Viis household died of the plague, its servants were blamed and burned alive. Fortunately in these modern days, it was now known that the Dancing Death was a genetically based virus that attacked certain cells within Viis blood. But no vaccine had been developed to counteract it. Now Ehssk was trying a revolutionary new approach. While Ehssk's aims might be noble, his methods were not. Ampris thought about becoming a lab animal, spending the rest of her life in a cage, helpless, while she was experimented on.

A shudder passed through her, and her heart began to thud. "I—I have heard of him," she said, trying not to show her fear. "I have seen reports about his laboratory on the vidcasts."

Halehl flicked out his tongue. "A place of horrors. His work has been honored by the Kaa, but how can the creation of monsters help stop a disease? It makes no sense."

His criticism increased her horror. Ampris lowered her head. She knew she was not supposed to ask questions, but Halehl seemed in a mood for conversation beyond the training maneuvers they were supposed to be discussing. And besides, she could not hold her tongue. "What have I done, to be sold to him?"

"It seems he admires your vigor and strength," Halehl said.

Again she shuddered. "But—"

"Ampris, take off that whipped look," Halehl said with a smile. "Lord Galard refused the offer, naturally. He isn't going to sacrifice a good fighter like you to Ehssk's house of butchery."

Relief swept her in a wave so intense she had to blink. She wondered why Halehl hadn't said so from the first. Yet was there any Viis living who did not enjoy toying with his slaves? As a joke, Halehl's little game held no amusement for her. But just then, her relief was too great for her to feel anger.

"So, Ampris," he continued. "You may be champion, but this season you must prove yourself to be worth the million ducats Lord Galard turned down. Do you understand?"

"Perfectly, Master Halehl," she replied, keeping her voice meek and courteous. But inside she felt insulted by the remark. As though she had not brought Galard millions in the wagers he had won. Couldn't Halehl see that as a motivator, his approach today fell very short?

But Halehl was tapping a schedule on his desk. "Lord Galard has suffered some losses recently in other ventures. He wants us to concentrate on bringing home monetary prizes this season instead of prestigious trophies. That means a change of schedule."

She grew very alert and stared at him intently. "Last-hour changes are fined, aren't they?"

Halehl dismissed this consideration with an impatient gesture. "We can't cancel many competitions, because of the penalties, but we can add to the schedule."

Ampris drew in a sharp breath. They were already heavily booked. Halehl had always been meticulous about allowing rest days in case of pulled muscles or more serious injuries. If he forced the team to fight without sufficient rest and recovery, it would mean mistakes. It might mean defeats.

Equally bad was what these changes would mean to her own carefully laid plans. At their third scheduled competition, which was supposed to be on Mynchepop, she had intended to meet with a Myal subversive named Vome during her free time. Normally her movements were restricted by her Toth bodyguards and Halehl's paranoid security measures. While she was too well-known to be actually stolen by a competitor, she could be kidnapped and held for ransom. Or, even more likely, she might be attacked and crippled, or poisoned. Now she realized that if word spread about Ehssk's offer for her, she could be stolen and sold to the laboratory. Security was likely to be stepped up even further. However, because Vome worked within the arena compound in Mynchepop's capital city, Ampris believed she could smuggle him into her quarters with minimal risk. It had taken much effort and negotiation through her secret communication routes to arrange this meeting. If Halehl changed the date, or opted for a competition more profitable than the one on Mynchepop, it would ruin everything.

"I'm adding competitions on Lapool, Veltai, and Shrazhak Ohr."

Ampris swallowed a sigh. Her disappointment lay bitter on her tongue. "Shrazhak Ohr means we must give up Mynchepop."

"True. But the prize for Shrazhak Ohr's Triad Sweeps is huge, more than enough to cover the penalty for canceling Mynchepop."

Apprehension touched her. Lord Galard must be in grave financial trouble, she reasoned, if he was willing to surrender Mynchepop's prestigious competition. Although in recent years the planet was blighted by severe economic troubles, the best teams still fought there. The crowds were smaller but still generous in showering prizes on the victors. Many product endorsements came to teams from promoters on the pleasure planet. The absence of the Blues would be noticed, even considered an insult. But what about the insult to the Blues themselves? Gladitorial combat on Shrazhak Ohr was savage and dirty, a competition for second-tier fighters who didn't care about skill or finesse. It was the lowest of the low, with the Triad Sweeps a grueling three-day competition that included everything from Zrheli-baiting to sword relays. It was about pleasing the crowd with fakery and wholesale slaughter.

Her team was comprised of skilled fighters, consummate artists. They were not common brawlers, and she felt they should not be expected to slaughter condemned political prisoners too unimportant to merit official executions. As a champion at the peak of her athletic ability and skill, Ampris could not believe Galard and Halehl were throwing the Blues down among the dregs.

Backing her ears, Ampris said hotly, "But the Blues have never dropped to this level. The sweeps are for second-rate—"

"All the more certain the Blues will win," Halehl said, cutting off her protest. "You are not permitted to question the orders of Lord Galard."

"Is the prize money that good, to merit ruining the reputation of a champion team—"

"Be silent," Halehl said, his rill rising behind his head. "Or would you rather Lord Galard recouped his finances by selling you to Ehssk?"

Ampris closed her mouth with a snap of her teeth. Fuming, she swallowed the rest of what she had meant to say. She recognized a threat when she saw it. Anything was better than going to a laboratory.

"The placement on the schedule is not so bad," she said, choosing her words with care. "Shrazhak Ohr is a space station, I think?"

She acted ignorant on purpose, and was relieved when some of the crimson faded from his rill. He nodded, and the expression softened in his eyes. "*The* station," he said quietly, his thoughts drifting away. "The shrine of hope. You should be honored, Ampris, at the chance to see our gateway to the promised land. Ruu-one-one-three, the future of all Viis."

Ampris was surprised to hear him talk that way. Halehl was such a practical male, always concerned with the here and now. She'd never realized he believed in the old legend of Ruu-113, a planet that supposedly looked exactly the way Viisymel used to centuries ago, before the Viis stripped it of its natural resources and damaged most of its natural ecology. Viisymel was now so exploited and so depleted across most of its land and sea masses that it had to depend on imports from its colony worlds in order to survive.

Ruu-113 had been discovered about a century ago, and was reputedly verdant, unspoiled, flowing with abundance, and unpopulated. It had been declared the second Viis homeworld. Colonization permits had been issued to aristocrats of the first rank, from the Twelve Houses only. Plans had been implemented to establish enormous plantations that would send food, minerals, precious metals, lumber, and other resources from Ruu-113 straight to Viisymel, so that it need not ever again be dependent.

Shrazhak Ohr, a large space station orbiting Viisymel, was once the grandest in the empire, once the busiest, once the most magnificent. Its jump gate—legendary, especially because of its large size that could accommodate enormous space-going cargo barges—led only to Ruu-113.

But the jump gate no longer worked. Ampris did not know why it had failed—probably because of faulty technology or poor maintenance. Every daily vidcast supplied a report on the progress of repairs, and had done so for years, but the gate was still not fixed. Ampris and most of the abiru folk did not believe the gate would ever again be functional. Ruu-113 was now unobtainable, as though Fate had cast its judgment on the hopes and future of the Viis empire.

But Ampris said nothing about any of that. She betrayed none of her knowledge, knowing it was best if Halehl never realized how intelligent or educated she actually was. Besides, the Viis could be touchy about the subject of Ruu-113, permitting not the slightest abiru criticism where it was concerned.

Drawing a deep breath, she said instead, "If we fight on the station, we will need time to train for the gravity fluctuations there, especially if the systems fail or—"

"The Greens will be there too," Halehl said, interrupting her. "We're not the only superior team to take this course. You need not look so offended."

Ampris bowed. "As the master commands," she said formally. "I'll speak of this to the team."

"These are a series of moves suitable for the competitions on Lapool and Veltai—most especially on Shrazhak Ohr." He handed her a schematic picture of the fighting positions. Unaware that she could read, he always gave her graphics instead of text, which amused her. "Discuss them with the team. I have already instructed the subtrainers to obtain vids so that everyone can review these different fighting methods. You agree?''

"Yes, Master Halehl." She took the diagrams with barely a glance. "We'll be in top form."

"Excellent. I depend on you."

Dismissed, Ampris strode out. As soon as Halehl's office door closed behind her, Ampris flattened her ears to her skull and narrowed her eyes to slits. Her pride hurt, and her secret plans lay shredded. With every step her morale dropped another notch. The team would hate this as much as she did. They did not deserve a season like this. It would be harsh and brutal, far more so than usual.

She tried to tell herself this was a positive sign. The Viis empire really was falling apart, its cracks reaching now to the pockets of the wealthiest members, such as Lord Galard.

But at the moment she felt little satisfaction. It was one thing to plot and assist the downfall of an oppressive empire built on the backs of slave labor. It was another thing not to get crushed when the empire fell.

She suddenly realized with absolute clarity that she must do her best to make sure Lord Galard never needed or wanted to give up his fighting team. She had no intention of becoming a lab animal as long as there was anything she could do to avoid it.

CHAPTERTWELVE

The cargo shuttle docked sloppily into a loading bay at Shrazhak Ohr, coming in slightly canted on its port side. While it was still bumping to a halt and relinquishing controls to electronic lines that would draw it the rest of the way to its berth, Halehl was already marching down the center aisle, pressing the control on each seat to release the belt locks.

As each one in turn clicked release and whirred up above the seat occupant's head, the gladiators stretched and got to their feet.

"Hurry," Elrabin said softly to Ampris as she fumbled with a gear bag. He took the bag from her hand and gave her a gentle pat on her shoulder. "Leave this to me."

The shuttle bumped again, nearly knocking her off her feet. Beside her, Nink half fell over the seat in front of him and snarled.

"We're too late," Omtat mumbled beneath his breath. "Waste of our time, rushing in late."

"Can't believe we gave up Mynchepop for this," Lamina said. A spotted, slender young female Aaroun, she'd been purchased to replace Ylea on the team six seasons back and had proved herself to be competent but unimaginative. She'd been repeating the same complaint the whole flight. "Mynchepop has the most breathable air in the empire. So many negative ions to inhale. This place is probably nothing but recycled air, full of toxins. The outgassing alone from—''

"Shut up," Teinth told her with a growl. "Keep your damned toxins and ions to yourself."

Lamina narrowed her eyes at him while they lined up to disembark. The servants squeezed past them, harried and quick as they pulled more gear bags from storage bins. A ready light flashed on, went out as though it had a short, then flashed on again. The hatch popped free with a hiss of escaping air and pressurization.

Ampris felt her body lift slightly as the gravity field within the shuttle faltered. She gripped the back of a seat for support and gritted her teeth against the ache of her sore muscles.

Finishing the competition at Lapool, they had gone straight from the arena to a ship destined for the homeworld system. It was supposed to be a rapid flight, with a single, direct jump, but the ship developed a serious navigational malfunction just as it emerged at the outer edge of the solar system and was denied entry into the heavily trafficked areas. Halehl had spent hours on the linkup, pulling all the influence Lord Galard possessed to get a communications line ahead of other passengers. Finally, after a three-day delay, he had managed to hire this cargo shuttle to complete the journey.

The shuttle, however, was slow and in poor repair. It limped along at half speed, taking five days to cross the system while Halehl paced and fretted. With the master trainer so nervous, the gladiators themselves couldn't help but worry.

Ampris knew that more was perhaps riding on this competition than even Halehl had admitted. She had never seen him look so haggard. There had never been so many difficulties before with travel arrangements. There had never been so many things that went wrong. It had unsettled them all. Plus they were finding the rough schedule even more taxing than they'd expected. All the members of the team were in peak condition, but even so they were beginning to tire.

This journey had been anything but restful. Ampris was aching for a deep massage. Their seats converted to berths, but the noisy, rough-flying shuttle made sleep difficult. Chemical baths took care of basic essentials, but still left her feeling unclean. The food tasted like its storage cartons. Ampris wasn't sure they'd even arrive in one piece.

But they made it, although they were late. This was the first day of the Triad Sweeps, and Halehl was still on his hand-link as they disembarked and moved awkwardly up the tunnel into the station terminal. Ampris overheard snatches of his conversation and wasn't sure they could keep their entry status since they were so late.

"The fighting has started," Halehl reported, closing his link at last. "Everyone, stay calm. We've enough time yet to get there. I have negotiated a switch in the lineup with another team. We don't go into the ring for another hour."

"Reassuring," Teinth muttered to Ampris as they trudged along, half striding, half bounding in the odd gravity field of the disembarkation tunnel.

Ahead of them, a Viis station official in black uniform hurried to block their path. "Stop! Stop!" he said in Viis. "These slaves must be in restraints. Who is in authority here?"

Sanvath and Lamina were in the lead. Not understanding what the official was actually saying and clearly not caring, Sanvath tried to brush past the official, but the Viis dropped back and drew a stun-stick. Growling, Sanvath dropped his left shoulder and started to charge with a blocking tackle, but Halehl's voice rang out.

"Sanvath, halt!"

The big Aaroun growled again, but he obeyed. He stood glaring at the official, whose rill was standing at full extension behind his head.

Halehl hurried forward to argue with the official, who

was pointing at the team and shaking his head.

Ampris sighed and rolled her eyes. "Another delay. If we're detained in customs, we'll never get to the arena."

"Don't much care," Teinth grumbled hoarsely. "At best, we'll have to go straight there. No time for anything else . . . now."

Meaning no time for a quick bath. No time for a massage. No time for a decent meal.

"We have to warm up," Ampris said in annoyance. "We need some time to prepare."

"Dreaming for the good old days," he said and scratched his ear.

Halehl apparently won his argument with the official, who stepped aside with visible reluctance. Halehl rounded them up and glared at all of them.

"I have persuaded them to let us go straight to the arena through the central axis of the station," he said, his voice low and urgent. "We have just enough time to make the opening displays. Our entry contract calls for it, and I don't intend to lose any possible prize money because we miss easy work."

Ampris looked at him in rising suspicion, but Halehl was hustling them forward.

"I have given assurances that there will be no trouble," Halehl said to them all while he waved the Toth bodyguards ahead. "See that there is none."

Giving them no time to answer, he hustled them forward. The station was indeed larger than any Ampris had seen before. The central axis was an engineering marvel spinning slowly within the vast boundary hull. Ampris got a rushed impression of vaulted ceiling, brushed metal walls, crisscrossing passenger conveyors linking the multiple levels of shops. Craning her neck, she hurried along while Viis tourists not already within the arena stands backed out of the team's way and stared, pointing and murmuring to each other. Shops featuring wares of all kinds crammed every available meter of space, the merchants haggling busily.

When they reached the far end of the axis, they found a huge bank of observation ports overlooking the magnificent panorama of space itself.

Despite their hurry, everyone slowed down and stared. Here was the famous shrine to Ruu-113, now a fable even for the few Viis who still believed in it. Brightly colored pledges of Viis hope were fastened to the observation ports. A Kelth wearing black station coveralls came along, dragging a floating trash receptacle behind him. He set to work plucking the pledges down and throwing them away. Then he started scrubbing away the scrawled inscriptions. While he worked, a Viis female robed in expensive traveling clothes came up with her attendants and fastened a trinket of dyed feathers and beads to the shrine. She stared at the view no more than a second before hastening away.

The Kelth janitor took her pledge and tossed it in the trash, then went on scrubbing.

Halehl summoned the nearby lift, which was slow in coming. That gave Ampris the opportunity to stare longer through the ports. The view was so beautiful, she wanted to drink it in forever. For a moment she felt renewed in spirit, almost young again.

The station arms reached out on either side of the boundary hull, pincherlike, to form the jump gate, which was larger than any Ampris had seen in all her travels. She could imagine what an engineering marvel it had once been. Now the accelerator rings hung black and unused, just one more testament to the darkening future of the Viis empire.

Clutching her Eye of Clarity, Ampris whispered a prayer of her own, "Your despair is our hope."

Then she hurried on to catch up with the others.

The arena was an elliptical structure at the bottom of the station, reached only via lifts that plunged down deep shafts at dizzying speeds. By the time the lift doors slid open, Ampris could hear the frenzied shouting of the crowd, punctuated by roars of excitement.

Her blood began to pound in anticipation. Tired as she was, she still responded instinctively to the sounds and smells of battle.

"Quick," Halehl ordered, shoving the fighters into a corridor lined with metal bulkhead ribs. "Elrabin, get out their glaudoons and take them to the chute."

Not giving Elrabin time to respond, Halehl turned away to flash his trainer's pass at an official and produce the entry documents.

"You're late," the official said.

Ampris heard nothing else, for she was being hustled along by the Toth bodyguards. As she jogged along into the chute, she shrugged off travel garb in exchange for her fighting harness and sword belt.

"Hey!" shouted an arena guard, noticing what they were doing. "You can't arm those fighters here. Who's in charge?"

Elrabin cast Ampris a wicked look and stepped in front of the guard with an obsequious bow. "Please, good sir. Our trainer be coming right away, see? We're the Blues, from Galard Stables."

"Don't care if you're purple, from the gutter," the guard retorted. "You can't arm those fighters out here."

While the argument continued, Ampris and her teammates continued to pull out weapons cases and wrist guards.

"Fine way to arrive," Sanvath muttered. He and Teinth exchanged dour glances. "Fine way to look, and us champions."

"Keep on fighting in these dives," Omtat said, tugging on his wrist guards with his teeth, "and we won't be champions long. Should have gone to Mynchepop."

"Clear the way!" bellowed a voice.

Ampris looked around and scrambled to one side as arena guards came bustling past. They were escorting a pair of Gorlicans who carried a Zrhel trussed in a net. He wore a black smock that identified him as a station employee.

Dropping feathers and snapping viciously with his beak, he struggled and screamed curses.

The gate ahead swung open, letting in the cheers of the crowd and the death cry of a victim in the arena. Ampris's blood ran cold. She froze with her sheathed glaudoon in her hand.

"Zrheli-baiting?" she asked. She swung around ferociously, her ears back and her eyes flashing. "Is that what we are doing today? Slaughtering helpless victims?"

Halehl came striding up, his rill flared out, his tongue flicking in and out. "Ampris, be silent," he ordered. "The rest of you, get ready. We're up next."

Ampris stepped in his path, forgetting all about obedience and humility. "We're champions, not executioners. We're fighters, not—"

"No speeches, Ampris," Halehl said impatiently, gesturing for them to line up. "Shut up and take your place."

Something in her snapped. She backed her ears. "I won't. What have these Zrheli done, to be killed like this? If they've broken laws, why aren't they executed by the authorities? Why force us to do the work?"

Her questions were designed to needle Halehl. She already knew the answers from her network. The Zrheli on this station were quantum engineers assigned to repair the jump gate. As a race, Zrheli were rude, stubborn, independent, and unlikable. Their spindly, lightweight frames and hollow skeletons made them unfit for manual labor. But their minds were brilliant. They made superb engineers, ship pilots, and navigators. They kept to themselves, associating only with their own kind, and generally refused to even call themselves abiru with the other assorted slave races. Never had she been able to get any Zrheli involved with her rebellion network. The Zrheli had their own methods of causing their Viis owners trouble. They failed to report maintenance problems, rewired circuitry and sabotaged machinery to malfunction, and worked with deliberate infinitesimal slowness on the repairs to the Ruu-113 jump gate.

Periodically they were caught at sabotage, and a whole staff of engineers would be condemned and thrown into the arena for slaughter. The deaths of their comrades were supposed to spur the survivors to genuine effort, but to Ampris's knowledge it never worked. Zrheli defiance never waned; they seemed to consider death a small price to pay for giving continual problems to the Viis.

Ampris thought of all she'd worked for these past seven years. She thought of the risks she'd taken, of the rebellions she'd tried to foster. To enter the arena today and slaughter some helpless engineer would be to betray all she'd worked so hard and so long for. Every abiru on this station would know her for a hypocrite.

"It is wrong," she said, her voice thick with emotions. "It is immoral. I won't do this, no matter what prize money we have been offered. And neither will my teammates."

A jolt hit her throat from her restraint collar, jarring her teeth together and knocking her off her feet.

Ampris landed hard and lay there gasping for air. It took her a moment to realize what had happened.

She hadn't been disciplined by her restraint collar since her first season. Now, rolling her eye back to see Halehl looming over her, she felt her fury burn hotter. Growling, she pulled herself to her feet.

Elrabin darted up to her and gripped her harness. "No," he whispered, trying to warn her. "Don't do it—"

She pushed him aside and turned on Halehl. The Viis trainer stood his ground, his eyes stony. She took one step toward him, and he tapped the transmitter with his finger.

Again the jolt hit her in the throat. Again she was knocked off her feet. This time she lost consciousness for a moment. She came to because Halehl kicked her in the side.

"Get up and take your place in line," he said in contempt. "If you speak again, I'll have you whipped. Get up!"

Slowly, feeling dazed, Ampris staggered upright. The world looked unsteady around her, and she was panting for air. She still clutched her sheathed glaudoon in her hand. For a white-hot moment she was tempted to draw it and attack. She could slit him from gullet to tail in a single stroke, but a glance at Elrabin's horrified face brought her back to sanity.

She looked at her teammates, resenting them for not joining her. But they stood quietly, refusing to take sides, refusing to protest their orders. She hated them for being such cowards.

After all the grumbles, after all the resentment they expressed in private, still they would not stand against this wrong. In that moment, Ampris told herself they deserved to be slaves. Talk was easy, but no one was willing to work for freedom, or fight for it, or sacrifice for it. No one, it seemed, but these pathetic Zrheli engineers.

"Let me deal with her," Elrabin was saying to Halehl. He cringed and bowed, holding out his hands in supplication. "Please, master. I can calm her back to reason."

"See that you do it," Halehl said. "We've only a few minutes left."

Elrabin swung to face Ampris. With both hands, he gripped her by the front of her fighting harness. "Ampris, listen to me," he said, his voice low and urgent. "You've worked too hard to get where you are. Don't throw everything away now."

His eyes pleaded with her as he spoke. Ampris was well aware of the double meaning in his words. She shook her head, more to clear it than in argument, but Elrabin misunderstood.

"You want to get yourself sold as a troublemaker?" he asked, his voice shrill and frantic. "You want to go to some low-rate team that gets more beatings than grub? You want to lose your privileges, your status, your chance to travel?

You been places, Goldie. You done a lot. You got it so much better than most, but now you want to throw that away? Goldie, use your sense.''

Tears stung her eyes. Tears of helplessness, frustration, and rage. They spilled down her muzzle, and she sniffed. ''It's wrong,'' she insisted, her voice hoarse. ''They don't stand a chance against us.''

''And you don't stand a chance against the master,'' Elrabin said, his voice low and furious. He glared deep into her eyes. ''Think, you! What right you got to throw yourself away? Can't do nothing about this, see? Can't do nothing!''

He was right, and that galled her the most. Slowly, her emotions tangling in her throat, Ampris nodded and hunched her shoulders. She had no choice. Elrabin was absolutely right.

But her disgust ran through her in hot waves. She wanted to roar. She wanted to turn on Halehl and drive her claws deep.

If only her teammates would back her, but they weren't even looking at her now. In silence, they stood against the wall and stared at nothing. They were cowards, but so was she . . . because she slowly hooked her sheathed glaudoon on her belt and lifted a gaze of surrender to Master Halehl.

''I will obey,'' she said sullenly.

He said nothing, did not even bother to acknowledge her obedience or what it had clearly cost her. Gesturing impatiently, he turned away and strode ahead to the gate.

''Make way!'' shouted a voice.

More arena guards jogged past, followed by a herd of Skeks being driven along by more Gorlicans. The Skeks jostled and shrieked in panic. No taller than Ampris's knees, they scuttled along on their multiple legs, holding their arms aloft in terror and letting their hands flop almost bonelessly. They milled around in all directions, forcing their Gorlican herders to close ranks to keep them from doubling back and escaping the way they'd come.

One of the creatures rammed into Ampris's legs, nearly knocking her off balance. Its fear-crazed eyes met hers, and it jabbered something rapid and incomprehensible, patting her with its soft, repulsive hands before a Gorlican struck it hard across the back with his staff and drove it onward.

The Skeks were driven into the gate with much commotion and struggle, then they were released into the arena, spilling forth in all directions.

Laughter and shouts rose from the crowd. Applause followed.

Beside Ampris, Teinth growled deep in his throat. "You protesting Skek-baiting too?" he asked, his voice low with contempt.

She did not look at him. She did not answer.

"Skeks," Lamina muttered in disgust. "That's what we're down to? Killing Skeks for money?"

Her teammates would not risk punishment and protest Zrheli-baiting. They would not refuse to kill intelligent, sentient, unarmed individuals of value. But they grumbled at the prospect of hunting down brainless, useless, thieving, gutter-life Skeks. Ampris closed her eyes. She didn't want to harm the stupid creatures either, but the distinction seemed lost to everyone but her.

"Just how deep in debt has Lord Galard really got himself?" Teinth asked. "We've hit bottom, Ampris. We really have."

Ampris opened her eyes and saw Halehl gesturing them forward.

"Time," he said. "All of you, get inside."

She pivoted on her heel to lead the gladiators into the gate. "No, Teinth," she said softly over her shoulder. "Bottom can go a lot lower than this."

On Viisymel, inside the Imperial Palace, Israi swept through the long audience hall with a loud rustling of her gown. Her train swept the ground behind her. Every rapid step of her gold-embroidered slippers made the tasseled bells on the toes jingle merrily.

But there was nothing merry in her heart. Grim with alarm, she hurried past the gawking courtiers without heed for what they thought or their spoken speculations. The Kaa had collapsed suddenly during his audience and had to be carried out.

Now his physicians were with him, and as yet Israi had no word except that he had been taken seriously ill.

Reaching the Kaa's imposing apartments, she found the outer chambers choked with lords in waiting, idle servants, ambassadors, guards, and members of the imperial court. The loud buzz of conversation filled the air.

Israi's escort had to shout orders to clear way for her before anyone even noticed her arrival.

Her rill stiffened behind her head and darkened to deep indigo. She curled her tongue inside her mouth, seething at having to force her way inside like a mere courtier. As people became aware of her presence, they moved aside and bowed to her with open speculation in their eyes. Then their gazes returned to the tall, gold-embossed doors leading to the Kaa's private chambers.

Israi reached these, and they were opened for her without delay. As soon as they shut behind her, she was conscious of a profound silence that contrasted markedly with the noise outside.

The lights had been turned down until the room's interior was dim and shadowy. Chancellor Temondahl and Lord Huthaldraril stood conferring on one side with a tall, red-eyed male whom Israi had not seen at court in several years.

Recognizing her uncle, Lord Telvrahd, who had been exiled from court years ago for his affiliation with the Progressionist Party, she felt a jolt to her self-confidence. How dared he return? How had he heard of the Kaa's collapse so quickly? She knew he had once had aspirations to the throne himself, and finding him here now, at this fragile time, seemed a portent of political danger.

On the opposite side of Telvrahd stood another figure. This one leaned back to glance at her, and Israi realized it was Oviel.

She received another internal jolt. Oviel had managed to recover his standing at court despite his cowardice during the Malraaket riots years ago. While Telvrahd could not legally take the throne, since the Kaa had living progeny, Oviel was a far different matter. He was not the chosen successor, but he remained capable of causing her much trouble. Seeing him with not only a recognized trouble-maker but also with two of the most influential members of the council seriously alarmed her.

But there were other matters to attend to first. She turned herself toward the towering bed of state, with its carved columns and hangings of gossamer silk gauze. Physicians were bending over the Kaa's still figure. Israi approached her father's bedside and found him lying curled on his side with his eyes closed and sunken. His breathing came harsh and ragged, as though his lungs struggled. His bronze skin, always so resplendent, had turned an ashen shade of dingy gray.

Israi, so impatient with her father of late, so eager to sweep him aside to take the throne for herself, now found herself face-to-face with the possibility of his death. She felt stunned and shaken, as though she'd walked into an invisible force shield. In that instant she forgot about suc-cession and imperial privilege and her own impatience to live and do as she pleased. She forgot all her clawing am-bition, all her scheming, all her plans for the future. And instead, she saw her father, always so tall and magnificent, always so indulgent of her whims and fancies. Once he used to carry her about the palace in his arms or on his shoulder, in defiance of imperial protocol and custom. He used to take her for rides in an open-air litter along the river, ordering the driver to fly them as fast as possible until Israi squealed with delight. He used to give her private lessons of statecraft in his study, teaching her how to pick loyal advisers, how to eliminate her political enemies, how to rule always with the benefit of the throne foremost in her mind. Her father had loved her, and she loved him. In that moment, she ached inside with a tangling of fear and grief.

The chief physician stopped what he was doing and turned to bow to her.

"Is he dead?" she asked, her voice cracking as she spoke.

"No, highness."

She closed her eyes, not certain whether she felt relief or disappointment. A strange feeling of destiny had settled over her like a mantle. It was time, or very near now. Soon she would be ascending to the throne. Soon she would carry the weight of her father's endless responsibilities. Her throat closed up, and she swallowed hard, trying to find words.

"What's the matter with him?" she asked, her voice still a whisper. "What illness has suddenly struck him down like this?"

For a moment she had the panicky thought that this might be the Dancing Death, which she had never seen, but the physician's answer immediately negated her supposition.

"This is no sudden illness, highness," the physician replied. "He has been suffering from a weakness in his lungs for quite some time. This attack, however, has been the most severe."

"*This* attack?" she echoed, her voice rising slightly. She felt ignorant, a fool. "What do you mean? How many others? Why wasn't I informed? Chancellor Temondahl, have you known of this illness?"

The chancellor came to her at once, his movements slow and deliberate, his eyes filled with a calm sadness. "Yes, highness," he said, bowing low to her. "I happened to be in the Imperial Father's presence when the first attack occurred some years ago. Otherwise, I should have been equally uninformed.''

That he knew something this important when she did not infuriated Israi anew. She hated being shut out, hated any reminders that she was not yet the Supreme Being she felt herself to be.

''I should have been told,'' she said.

''The Kaa wished no one to know,'' the physician told her.

She glared at both of them. ''When was the first? How many times has this happened?''

''A dozen or more, usually following a period of stress or crisis,'' the physician answered. ''Each one has depleted his vital force more.''

''The first occurred during the Imperial Daughter's visit to Malraaket, several years ago,'' Temondahl said.

Israi's rill stiffened. Was he implying that her misfortune had brought this weakness to her father? Was he saying this was somehow her fault? Her anger grew, but she controlled it. After many years, Israi had learned that her temper should not always be unleashed.

''To be out of control,'' old Chancellor Gaveid had said to her once after one of her furious tantrums, ''is to allow others to control you. Take care that you remain in charge of your destiny, not others.''

She remembered that sage advice now, and drew a breath so deep it hurt. ''Will he recover?''

''That remains to be seen,'' the physician said, his voice grave. ''He is seriously afflicted. His vital force lies low. He should be moved to the infirmary, where he can be—''

''No!'' she said sharply. ''The Imperial Father would not wish that.''

''True,'' Temondahl agreed with a sigh. ''It is not in keeping with the imperial dignity.''

''Perhaps we should worry more about saving the imperial life,'' the physician retorted.

A glare from Israi made him bow hastily, his rill very

red. She said, "Let what equipment is necessary be brought here. Attend him with all your skill. The Imperial Father must be saved."

"All that can be done will be done," the physician replied with another bow.

He turned back to his patient. Temondahl gently gestured for Israi to step aside.

She did so, allowing him to lean his head close to hers. "The Imperial Daughter should make herself ready," he murmured. "While all hope for a full recovery must be held to, it is equally wise to take precautions."

She thought again of how he had been talking to Telvrahd and Oviel before she arrived, and wondered if he could be trusted. "Explain," she said.

Temondahl's gaze flickered evasively. "Privacy is not sufficient here," he said, sounding almost disappointed in her. "The Imperial Daughter should know what to do. Excuse me. I must prepare an official statement for the court and the public vidcasts before a panic can begin."

"Yes, do so," she commanded.

He bowed and walked away from her, leaving Israi to pace back and forth in rising consternation. She had pretended ignorance instinctively, without thought. But she knew exactly what he meant. Years ago, the Kaa had instructed her that the transition of power from kaa to kaa was seldom an easy one. Although she was the named successor, acknowledged by all, she still had enemies, many of whom she would never know or meet. It was up to her to grab the throne with both hands and not relinquish it.

Glancing up, she found Oviel gazing at her. There was a trace of a smile on his narrow face, and definite mockery in his eyes. How bold he had grown in displaying his contempt of her.

Israi did not attempt to stare him down. She turned her back on him and went straight to her father's study. The guards stationed there in front of the locked doors allowed her access.

From memory Israi entered the code with her own hand, and the locks released.

She slipped inside and locked the doors after her, aware from the corner of her eye that Oviel—too late—was trying to follow her.

He knocked on the doors, calling her name once before the guards hushed him. Smiling to herself, Israi strolled over to her father's massive desk. Oviel might be sly and clever, but he had not expected her to act this quickly, or this publicly.

Running her hand along the polished surface of her father's desk, Israi allowed her tongue to flick out in satisfaction. She sat in her father's crimson chair, finding its contours too large for her more slender form. For a moment she let herself relish the sensation, then she recalled herself to the task at hand.

Temondahl's warning had been clear. She did not have much time.

Locating the lock on the desk, she entered the codes, her fingers faltering only momentarily. A secret drawer opened, and she plunged her hand inside to lift out a small box of expensive songwood. The wood whispered melodically at her touch. She opened the lid and peered inside at the contents.

The box held a gold-colored key; a red rectangle shorter in length than her hand; the actual imperial seal, made of extremely heavy truvium; and a list of principal security codes for defense installations across the empire. The gold-colored key gave her access to the imperial treasury. The red rectangle controlled access to the Chamber of Treaties. The imperial seal was equal to the Kaa's signature. The defense codes gave her power over the military.

Israi held each item in turn, gloating to herself. There was only one more thing to find. She turned the box of songwood over and felt along the bottom until she found the hidden catch. The false bottom opened, and she took out the access key to her father's personal fortune.

It was forbidden for anyone except the Kaa to possess these items. Until her father breathed his final breath, Israi could not legally touch them. Yet this was a moment for risks. If she let her courage fail her, if she waited until the Kaa was actually dead to seize this chance, then she would be a fool who deserved to have the throne taken from her.

Israi hesitated no longer. The trick was now to make sure no one knew she had these things. She lifted her voluminous skirts with their multiple layers and felt along the deep hem of her underskirt. Finding a seam, she tore it open with her fingers, breathing quickly in excitement, and tucked the items into the hem. Taking a tube of stickant from the desk drawer, she resealed the hem and shook down her skirts, smoothing them quickly into place.

She closed the songwood box, ignoring its melodic response to her touch, and replaced it inside the secret drawer. With all back in place as it should be, she glanced around the study, then crossed the room and took down several scrollcases containing her father's favorite poetry.

Clutching these in her hands, she emerged from the study, locking it behind her, and found Oviel waiting there with his eyes narrowed in open suspicion.

"What are you doing, Israi?" he asked. "Why do you not attend your father?"

She glared at him in contempt and did not bother to answer. When she started to step past him, however, he did not move aside.

"I ask you again, Israi. What were you doing in there? Stealing his scrolls? Looting his study like a common thief? How greedy you have become. Have you no thought for Sahmrahd Kaa at this time? Have you no thought for anyone but yourself?"

Her anger burned her throat, but she glanced at one of the impassive guards instead. "Clear this courtier from my path that I may return to my father's side."

The guard moved immediately to obey. Wide-eyed,

Oviel stepped aside before the guard could grip his arm. He flicked out his tongue and bowed.

Head held high, Israi swept past him, carrying the scrolls back into her father's bedchamber. She was conscious of the stolen badges of state bumping against her ankles with every step, conscious of the jingling of her slipper bells, conscious of her heart beating too fast. But she kept her imperial composure and ordered a chair placed by her father's bedside. Calmly, while everyone stared, she seated herself, arranging her skirts prettily, and unrolled one of the scrolls. While her father lay unconscious, struggling to draw every ragged breath, Israi read to him from exquisite poems in a voice melodic and low, looking the very picture of a most devoted daughter.

She had all the time in the universe now to wait on him. She felt both calm and exhilarated, the reins of power close within her grasp.

CHAPTER THIRTEEN

The crowds of Shrazhak Ohr were cheering for the Crimson Claw and stamping in unison on the benches. "Kill! Kill! Kill!"

She flicked her ears back, circling her staggering opponent with lithe, deadly intent. He was a Gorlican, awkward on his stumpy legs, his shelled torso showing a bright yellow gash where her parvalleh had struck deep in the first flurry of blows. His blood dripped steadily on the dirty sand, and his orange eyes were glazed over with pain and fear. His scaled hands held a stave and a cheaply forged glaudoon. He looked like a common laborer who had been shoved into the arena without any training. He didn't even know how to swing his glaudoon properly.

Armed with her parvalleh and glevritar, Ampris had sized him up in a single glance the moment she strode into the arena. She could have struck off his head in the first blow, which was the swiftest, most efficient way to kill a Gorlican. It was also the kindest death, but she had her instructions from Halehl.

The Gorlican was condemned to death for having struck his Viis owner. Ampris was to spin this out as long as possible, giving the crowd maximum enjoyment.

So she'd struck the first blow at his shell, gashing him deeply but not letting it be a mortal strike. Since the Gorlican's blood had begun to drip the crowd had been constantly on its feet. Halehl's voice whispered to her through her collar, praising her.

"Time for another blow," he murmured to her now. "Stalking is good, but it's gone on long enough."

Backing her ears, Ampris sprang at the Gorlican with a roar that startled him. Yelling, he stumbled back and lost his balance. Dropping his stave, he windmilled his arms frantically to keep from toppling over as Ampris closed in.

She knew if he fell on the ground she would have to finish him, and Halehl would be displeased with her.

Growling, she reached out and blocked his wildly swinging glaudoon, nearly getting her ear nicked in the process as she pulled him upright. With her other hand, she swung the glevritar up and down, making the serrated blade whistle, and hacked off the outer edge of his shell in a long, gleaming strip.

He cried out, and the crowd went wild.

The chanting resumed. "Ampris, kill! Ampris, kill!"

More blood dripped. The Gorlican was staggering heavily now. His beaked mouth opened in distress. "Kill me," he pleaded hoarsely. "Have pity. Make it quick."

Ampris could not bear his begging. Closing off her pity, she snarled at him. "Hold up your weapon, fool! Make this look good for the crowd."

But he barely seemed able to focus, much less hold up his glaudoon. "Why should I please them?" he said, his orange eyes flashing in momentary defiance before pain clouded them again. "Why should I care?"

"Circle him, Ampris," Halehl whispered through her collar. "Close in, and toy with him."

She gouged the Gorlican in his leg with the tip of her glevritar, and again the crowd cheered. Ampris felt sick to her soul.

"At least defend yourself!" she shouted at him.

"Kill me, please."

Ampris could bear it no longer. Compassion swept her.

She knew there was only one thing she could do now for him.

"Listen to me," she said. "I'll finish you with mercy if you will help me."

"Anything," he panted, his voice weak and desperate. "Please."

"Attack me," she told him. "Lift your glaudoon high. No, change your grip."

Again she sprang in and out, nicking him to keep the crowd and her trainer happy. She despised herself.

"Change your grip!" she said angrily. "Look like you can fight. I can't do anything to help you if you don't appear to challenge me."

"Just kill me," he whispered.

"Raise your glaudoon and charge at me with all your strength and speed. Come at me fast and hard, and I will make it quick and merciful."

Although her voice was cold, inside she wanted to weep for this pathetic doomed creature.

Fire kindled in his eyes. He raised his glaudoon as she instructed, and suddenly released a shrill yell that startled her. He charged, full tilt, coming at her with more strength and speed than she had expected.

Caught slightly off balance, Ampris pivoted on her back foot and swung the glevritar aloft with a swift flourish that made the blade flash in the lights. The blade hit the Gorlican's neck between jaw and shell and sliced cleanly.

His head went rolling off in a shower of blood, and Ampris moved smoothly to one side like a dancer as the Gorlican's body crumpled to the ground.

The crowd roared acclaim, and Ampris brandished her bloody sword in a champion's salute, swaggering around the arena in victory the way she'd been taught. But tears ran down her muzzle for the Gorlican lying behind her on the sand.

.   .   .

In the Kaa's palace, all lay hushed and quiet. Servants crept about their duties, hardly daring to make a sound. Courtiers clustered in knots, worried and chattering in low voices. Members of the council came and went, looking grave, speaking to no one idly.

Outside the palace, Viis citizens began to assemble at the gates, keeping vigil. Newscams hovered, reporting rumors and speculation as to the state of the Kaa's health. The sri-Kaa emerged from the palace in the afternoon of the second day of the crisis, attired magnificently, and rode in a processional litter of state with the imperial wives and members of the council surrounding her. The procession went to the Temple of Life in the historical district, where Israi and other ladies delivered ceremonial prayers to the gods on behalf of the dying Imperial Father.

When the procession returned to the palace, spectators saw that the sri-Kaa rode veiled and motionless. As was proper, she did not wave to the crowd.

As soon as Israi was back inside the palace, she stepped down from the litter and tossed aside her veil impatiently. "What news?" she asked Temondahl.

He bowed to her and shook his head. "No change."

Wearily, Israi sighed. She was fatigued and feeling cranky from the strain of this vigil. On the first day it had pleased her to sit at her father's bedside, reading to him. But when he made no response and seemed completely unaware of her presence or her efforts, she found herself losing interest. This morning he seemed no better. If anything his vital force had dimmed even more. Had Temondahl said he was better, she would have gone straight to his bedside. But now, tired and wind-whipped from riding in the open litter, she wanted her rest.

"I shall be in my apartments momentarily," she announced. "Inform me immediately of any change. Instruct the physicians that I shall soon join my father's side."

"Your concern is most commendable, highness," Temondahl said in approval.

"I shall be there as soon as I can," Israi said and left him.

In her bedchamber, she dismissed her ladies in waiting and allowed her slaves to undress her. Old Subi had died during the past winter, and today Israi missed her servant. She felt isolated and alone. No one had ever understood her as well as Subi—or Ampris.

Swiftly Israi closed the thought of Ampris from her mind. She would not think of the golden pet of her chunenhal, now turned into some common gladiator cheered by the masses. But for just a moment, as she wandered to the tall windows and pressed her brow ridge against the cool, smooth surface, she longed for the past, when her life had been simple, when her father had been strong and handsome, granting all she desired, when Subi had cared for her exactly the way she liked best, when Ampris would have caressed her and soothed her, adoring her without question.

Then Israi stiffened her spine and pulled herself erect. She closed off the past, reminding herself that to reach behind her was to be weak. She had to be strong now. She had to be ready for the moment when it came.

But, oh, why did her father linger? Why did he not release his vital force into the hands of the gods and just *go*?

Then she could mourn him. Then she could get on with her life.

Ampris shifted restlessly on the hard bench, bumping Teinth with her shoulder without meaning to. He lifted his hand and gripped her shoulder affectionately for a moment before releasing her. At the other end of the bench, Nink was groaning and flexing his bandaged leg.

They were waiting for Halehl's training lecture on what they'd have to do tomorrow for the final day of the Triad Sweeps. Their quarters on the station were cramped and uncomfortable. Ampris and Lamina were sharing quarters. Teinth and Nink had been paired, although Teinth had asked to share with Ampris. Sanvath and Omtat took the third compartment. Elrabin and the other servants had to sleep on the floor here in the conference room, which also served as massage and mess area. Halehl's temporary office was located on the opposite side.

Ampris glanced over at Elrabin now, where he was crouched on the floor against the wall with the other servants. He looked cranky and was rubbing his slim muzzle thoughtfully. She wondered if he still intended to slip away tonight after everyone was bunked. It was risky, but Elrabin was an expert at getting out. He claimed he'd found a schematic for the ventilation system of the station and he thought he could make his way to the central axis shops without being seen. Then he would meet with a representative of the station's abiru workers and slip back to their quarters before day shift.

Although Ampris had given him permission to try to keep this rendezvous when he'd first asked her, now she had doubts. She wondered if she'd been wasting her time, trying to unite the abiru folk. What good were the old legends or the heroes such as Zimbarl or Nithlived? The Viis were never going to let their slaves go. They were too dependent, too lazy to do much work. They had built their empire by harnessing the talents and creative ideas of other races, but what could they do themselves?

"Cheer up," Teinth murmured to her hoarsely, elbowing her as Halehl came in. "Only one more day, then we be off this space derelict."

Ampris sighed and nodded, trying to shake off her sense of depression. She did not know why, but Shrazhak Ohr gave her a strange feeling of impending doom. She had felt it from the moment of their arrival. It was even more oppressive now. Absently she stroked her Eye of Clarity, sitting erect and pretending to listen as Halehl started his lecture. But her mind remained parsecs away, drifting and unfocused, unable to concentrate on what was said.

•   •   •

An insistent tapping on her chamber door awakened Israi from a deep, dreamless sleep. She sat up, scattering her sleeping cushions, and let her robe drop heedlessly off one sloped shoulder. The room was very dark, its lamps unlit.

Israi hated waking up in the dark. "Lights on, dim," she commanded, and several lamps came on to cast soft, ambient illumination about the room.

"Highness, forgive me for disturbing your rest." It was Lady Moxalie, her chief lady in waiting after having replaced Lady Lenith years ago. She entered now, wrapped in an exquisite embroidered robe, her head and rill swathed in an oil-saturated cloth to pamper her skin at night. "Chancellor Temondahl has requested your presence immediately."

"Is it—" Israi cut off her own question. One glance at Lady Moxalie's wide, frightened eyes told her enough. Besides, speculation only fed rumors, and there were enough of those circulating through the palace already. "My clothes, quickly."

A slave came to help, and in a few minutes Israi was dressed in a plain gown of soft rose velvet that made her golden skin glow. She did not bother with accessories or jewelry aside from a rill collar of plain gold studded with green Gaza stones.

Guards in their distinctive bright green cloaks stood waiting outside her apartments to escort her. In silence they hurried to the chambers of the Kaa.

When Israi entered, all the low, murmuring conversations ceased as though cut off. Israi stopped breathing. Her gaze flashed around the room and landed on Temondahl.

He went to her at once, bowing low. "Highness, your father has called for you."

The clenched knot inside her torso eased, and she began to breathe again. The Kaa was not dead. Perhaps he was mending, especially if he was able to speak. Yet the faces around her looked grave indeed. Her mind felt tangled, unclear.

She walked forward, past the bowing physician, and approached her father's bedside with trepidation, afraid too many of her conflictful emotions were revealed on her face.

The Kaa had been robed in formal sleeping attire of crimson silk embroidered heavily with thick gold thread. He wore no collar and his rill lay in flaccid folds across his shoulders. Although he had been propped up high on cushions and lay on his side, his breathing remained hoarse and labored. His skin, once a gorgeous iridescent shade of bronze, had turned ashen and pale. She had never seen him look so ugly, so weak.

She stepped up beside him, hesitated, and was prompted by Temondahl's nod.

"Father, I am here," she said. "I, Israi your daughter, have come as you requested."

The Kaa dragged open his eyes. They remained as deep and as brilliant a blue as ever, startlingly so in contrast to his gray skin. Israi felt the force of her father's will travel through his gaze, boring deep inside her. For a moment it felt as though the Kaa could see into the very depths of her mind. Did he know what she had done? Did he suspect?

His hand moved weakly toward her and stopped.

"Take his hand, highness," Temondahl coached her.

Israi realized her own hand was trembling as she reached out and gripped her father's fingers. They moved against hers without strength.

She knew then, with absolute certainty, that he was dying.

"Father," she began, then stopped. She could not command her voice.

"Israi," he whispered, and his voice was no stronger than a sigh against his labored breathing. His eyes closed a moment, then opened again. "Our daughter."

"I am here, Father," she said, trembling all over now.

"Take our vital . . . force into . . . yourself," he gasped. "From our hand to yours. From us, receive the throne. Let history . . . judge . . . you as it will . . . judge us. Israi . . ."

Her name sighed from his mouth, and the labored breathing stopped. His blue eyes stared at nothing until the physician reached out to brush them closed.

Israi stood there frozen, unable as yet to believe he was truly gone. She had never seen death before, had never witnessed its finality.

In the distance, a drum began to throb, low and steadily, carrying the news to all within the palace.

Temondahl glanced at Israi, still clutching the Kaa's dead hand, then stepped around her and murmured to a guard. "The Kaa's flag must be struck. Let word go forth to the city, to the empire, that Sahmrahd Kaa is dead."

The guard saluted and hastened out, his eyes staring in shock.

Temondahl faced all those present in the room and lifted his staff of office. "The Kaa is dead. Long live the Kaa!"

Their voices rose in ragged, uncertain unison: "Long live the Kaa!"

A commotion broke out beyond the doors. Wailing could be heard from the servants, a raw, ugly sound.

Israi turned at last, releasing her father's still hand and laying it gently against his side. For a moment she was blind with grief, with a sense of loss so intense it felt as though she had been struck.

Somehow she turned around to face the others, her body moving stiffly and unnaturally. She could not think of what to do. Her mind felt frozen. Protocol, so stiff, so boring, supported her now, and for the first time in her life she was grateful for it.

She would be required to walk forth from the Kaa's apartments. She was to go straight to the throne room. There the chancellors would declare her rights, and the courtiers would declare their acceptance of the changing order. Her flag would be raised over the palace . . . only she didn't have a flag, not the proper one. The sri-Kaa's banner could not fly.

"Temondahl," she said in alarm. "My flag . . . it's all wrong—"

"All is prepared for the Imperial Mother," Temondahl said smoothly. His eyes were kind and sympathetic. "It is time to go forth. Not until the declarations are made can the grieving begin."

She blinked, remembering the procedure as she had been taught it. "Yes," she said numbly.

"Come," Temondahl said.

Israi swallowed hard, coiling her tongue inside her mouth, and walked forward. She moved slowly, stiffly, with great dignity. It was as though the weight of the empire suddenly had fallen on her shoulders with crushing force. *Imperial Mother,* her mind thought dizzily. Temondahl had called her Imperial Mother. It had happened, really happened. She was now the Mother of the Empire, the Supreme Warrior, the Guardian of the Golden Seals, the Ruler of All Things. Israi felt that she had just been hatched. She emerged from the Kaa's chambers a new person, all her past shed behind her like an unwanted skin. Israi's head lifted and her shoulders straightened. Her grace returned to her, and she lengthened her stride.

But before she reached the end of the corridor she was met by a phalanx of Palace Guards, grim-faced and marching in unison.

Beside her, Temondahl hissed in alarm. His rill shot up.

Israi stopped in her tracks, but Temondahl urged her forward.

"Courage, majesty," he murmured.

But Israi was afraid. She could feel her heart thudding inside her torso. Had Oviel succeeded with his plotting? Was this the coup she had dreaded? She reached out and snagged Temondahl's sleeve.

"Chancellor," she said, her voice low and urgent, "tell me the truth now. Are you loyal to me? Where do I stand with the council?"

Lord Temondahl turned his calm, sympathetic face to

meet her gaze. His tongue flicked out. "That, majesty, has yet to be decided."

Israi stood there, stunned by his unexpected honesty, while Temondahl advanced to meet the captain of the guard. "Have you come to escort the Imperial Mother to her throne?" he demanded.

The captain saluted stiffly. His gaze swept over Israi, giving her no loyalty as yet. "We have come to offer our protection and escort. The throne is being claimed by another."

Rage swept Israi as though she had been ignited by fire. She stepped forward, her rill stiff and tall. "What?" she demanded. "Who dares to oppose me?"

The captain did not hesitate with his answer. He met her furious eyes without fear. "Lord Oviel, son of the Kaa," he replied. "He waits in the throne room for his declaration at this moment."

"Get up!"

A swift kick thudded into Ampris's side, knocking her from her bunk. Startled from sleep, she snarled and sprang up, but another blow across her shoulder drove her to her knees.

Across her quarters, Lamina was being dragged from bed with equal roughness. The door slammed open, spilling light into the cramped room, and Ampris saw Viis patrollers in black body armor and helmets surrounding them.

"What is this?" Ampris demanded. "Where is Master Halehl?"

"Shut up!" One of the patrollers struck her in the jaw with his inactivated stun-stick, knocking her back and making her head ring. "On your feet! Now!"

Ampris staggered upright and was shoved outside into the conference room. The rest of her teammates were there, Omtat nursing a bloodied ear, Teinth growling steadily with his eyes like burning coals.

"Stealing us," he said while Lamina roared in outrage.

Afraid that he was right, Ampris glanced around swiftly, wondering if Elrabin was still out on his venture or if he had returned. She saw him across the room, cringing and massaging his shoulder where he'd been struck. Ampris wasn't certain whether she was relieved to see him taken prisoner or not. Her head was aching. She had no idea of the time. But the absence of Halehl and the Toth body-guards made her worry.

The patrollers locked them in restraints and marched them out. They were herded down a corridor thronged with other abiru folk of all kinds. Ampris's puzzlement grew. She did not understand what was happening, why all abiru on the station—whether fighters, servants, station workers, engineers, dock cleaners, shopkeepers, or laborers—were being thrown together like this.

As they were marched along, their numbers continuously swelling as more abiru were added at every corridor junc-tion, Ampris no longer believed they were being stolen. No, something else was happening, something sinister and alarming.

In the distance she could hear loud wailing coming from Viis throats. A pair of well-dressed tourists rushed past, tearing at their clothing and crying out as though they had gone mad.

Indeed, all seemed like madness. Jostled and pushed along with the others, Ampris became separated from her teammates and struggled to keep her feet as the crowding grew worse.

The patrollers swore at them and beat them indiscrimi-nately to keep them moving.

Finally they reached the end of a corridor that stank of machinery lubricant and were shoved through open bay doors into an icy cold darkness.

Some of the abiru, obviously fearing that they were go-ing to be ejected into space, screamed and fought to double back, but the patrollers shoved them forward, shouting as they hit anyone who hesitated.

Ampris stumbled into the darkness, finding herself almost blinded except for what light filtered in behind her from the corridor. She had an impression of enormous space. The smells of machinery crisscrossed each other and mingled with a confusing myriad of other scents, some ordinary, some exotic. Ampris heard no humming sounds of engines, only the cries and frightened babble of the abiru being thrust inside.

Lights flickered on, spaced far apart and casting only a dim orange glow, but it was enough to see by. They were inside a cargo bay, a long narrow space with a high ceiling of metal fretwork and catwalks. Stacks of crates and shipping pods lined the bay on both sides. At the opposite end, Ampris could see the sealed air locks that opened to space itself.

"We're going to die!" wailed a Kelth station worker. "The world has gone mad. They mean to eject us!"

"Shut up!" Ampris shouted over the cries and hysteria. She roared, deepening her voice so that she could be heard over the din. "Everyone, stay calm. We haven't been ejected yet."

Someone swore at her, but in general the station workers calmed down or were smacked into silence. More gladiators poured in, snarling and struggling against their restraints. Ampris even saw her Toth bodyguards towering over others. She made no move to go in that direction and instead looked around for Elrabin.

The doors were closed finally on the last of the abiru. Locks engaged with echoing thuds, and all the prisoners fell into an uneasy silence, exchanging wary looks, fear flashing in their eyes.

Most of them stood without moving for several minutes. It was as though they believed that by remaining motionless they would avert the expected disaster.

Elrabin, however, came threading his way through the crowd to Ampris.

She smiled, glad to see him. "What do you think is happening?"

"Hey, nothing good for us," he said, rubbing his shoulder again and swiveling his ears. "These station workers be going crazy on us. Going to cause problems, if we let them."

"Do you think they know what is happening?" Ampris asked.

Elrabin snarled with scorn. "Not likely."

Something thudded against the wall, sending Ampris and others whirling around. Shouts came from outside the locked doors, and someone banged on the doors as though trying to break in.

"What they saying?" a Kelth female in black coveralls asked breathlessly. She panted, fear in her eyes. "What be happening to us?"

Elrabin gripped Ampris's arm. "Hey, Ampris here understands Viis talk! Put her over there so she can listen. Make way! Move your fur, you! Let her through."

Ampris was shoved over by the doors. She pressed her ear to them, jumping back as the thudding came again. She listened to the hysterical shouting and wailing. Most of it was Viis babble, but what she understood disturbed her.

After a moment, the Viis trying to break in left, arguing and fighting among themselves. Ampris swung around and found all the prisoners staring at her.

She blinked at them and drew a deep breath, knowing she must keep things simple and clear. "They are mourning someone important. I don't know who. I think they're looting the station."

"Be it the Dancing Death come for them?" piped up a voice from the crowd. "Be it the judgment?"

"I don't know," Ampris replied. "I couldn't tell much from what they were shouting."

"Over here!" a gladiator called. He was standing by the wall and he lifted his bound hands to point. "There's a

ventilator grille here. Stand by it and see if you hear anything else.''

Ampris stationed herself under the grille, which was too
small for anyone to crawl through. She listened for what
seemed like hours while Elrabin squatted next to her and
tried to pick the lock on her restraints.

''They keep crying out, 'He's dead. He's dead,' '' Ampris reported whenever a faint and distant shout echoed to
her through the ductwork. The echoing made it difficult to
translate. ''It's like their world has ended.''

''Maybe empire be ended,'' Teinth said. ''That be what
you preach, eh, Ampris?''

''They'll kill us,'' a station worker declared vehemently.

More wails echoed down the ventilation shaft, eerie and
strange enough to make the fur stand up around Ampris's
neck.

''You're fools, the lot of you,'' said an unfamiliar voice.

Ampris glanced up to see an older male Aaroun wearing
the insignia of the Greens standing before her. She rose to
her feet in respect for a professional colleague. He inclined
his head to her in response.

''You know something about this situation?'' Ampris
asked.

''If someone important has died—and that could be anyone from the station manager to a minister of state—then
there will be a period of mourning. We'll be kept here until
the mourning is over. Then the competition will go on.''

The Aaroun sniffed scornfully, raking the crowd of worried faces with his fierce old eyes. ''What have you to fear?
If they meant to kill us, they would have shot us in our
bunks.''

Ampris hoped he was right. She felt greatly reassured,
yet saw that many remained afraid.

Not everyone could hear what the Aaroun of the Greens
had said. Clearly not everyone was ready to believe it.

''Let's keep everyone calm,'' Ampris said to Elrabin,

who swiveled his ears and nodded nervously. "People need something to do."

"Yeah, organize the lot, Goldie," he said in agreement. "What first?"

"Let's see if we can find any food in the cargo pods," Ampris said, wrinkling her nostrils. "I smell something promising. We need to find the available food, then ration it so that there's enough for everyone."

She glanced over her shoulder at the Aaroun of the Greens. "How long do you think we'll be imprisoned here?"

He backed his ears. "Can't say. Depends on who died."

They set to work, and Ampris soon found many eager volunteers. Now that the initial panic had calmed down, a spirit of cooperation rose in its place. The abiru sorted themselves into groups and made a systematic search through the cargo pods they could reach. Elrabin and other Kelths worked at breaking them open until some of the Toths pushed them aside and smashed the pods apart with brute force.

By the time everyone was fed a small portion, Ampris moved back to her place under the ventilation grille. A noise echoed down to her. She raised her hand at once. "Hush! I hear something."

The babble of voices grew silent immediately. Everyone strained to hear while Ampris concentrated on deciphering the echoing, distorted voices.

She drew in her breath sharply and dropped to her haunches as though her legs had failed her.

Elrabin gripped her shoulder, his eyes concerned. "What is it, Goldie?"

Ampris felt hollow inside. Her mouth was suddenly parched, and she longed for a lap of water.

Somehow she forced herself to look up. "It's the Kaa," she said, stunned by the news. "The Kaa is dead."

The word passed swiftly across the cargo bay. At the rear of the crowd, the Toths bellowed a ragged cheer. Some of the abiru were grinning. Others looked worried. Some clearly did not care.

Ampris turned away for privacy. She remembered the Kaa, how tall and majestic he had been when she was a small cub. He had been kind to her at times, giving her an absent caress on his way to scoop Israi into his arms. He had been the most splendid being she had ever encountered. She recalled the way he used to look in processionals, his skin glistening in the hot sunshine, his eyes as deep a blue as the evening sky, his breathtaking jewels and gold adornment glittering upon him.

But he was also capable of tremendous cruelty and ruthless indifference. He had been a selfish creature, spending fortunes on his restoration projects, oblivious to how his city and his empire crumbled around him. He had spoiled Israi, indulged and pampered her, then grown angry when she misbehaved. He had ruled his empire in much the same way.

And now Israi would take the throne. Ampris closed her eyes, squeezing her fist tightly around the Eye of Clarity which Israi had given her so long ago.

Israi would be in the audience hall now, receiving the declarations of loyalty from her new subjects. Surrounding her would be the favorite wives and the multitude of the Kaa's young progeny. All would be in mourning. There would be much ceremony, much panoply. Israi would be crowned Imperial Mother of the empire. How her vain head would swell as more attention was showered upon her than ever before.

She had inherited a great responsibility. She had the abilities to be a just and capable Kaa. But would she exercise those abilities or would she indulge herself in idleness and pleasure? Would she squander her riches while the empire fell apart around her? Or would she hold it together?

Ampris found that she did not really care. After such a long time of shutting away her memories, of shutting away the pain of betrayal and separation, Ampris now found that thinking of Israi did not hurt her the way it once had.

She thought she would envy Israi, now privileged above all others. But instead she felt nothing. Inheriting the throne would make Israi very happy, but Ampris no longer cared about her former friend's happiness. Israi, so selfish and cruel, cared only for herself. Now that she was the Imperial Mother, her general indifference to the plight of those less fortunate than she would probably increase. There would be no one to calm her tantrums, no one whose advice she would willingly take.

Ampris hoped Israi found that possessing the throne was nothing so great, after all.

CHAPTER FOURTEEN

Israi entered the audience hall with an escort of guards that might soon turn and arrest her should this go wrong. Temondahl walked the correct pace behind her, tapping his staff of office on the floor with every other step.

A dozen ploys and strategies went through Israi's mind with lightning speed. She felt it was a mistake to come here like this, with Oviel already standing beside the throne. Yet she had no choice but to confront him here and now. It was time the rivalry between them was finished, forever. He must learn he had no chance, and would never have a chance.

The members of the council stood to one side before the throne. Courtiers, their rills stiff with shock and grief, had retreated from its proximity. Several were sobbing. Others stared into space as though frozen.

Seeing so many devastated faces, Israi felt her own grief fill her throat. She swallowed it ruthlessly. She could mourn her father later. Now she must survive.

Oviel stood beside the throne, which was covered with a black cloth to indicate the death of the Kaa. Only the successor had the right to remove that cloth. But already Oviel's hand rested lightly, possessively on the back of the throne.

Israi burned with rage. She wanted to hurl herself at him,

screaming, but she battled with herself to remain in control. She had the advantages, she reminded herself. The court would support her, for she had been her father's choice. Oviel had only his own ambitions and his self-delusions to support his claim.

He looked up at her entry, and smiled. "Ah, captain," he said, pitching his voice so that it rang out across the audience hall. "I see you have brought my egg-sister. Excellent. Now we can begin."

The smug triumph in his voice warned her. Israi glanced at the captain, who remained impassive. She knew he had not given her his allegiance. But was he in the service of Oviel?

Fear pierced her, as cold as ice. If she lost the Guard, she might indeed be lost. Temondahl, she realized, would side with whoever appeared the strongest. She must win this, Israi told herself, rigid with determination as she continued to walk forward. At all costs, she must win. And once she did, she would see that the executioner broke Oviel's scrawny neck.

The guards halted before the throne. Israi, however, stepped around them and continued forward, taking her place beside the chair opposite Oviel. To match his insolence, she also placed her hand on its back, then stared at him with a bold confidence she did not entirely feel.

His evil smile faltered. He glared at her, his rill stiff and crimson behind his head. "You have no place here, Israi," he said. "The throne cannot possibly go to you."

"I am sri-Kaa, chosen successor to Sahmrahd Kaa," she said, making her voice clear, distinct, and fearless. "Into my hand did his vital force pass. My name was the last word he uttered."

Fresh sobs broke out from some of the courtiers. Others crept closer as though to make sure they missed nothing.

"The Palace Guard has chosen me," Oviel said angrily, his rill redder than ever. "The empire is in trouble. It needs a ruler who is strong and capable of—"

Israi's contemptuous laugh cut him off. "What strength have you? What capabilities have you? Only ambition beyond your place, nothing more."

"The Kaa chose me!" Oviel insisted. "I have been his confidant in recent times. I have become his favorite. He appreciated my assistance in various matters. He knew I was more worthy than his empty-headed daughter."

Her rill stiffened. "You go too far," she said, her voice dangerous. "You dare too much."

"Yes, I dare!" he shouted, not backing down. "Because I care about the fate of the empire! This is not a game, Israi. This is not about choosing new jewels or what gown to wear to a banquet. This is about—"

"What are the security codes to our principal defense installations?" she broke in furiously, glaring at him. "What are they? Can you recite them?"

Oviel's eyes shifted to the captain, then back to her. "Of course not," he said stiffly. "I have not yet had access to information given only to the Kaa and the Commander General."

"Haven't you?" she said sweetly. "Where are the defense installations? Name them!"

"I—I cannot," he stammered, his eyes full of loathing. "Nor can you—"

"How many are there?"

"Twelve," he snapped, then hesitated with visible doubt. "At least that many."

"There are forty," she replied, her voice as sharp as a whipcrack. "Starting with Suvedi Prime—"

"May I have leave to interrupt the Imperial Mother!" a gruff voice rang out.

Commotion filled the hall, and many craned to look at the officer striding inside. Israi took one glance at the scarred Viis and recognized the Commander General with a feeling of relief. She did not know Lord Belz well. She did not know how his loyalty would fall, but she was sure Oviel would not have been able to bribe him.

"Greetings, Lord Belz," she said warmly. "You are most welcome here."

"Indeed," Oviel said, but his voice held strain. "You were about to say, Israi—"

"That's the Imperial Mother to you, Lord Oviel," Belz said in a voice like iron. He stepped onto the dais and drew his side arm before anyone realized what he was doing. His rill lifted behind his head in stiff aggression as he pressed the end of his weapon to Oviel's throat.

"Take your hand off the throne," he said. "It does not belong to you."

Oviel's rill dropped as though deflated. Fear flashed in his eyes, but he tried to bluster. "You dare!" he sputtered. "You have no right to threaten me in this way. Guards!"

"They won't help you," Belz said without even glancing at the guards behind him. "I have not brought the imperial army into the palace, but by the gods, I will if necessary. Remove your hand!"

Oviel made a queer little hissing noise and dropped his hand from the throne.

Belz gripped him by the front of his elegant coat and pulled him off the dais. Only then did the Commander General release him and lower his side arm. No one else in the hall dared move, not even the guards.

Belz glared at them all, especially the members of the council, who stared as though stricken dumb. "What madness is this?" he demanded. "What treason do I see, that you would allow this piece of puffery one second's hope of sitting on that throne?"

Lord Brax stepped forward. "We must consider the greater good of the empire. Lord Oviel has some well-argued points to—"

"Well-argued . . . in his own interests," Belz said scornfully. He glanced up at Israi, who still stood next to the throne. "You were about to reveal classified military information, majesty. Even in a moment of duress, that is unwise."

She took the rebuke without annoyance. She was too grateful for his intervention, and his support. "The Commander General is correct," she acknowledged and had the satisfaction of seeing respect enter his fierce eyes.

He swung around to glare at everyone. "The successor must be able to produce the imperial seal. Do you have it, Lord Oviel?"

Oviel opened his mouth, his tongue flicking out helplessly. "No," he said after a moment, although the admission clearly hurt his pride. "But neither does she."

"I do!" Israi declared.

"One moment, majesty," Lord Belz said. He shot her a look of warning, and Israi realized she was failing to keep her imperial dignity. The court would not respect her if she haggled and squabbled with Oviel at his level of desperation.

"She lies," Oviel said.

The guards reached for their weapons, and Oviel lifted his hands in fear. "I may speak freely. The throne is not yet taken."

"Guard your tongue," Belz warned him. "Give her the proper respect that is required."

"She does not have the seal," Oviel insisted.

Israi lifted her head very high, seething, but she waited until the Commander General swung his gaze in her direction. She understood now what he wanted to hear, and that is exactly what she said. "The Imperial Father gave it to me with his last breath. His hand placed it in mine."

"Was this witnessed?" Oviel shouted. "Who saw this done?"

"Were you present at the Kaa's deathbed?" Belz asked.

Oviel sputtered and fell silent. He glared at Israi, who reached into her pocket. She pulled out the seal, taking care not to reveal the key to the treasury or the other important items she had taken from her father's desk. This small lie was workable, but it would all fall apart if anyone realized she had the keys and security codes. No one would believe the Kaa had been able to give her all those things.

Israi held up the seal, and the hall fell completely silent. No one spoke, and she wondered if they were going to doubt her after all. For Temondahl—the one witness present—had only to deny what she had said to wreck her story . . . and her future.

It took every ounce of willpower for her not to look at the chancellor. He would do what he would do. She held her breath, showing the seal to all present.

Temondahl said nothing, and Israi began to breathe again.

Lord Belz was bending his knee to her. He bowed his scarred head. "The Imperial Mother," he said.

Chancellor Temondahl also knelt. "The Imperial Mother."

Murmurs of declaration rose through the hall as courtier after courtier knelt. The guards knelt, then at last the members of the council sank before her. Only Oviel was left standing.

"No!" he shouted. "No!"

Israi's heart sang with triumph and satisfaction. She had won. But she let no smile cross her face.

Grimly she gestured, and two of the guards jumped up to take Oviel from the hall. Struggling and shouting curses, he fought them all the way.

Belz pulled himself stiffly to his feet. "Long live the Kaa!" he said.

The others rose. "Long live the Kaa! Long live the Imperial Mother!"

The acclaim rang in her ears. Israi swelled with it, savoring it, and knowing that at long last she had come into her own. She had been born for this. She had spent her life waiting for this. Israi knew already in her bones that her reign would be long. She would have to be fierce and wily to hold it, but hold it she would.

Only then did she look down at the seat of the throne, where the black cloth lay. Israi bent down and twitched it off, letting the dark silk square flutter to the floor. She seated herself, the seal still in her hand, and felt ultimate satisfaction flow through her body.

The throne was hers now. No one would take it from her. From this day forward, her word was supreme law. Never again would she have to answer to anyone. Never again would she be held back from what she wanted.

"Let the mourning begin for he who ruled before us," she declared. "Five days may the empire mourn. So says Israi, Kaa of the Viis."

On the sixth day after their incarceration, the cargo bay doors of Shrazhak Ohr were unlocked and the abiru prisoners released.

They emerged, blinking in the bright lights. They were wary, unsure of what to expect. Trainers, handlers, and station supervisors came to sort out the various abiru. The gladiators were reclaimed with scanners, documentation, and qualifiers.

Halehl, looking impatient and haggard, watched like a raptul as Ampris and her teammates were brought forth. Ampris noticed a long scratch down one side of his neck and wondered if he had been fighting. Unable to believe it, she decided her imagination was running away with her.

In curt silence Halehl led them through the station back to their quarters. The station looked wrecked. In every direction Ampris saw destruction and the aftermath of pillaging. Shops lay dark, their wares spilling out into the central axis. Wall panels hung open, exposing torn circuitry. The floor was scored and stained. Dead Viis still lay where they had fallen, not yet cleared away. Injured Viis, their clothing torn and blood-soaked, lay groaning with no one to care for them. The stench of death, charred cloth, and chemical spills choked the air.

Shocked and appalled, Ampris stared at the carnage and destruction, unable to believe that the supremely civilized Viis had done this to themselves. Yes, she could understand grief. Yes, she could even understand the urge to release that grief by hacking at walls and tearing apart furnishings. But she could not understand how the Viis could turn on each other. Stepping over a moaning Viis official with a battered face, Ampris contrasted what she saw now with how the frightened abiru folk had behaved during their incarceration. They, the inferior species, had not fought, had not stolen one another's meager rations, had not preyed on each other. Surely this indicated that they could indeed form an alliance and work together for freedom. If the Viis had turned on one another with this kind of savagery, perhaps they could one day be tricked into doing it again.

Ampris paused a moment by the defaced shrine to Ruu-113, as they waited for the lift to come.

"All the workers were imprisoned," Elrabin whispered to her. "So they haven't even cleared their dead. What kind of folk can do that to each other?"

Ampris gazed out the observation port at the dead accelerator rings. Were they indeed unable to function, or had the Zrheli sabotaged them? She'd hoped to talk to some of the engineers, but none of the Zrheli had been incarcerated with the main group of abiru.

Ruu-113 did exist. She had studied it long ago with Israi. To the Viis it had become a legend, hardly a place that seemed real anymore. But Ampris wondered why it could not be a new world for the abiru folk who had lost their homeworlds. The Aarouns, if they were ever freed, could not return to their place of origin. But they could perhaps one day go to Ruu-113. It was a dream, she knew, the largest dream she'd had yet. But as she stared out at space, clutching her Eye of Clarity in her hand, she felt the pendant warm slightly against her palm, and knew this goal was right and good.

"Someday," she whispered, making a promise. "Someday."

"Ampris!" shouted a voice. "Come on!"

She turned and hurried onto the lift, descending back into her normal life of combat and bloodshed.

Israi leaned forward and struck her fist upon the desktop. "Here!" she cried, tossing the gold-colored key to the imperial treasury onto the wood. It bounced and spun on the polished surface. "Here is the key. Tell me why the treasury cannot be accessed?"

Chancellor Temondahl puffed out his air sacs and looked grave. "Shall I call in the Minister of Finance to explain?"

"No! You explain it to me. You explain!"

Temondahl began talking, his voice droning through the long explanation. Israi settled back in her chair, feeling fury burning to the tip of her tail. Her rill stood up stiffly behind her head. It had been at full extension all afternoon, since this session began. It ached, but she was too angry to let it go down.

Although she made Temondahl run through his explanation of finances, military campaigns, extravagances, poor investments, lack of interest, and shortsighted policies, Israi already grasped the situation perfectly. She had inherited a bankrupt empire. Most of her nobles were ruined, unable to pay their high court expenses, unable to recoup their losses even by selling their ancestral estates. The city of Vir was operating at an annual loss. Issued credit was practically worthless. The economic sanctions leveled against Malraaket had not only ruined that prosperous city but had ruined the economy of Viisymel also.

Even worse, Israi's personal inherited fortune was practically gone. She stopped listening to what Temondahl was saying and wanted to jump to her feet, to scream and throw priceless treasures at the walls. How could her father have spent it all? She had listened to reports until her ear canals rang. What had he spent it on? His stupid restoration projects? How could he have been so foolish? When she learned that he had deliberately withdrawn the treasury from Mynchepop, leaving his aristocracy to face ruin without any warning, and had refused to reinvest it, so that inflation ate away a huge portion of it, she wanted to rush to his tomb and throw his corpse into the river.

"Shall we move on to other matters on the agenda?" Temondahl asked tactfully.

Israi glanced at him and realized he must have stopped talking without her realizing it. She gestured for him to continue.

"Military dispatches from the rim world rebellions," he announced. "The conflict on—"

"Why do we not simply destroy those planets?" Israi interrupted. "We would lose a few worlds but the others would be frightened into new obedience. It would save time and costs."

Temondahl stared at her as though he saw a monster. It took him a moment before he seemed able to speak. "Yes, indeed," he finally said. "But—"

"Which of the defense installations is closest to galactic border nine?" Israi demanded. "Simply withdraw our forces and order a strike. If I recall my last study of the imperial star charts, we have an installation not far from—"

"It does not work, majesty," Temondahl said.

His voice was so low, Israi was not certain at first that she had heard correctly. "Repeat that."

"It does not work."

She stared at him, her rill so rigid she thought it might snap off. "Explain."

"We have forty of these secret installations scattered around the empire."

"Yes?" she said, flicking out her tongue and wishing he would get to the point.

"Only twelve of them are actually operational."

She felt as though she'd been gripped in a nightmare without end. Was there nothing right? Was there nothing working as it should be? "Twelve," she repeated in disbelief. "Why?"

Temondahl made a gesture. "Who can say why some

equipment fails and others continue to function.''

''You mean no one has maintained them properly,'' she said icily.

''As the Imperial Mother says.''

Israi slammed her fist down on the desktop again. ''We have nothing!'' she screamed, her rill darkening to indigo. ''Nothing at all! We rule an empire that is a ghost! It is dead. It is lost. How long until the people learn the truth, that we can hold nothing that is ours, that we can pay for nothing that should be ours? How long?''

Temondahl met her eyes without flinching, his composure unshaken by her temper. ''With sufficient cleverness by the Imperial Mother and her council, the people will never know.''

Israi choked back something and rose to her feet. ''We hate this,'' she said bitterly. ''You mean we are to perpetuate a lie.''

''Exactly, majesty.'' Temondahl's gaze followed her. ''That is what it means to rule. Nothing is ever what it seems to the public.''

She flicked out her tongue, feeling overwhelmed. ''We did not anticipate so many problems, chancellor. We thought the solutions could be applied quickly.''

Temondahl hesitated a moment, then said, ''There are two types of kaas, majesty. One type will work hard, serving the people—''

''The people exist to serve us!'' Israi cried.

''No, majesty. The people are the children of the Imperial Mother. She works hard to protect, guide, and keep them safe.''

Israi glared at him, hating this lecture as she had all his others. ''And the other type of kaa?'' she asked in a voice like silk.

''The other type defers that which is difficult, ignores that which is troublesome, delays that which is inevitable. The problems become cumulative, and eventually insurmountable.''

Seething, Israi said nothing. She understood his point perfectly, and she did not like it. She hated drudgery, hated these long hours in her study, closeted with Temondahl, who never ran out of reports or problems. There was no end to the work, and she hated work. She longed to be in her garden, lying in the sun, while musicians played soft flyta tunes.

Temondahl said, "Although the empire teeters on the brink of ruin, it is my belief that we can save it, majesty. With hard work and sacrifice, such as—"

"You are a joyless creature," Israi declared. "Have we not sacrificed enough, waiting all these years to inherit the throne from our esteemed father? Have we not been patient? Have we not endured?"

Temondahl's pupils narrowed to very small dots of black. "Sacrifice, majesty, such as reduction of the imperial household expenses, the elimination of waste and duplication in the military budget, especially inherited officer rankings for the aristocracy, suspension of restoration in the old palace, the closing of unproductive space stations such as Shrazhak Ohr, and the—"

"Enough!" Israi said, raising her rill. "We will hear no more of this today."

Temondahl bowed at once. "Very well, majesty," he said, closing the dispatch box. "But the problems not dealt with today will have multiplied as fast as Skeks by tomorrow."

She glared at him, feeling furious and trapped. A chasm seemed to yawn before her. She knew she had a momentous decision to make, one that might make the difference to the very survival of all she knew and held. But she was tired and too distressed by all she had learned today. She felt that Temondahl was being unfair, dumping so much on her at once.

"Tomorrow," she said. "We will resume this tomorrow."

Temondahl's rill sagged with disappointment. He bowed

without protest, his eyes meeting hers in silent criticism. "As the Kaa commands," he said and left her.

To the sound of cheers, Ampris jogged into the arena for her final appearance at Shrazhak Ohr. She carried her glaudoon, which she brandished aloft in a salute to the crowd. It amazed her how the Viis had resumed the games as though the Kaa hadn't died, as though they hadn't been rioting, looting, and killing each other only a few hours ago.

But Ampris spared little thought for the morally corrupt Viis. Instead, she felt pumped by renewed optimism and inspiration. She believed now that the abiru folk really did have a chance at freedom. But they would have to make a real alliance and take action instead of just talking about it.

Now she focused on her quarry. The Zrhel engineer crouched on the opposite side of the arena, his gray eyes huge with fear and hostility. From his narrow, domed skull covered with tiny, plush feathers, to his thin shoulders, to his knobby legs, he clearly possessed no athletic ability at all. As soon as he backed away from her purposeful advance, Ampris gauged his movements and knew he had no chance at all to spin this out.

Being condemned, the Zrhel was unarmed except for his talons and huge, curved beak. Ampris swung her glaudoon about, making showy motions to please the shouting crowd while she closed in.

Again he backed away from her. She circled him, growling to get his attention.

"Hey, Zrhel," she said softly under the noise of the crowd. "Listen to me. We must talk."

He squawked in alarm and scrambled away from her. Ampris circled him again, driving him back to the center of the arena, away from the walls.

"Listen," she said, lunging at him with a flurry of sword movements that ended in a whack at his legs with the flat of her blade.

The crowd booed her. Ampris backed her ears but ignored them. Halehl began murmuring instructions through her collar, but she ignored him too.

"Listen," she said once more while the Zrhel glared at her, his beaked mouth open. "I am Ampris. I am friendly to the cause of the Zrheli. Answer me one question, please."

"Liar!" he shouted at her. "Why don't you execute me and get it over with? Then you can go back to your fancy living, the pet of your accursed masters."

"I am not here by choice," she said.

He charged her, squawking and scattering feathers. Ampris whacked him with the flat of her blade, sending him tumbling to the ground.

Again the crowd booed.

"Ampris," Halehl said through her collar. "Make this quick. We're paid by the number of Zrheli you kill, not by the show itself."

She ignored the trainer, focusing all her attention on the engineer scrambling to his feet. "I didn't choose to be a gladiator," she told him, anxious to make him understand. "I am a slave, just like you."

"Slave, hah!" His contempt came hot and furious. "Do you die for your convictions, the way Zrheli die? You talk, Ampris, but you don't act."

"Can you fix the jump gate?" she asked, knowing she couldn't delay killing him much longer.

The crowd had seated itself and was booing her constantly now.

"Kill him!" Halehl commanded her.

"There isn't much time," Ampris said to the engineer. "I will be merciful to you. I promise. But can your people fix the jump gate so that the abiru can escape to freedom at—"

Screaming curses, the Zrhel attacked her. Ampris thrust him off with her arm, refusing to use her glaudoon until he answered her question. Again he went tumbling across the dirty sand. She tackled him before he could rise, and pinned him to the ground.

He thrashed beneath her weight, snapping viciously with his beak, his talons clawing at her.

"Can it be fixed?" she shouted at him. "Could it be used for the abiru?"

He went on screaming curses, too panicked to listen to anything she said. Growling, Ampris let him up, thinking he would scramble away from her. Then she would be able to ask him once more before she had to run him through.

But when she released him, the Zrhel instead turned on her, clawing across her chest with talons that sliced razor sharp. Ampris roared in pain and gripped him by one feathered arm. But he dived across her, ignoring the sudden snap as her grip broke his arm.

His beak cut through the tendons at the back of her knee before she could stop him. Roaring again, Ampris rolled with him, trying to dislodge him. But the Zrhel clung to her like something demented, gashing her again and again with talons and beak.

She was losing blood and strength. She had dropped the glaudoon as they rolled and tumbled. It was useless at such close quarters anyway. Elrabin had not armed her with a dagger, as she wasn't supposed to need it. Thrusting the Zrhel's snapping beak away from her throat, Ampris bared her fangs and bit his shoulder.

She got a mouthful of skin and feathers, her powerful jaws crunching through bone. The Zrhel's screaming grew shrill and louder, then it abruptly cut off as Ampris snapped his neck.

Panting hard, the world swimming around her, she thrust his lightweight body away from her and tried to climb to her feet. Her left leg refused to support her weight and she fell.

The crowd booed her more loudly than ever.

From the corner of her eye, Ampris could see medics and handlers running out to her. She shook her head, trying to clear her cloudy vision. Again she tried to rise. Again she fell.

Pain skewered her, a fiery throbbing pain. Her golden fur was smeared with blood, her own blood. Ampris lifted her head and roared defiance at the booing crowd. Then the handlers reached her, tossing her bodily onto a stretcher and sending it bobbing out of the arena with the medics.

Ampris kept hoping they would give her something to null the pain, something that would knock her unconscious, but they didn't. She was shoved through a tunnel jammed with trainers, servants, handlers, and waiting gladiators. Everything was a blurred confusion of shapes and noise. She was still bleeding, her senses spinning around her.

For an instant she managed to blink her vision clear and glimpsed the veteran Aaroun gladiator of the Greens. He stood in fighting harness, waiting to go in with the slouched patience of a professional. His gaze met hers, briefly, full of pity, and he gave her a tiny salute of farewell as she was carried past.

Not until the medics bumped the floating stretcher against the infirmary doorway in their haste, jolting her weight onto her injured leg, did Ampris think she might finally pass out. Writhing, she screamed in agony, and rough hands pressed her flat.

"Be still," someone told her without sympathy.

Ampris could hear the hum of a medical scanner. Someone close by was moaning and whimpering. She gritted her jaws to hold back any sounds of her own suffering.

Temporary bandages were stuck over her lacerations and gashes. By then Fuvein was there, bending over her and giving the medics a rapid series of instructions. They yanked her leg straight, and Ampris cried out, arching her back in pain.

Again they pressed her down, and this time restraint cables were secured around her to hold her immobile. She heard Fuvein's voice arguing with Halehl's, both sounding very far away, then a mask was placed over her face, and she knew nothing else but oblivion.

CHAPTER FIFTEEN

Shivering with nerves, Elrabin compressed himself even more tightly in the narrow space between the desk and a box of training gear in Halehl's office. He had hidden there to avoid being caught searching Halehl's desk. Now he tried to stay still, not even breathing more than he absolutely had to, and cursed the trainer in his heart for having come in at this critical moment.

Halehl seemed to be in a hurry. Activating only a single lamp, much to Elrabin's relief, he switched on the linkup. By turning his head minutely to the side, Elrabin could just glimpse part of the small screen.

The station's operator could be seen on it. She said something in Viis, and Halehl replied, looking at his timepiece as he did so. Static blurred the screen, then an icon blinked, indicating an incoming transmission.

Elrabin moaned silently to himself. If he got himself caught in here, eavesdropping on the master's conversations, even if he couldn't understand what was being said, then it would be worse than the whipping post for him. Elrabin figured he would get the rod, and the thought of even minor electrocution made his heart quail. Oh, Master Halehl was always imaginative when it came to dealing out punishments. But Elrabin was here to help Ampris. All he needed was a pass from Halehl's desk, and he would be permitted into the station's infirmary to see what had become of her.

Halehl was standing in front of the screen, which now showed the furious visage of a Viis aristocrat. His skin was variegated in shades of green, dark blue, and yellow, and his rill stood up tall behind his head. His yellow eyes were the coldest, most ruthless Elrabin had ever seen.

It was Lord Galard. Elrabin recognized his features from vidcasts he'd seen. Elrabin panted, then gulped and forced his jaws shut. *Be quiet. Be quiet,* he told himself.

Halehl bowed to the face on the screen. Static obscured it momentarily, then cleared, losing part of what Galard said.

Halehl spoke briefly, keeping himself partially inclined in obeisance.

"Chuh-ha!" Galard said vehemently.

Elrabin's ears perked forward. He knew that word. It meant stupid. He grinned in delight. Was Halehl being blamed for what had happened to Ampris? So maybe justice still existed.

But Halehl was nodding. *"Chuh-ha,"* he said in agreement.

When Elrabin realized Halehl was not getting a reprimand, his ears flattened and he mouthed a silent curse.

The two Viis discussed matters for a few seconds more, then Galard's image blanked off the screen.

Halehl stood there a moment, breathing hard, his tongue flicking in and out. He swore in Viis and kicked his desk with a thud that startled Elrabin.

The box of gear scooted slightly, and Elrabin froze, except for the thundering of his heart. His mouth was suddenly so dry he could not swallow. He had to clench his jaws shut to silence his involuntary whining.

The lights flared on, and the gearbox was shoved aside. Elrabin looked up at Halehl towering over him. Halehl's rill was flame red and stiff.

"Get up," he said in a voice of fury.

Fear grabbed Elrabin's entrails, but he forced himself to jump to his feet. He bowed to Halehl, cringing a bit, and said rapidly, "May the master forgive me. I was just checking the gearbox for—"

"You were spying," Halehl said, his tone as sharp as a whipcrack.

Elrabin flinched. "Please, I—"

"Never mind. There isn't time to beat you now," Halehl said shortly. "Our shuttle is departing in two hours. See that the fighters are informed. Make sure all the gear is checked and accounted for."

"At once, master," Elrabin said, starting to breathe normally again.

Halehl glared at him. "What are you waiting for? Go!"

"Yes, at once. As the master commands," Elrabin said. He scuttled around the desk, relieved to have escaped so lightly, yet he couldn't bring himself to leave as commanded. "Please," he said hesitantly, swiveling his ears back. "Please, master?"

"What?" Halehl asked without looking up from the manifests he was collecting from the desk. "I ordered you gone."

"Yes, master. At once, master." Elrabin moved toward the door, then once again turned back. "How do I collect Ampris from the infirmary?"

Halehl's rill flared out and he pinned Elrabin with a suspicious glare. "So that is what you were after."

Elrabin opened his mouth, panting, and found himself unable to deny it. Once, long ago when he was just a young grifter in the Vir ghetto, he could feed anyone a line of patter as slick as could be. But he was older now. There had been too many beatings, too much cruelty. Besides, Halehl had always had the knack of being able to probe straight to the depths of any slave in his keeping. Lying to him was almost impossible.

Bowing his head, Elrabin whispered, "Yes, master. I been worried about her. You ain't told us nothing, not how bad her injuries are or if she's healing good. I thought—"

"You are not expected to think," Halehl snapped, red burning in his rill. "You do what you are told."

"Yes, master. But is she going to be released in time to go with us?"

Halehl puffed out his air sacs. "No. Ampris is no longer on the team. She was stupid to let that Zrhel get close to her. She knew better."

Elrabin sighed. Yes, Ampris had known better. She had been up to something out there in the arena. He had seen a light in her beautiful eyes that had been absent in recent months. She had been fired up, enthusiastic again. But when she was carried out of the arena, bleeding and torn, her face contorted with agony while the fickle Viis booed their once beloved champion, Elrabin had wanted to howl in anguish.

What a waste, a stupid waste. The Zrhel hadn't been worth it. Now the beautiful, incomparable Ampris was crippled, ruined, and all they had worked so hard for was being destroyed with her.

"Not on the team, master?" Elrabin said softly, hoping that Halehl would explain. Inside, he was frantic, trying to think of what he could do. If Halehl was only angry at Ampris for having disobeyed him, then perhaps the situation could be salvaged. "She going into service for the Blues, going to be part of the training staff? She could be—"

"Ampris will be sold," Halehl said.

Elrabin's jaws parted and his ears snapped forward. "Sold?" he yipped. He felt stupid, unable to comprehend it. *"Sold?"*

Halehl gestured furiously. "She is crippled for life. Her career is over. Now we must recoup what we can from this disaster." Frustration burned through his voice, then he glanced up and glared at Elrabin. "Get to your duties. Your service to Ampris is over. Let her name be mentioned no more. Go now. I have calls to make."

Elrabin scuttled out as fast as he could, while his brain

whirled in dismay. Ampris to be sold? Ampris to be gone forever? He couldn't believe it, couldn't accept it.

He didn't let the door close completely behind him, but instead paused there with his ear pressed to it, listening while Halehl swore long and low to himself. Then the linkup was activated. Halehl spoke rapidly in Viis, but Elrabin recognized one thing he said: Vess Vaas.

It was the name of the research laboratory on Viisymel. Horrified, Elrabin stumbled away from the door, letting it close. He tried to imagine Ampris caged like an animal, helpless while Viis scientists conducted atrocities on her, and couldn't. His brain would not accept the idea.

"Elrabin!"

The shout came from behind him.

Elrabin halted with his shoulders hunched. He turned around and saw Halehl standing in the office doorway. Fear shot through Elrabin, but before he could speak, Halehl pushed the transmitter that controlled his restraint collar.

Energy jolted through Elrabin's throat, making his body arch backward. He fell to the floor, convulsing helplessly as Halehl jolted him again and again.

When the punishment finally stopped, Elrabin lay there, sobbing soundlessly with tears of pain streaming from his eyes. His body hurt all over. He could not stop trembling.

Halehl placed his foot on Elrabin, holding him down. "There is not time before our departure to use the rod," he said in a voice as cold as space. "But you've made your last mistake. One more transgression, and you will be a rug on my floor. Am I understood?"

Elrabin dragged in a shuddering breath, unable to speak.

Halehl kicked him. "Am I understood?"

"Yes, master," Elrabin whispered, weeping. He despised himself for his weakness. He wished he could fight, could attack Halehl and tear him apart.

The trainer kicked him again. "I did not hear you."

"Yes, master!"

"You are a defiant fool," Halehl told him angrily. "Take care, Elrabin. I will not warn you again."

He walked back into his office and let the door snap shut behind him. Elrabin slowly levered himself to his feet, wincing in pain, and limped away.

As he walked, he shook with hatred. He crossed the conference room, then stopped, too dazed to remember what he was supposed to do.

The door to Teinth's quarters opened, and the big gladiator stuck out his head. "What's the word?" he asked. "You find out anything about her?"

Elrabin's shoulders hunched. He was still trembling from head to foot. He could not answer, could not even look at Teinth.

The big Aaroun growled at him, then reached out and snagged Elrabin by the arm. "Hey! He use the rod on you? Or he just cut out your tongue?"

Elrabin stood there, seething and shocked. His fists clenched at his sides, and he drew his lips back from his teeth. Lifting his head, he looked right into Teinth's eyes.

"Halehl is selling Ampris to a lab," he said, his voice low and ragged. "You love her, Teinth. If I unlock the weapons case and give you a glevritar, will you murder him now?"

Teinth's eyes widened. He said nothing.

Elrabin waited, but then he realized Teinth's very silence was a refusal.

"I'm serious," Elrabin said, growling.

Teinth's ears flattened, and great sadness entered his eyes. Saying nothing else, he retreated into his quarters.

Elrabin snorted to himself, baring his fangs, and stared around at the deserted conference room. He could knock on the doors of the other fighters, but the answer would be the same. Elrabin took a couple of steps toward the storage bins, trying to make himself follow Halehl's orders. Forget her, he told himself savagely. She's history. She's gone. She had it good, and she ruined her own life.

He jerked open a bin, letting the contents spill at his feet. She would be replaced soon enough, and he would be assigned to serve the replacement. He'd do a good job. He'd adapt like he always did. He'd go on sneaking his bets in and hiding his slowly accumulating fortune. It wasn't enough yet, for his purposes, but he was getting there. Sure, he could go on, the way he always had.

Elrabin's vision suddenly blurred, and he pressed his hands to his eyes. He could hear himself keening silently. Again and again, images of Ampris flashed through his mind. Her grace and athleticism as she bounded and attacked in the arena. Her well-modulated voice stumbling over some archaic Kelth phrase as she strove to teach herself the language of his ancestors. The radiant flash of her smile. The sweep of her long lashes over the keen intelligence in her dark brown eyes. The innate kindness as she stopped what she was doing to speak a word of encouragement to Okal after he was punished for using his own remedies on her hurts.

Lowering his hands from his face, Elrabin tilted his head back and shuddered. She was the best friend he'd ever had, the only true friend he'd had. Always before, he'd linked up with folks that betrayed him, but not Ampris. Her heart was true. She didn't lie. She didn't betray. A promise was a bond to her. So what if she was crazy with idealism? She didn't deserve to be thrown away like this, abandoned, with no one to help her.

It had been good here, too good. He got regular meals. He had easy work. But the good life was over.

Elrabin knew he couldn't go on being a hypocrite, living with the Blues, wearing the restraint collar like a good little Kelth, eating decent food and enjoying luxuries while Ampris lived in a cage.

Something inside him snapped, the way it had when he was just a young lit and one day had walked out of his tenement house, never to see his mother and siblings again. Elrabin turned and left the conference room. He did not get out the gear bags. He did not tell the fighters to prepare themselves for departure. He went through a small hatch into the cramped storage area, shoving aside extra gear bags and weapons cases, to uncover the ventilation grille that he had loosened earlier.

Only then did he stop, feeling his momentary courage fail him. How did he think he was going to get away? How was he going to get rid of this restraint collar?

Then he shook away his cowardice and told himself to start thinking. He couldn't just cut the collar off, for it was rigged to fatally electrocute the wearer if broken or tampered with. No, he would have to find someone who knew how to remove it safely. So what? It wasn't the first time he'd found a way to evade detection. He'd manage somehow.

Once he lost the collar, the space station would be an easy place to hide himself in. People came and went constantly. He figured he could tag along as just another slave in someone's retinue in order to stow away aboard a planet-bound shuttle.

Of course, once he ran away, he would be labeled a fugitive slave, with a price on his head for the bounty hunters. Halehl probably would not pay for his recovery, finding it simply cheaper to replace him. In that case, Elrabin would be marked for shooting on sight. He shuddered, but he pushed open the grille and climbed inside. He was tired of being a coward, or maybe he was just becoming a fool. Either way, no matter what it took, or how long it took, somehow he would find a way to help Ampris.

The painkillers wore off during the flight from Shrazhak Ohr to Viisymel. Curled inside a cargo pod with cold food and stale water, Ampris gritted her teeth and tried to endure the throbbing agony in her left leg. The medics had patched up her other injuries, and they no longer troubled her. But her leg was a crippled, drawn thing, healing crooked.

Being jolted around in transit inside the windowless pod

was agonizing. Ampris suffered, but she also forced herself to stretch and exercise the leg, gritting her teeth as she kept flexing it, trying to prevent it from healing stiff and useless.

No one had told her anything. Halehl had not come back to the infirmary, nor had Elrabin, nor the rest of her team-mates. She understood she had been sold, although no one on the infirmary staff would answer her questions. Clamped into restraints, she had been loaded into the cargo pod and shipped.

Ampris suspected where she was going. Would the scientist Ehssk still pay a million credits for a crippled Aaroun? Her genes were not crippled, so perhaps she was still worth something.

She could not bear to think about going to the research laboratory, however. Each time it entered her mind, fear burned sour in her mouth and she wanted to howl.

So she sang to herself the old Aaroun prayer-songs she had learned. She recited the old legends. She talked to herself, and slept, and stretched her aching leg, trying not to be afraid.

When she made planetfall, she was shipped far into the barren plains of Viisymel, all the way out to a dusty pro- vincial town called Lazmairehl, then onward a few more klicks to a cheaply constructed installation of rectangular, flat-roofed buildings at the base of a jagged mountain range. A road curved away into the distance, but no other evidence of civilization could be seen.

Ampris stood on the landing dock, her fur ruffled by the blowing wind, and stared at the desolate scenery. The air smelled of dust. She saw no vegetation growing and won- dered if this was one of the blighted regions of Viisymel so ruined, poisoned, and exploited in past centuries that it was now considered uninhabitable.

The sign in Viis characters over the top of the largest building said Vess Vaas Research Laboratory.

Ampris backed her ears and shuddered in fear. It was true, then. She had reached the bottom. Try as she might, she could not imagine a worse fate than to be condemned to this place.

Toth handlers came with charged nooses attached to poles. Fitting the nooses around her neck, they shoved her forward, faster than her crippled leg could go. Ampris fell in the dust, and they bellowed curses at her, dragging her upright and nearly choking her in the process.

With her arms bound by restraint cables, she could not protect or defend herself. Choking and crying out, she limped forward, staggering in pain.

Viis lab technicians in white smocks stood just inside the double air locks to witness her arrival.

"Careful with her!" one of them said sharply to the Toths. "Take her to Section B, the cage at the end. No, don't choke her, you fools!"

The tech jerked at one of the poles, berating the Toths until they stood with their massive heads lowered, flicking their long ears back and forth in puzzlement. One of them ran his thick tongue up into his broad nostrils and grunted.

"Go on," the tech ordered in annoyance.

Ampris was too tired and frightened to even snarl. She limped down a bare corridor that stank of chemicals, urine, and fear.

Through another set of sealed doors, she found herself being led past row after row of cages. On one side they were small and stacked atop each other, containing numerous small animals, reptiles, rodents, and birds. These creatures screeched in panic at the sight of the Toths, and hurled themselves at the wire sides of their cages.

On the other side, the cages were quite large, the size of small security cells. They contained mostly Kelths, a pair of Samparese who paced in perpetual restlessness, a single Phivean, and a few Myals. Ampris seemed to be the only Aaroun, and she felt very alone.

Disheartened, she was suffering too much to give the Toths any trouble as they yanked the nooses off her and shoved her into a large cage in the corner. A small white sign was fastened to the door. The Viis letters said EHSSK PROJECT 1. It was located at the very end of the row, with a solid wall on one side and the wire fence of her cage on the other. The back wall had a heavy metal door. She tried it, but it was locked.

Her neighbor was a Myal female who had pulled out her entire mane and most of her fur. Crouched in one corner, the Myal held her tail in her hands and twisted it one way and then the other, over and over, endlessly. Now and then she mumbled something to herself, but her eyes were quite insane.

Ampris's fear returned. Panting, she limped around her cage once, taking note of the suspended shelf that clearly served as both chair and bed. The floor had a drain set in its center and was covered with straw that rustled beneath her feet. Ampris backed her ears, sniffing a mixture of unpleasant odors, and knew the cages were not cleaned often enough.

Despair washed over her in a flood, and she lowered herself awkwardly to the shelf, massaging her aching leg with her hands. She was not sure she had the courage to cope with this place of horrors.

"Welcome to Vess Vaas, Ampris," said a Viis voice.

Startled, Ampris looked up and saw a green-skinned Viis male standing by the door to her cage. His rill was standing behind his head in excitement. His green eyes gleamed at her. Flicking out his tongue, he rubbed his slender hands together.

Ampris wondered if she was expected to rise to her feet and bow to this individual. She hurt too much. She did not move.

The gleam in his eyes only brightened. "Aha, that defiant spirit, that fire in you remains. Excellent. Excellent. I have great hopes for you, Ampris. You are the epitome of your species. Strong, well-proportioned, intelligent, beautiful, ferocious, yet gentle. So many qualities. So many possibilities. Excellent."

Ampris felt the fur around her neck bristling up. She did not know who this Viis was, but she did not like him. There was a smell of evil upon him. Despite his praise, she felt soiled by what he had said.

"Who are you?" she asked rudely.

Unlike most Viis of his rank, he seemed uninsulted by her bold question. "I am Ehssk, director of this facility."

Ampris snarled and rose to her feet, backing awkwardly away from him.

He seemed not to care about her reaction. Instead he stared at her injured leg. "Are you in pain, Ampris? They did a hasty job on you, didn't they? Pity. Still, it won't interfere with my experiments. We'll start tomorrow, drawing blood and tissue samples. Should those align with the preindications of my latest theories, then we'll be able to begin on the actual experimentation without delay."

Ampris did not want to ask, but she could not hold back the question. "What will you do to me?"

He rubbed his hands together briskly, almost laughing. "At last, at last," he said jubilantly. "This time I am so close to the solution. Every instinct tells me so. And you, Ampris, are going to help me reach that solution. You will help my name land on the scrolls of history. Together, we will save my people from the Dancing Death."

Ampris said nothing. Right then she wished the Dancing Death would come and smite him where he stood. She glared at him, envisioning how he would look, shaking from head to foot with ague, his skin turning a dreadful color, his eyes filming white as the plague destroyed his nervous system. Oh, yes, she would rejoice to see him die.

Ehssk puffed out his air sacs. "Well, you are a magnificent specimen. I realize you can't follow what I'm talking about. You will probably never understand your contribution to science, but you should be honored at having been selected."

Narrowing her eyes, Ampris bared her fangs and snarled at him. If he thought her nothing but a stupid animal without intelligence or education, she saw no reason to inform him differently.

Making a satisfied sound in his throat, Ehssk smiled at her again and left as abruptly as he had come.

Ampris glared after him, and was still growling even when he was long gone. She paced back and forth, snarling and slamming her hand against the wire front of her cage, until her aching leg drove her back to the shelf to rest.

At the end of the room, a door slammed. Again the animals shrieked and hurled themselves around their cages. Ampris listened to the echoing approach of footsteps. The smell of food made her nostrils wrinkle. Synthetic meat globes . . . revulsion filled her.

Although the other abiru prisoners stood at the front of their cages, acting eager to receive their meal, Ampris remained seated. She could see a Kelth malc wrapped in a dingy smock. He pushed a wheeled cart filled with large, covered tubs and stacks of metal bowls.

Ampris could not help but think of how only a few days ago she was being served an exquisite, nourishing dinner on pretty ware by her own personal servant. Then she slammed away those memories, knowing that if she did not it would be unbearable.

"Niruo!" wailed a voice from down the row. "You damned *nolo*! You shorted me again!"

The Kelth rolled his eyes back slyly but didn't answer. He stopped his food cart in front of the insane Myal's cage and rapped loudly on the wire. "Lua!" he said, his voice shrill and cruel. "Come and get your bowl."

The Myal female ignored him, rocking herself from side to side and twisting her tail in her hands.

"Lua!" Niruo called cajolingly. "Come and get your bowl. If you don't come, you'll be hungry."

With growing annoyance, Ampris watched him continue to tease the unresponsive Myal. "Hey," she said at last. "Give her the food and get on with your work."

"Ooh," Niruo said, turning on her with his teeth bared.

She noticed that several were missing, and the rest were yellow and rotting. He smelled like a dust addict, and she backed her ears in revulsion.

Niruo came over to her cage and leaned one arm against it, standing there slouched while he leered inside at her. His yellow eyes held nothing but cruelty. "You speaking to me?" he said.

Ampris met his gaze steadily. She had nothing to prove. She knew that even with her crippled leg she could break him in half if she had to.

"You speaking to me?" he repeated more loudly.

"Yes," Ampris replied. "I am speaking to you." From the corner of her eye she saw Lua creep forward in her dirty cage, then retreat. Pity swelled inside her. "Feed this poor creature. She's hungry."

"Hey!" Niruo said angrily, straightening. "You don't run this place. You're in there, locked up. I'm out here, free. You got me?"

She said nothing, only went on staring him down.

He lifted his muzzle, twitching in a brief, involuntary muscle spasm. When it ended, his gaze dropped away from hers. "Nothing for you," he muttered, turning away.

Ampris limped forward until she was only inches from the front of her cage. "Does Ehssk run this lab?"

He ignored her, banging the empty bowls on top of his cart and lifting it to wheel it away.

"Isn't Ehssk in charge?" Ampris persisted, speaking to his back.

Beside her, Lua crept forward again, making a pathetic mewing sound, then retreated.

"He's a very famous, very important scientist," Ampris said while Niruo turned his cart around to leave. "And I'm his priority project. Did he order you to withhold my meal?"

Niruo stopped his cart so suddenly, some of the empty bowls on top fell off with a clatter. The Kelth swore, bending down to scoop them up.

"Shall I report you for withholding my food without authority?" Ampris asked again, her voice harder.

He whirled around, glaring at her. "You ain't reporting me to nobody! You can't—"

"Can't I?" she asked, not backing down. She knew how to handle bullies like him. "Why not?"

He snarled at her, but he had no answer to that. He grabbed one of the bowls that had fallen to the dirty floor, flipped open the lid of a food bin, ladled a sloppy portion into the bowl, and came over to her cage.

Without warning, he rapped the wire forcefully right by her face, but Ampris did not flinch. She stared at him implacably, her eyes intent and dangerous now.

The cockiness faded in Niruo's yellow eyes. Looking sullen, he opened a narrow opening at the bottom of the cage and stuck her bowl inside, slamming it on the floor.

"Now give Lua her portion," Ampris commanded.

But Niruo backed away and shot her a rude gesture of defiance. "You want her fed, you give her yours," he said and pushed his cart away.

When he was gone, Ampris bent and picked up her bowl. She sniffed the contents. Yes, synthetic meat globes that weren't fresh. The heavily spiced sauce coating them was designed to mask how old they were.

Revolted, she turned around and saw Lua's mad eyes peering at her. At once the Myal broke eye contact and retreated.

Ampris sighed and put her bowl on the floor next to the wire partition that separated their cages. She backed silently to the far corner of her cage and made no move while Lua finally crept forward and slid her dirty hand through the wire.

Greedily, she scooped out the food, sauce dripping through her fingers, and shoved it in her mouth. In seconds, the bowl was empty, then Lua scuttled back to her corner and began to rock herself from side to side.

Ampris noticed one of the imprisoned Kelths watching

her from the cage on the other side of Lua's. He met Ampris's gaze and shook his head.

"Don't waste your food like that," he told her. "Lua's a goner. Take care of yourself. That's the rule around here."

"Why not help each other?" Ampris countered, her voice ringing out clearly over the noise made by the animals across from them.

A few of the prisoners laughed mirthlessly.

"How long you want to stay here?" the Kelth asked her. Like Lua, he was missing patches of his fur. One side of his narrow face had been shaved recently, his skin showing pink and covered with scabs. "Better to die quick. It's the only way out."

Ampris backed her ears. She didn't want to hear such talk. "I don't believe that," she said.

The Kelth yipped. "We heard of you. Ampris of the Freedom Network. That be you?"

"Yes," she said with quiet pride. "That's me."

"You ain't free," he said, disillusionment strong in his voice. "You in here. You condemned."

She didn't flinch from him any more than she had from Niruo. "Then I have nothing to lose," she replied.

Silence fell over the rows of cages. Even the animals stopped their noise, as though instinctively they understood.

But the Kelth was shaking his head. "Wrong, Ampris," he said sadly. "You got a lot to lose. Wait and see."

CHAPTER SIXTEEN

At dawn, Ampris learned what her fellow inmate had meant. Viis lab techs in smocks came to her cage and used a stun-stick on her. Lying helplessly on the straw floor, paralyzed and fighting nausea, Ampris could not defend herself as they moved decontamination wands over her, then shaved patches of her fur prior to drawing blood and tissue samples which were labeled on site and placed in a metal box. They left her on the floor, locking her cage and walking away in an earnest discussion in Viis about a procedure she did not understand. Numb and unable to move for nearly an hour until the stun effect wore off, Ampris raged inside at her helplessness.

That afternoon, the same procedure was repeated. The rest of the week, Ampris was scanned, examined, and humiliated by the impersonal procedures performed on her. Ashamed and bitter, she withdrew into herself until Niruo came along with their daily ration of food, laughing and jeering at all of them.

Then Ampris forced herself to stand up and face him as she had done before. She refused to let him see any weakness in her.

The second week, Niruo unlocked her cage and motioned her out. Suspicious, Ampris refused to budge.

"Come on. Come *on*," he said with irritation, rolling his

eyes. "You're assigned to cleaning detail this week. You get busy."

Walking away, he left the door to her cage open. Ampris hesitated, then stepped out to follow him to a storage bin, where he handed her cleaning supplies and put her to work.

Recalling her short life as a household slave in Malraaket, after Israi discarded her as a pet and sold her to a middle-class Viis family, Ampris set about expertly scrubbing floors and hosing down cages with disinfectant. Her crippled, aching leg made her slow, but her hard, well-developed muscles allowed her to handle the equipment with ease. She was twice as efficient as Niruo.

He glared at her, but he said nothing as he escorted her back to her cage at the end of the duty shift. That night, when the food rations had been eaten and the overhead lights dimmed, the Kelth caged on the other side of Lua called out to her.

"Hey, Ampris! Ampris."

She hurt all over and her leg was paining her from the day's exertions, but she lifted her head. "Yes, Paket?"

He was looking at her with a new expression, no longer as dubious or as suspicious as before. In fact, she almost thought she saw respect in his eyes. "You scrub this place good."

She wanted to laugh in astonishment. Was that all it took to win the friendship of her fellow inmates? Didn't they think she knew about hard work? Maybe not, if they only knew that she'd been famous in the arena.

But she didn't laugh. Instead, she ducked her head, accepting the compliment for what it was. "Thanks, Paket. I haven't scrubbed floors in a long time."

"You remember how," he said in admiration. "Is good to be clean."

"Yes," she agreed wholeheartedly. "It certainly is."

She spent the rest of the week on cleaning detail, along with four other inmates. Ampris learned that all fifteen of the prisoners worked on weekly rotations, cleaning cages and labs, disposing of biohazardous waste, hauling in deliveries of supplies and storing them, plus doing any other chores the Viis scientists wanted to assign. Ampris welcomed the work, being willing to do almost anything to get out of her windowless cage with its stink of desperation. Besides, when she worked on cleaning detail, she was exempt from the experimentation, which left her tearful and shaking with shame.

The facility actually consisted of several labs. Ampris learned that Vess Vaas was the pride of the small Viis scientific community, with full backing of the imperial government. It contained a rookery of Zrheli engineers assigned to work on the theoretical puzzle of the failed jump gate. Ampris learned that these engineers came up with procedures, which were then relayed to the engineers working on implementation attempts at Shrazhak Ohr. The facility also had an animal behavior lab that supposedly was researching better, more lasting ways to train abiru. In reality, it was a place where the most barbaric atrocities were conducted. The main lab was the medical section headed by Ehssk, whose obsession remained the genetic recombinant DNA experiments that were so well-publicized across the homeworld, especially since they were authorized by the Kaa.

Ampris looked for ways of escape, but the place was well-secured with both Toth enforcers and security force shields. Even her outdoor run was secured, with wire top and sides, plus pavement that kept her from digging out. She never knew when she would be allowed outside for the welcome treat of fresh air and sunlight, but Ampris always seized those opportunities to exercise as much as her sore body would allow. Still, the chances to work out were limited. That, combined with the poor-quality food, began to tear down her conditioning. Her fur grew dull. Sometimes it would fall out, especially after she'd been given certain drugs. Afflicted with nightmares, she slept poorly.

There came a day when she, Lua, and a Kelth female so
young she was hardly more than a half-grown lit were each
stunned and lifted onto floating stretchers. Paket raged and
slammed himself against his cage door, shouting curses at
Niruo, who was helping the Viis techs take them away.

Ampris tried to look around, tried to see where she was
being taken, but her neck was paralyzed and she could not
move her head. Lua was making a muffled grunting sound
of terror, and Shevin, the young Kelth, rolled her eyes so
that the whites showed.

They were shoved into a tiny chamber and lifted onto
medical tables. Arrays of equipment surrounded them, and
the air was icy cold. For one panicky moment Ampris wondered if they were about to be dissected. She screamed, but
all that came out was a muffled grunt.

Although they were still stunned, Niruo bound them
tightly to the tables with restraint cables. He laughed softly
to himself, his eyes gleaming.

"Lua knows, don't she?" he crooned to the grunting
Myal. Her eyes rolled crazily, wild with terror. "Lua's been
here before."

Ampris burned to shut him up, but she couldn't move
and couldn't speak. Niruo leaned over Shevin, who was
panting with fear, her young eyes wide. He licked her muzzle, whispering something to her that made her moan.

Then he came to Ampris, yanking the restraints extra
tight. "You're going to love this, fanciness," he said,
laughing again.

She glared at him, longing to tear out his throat. He knew
it and exulted in her helplessness.

One of the techs came back in and tapped his shoulder.
"You're done here. Get out."

Niruo's eyes grew sullen. He slouched away, and Ampris
had no time to think further about him as the techs set to
work on her.

Later, weeping with raw humiliation, she was wheeled
on her table into another small room. There, she and the

others were kept, bound and unable to move, for three days. The stun wore off, but their restraints were unbearably tight. They were given water through tubes inserted into their throats, but no food.

Lua moaned and jabbered incessantly until Ampris thought she would go mad herself. Shevin just wept softly.

"Don't cry, little one," Ampris said to her, wishing she could herself crawl into a small, dark place and never emerge again. "Don't cry. We will survive this. You don't think so right now, but we will."

Shevin sobbed. "There's no hope for us. Why do you lie?"

"I'm saying only what I believe," Ampris told her. She ached, but she kept talking, to reassure herself as much as the young one. "I will not be defeated."

"Crazy as Lua, you are," Shevin said wildly. "Look at her. We'll be like her soon."

"No," Ampris said.

"But—"

"No!" Ampris lifted her head as much as the band encircling it would allow. "You listen to me, Shevin. You must find strength inside yourself and hang on. There is hope."

"Ampris the preacher," Shevin said with scorn, then began to cry again. "Wish I believed you. Why they be so cruel?"

"It will be their downfall," Ampris said.

"Can't live on hope!" Shevin cried. "Only got now, and how much worse can now be?"

Ampris sighed, understanding the youngster's logic all too well. She fell silent and let Shevin go on weeping.

At the end of the three days, the techs examined them again, making notations and running tests.

Listening to them discuss the situation in Viis, Ampris understood that she was now pregnant, as was young Shevin. Lua's procedure had been unsuccessful.

"Do we attempt it again?" one of the techs asked.

The other one checked back through his notes. "Eight term pregnancies with Lua, seven miscarriages. The last two procedures have been unsuccessful. She's not worth it."

The first tech made a notation. "Termination notice for Lua. We'll have to requisition a replacement. Ehssk won't be pleased."

As though she sensed they were discussing her, Lua began to howl. The second tech struck her across the mouth, and she fell silent. "Then let him authorize another attempt. As low as our supplies are, I'm not going to risk a reprimand for waste."

Ampris turned her head away and stopped listening. In her heart she grieved for poor Lua. What had become of her babies? Small wonder the Myal was insane, if she'd been put through this so many times. Ampris turned her senses inward, questing to see if she did indeed carry life. She could not as yet tell, but she worried just the same. She was strong. She was a survivor. That, she had proven to herself. But if she bore cubs, what then might become of them all?

Ampris and Shevin were returned to their cages after that, while Lua vanished. They were fed special nutrients, their food brought by a Viis tech who shoved it at them with disdain, then recorded how much they ate of it and how quickly.

Ampris was taken off the cleaning detail and instead allowed outside daily for fresh air and exercise. While she stretched and did her calisthenics, she studied the mountain range curving behind the installation and the featureless arid plains. On a clear day she could see a smudgy haze on the horizon that was Lazmairehl. Sometimes black columns of smoke rose upward from the city. Ampris wondered if part of it was on fire.

Throughout the research facility, newscasts were allowed to run via the communication speakers. So although Ampris had no access to vids, she could hear the news of the empire and homeworld. The reports were grim ones. Economic ruin continued. Colony worlds responsible for growing most of Viisymel's food had suffered poor harvests this year. Taxation increased again, while abiru riots broke out in Vir's ghetto, forcing patrollers to enter that sector to quell them. Countless abiru workers had been killed. New force shields were being installed around the perimeter of the ghetto, and the Viis districts of the city were declared safe. Other cities on Viisymel reported difficulties with bands of Rejects, who were marauding and looting with increasing boldness.

At night, when the lights were dim and the facility lay quiet, Ampris and the other prisoners talked. Ampris was planning a breakout. As her body swelled and changed in the advancement of her pregnancy, she grew increasingly desperate to get away.

Lua had not been replaced, leaving fourteen inmates. Ampris was considered one of them now, especially since she'd become pregnant. Paket, who had once worked in a rock quarry, hewing out massive stones for shipment to the former Kaa's palace restoration project, told them that a free abiru settlement was located over the mountains behind the lab.

"That's not far," Ampris said excitedly.

"But winter is coming on," Paket warned her. "It snows here, very deep. There are storms."

Shevin paced her cage restlessly. "My lits will be born soon, sooner than Ampris will have her cubs. We can beat the storms."

"What did the Myal delivery workers tell you today when they came?" Ampris asked another Kelth male, named Matiril.

He rubbed his muzzle. "Not much. He said the deliveries from Lazmairehl are changing schedule."

Everyone groaned.

"These Viis," Paket said in exasperation. "No sense of organization. No efficiency. No sooner do they make a schedule than they change it. What's wrong now?''

"What ain't wrong?" Matiril replied with a scornful yip. "Everything be a mess. The delivery workers said there be riots going in Lazmairehl."

"I saw the smoke when I was outside yesterday," Ampris said. "What kind of riots? Abiru or Viis?"

"Rejects, mostly," Matiril reported. "They be causing lots of trouble. Seems the Viis ain't giving them free grub no more. They don't like that, them."

"Good," Ampris said. "It's time the Viis dealt with the problem. Rejecting their own kind because they're not pretty enough. It's unnatural."

"I would never reject my own lits," Shevin said, rubbing her bulging sides protectively.

Ampris felt life stirring inside her as her cubs turned in her womb. She smiled to herself, feeling a surge of love for them. This, after all, completed the circle of life, from birth to birth.

"Ampris? You listening?" Paket asked sharply.

She looked up, pulling her attention back to the conversation. "What?"

"Matiril has a question for you."

She looked down the row at the Kelth. "What is it?"

"When I be cleaning down Zrheli row—," he began, but everyone groaned, interrupting.

Shevin made a gagging sound. The Phivean, who never criticized anyone, flailed her tentacles, and Paket backed his ears. Pacing, the Samparese female, called Chean, emitted her gruff cough of scorn.

"Niruo did that to you again?" Paket asked Matiril. "What you done to him this time, he got it for you so bad?"

Matiril yipped. "A Zrhel is a Zrhel. Nasty, filthy things. That rookery ain't never going to be clean. But that don't be what I want to ask. In their lab, there goes through a big pipe, shielded, and it goes through the wall into a Viis lab on the other side of the wall. It making a weird sound today. I start thinking something be wrong, so I go over there to sniff it."

He shook his head, wrinkling his nostrils. "Terrible smell, like a gas escaping. I asked what it is, but the Zrheli just laughed at me. They said not to worry about a little zeron—"

"Zeron?" Ampris echoed, her voice suddenly sharp. She pricked her ears forward, staring at him intently. Fear curled cold tendrils around her heart. "Are you saying there's zeron gas here?"

Matiril swiveled his ears. "Yeah, I guess. What it be? I figured you'd know."

Ampris told herself not to panic. There was no point in worrying the others about something they couldn't do anything about. But neither was she going to lie. Her determination strengthened, and she knew she had to escape soon.

"Zeron is a radioactive gas," she explained. "It's very dangerous, unless it's shielded properly. Matiril, did the Zrheli actually say there was a leak?"

Matiril was panting in alarm. He flattened his ears. "No, they said not to worry."

"They should know," Ampris said, but inside she was not so sure.

"I smelled it," Matiril said worriedly. "My nose be going to fall off?"

Paket yipped with laughter, and Matiril growled at him.

"No," Ampris said before they could throw themselves at the wire partition separating them. "You smelled a companion gas that's used to encase the zeron. I can't explain how it works. One gas is heavier than the other, or their molecules bond somehow, but the companion gas is part of the protective shielding. I think if you smelled it, that meant everything was well."

They all stared at her, worry in their eyes.

"You don't sound sure," Paket said.

"I'm not sure," she replied honestly. "That's what I

remember from my science lessons. But listen. The Zrheli wouldn't be calm if they thought they were in any danger.''

Even as she spoke the assurance she wasn't sure she believed it. She knew all too well that the Zrheli were brilliant and fanatical. They were perfectly willing to die if it meant accomplishing their goals. Perhaps the engineers had made a suicide pact and were sabotaging the protective shielding around the gas.

Her heart shrank inside her, but her comment seemed to calm the others. They relaxed visibly and began to chatter.

"Besides," Paket said, "we're going to be out of here before winter. Right?"

"Right!" they agreed, laughing.

"But how?" Shevin asked.

"That Kaa, she don't be able to keep her throne much longer," Paket said with relish. "The newscasts got all that official talk about new programs and reforms, but she got too many enemies around her."

"Yeah," Matiril agreed. "The Myal workers today were saying things are bad in the government. Maybe she get herself overthrown. Abiru can fight if they get the chance. That be a good chance then."

"But that's nothing to do with us," Shevin said worriedly. "How we getting away before I have my lits and Ampris has her cubs?"

"Shevin, you got to look at the whole picture," Paket said.

She backed her ears. "Got to look at me and my lits. That be what matters, not some kaa on a throne somewhere I ain't never going to see."

"We can't count on Israi being usurped," Ampris said clearly over their argument. "She has problems, yes, but she should never be underestimated."

"What else we got to hope for?" Matiril asked.

"We can count on ourselves," Ampris said. "Now—"

"What's all this?" demanded Niruo. He suddenly appeared in the doorway, shining a handtorch into their eyes so that they had to squint and duck away. "What's this noise? What are you doing?"

They fell silent, staring at him with their ears backed in resentment.

Ampris wondered how much he had overheard. Niruo had no loyalty at all to his own kind. He would betray them without hesitation if he got the chance.

"What are you doing?" he asked again, more loudly. "Plotting? Trying to think up ways to escape? You fools, you can't get out of here."

"Maybe we can," Matiril said hotly.

Ampris growled to herself. Why couldn't Matiril hold his tongue? Niruo knew nothing as yet. He was just trying to provoke them into betraying themselves.

"You can't," Niruo said. "You're locked in. Every building is locked. The Toth guards patrol the outside day and night. And there's the compound wall. You're going nowhere. So shut up and get to sleep."

"Go lick Ehssk's toe," Paket muttered.

Ampris snorted in amusement. She ducked her head, trying to control herself, but then she guffawed.

Everyone stared at her in shock, then Paket laughed too.

Matiril joined in, then the Phivean, then the rest, all laughing and banging on their cages.

Niruo glared at them, his jaws parted helplessly. His ears snapped back, but there was nothing for him to say. After a moment, he retreated to his cramped closet, which he grandly called the trustee quarters.

Their laughter rolled on for several minutes more, until they were spent and gasping for breath.

Ampris wiped her eyes, feeling fond of all her comrades. "Now," she said, her voice low and no-nonsense. "As soon as the next deliver transport comes in from Lazmairehl, we must find out the new schedule. Then Matiril and Ophah should use their cleaning details to work on scouting what kind of locks are used on the doors."

"Automatic locks, security grades one, four, and nine," Matiril reported proudly.

She grinned at him, and if she could have reached him at that moment she would have licked him between the ears. "Well done. You know how to pick locks, then?"

"Not those kind," he admitted, rubbing his muzzle. "But I'll study on it. Can't be much different from security grade two locks, which is mostly what I know."

Ampris wished with all her heart that Elrabin was here. He could have handled the locks with ease. But at the same time she was glad Elrabin would never know this kind of nightmarish place.

A whirring noise overhead made her look up. "Cams," she said in warning, halting the discussion.

They all went silent immediately, arranging themselves on their shelves as though they were idle and innocent.

Seating herself, Ampris stretched her leg and settled back to rest. Overhead, the cam whirred back and forth on a tiny track attached to the ceiling. A red light winked on it, showing it was active. The surveillance cam was seldom activated. She guessed Niruo had reported they were talking too much.

She sighed. Niruo presented a problem. As long as they feared him, he stayed happy and not too observant. But their having laughed at him was probably a mistake. He would hate them—particularly her—more than ever.

The ancient transport lurched and weaved as though it might topple over and crash to the ground at any moment. Rusted through in spots and looking ready for the scrap heap, it wheezed and clanked across the Dry Sea and finally turned its nose toward a dusty heap of buildings clustered on the horizon.

Coated with dust, frozen through, and stiff from sitting hunched up in the back scoop on the rear of the transport, Elrabin sneezed and flattened his ears miserably. He squinted against the blowing dust, and told himself to hang tight another hour or two. He'd been hitchhiking and stealing rides for days on the long journey cross-country from Vir to Lazmairehl. He was expert at stowing himself aboard, knowing how to pick the oldest and slowest transports since they were less likely to be decked out with surveillance equipment or robotic guards. Never mind that if he could have bought a ticket for a shuttle, he'd have reached his destination in a matter of hours.

Slow and careful, he reminded himself, feeling his stomach growl with acute hunger. He was shaking with cold, despite the shelter within the scoop. Slow and careful. He'd gotten this far by not rushing things. He wasn't going to take a stupid chance and ruin himself now.

Which meant, with maybe two more hours of air time for the wheezing old transport, that it was about time he rolled off this ride.

Sitting up with a groan, Elrabin squinted at the sky, gauging the sloping angle of the sun. It was already cold, and the temperature would drop sharply come nightfall. He had nothing on him but a thin, city-weight coat, his possessions belt, and a light rucksack. The idea of another long night walk daunted him.

Worrying, he rode for another hour, then decided he couldn't risk it any further. When the transport dipped into a shallow canyon and slowed down to sputter up the other side, he dropped out of the scoop and went rolling head over heels to the bottom of the canyon.

By the time he climbed to the top, panting and slapping dust off his coat, the transport was barely in sight. It dropped into another dip and vanished, but Elrabin could hear it clanking and wheezing for quite some time.

Then there was only silent, eerie desolation and the empty whistle of the wind. Elrabin stood there and looked in all directions. There was absolutely nothing to see, no sign of civilization or life. Weird sandstone formations stood like lonely sentinels, and canyons split the ground in all directions. No vegetation grew except some occasional ankle-high scrub that prickled when he brushed past it.

Slinging his rucksack over his shoulders, Elrabin realized that the uneven ground and canyons were going to make this hike a lot longer than he'd anticipated. But it wasn't going to get any shorter as long as he stood here. So he ducked his head against the low, slanting glare of the sun and trudged forward.

It had taken him months to get off Shrazhak Ohr, much longer than he'd anticipated. When he ran away from Galard Stables, he'd gone straight to an abiru bar on the lower level of the central axis, an ill-lit dive tucked into a back corner. The place was crowded, smoky, reeking of illegal dust, and noisy with babbling conversations and the squeal of music.

Elrabin edged his way cautiously around to the back, where the proprietor of the place, a masked Gorlican with a thick, spotted torso shell and fleshy, scaled arms, sat at a table with a number of Kelth females dyed various colors seated around him.

Before Elrabin reached the Gorlican, an Aaroun bodyguard stepped into his path and gave him a shove backward. "Get lost," he snarled.

Elrabin held up his hands in the universal gesture of peace, desperately aware of time running out. He had to get this restraint collar taken off before his absence was discovered. "Hey," he said to the Aaroun. "Back off, see? My business here ain't with the likes of you."

The Aaroun shoved him again, nearly pushing him off his feet. Elrabin staggered back and barely kept himself from falling across another patron's table. Nimbly, he dodged to one side, darted around the Aaroun, and reached the Gorlican's table just as the bodyguard grabbed him by the back of his coat.

Elrabin gripped the edges of the table. "I need my restraint collar taken off in the next twenty-seven minutes," he said as fast as he could before the Aaroun dragged him back. He struggled in the bodyguard's grip. "I can pay!"

"Chofa," the Gorlican said, his orange eyes glowing with greed through the slits of his face mask, "drop him."

The Aaroun released Elrabin so fast, he nearly fell to the floor. Righting himself breathlessly, Elrabin shook out his coat and gave the Gorlican his most ingratiating smile. "Thank you," he said, pouring on the charm. "Now what kind and how fast of a deal can we make here?"

"What grade restraint?" the Gorlican asked, cutting to the bottom line.

Elrabin sucked in a breath, knowing he was going to have to pay dearly for this. "Grade eleven."

The Kelth females looked at each other and giggled. The Gorlican grunted. "Tough."

"Yeah, but not impossible for the one who knows how. You set this up, get it done, and I'll pay—"

"Price set by me," the Gorlican announced curtly.

Elrabin shut up, knowing he didn't have time to bargain. "Fine," he said desperately. "So how fast can we get this done?"

"You work for me," the Gorlican said. "Deliver dust—"

"No way," Elrabin said automatically, flattening his ears. "I been down that road before. It ain't—"

"Ten months you work."

"Two."

"Seven."

"Four," Elrabin countered, feeling his fur itch as time kept on ticking.

"Seven months."

They stared at each other, but Elrabin's gaze dropped first. Seven months, trapped on this scrap heap with its stale air, dealing dust and probably doing every other kind of dirty job the Gorlican could think up.

"Done," Elrabin said.

The Gorlican gestured, and the Aaroun bodyguard stepped up behind Elrabin, tucked his fingers inside the narrow wire restraint collar around his throat, and clipped it in half with a palm-sized cutter.

Expecting his head to explode, Elrabin yelped in panic. "Hey! Be careful—" He broke off as he saw the thin collar dangling from Chofa's powerful hand and realized he was safe. Elrabin's shoulders sagged with relief and dawning astonishment. Maybe the collar hadn't been rigged after all. And here he'd just traded away seven months of his life.

Laughing, Chofa looked at Elrabin as though he could read his mind. He ambled over to a disposal door next to a wall bulkhead and tossed the collar inside. Then he pressed something on his cutter, and a muffled boom sounded within the disposal chute. The door dented, and Elrabin found his throat suddenly too dry to swallow. Seven months seemed a bargain.

"Your name?" the Gorlican asked.

"Elrabin."

"Now you called Frade. Now you work for me. Over there." He pointed, and Chofa clamped a hand on Elrabin's shoulder to hustle him to his first task.

Now, trudging across the Dry Sea of Viisymel with dust thick on his tongue, down inside his ears, and even gritty in his eyes, Elrabin told himself to lose that memory along with plenty of others. He'd done what he had to do, and at the end of his seven months of service he'd struck another deal with his boss, spending half his secret hoard of credits to secure semilegal passage down to the planet.

It had taken plenty of dodging and all his skill to keep from being picked up by patrollers around the docks, but he'd managed. Then he'd caught a transport headed out, and was on his way.

Now he was close to Lazmairehl, close to Vess Vaas. He just hoped that Ampris was still alive after all this time.

CHAPTER SEVENTEEN

Exhausted, but supremely content, Ampris lay curled in the maternal bed with her three newborn cubs. They nuzzled weakly against her, making their soft mewing cries, while she caressed them and crooned to them with love.

Never mind the shock of their first appearance, when she realized that they were not entirely Aaroun. Never mind how they looked, so bizarre with their flat faces and hairless heads with only vestigial nubs for ears. Their tiny hands looked strange, too slender and long-fingered for Aaroun hands, yet their bodies were Aaroun-shaped. They were covered with a golden downy fuzz instead of dense fur. In that initial moment of realization, she had felt a flash of sheer horror, then she had inhaled the birth smell and each of their scents. Her maternal instincts had kicked in, so powerful they consumed her.

Now she crooned and took care of her babies, adoring them no matter what they looked like. They were hers, these two males and one female. They were healthy and strong. Already the female was trying to lift her bobbing, unsteady head and open her eyes.

Ampris scooped her up and cradled her close. Looking into her daughter's precious, birth-blue eyes, Ampris recalled her earliest memory of her own mother, who had nuzzled her and sung to her.

"You are *my* golden one," Ampris told her cub. She licked her daughter's hairless face, imprinting her scent forever. "My precious, beautiful, golden one. You are mine, you and your brothers. Together, we shall be a family. I will teach you all that I know, and you will grow up strong and fearless and free. Someday."

She backed her ears, thinking with regret of how their escape plans had gone awry. The delivery of supplies from Lazmairehl continued to come at random times and days. Often now, the Toth guards were ordered to unload the supplies, so that Paket and Matiril had no chance to talk with the Myal workers on the transports. Ampris and the others blamed Niruo for having betrayed their intentions. But they intended to come up with something else.

Ampris turned back to her daughter and smiled. "It won't be forever," she said. "That, I promise you, sweetness."

The cub stared at her and mewed, then reached up a wavering, uncoordinated hand. Ampris took it, marveling at how tiny it was, yet how strongly those little fingers curled around hers.

A bright overhead light snapped on, startling Ampris and making her cubs cry in panic. Snarling, Ampris gathered all three of them close and tried to shield their tender eyes. "Niruo!" she shouted furiously, yet when the door to the tiny birthing chamber opened, it was not the Kelth who stood there, gazing in at her, but Ehssk.

The Viis scientist, clad in a pristine lab smock, his multihued skin shiny with oil, stared at her with eyes that shone with fanatical satisfaction.

"Ampris, Ampris, you sly Aaroun," he said in mock disapproval. "You had your cubs while I was away attending a conference. Why didn't you wait for me, so that I could watch the birth?"

A ridge of hair stood up along her spine, and the fur around her neck bristled. Still shielding her cubs protectively, Ampris growled.

Ehssk laughed and came into the chamber. "Now, now, you mustn't be a bad-tempered Aaroun. Let me see what you have."

"Get away," she said, her eyes slitted dangerously. "This is a private time."

It was as though he didn't hear her. He paid no attention and came right up to the bed, peering down at the cubs with glee. His tongue flicked out. "Three in your litter. Excellent. No stillborns, according to the report. All healthy, and measuring sixes and sevens on the Tefert Scale."

Ampris growled again. No one had touched her cubs since that initial examination. It had taken her hours of licking to clean away the stench of Viis hands on her babies. She wanted no more Viis stink on them, ever.

"Get away," she said.

"Ampris, you will be a good Aaroun and cooperate with me," he said, his voice more stern now. He met her eyes and his rill rose behind his head. "Let me have your cubs."

Her ears flattened against her skull. She glared at him through slitted eyes, her lips curled back from her teeth. She was past warning him. If he came closer, she would attack.

"The report says two males and one female," he went on, his voice calm and unafraid. His eyes remained as implacable as hers. "Pity it isn't the other way around. It's the females I need for my study."

The cubs mewed and shifted beneath her hand. Ampris tightened her grip on them, fear starting to squeeze her heart.

"But although there's only one female to dissect this time, there will be others the next time you give birth—"

Roaring, Ampris sprang at him, intending to sink her fangs in his throat. But her weakness made her slow, and Ehssk jerked a stun-stick from his pocket and jolted her with it, full charge.

The jangling paralysis gripped her, and Ampris fell

across the bed, helpless and raging while Ehssk hummed to himself and took his time lifting and examining each cub in turn. He put down the males after the most cursory look.

"Pity," he said, then scooped up the female.

She lifted her wobbly, misshapen head and spat at him.

Ehssk tucked her in the crook of his arm and walked out. The door slammed shut, and the bright light dimmed.

With all her might, Ampris strained to lift herself and go after him, but she could not move. She lay there for hours until the stun finally wore off, with her remaining cubs nuzzling her and crying for comfort. And Ampris wept for the daughter she would never hold again, for the daughter she would never see grow up tall and strong, for the daughter now lost to her forever.

"Oh, little one, little one," she sighed, while her tears ran unchecked and she gathered her frightened sons closer.

How could the Viis be so cruel, so heartless? How could they deliberately create and destroy innocent little ones for their own selfish ends? Was Ehssk's research worth such a sacrifice? Paket had told her that Ehssk was good at making vid appearances and getting government support, but that most of his experiments didn't really work. He lied and covered up his mistakes. He was a fake, a hypocrite, and a charlatan.

And now he had taken her daughter, as she had been taken from her mother. But Ampris's little one would never be adopted by a lonely Viis chune, would never have a chance to play or grow up. Ampris's daughter was born condemned, and she knew that at any time these other two cubs could be taken away to satisfy some Viis whim.

Grieving, Ampris soothed and tried to comfort her sons, while in her heart she hated Ehssk, with a burning, relentless hatred deeper and stronger than any emotion she had ever felt before. He had gone too far. He had taken too much. If ever justice returned, she vowed, let there be a curse on this place and the Viis barbarians in it.

Two days later, Ampris was taken back to her cage,

along with her sons. The other abiru folk stayed quiet and left her alone with her grief. Even Niruo did not torment her, but simply brought her food and went on about his duties.

Ampris spoke to no one but her cubs. She kept them close to her side, and each time a Viis tech came near her cage, she was swept with panic that he was going to remove her sons. She would spring at the wire, snarling and snapping her teeth viciously until the tech retreated. It took days for her to calm down, days for her to start believing that her remaining cubs were not wanted for any experimentation. But as the Viis staff continued to leave her alone, Ampris gradually settled and regained her mental balance. She named her sons Foloth and Nashmarl, after the Aaroun words for hope and courage. They lost their newborn scent and began to fill out, their stubby legs growing stronger and more sturdy daily. As they crawled about the cage, exploring at first, then learning to play and tumble each other at her feet, she always kept a vigilant eye on them.

Then there came one evening when her mind grew clear, and once again she gave thought to the future.

"Paket," she said softly.

He responded at once. "Yes, Ampris?"

"Are the deliveries still random?"

"Yes. We think they have a rotating schedule. Matiril is working out the pattern of it, but he will have to make sure for a few more weeks."

"Forget that plan," Ampris said. Even to her own ears, her voice sounded harsh. "I have another."

All the abiru inmates sat up and looked at her.

"A new plan?" Paket said. "What is it?"

She met their eyes without doubt or hesitation. "It's no longer enough to simply get away. We're going to destroy this place."

Someone laughed in despair. Others began to talk among themselves, but Paket's gaze never wavered from hers. "How?" he asked.

A corner of her heart warmed to him. Good, steady Paket. He was the best of the bunch. She smiled at him. "Remember the zeron gas? Remember the pipe that goes through the Zrheli rookery?"

The others fell silent.

Paket's eyes widened, but he didn't flinch. "Yes."

"Follow that pipe, the next time you're on cleaning detail. See if you can find out where it originates and where it goes. Does it pass through any other easily accessed areas besides the rookery?"

"I'll find out," Matiril volunteered before Paket could answer. He looked uneasy. "It be a dangerous thing, Ampris. You sure—"

"What have we to lose?" she asked harshly.

Paket pointed at Foloth, who was clinging to her leg and trying to pull himself upright. "You got little ones to think of now."

"I am thinking of them," she said. "When they are weaned, they will be taken from me and destroyed."

They stared at her, and her impatience grew. "Don't you understand? Lua is gone. Shevin's lits were taken. Now Shevin herself is gone. Ophah the Phivean is gone. No replacements have been bought."

"That's because they spent all their funds on you," Niruo's voice muttered.

Ampris looked around with a snarl, and there stood the Kelth in his dingy smock, trying to be a Viis for some kind of twisted, pathetic reasons of his own.

She glared at him. "So, Niruo, you've come to betray us again. When will you learn where your allegiance should lie?"

"With you, fanciness?" Niruo sneered. "How would Ehssk like it if I told him his special Ampris is plotting to destroy his lab?"

"Ehssk won't punish me, if that's what you're after," she said boldly. "I'm still valuable to his plans. But you aren't. Have you considered that? Maybe if they're short on funds, they'll put you in one of these cages and inject acid in your veins to see what happens.''

Niruo's ears snapped back and he snarled fearfully. ''You'd like that, but it won't happen. I got—'' He stopped, as though aware he was about to say too much. He glared at her, and vanished.

''Off he goes, to tell the whole plan,'' Matiril said scornfully. ''Ought to break his scrawny neck.''

''That may be necessary, when the time comes,'' Ampris said, her cold tone making them stare, first in surprise, then in appreciation. ''Now, back to the plan. First we find the access points of the gas pipe, and any weaknesses. Look for places of poor maintenance. Who's been assigned to clean the offices this week?''

''Me,'' said Robuhl, an elderly Myal. He had once been a scholar and archivist at a Viis university. Now he was here because of political sabotage. Ampris nodded at him. He was perfect for her purposes.

''Good, Robuhl,'' she said. ''Do you think you can find a manual for the building's safety and emergency evacuation procedures?''

Robuhl's cage was at the far end of the row from hers, but Ampris could see him nodding vigorously. ''I have seen it, both in hard form and a labeled data crystal in the storerooms. The techs never look at such materials. It is easily obtained.''

''Good. As soon as you can, please get it to me,'' Ampris said.

''Can you read Viis, Ampris?'' he asked her.

''Yes.''

Robuhl beamed and shook back his gray mane. ''The power of learning is once again proven—''

''Shut up, old one,'' Matiril said impatiently. ''What good does a book be to us?''

''I'm not sure yet,'' Ampris told him. ''It depends on how the building was designed to be evacuated.''

''What do you mean?'' Paket asked her. ''How we going

to get past the Viis techs to do these things?''

''You'll see,'' Ampris said. ''I'll give you the details later, when I'm sure it can work. Matiril, examine the pipe. See if you can find any places where the Zrheli have broken the casing or tampered with the shielding.''

''I'll do it,'' Matiril said.

''You think the Zrheli will help us?'' Paket asked her.

She backed her ears. ''No. I wish they would, but we can't count on them. If their plan is similar to ours, it doesn't matter. We're going to take it from them and speed it up.''

Several yips of protest broke out. ''You don't expect us to kill ourselves in here with the Zrheli, do you?'' Matiril asked in horror.

''No,'' Ampris said. ''We're getting out. Count on it.''

Snow blew through the streets of Lazmairehl, whipping around the tall ears of Elrabin and sticking with fluffy whiteness to his coat. He pressed himself deeper into the doorway of the abandoned building, shivering and tucking his hands under his arms to keep them warm.

He was in the Skugvo, the derelict, dangerous side of town where empty buildings made of cheap metal construction stood rusting. Some of them were hardly more than shells, with their walls and roofs stripped away by scavengers. Windows were broken out. Doors hung askew and broken in. The wind blew without ceasing along the empty streets, and now and then a broken piece of dead scrub tumbled by.

The desolate place creeped Elrabin, but he'd learned that the sniffers didn't patrol the streets in the Skugvo. After narrowly evading capture and arrest several times for stealing food in the main part of town, Elrabin had ducked into this sector to let things calm down. He'd been in Lazmairehl almost three weeks now; winter had definitely set in, with frequent snows and a wind that sawed through him with bitter cold. Food was hard to come by. Worse, he'd had little luck getting past the suspicions of the main band of troublemakers in town.

Abiru thieves and Viis Rejects had joined forces in the recent hard times. Growing constantly bolder as their desperation increased, they now raided the respectable side of town frequently, burning and looting until patrollers drove them back.

Elrabin had sought them out when he'd first slunk into town, footsore and weary to the bone. But they had no interest in helping him rescue an Aaroun female, not even one as famous as Ampris had been. And when Elrabin was forced to admit he didn't even know for sure if Ampris was still alive, they beat him up and kicked him out. Groaning in the gutter and fending off the Skeks trying to steal his rucksack, Elrabin ended up almost being arrested for vagrancy by a patroller. He got away, but it took considerable dodging to evade pursuit.

Now Elrabin had to subsist on the fringes, avoiding everyone. He was starving, cold, and lonely. A new squad of patrollers had arrived in town this week, supplemented by the imperial army assigned to keep order during the imminent Hevrmasihd Festival, the main winter celebration of the Viis.

Elrabin had been haunting public vids, keeping himself informed about the local news. He eavesdropped and spied, especially around the supply depot, where irregular transports departed with deliveries for Vess Vaas. It was tempting to steal aboard, but he knew he could do nothing to help Ampris by himself. He had to have assistance.

And now he'd returned to Skugvo with an idea and the goal of asking the Rejects one more time for help.

Finally, the hours of watching and shivering in this dank doorway paid off. Just before dusk, Elrabin saw a tall, hooded figure hunched over and hurrying down the empty street. Elrabin's ears pricked forward. He drew in a deep, intent breath and rubbed his muzzle as he stepped silently out of the doorway and followed.

Deep shadows crisscrossed the streets and pooled around the bases of buildings. The hooded figure was cautious and careful, stopping often to glance back, zigzagging back and forth to avoid the deepest shadows, where ambush might lie in wait. But Elrabin was an expert at following stealthily. He made himself a ghost, silent, able to anticipate when his quarry was going to glance back so that he could duck out of sight.

He followed down numerous, twisting streets, darted along a section of recently burned buildings, where the stink of charred timbers still hung heavy on the air. The snow swirled around him, stinging his face and making his fur wet, but Elrabin grimly refused to give up.

Finally, his quarry ducked down a flight of steps leading into a hole between two buildings. Pausing in the street, Elrabin watched as the hooded figure rapped in code on a door.

It slid open, spilling out a narrow oblong of golden light and warmth before the hooded figure darted inside and the door slammed shut.

Elrabin crept down the steps, finding them crumbly and unstable in the darkness. He waited an interval, feeling his hands and feet turning numb. The snow drifted across the steps behind him, and his breath steamed about his muzzle.

Telling himself to find his courage, Elrabin stepped up to the door and duplicated the pattern of the knock the hooded figure had used.

The door slid open, and a face in shadow peered out at him. Elrabin said nothing, but instead tried to dart inside.

He made it halfway in before a hand gripped his arm like iron and tried to thrust him out.

Swearing, Elrabin ducked his head and bit the wrist, tasting sour Viis blood. The door guard hissed and reached back to draw a weapon, but Elrabin ducked and tumbled himself across the floor to take cover behind a stack of kegs.

"Hold on!" he cried as the other occupants in the room

dropped what they were doing and rose to their feet. "I'm a friend, a friend! Remember me? Elrabin? I came to you before—"

"Yeah, and we beat you for your trouble," replied a hoarse, gravelly voice.

Looking across the room, Elrabin got a swift impression of rough-hewn timbers supporting the low ceiling, a scattering of tables and chairs, a roaring fire in a crudely made hearth that gave out welcome heat and light, the smell of food on platters, and about fifty abiru and Rejects gathered before him with crudely made daggers and stolen side arms glinting in their hands.

A low whine grew in his throat. Elrabin swallowed hard, then panted. Slowly, making no sudden moves, he rose from his hiding place behind the kegs, keeping his hands up and in plain sight.

"I'm a friend," he said, his voice shrill with fear. "I come to offer a deal."

The Reject who led the band was a tall, yellow-skinned Viis with webbed fingers and a rill that lay too flat on his neck. Named Sollusk, he was mean, unpredictable, and hostile.

Shooting Elrabin a look of contempt, he drew his hand swiftly across his throat.

A pair of Kelths streaked toward Elrabin. Yelping, he ducked to one side and ran toward Sollusk. The Reject drew his side arm and aimed it at Elrabin. Horrified, he skidded to a halt, and the Kelths grabbed him.

"A deal! I offer you a deal!" Elrabin said desperately.

Sollusk flicked out his tongue. "Your deals do not interest me, furred one. I care nothing about your friend."

"What about loot?" Elrabin asked, yelping as his arm was twisted behind him. "What about chemicals to sell on the black market, food, equipment—"

"You have nothing," Sollusk said in contempt. "You have none of these things."

"The Festival be coming, see?" Elrabin said hurriedly,

watching the minute leap of interest in Sollusk's eyes. "Everyone at Vess Vaas will be gone on leave. The lab will be empty. It's gotta be a perfect time to break in, see?"

"Lies," Sollusk said. "Still trying to rescue your friend."

"Hey, this is a deal for me, and a deal for you," Elrabin said. "Yeah, okay, I want to get her out. Something wrong with that? Why should you care, as long as you get to loot the whole place, see? No one there—"

"Shields," Sollusk said. "Locks. Security systems. Guards."

"The guards are abiru," Elrabin said. "I walked out there last week and looked the place over. Not as secure as advertised. A snap to get in."

Laughter broke out among the thieves.

"Like you know," Sollusk said.

Elrabin lost his temper. He glared at the Reject with his teeth bared. "Like why shouldn't I know? Like I didn't used to be a thief myself in the Vir ghetto? Like I didn't live ten years without a registration implant, coming and going where I pleased, working the street? Like I didn't run dust? Or operate gaming tables? Or smuggle? Or work scams on Viis marks up on Shrazhak Ohr? Like I ain't been around, on this world and a dozen others? Where you been, besides small-time, one-town trouble? What do you know to make you laugh at me?"

The room fell deathly quiet. Glaring, Sollusk pointed his side arm right at Elrabin's face.

"You so smart," the Reject said, "how come you're here, wanting my help? Why don't you go break in Vess Vaas all by yourself?"

Defeat burned inside Elrabin. It took all he had to swallow it, to accept it. He didn't beg. His pride hurt too much for that. "Sure," he said, swiveling his ears. "Guess you too busy to go out and take easy pickings. So I'll go alone. So thanks for nothing."

He tried to twist free of the Kelths and go, but they held

him fast. Elrabin snapped at them, nipping an ear and getting himself knocked against the head.

His hearing rang, and everything swam around him momentarily. When his senses cleared, he found himself flat on the dirty floor with someone's foot planted in the center of his back.

"Good idea you brought me," Sollusk said. "Maybe I'll use it. Maybe I won't. Either way, we don't need you."

Elrabin panted, too angry to be afraid now. "Yeah, you do. 'Cause I can pick the locks and run you past the security slick, see? Otherwise, you going to have an automatic alarm bringing out the army."

Sollusk said nothing, but finally the foot came off Elrabin's back, letting him up.

He scrambled to his feet, dusting off his coat. "So what's it to be? We got a deal?"

Sollusk flicked out his tongue. "Deal," he said without enthusiasm. "But hear this. If we don't get in or there's nothing out there worth our trouble, then your hide, furred one, will make me a winter coat."

Elrabin's ears swiveled, and fresh doubts filled him. He was gambling plenty on the unknown, all right, but as he'd once told Ampris, the risk made the gamble worthwhile. Now he was about to put that to the test.

Masking his fear, he met Sollusk's cold Viis eyes and drew a deep breath. "So let's get to it," he said.

CHAPTER EIGHTEEN

Ampris moved slowly along the corridor outside the offices, making steady swaths with the floor polisher. Its engine hummed loudly, clanking each time she made the return sweep. On the opposite side of the corridor, a trio of techs emerged from their offices, talking about their Festival plans. As Ampris had guessed, the whole staff had been given leave to spend Festival in Lazmairehl or elsewhere, if they could afford shuttle travel to one of the larger cities. All experiments had been suspended, and Ehssk had already departed the facility earlier that day, bound for parties with the noble and influential in Vir.

While Ampris regretted his departure, for it meant she would not get the chance to sink her teeth into his throat, she put her own desire for revenge aside for the larger good. Besides, ripping out the throat of one evil Viis was less of a blow than destroying the premier research lab on Viisymel. All of Ehssk's work—his notes, the records of years of research—would be wiped away. And someday, if Fate was kind, she would once again meet him face-to-face to kill the murderer of her daughter.

She bared her teeth, growling softly to herself, and made her way toward the end of the corridor, unnoticed by the techs who casually tapped security codes on the keypads of their office doors and walked away. Ampris pretended to keep her attention on her work, but from the corner of her eye she saw that they used minimal security codes only. The full security required tapping in eighteen numbers, but it was considered too much bother by everyone on the staff except Ehssk himself.

Ampris went on sweeping the polisher back and forth, moving slowly and steadily. By the time the techs were out of sight, she had reached the far end of the office corridor. She stopped outside the door to a small janitor closet. Matiril had promised to pick the lock to it earlier during his chores. They knew none of the Viis ever bothered to check it. Niruo was unlikely to come this way, since his presence in the office area was frowned on by the Viis staff.

She glanced back, then reached out and pushed on the door. It swung open. Swiftly, Ampris darted inside. She looked around. The closet was cramped, dirty, and dark. A rusted, dripping water pipe stained the wall and floor. Outside, a bell rang in the corridor, and Ampris jumped violently. She was running out of time. That was the end-of-shift bell. If she didn't show up promptly, Niruo would get suspicious and come looking for her.

But where was the gas pipe? According to the lab construction schematics which Robuhl had found, the pipe was supposed to go through this closet. So where was it?

Growling to herself, her heart thudding against her ribs, Ampris shifted a stack of boxes aside, and there it was, running along the floor. Painted white, the pipe was equal in diameter to the length of her hand. Its contents were deadly. Fear rippled through her, but she mastered it. She had volunteered to take this risk, knowing she was the most qualified for the job.

Picking up the water bolt wrench which Matiril had slipped from the maintenance bin and left inside the closet, she hefted it in her hand, finding its balance and weight similar to a glevritar's. Bracing her feet, she swung it up and over, bringing it down on the gas pipe with a resounding clang.

The pipe seemed unaffected. Ampris swore under her breath, beginning to sweat beneath her fur, and lifted the wrench again.

"Stop!" a harsh, unfamiliar voice commanded her.

Startled, Ampris spun around with the wrench held upraised in her hands and found herself face-to-face with a Zrhel female. A pair of fierce, keen eyes glared at her above a vicious beak, parted now in aggression. The Zrhel's head was covered with tiny gray feathers edged in black in a beautiful pattern. But right now, Ampris didn't care what she looked like, only what she intended to do.

"What do you want?" Ampris demanded. "You have no business here."

The Zrhel held her ground. "You're the Aaroun, the one called Ampris."

Aware of passing time, Ampris backed her ears. "What of it?"

"Don't hit the zeron pipe again," the Zrhel said.

A chill sank through Ampris. Were the Zrheli going to betray them? "I'm just putting this tool away," she said, hefting the wrench in her hands.

But the Zrhel's gaze took in the scattered boxes and the dent in the pipe. "That is a water bolt wrench, size twelve," she said. "It belongs on rack three, left side, of the maintenance bin in—"

"Forget it," Ampris said gruffly. "I have work to do. Why aren't you locked up in your rookery, where you belong?"

"You will not do this, Ampris," the Zrhel said, tilting her head. One of her feathers drifted to the floor. "You are making a serious mistake."

"I don't know what you—"

"Stop it!" the Zrhel squawked furiously. "We know the plan. We monitor the surveillance lines when it suits us. The Viis never do."

Ampris opened her mouth in dismay, then closed it again. She stayed silent.

"Listen. This is an auxiliary line. If you break it, you will succeed only in flooding this wing with radiation. It will be sealed off from the rest of the lab, and you will have accomplished nothing. A more efficient strategy would be to tamper with the main power reactor located behind Building Three."

Unsure if this was advice or criticism, Ampris said slowly, "That's outside. I can't get to it."

"No, and you would not know what to do if you were there."

"Can you reach it?"

The Zrhel hesitated, then tipped back her head to rub it against her hunched shoulders. "No."

Ampris lifted the wrench. "Then this is all that I can do."

"No! Are you stupid? I have explained the fallacy of this procedure to you."

"What do you recommend?" Ampris asked impatiently. "There's no time to formulate another plan—"

"Why did you send the message to us?" the Zrhel interrupted with a sudden change of subject.

Understanding swept over Ampris. Over the others' objections, she had sent a cryptic message to the Zrheli engineers, advising them to seek escape at the first indication of trouble.

"You betrayed yourself," the Zrhel said. "Why?"

"Abiru folk should help each other. I'm not out to destroy innocent lives."

"Why not? You were an arena butcher."

The insult stung. Ampris snarled. "Not by choice."

"There is always a choice," the Zrhel said, fanaticism gleaming in her eyes.

"I don't like suicide as a solution," Ampris told her.

"It is the Zrheli way. It is the Zrheli belief."

Ampris rolled her eyes. "Fine. Your beliefs are okay for you, but not for me. At least I warned you. Now go, and let me do what I'm here to do."

The Zrhel edged closer. "I do not understand," she said. "One of my kind injured you. There is a direct correlation between that action and your presence here. Correct?"

Ampris narrowed her eyes to slits, not liking this conversation at all. But short of braining the Zrhel with the wrench, she saw no way to get rid of her. "Yes, that's correct," she said with a growl.

"You should hate all Zrheli for this."

Without realizing it, Ampris's hand reached up and curled around the Eye of Clarity that she still wore. "Maybe I should," she replied. "But you had nothing to do with what happened in the arena on Shrazhak Ohr. You weren't the Zrhel that attacked me. He was defending himself the best way he could. I didn't want to kill him like that, so I was careless." She shrugged, the memories churning unpleasantly inside her. "I will hate what he did to me until I die. I hate not being able to move like I once did. I hate the constant pain. I hate being weak. But why should I hate you?"

"The philosophy of Ampris," the Zrhel muttered, looking unimpressed by her statement. "You have spread much sedition in your Freedom Network. What good does it do?"

"Why do you ask me that?" Ampris replied in exasperation. "You and your kind keep sabotaging the repair efforts for the jump gate to Ruu-one-one-three. What good does that do?"

The Zrhel whistled in outrage, parting her beak. Ampris backed up a step, but no more than that. She kept her eyes cautiously on the Zrhel, prepared to defend herself if necessary.

"Ruu-one-one-three is sacred to us!" the engineer said vehemently, extending her arms and opening her talons. "All Zrheli are sworn to protect it to the death. While one Zrhel still lives and breathes, no Viis will set foot on it. It is a place of hope and beauty, not to be looted by Viis greed."

"I see," Ampris said thoughtfully. "This explains much

to me. Before, I could never really understand why your people would die just to thwart the Viis' plans. Was it your homeworld?''

"No," the Zrhel said, her voice still hot. "But sacred."

Ampris sighed, relinquishing her dream. "Then it isn't the solution I was looking for."

"What solution? Explain."

"Oh, I thought it might be a place for the homeless abiru to settle on one day. Folk like Aarouns and Kelths, who no longer have a habitable homeworld to return to."

"Gorlicans have no world. You let them live with you too?" the Zrhel asked scornfully.

"Why not? A planet is a large place. There would be room for everyone."

"And who would rule? Which race would lead? Your race?"

Ampris backed her ears. "Aarouns are no better than the others. Why not incorporate the talents of all the sentient races for the common good? Myals are thinkers and organizers. Aarouns are builders. Kelths are—"

"Kelths are thieves and troublemakers. Hah!" the Zrhel said in contempt. She belched and dropped more feathers. "Utopia is a dream for fools."

"I agree," Ampris said. "Utopias never work. We would start out with good intentions, then personalities would clash and there would be conflict and problems. But it would still be better than Viis oppression."

The Zrhel's eyes softened and she tilted her head. "You make an excellent point."

Outside, the second warning bell rang. Ampris growled. "I'm out of time. I have to—"

"Wait," the Zrhel said. "It was necessary to see you for myself before I could reach a decision. The solution you seek is to open a valve to the main line. The sudden pressure drop will trigger a reactor failure strong enough to activate the alarm system."

"Thank you!" Ampris said in gratitude. "Where do I find the valve?"

"You cannot," the Zrhel told her. "Such a valve is in our section. We know how to open it, but it is too complex a procedure for you."

Annoyed and increasingly desperate, Ampris started to argue, but she knew that would be futile. "Will you do this for us?" she asked. "Can your people get out in time?"

The Zrhel stared at her and did not answer.

"Is there a way simply to fool the alarm system, to trigger it without releasing the gas?" Ampris asked.

"It was your plan to destroy this lab," the Zrhel said. "Why do you change now?"

"I want this place blown to bits," Ampris said angrily, baring her teeth. "But not at the unnecessary cost of lives—"

"Even an arena butcher should know how to pay the cost," the Zrhel told her. "You are a strange one, Ampris."

"Will you—"

A distant sound made Ampris's ears snap forward. She listened, then swore to herself. "Niruo is coming. I have no more time."

The Zrhel stepped to one side, and Ampris had to brush past her to exit the closet. She did so, tensed and expectant, but the Zrhel did not attack her. Ampris leaned down and left the wrench in a corner.

She gave the Zrhel a searching look, wishing she could be sure the engineer was trustworthy. "If you decide to help us, thank you." The words seemed inadequate, but she could find no others.

A door slammed. She heard footsteps coming behind her.

Ampris lurched around, shutting the janitor closet and lifting her floor sweeper just as Niruo came into sight.

His yellow eyes narrowed with suspicion and he trotted toward her. "Ampris! Are you deaf? Both bells have sounded. What have you been doing? That closet is off limits to you."

Ampris stepped aside, attempting to walk away, but Niruo tried the closet door. Her heart froze inside her, but the door did not budge.

He grunted. "Good thing this is kept locked. You're always trying to steal something for your cubs. Hurry! Get your equipment put up now. The techs can't leave the lab until everyone is secured, and they're furious at having to wait."

Ampris concealed her relief and moved along as fast as her crippled leg would allow. She was panting and damp from nerves. Worse, she wasn't sure whether the Zrhel would really help her or not. *Have some trust,* Ampris told herself. But she was worried about depending on someone unknown and semihostile.

Niruo seemed too angry to notice her distraction. He hustled her along, swore at her while she shoved the sweeper into its correct bin, failed to observe that she didn't empty its tank of cleaner to avoid damaging it, and shoved her back to the inmate wing.

She'd barely stepped through the doorway before he wheeled around and headed away at a trot. "Everyone accounted for and secured!" he shouted.

Ampris peered through the window in the doors as he hurried into the main section of the lab, calling out his tally and wishing the departing techs a happy Festival.

Meanwhile, Ampris could hardly dare believe her luck, or his carelessness. No doubt he thought she would simply walk down the row to her cage, where her cubs waited, reared up with their slender hands clutching the wire. But Ampris acted quickly. She went along the row of cages, pulling out the locking pins on everyone's door, then entered her own cage.

"Mama, Mama," her cubs called to her, gripping her legs and butting their flat, naked faces against her with affection.

She smiled and scooped them up in her arms, licking their faces and ears to make them laugh. Foloth was the more affectionate of the two. He entwined his little arms around her neck and nuzzled her.

"Mama," he said. "Smell strange."

"Do I, sweetness?" she asked breathlessly, still aware that her heart was thumping too fast. "I'm sorry. There wasn't time to wash my fur before I came back."

Nashmarl butted his head against her cheek, trying to growl. "Me first!" he declared.

She stroked him soothingly. He was always so quick to get jealous, so constantly desperate for her attention.

"Did you grow today?" she asked him, knowing the question always made him puff out his little chest.

He nodded vehemently. "Me bigger than Foloth."

"Not!" Foloth said at once.

She jostled them gently in her arms to distract them from the quarrel, loving them so much it was an ache in her throat.

Nashmarl squirmed to get down. The moment she put him on the floor, he dropped to all fours and crawled rapidly across the cage to the rear corner. Gripping the ball she had made for them from some rags crudely wadded together and tied with twine, Nashmarl tossed it in the air and tried to catch it.

Foloth plucked at Ampris's arm. "Me down, Mama. Down!"

"All right, but just for a moment," she said, lowering him to the floor.

Tense with anticipation, she watched her cubs with only half her attention, glancing constantly at the doors.

Foloth, not as fast or as agile as Nashmarl, crawled to his brother and tried to pick up the ball. Growling, Nashmarl butted him hard in the side with his head, knocking Foloth over.

At once Foloth wailed, and Ampris had to pull them apart. While she was soothing Foloth and trying to correct Nashmarl, the doors opened.

Niruo came through, his eyes burning above an ugly welt

across his muzzle. He glared at them all, but they stood quietly in their cages. Ampris had coached them to offer him nothing to pick on tonight.

"What happened to your face?" Matiril asked, unable to keep quiet. "Little farewell caress from our Viis masters?"

Niruo's ears flattened to his skull, and he bared his rotting teeth. "I'm in charge!" he announced. "You all dependent on my care until Festival is over, so mind your ways."

"How 'bout some grub?" Paket asked gruffly.

Niruo tilted his head. "Hungry, are you? So what? This time I eat first, instead of waiting on you lot. In fact, I'm going to treat myself to real Viis rations."

"Hey!" Matiril said, shaking the front of his cage.

Ampris was afraid his door might swing open if he wasn't careful.

Niruo yipped at him, and the sound was ugly with derision. "For all I care, you can starve tonight."

Turning on his heel, he left.

The moment the doors shut and locked automatically, Matiril tilted back his head and yipped himself. "Can you believe how stupid that *nolo* is?"

"Never mind," Ampris said, swinging open her cage door and carrying her cubs out.

"Mama, where go?" Foloth asked. "Hungry."

"Me hungry more!" Nashmarl declared.

She hushed them. "We'll eat soon. You must be quiet now. Be good for Mama."

The others left their cages. Robuhl pointed at the animal cages on the other side of the room. "What about those poor creatures?"

"Forget them!" Matiril said impatiently.

Ampris glanced around. She hadn't planned for this. "Paket, prop your cage door open after we go through. I'll open their cages. It's up to them if they choose to follow us."

"They'll be in the way," Matiril argued.

"No. You'll all be out by the time I'm finished."

Paket nodded. Everyone stood there awkwardly, looking tense and anxious.

"You hit it good?" Paket asked. "The pipe?"

Ampris hesitated, wondering what to tell them.

Before she could reply, Paket said, "What happened? What went wrong?"

Groans went up, but Ampris shook her head at them. "The Zrheli are going to tamper with the main line—"

"The Zrheli!" Matiril said in horror. "They won't help us."

"Why'd you go to them?" Paket asked. "We said don't warn them, but you wouldn't listen—"

"See?" Matiril was yelling. "I knew it would go wrong. Always wanting to save folk. What they ever done for us? We can toss this idea good-bye—"

"Silence, all of you!" Ampris said sharply. "I think they will do what needs to be done."

"You think," Paket said, his eyes wide with disappointment. "Why—"

Robuhl coiled his tail around his leg. "Should we return to our cages and wait?"

"Stay where you are," Ampris said, but they were looking at her with resentment now, as though she had betrayed them. Ampris stared at the ceiling, willing the alarm to sound. "Come on. Come on," she muttered.

They waited, tense with anticipation, but nothing happened. Ampris swore silently to herself, and Nashmarl began to fuss. She licked him, trying to make him hush. The plan was that when the zeron gas escaped into the facility, the evacuation automatics would engage, unlocking all doors, including those to their outside runs. Paket's fence was rusted and weak. He had managed to break some of the wires and make a hole. If all went as planned, they would exit via Paket's cage and slip outside through the hole in the fence. Then they would only have to get themselves over the compound wall and head for the mountains in the falling twilight, hoping to be well-concealed in the wilderness before their absence was discovered.

But nothing happened. The plan was falling apart. Ampris wanted to howl.

"Come on," she whispered, trying to believe she hadn't been a fool for leaving this in the hands of the Zrheli.

Matiril growled restlessly, pacing back and forth. "It's not working. It's not working!"

Paket pulled him close and nipped his ear so hard Matiril yelped. "Shut up," he snarled. "We panic, and we be lost for sure."

They looked at each other, despair filling their eyes.

Ampris drew a deep breath, giving up. She'd been a fool. The Zrheli were probably laughing in their rookery at the trick they'd played. It was time for a contingency plan. "All right," she said. "We'll—"

A Klaxon blared, startling them all. Foloth and Nashmarl wailed with fright, burying their faces against Ampris's shoulders. The overhead lights flashed, went out, then came on red, bathing all of them in an eerie glow. The Klaxon continued blaring, an ugly, deafening sound that made the little animals go mad in their cages.

"Warning," a computerized voice announced over the speakers. "Hazardous conditions have been detected. All personnel to clear the facility. Warning. Hazardous conditions have been detected. Personnel have eight minutes to clear the area."

Someone in their group started sobbing while the red lights flashed over them. Paket reached out and gripped Ampris's arm so hard he nearly crushed it. She didn't care. Her heart was thumping in hope.

A hissing noise came from overhead. They all looked up and saw a white mist descending from the ceiling.

"Containment gas," Robuhl said. "Try not to breathe it."

They began to mill around. "We can't get out!" Matiril yelled.

Ampris wanted to bite him. If he panicked the others would also. "Keep your head, fool!" she shouted. "Paket, try your door. See if you can budge it."

"It's still locked," Matiril said furiously. "This isn't working. You've killed us, Ampris."

Paket, however, was already stepping into his cage. He put both hands on the latch of his outside door and yanked with all his might. But the door was not locked, although they had not heard the locks disengage. It sprang open so readily that Paket went sprawling.

Matiril yipped in excitement, forgetting his pessimism. He plunged into Paket's cage without heed for the others, who also tried to crowd inside.

Ampris grabbed at some of them, pulling them back. "Wait, wait," she said. "There's plenty of time. Remember the plan, and each of you take your turn."

They slowed down, but overhead came another announcement over the blaring Klaxon: "Warning. Hazardous conditions have been detected. Personnel have seven minutes to evacuate."

Ampris swung away to unlock the animal cages. The little creatures were hurling themselves about from side to side, harming themselves in their panic. One of them knocked open its cage door and went flying out. Others clawed frantically to follow suit.

Ampris stepped into one of the middle cages to open another outside door. The animals might not escape entirely, but at least they would be safer outside in the run than inside.

Then the doors to the wing opened, and Niruo stood there, screaming.

Ampris turned to face him with a growl.

His eyes were wide with fear and outrage as he bared his decayed teeth. "You can't do this!" he shouted. "You can't escape! I'm in charge!"

"We're going," Ampris told him. "There's a zeron gas leak. We'll all die if we stay here."

"Then die!" he snarled. "I'm in charge. They'll blame me if you escape."

"Not if you go with us," Ampris said.

Robuhl, who was at the end of the line exiting through Paket's cage, glanced back at her as he overheard. He opened his wide mouth to protest, then fell silent. Admiration for Ampris filled his eyes. "Mercy, even in the face of danger. Truly you do know the meaning of civilization."

Niruo didn't even hear the Myal. He shouted, "Join you? Become an escapee? Be caught and punished with you? Why should I?"

"Warning," the computer intoned. "Hazardous conditions have been detected. Personnel have six minutes to evacuate."

"Better to live as an escapee, than to die of radiation poisoning," Ampris said.

He snapped his teeth at her, growling with hatred. "The Viis trust me. They left me in charge. For the first time I have importance—"

Ampris felt pity for his illusions, but she had no time for kindness. The inmates were still filing outside. It was almost time for her to follow. With Foloth and Nashmarl tugging at her fur and wailing, she bounced them in her arms and said, "Niruo, face reality. You're in charge of nothing. This place has been left on automatic. You're as much a prisoner as we are. I know you want to feel important, and I'm sorry. But stop deluding yourself."

"You think I am not important?" Niruo yelled. "You think I can't call for help and bring patrollers from Lazmairehl?"

"Why bother?" Ampris said scathingly. "The computer will have already sent an emergency distress signal to the town. By the time help gets here, the place will be hot with radiation. No on can enter the site until it's decontaminated. By then, they'll think we're all dead. And we'll be gone where no one can find us."

"If I call Director Ehssk, you won't get away. They'll

come and hunt you down and make you beg for death.''

"Niruo, don't—"

Her cubs began to squabble for possession of the ball, distracting her. In exasperation, Ampris tried to take it from them, but the ball dropped to the floor. Foloth squirmed down from Ampris's arms to get it. She reached for him, but Niruo darted forward and grabbed up the cub so fast Foloth screamed in fright.

Ampris roared at him. "Niruo!"

But the Kelth whirled around with Foloth in his arms and ran back the way he'd come. Before Ampris could stop him, he was gone, taking what was more precious to her than life.

CHAPTER NINETEEN

She stood there, paralyzed with shock and horror.

"Ampris, come on!" Paket called. He gestured at slow old Robuhl to come outside. "We're all out! Come on!"

"He's got Foloth," she said, frantic. Knowing she had no choice, she set Nashmarl on the floor. Screaming, he clung hard to her, and she had to pry his little hands loose. "Robuhl, take care of Nashmarl for me."

Robuhl looked around in startlement, his mane swinging back from his face. "Ampris?"

Nashmarl wailed louder and reached up his arms to her, but Ampris was already running after Niruo and Foloth, desperate to get her other son back.

Robuhl and Paket both called after her, but Ampris didn't hear them. She thrust through the doors with her shoulder and plunged down the corridor toward the main reception area, limping on her crippled leg. Niruo had a head start on her, and she was too slow. She would never catch him in time. But she had to. The idea of his hurting Foloth, risking Foloth's life, enraged her past all caution or thought. She'd lost one cub to the evil in this place. She wasn't going to lose another.

From overhead, the computer's voice said, "Warning. You have five minutes to evacuate. You have four minutes and fifty-nine seconds to evacuate. You have four minutes and fifty-eight seconds to evacuate.''

Panting and ignoring the ache in her leg, she half ran, half hobbled, making her way toward the main section of the facility, knowing that Ehssk's office lay on the other side of it.

But before she reached the end of the corridor, she met a group of Viis clad in rags and ill-fitting body armor. Hooded and masked, they carried side arms, stun-sticks, bludgeons, and daggers, and were kicking in doors, smashing open storage bins, and yanking the security scanners off the wall in reception, causing great bursts of sparks as the wiring was snapped.

Bewildered, Ampris was knocked aside as more ran past her. She thudded into the wall and pressed herself against it to avoid being hit again. Who were they? Viis Rejects? Raiding the place?

She thought of riots and looters, and how the recent newscasts had been full of such trouble. Well, it didn't matter. She had to get to Foloth.

Limping past the entry air lock, she found it smashed and standing wide open. A blast of icy air and snow spilled inside. Ampris wondered if Niruo had gone that way.

Roaring in frustration, she paused long enough to sniff the air. No, his scent and Foloth's went the other way, toward Ehssk's office.

More bundled-up figures passed her, brandishing weapons and dragging loot. Someone had set fire to the padded benches in the reception area. Flames flared and grew, hungrily licking at the walls. More of the looters appeared, dumping their finds on the floor in front of the open air lock.

Pushing and shoving her way through them, Ampris ignored the mingled shouting of Viis and abiru voices. She got to the opposite side of reception and headed up the hall, oblivious to its fine carpeting and the awards of distinction hanging on the walls.

A Reject pushed past her, grabbing the awards and throwing them into a crude sack.

"You!" a gruff voice called to her as she went on. "Stop!"

An argument broke out behind her, but Ampris didn't pay it any heed, nor did she slow down.

Gritting her teeth against the pain, she forced herself on and reached the expensive wooden door of Ehssk's office. She could hear Foloth wailing inside and Niruo's voice, shrill with hysteria as he called for help on the linkup. Trying to open the door, Ampris found it locked.

Fury swept her like flame. Throwing back her head, Ampris roared and hurled her shoulder at the door, breaking through and falling inside as splintered wood rained down on top of her.

Niruo yelped and leaped back from the ornate desk, panic wide in his eyes.

Picking herself up, Ampris roared at him again and advanced. She barely saw Foloth sitting on top of the desk, wailing with all his might. She barely heard him. All she could focus on was Niruo, who had tried to harm her cub. Her blood burned in her and she bared her fangs, then leaped at him.

Her crippled leg threw her off balance, and Niruo was able to scramble away from her. He scuttled around the end of the desk, keeping it between them, and grabbed Foloth by his thin arm.

Ampris roared and lunged bodily across the desk, but her fingers missed Foloth by centimeters. Clutching Foloth against his chest, Niruo cursed her and ran, only to collide with a looter in the doorway.

"Hey!" shouted the looter. "Watch where you're going, you lop-eared—"

"My cub!" Ampris yelled in desperation. "Get my cub away from him!"

The slight figure in the doorway was shoved aside by a taller Reject, who hit Niruo with a stun-stick.

Screaming, Niruo toppled over, and Foloth's wails went abruptly silent.

Ampris's heart stopped. She came around the desk, flinging aside the slim Kelth who was kneeling over Niruo, and ignoring his startled, "Goldie? That you?"

Ampris rolled Niruo's paralyzed body over and pulled Foloth out from under him. The cub was alive. His eyes were huge in his misshapen face, and although his mouth stayed open he made no sound. Ampris sniffed him and felt his arms and legs rapidly, finding no injuries. She thumped him on his back, and heard the air whoosh back into his lungs.

Foloth screwed up his face and yelled with all his might.

Relief overwhelmed her. She clutched his little body tight and rocked him, weeping with joy.

The Kelth gripped her shoulder, shaking her, spinning her around. "Goldie! Goldie, you're alive!"

She stared at Elrabin, unable to believe he was there. Surely she was hallucinating. Maybe the zeron was starting to get to her; she could smell the companion gas, thick enough now to make her choke and sneeze. Elrabin could not possibly be here, not now, not when she most needed him. Yet it was his narrow face she saw. It was his hand gripping her arm. "You," she said in amazement, staring up at him over the top of Foloth's head. A broad grin parted her jaws. "You!"

Elrabin yipped, his eyes dancing. "Hey, Goldie. Looks like you didn't need no rescue after all."

"Rescue!" she said, her astonishment growing. "You came for me?"

Behind him she glimpsed more shadowy figures bustling back and forth. One of them ran inside the office, brandishing an emergency ax. "Anything worth stealing in here?"

Ampris opened her mouth, but Elrabin glanced around and said, "Lots. This be the jackpot. We'll clear out, see, and let you get to it."

As he, Ampris, and Foloth went outside into the hallway, the computer blared overhead: "Warning, you have two minutes and nine seconds to evacuate. Warning, you have two minutes and eight seconds to evacuate."

"What's happening here, Goldie?" Elrabin asked, his gaze darting around while one Reject ripped out the linkup with a shower of sparks and the one with the ax started hacking open the desk.

Ampris drew in a rapid breath. "Zeron gas leak. We have to—"

"Zeron!" Elrabin yipped. He yanked her away from the door. "We gotta get out. Now!"

Ampris clutched Foloth tight, praying the others were safely away. She started limping down the hallway as fast as she could while Elrabin darted back to Ehssk's office.

Elrabin leaned inside. "Ruoyon!" he yelled. "Tell Sollusk it's a zeron leak. The whole reactor may go."

Then he caught up with Ampris and put his hand in the center of her back to move her faster. "Come on, Goldie. Let's pick it up."

"Warning," the computer said. "One minute and two seconds to evacuate. One minute and one second to evacuate. One minute to evacuate."

Ampris's leg gave under her. She stumbled, grunting heavily, and barely caught herself from falling. Elrabin gripped her arm with both hands and pulled her upright, while she hung on to Foloth.

"Come on," he panted. "Gods, zeron! Come on!"

Ampris staggered forward, panting with pain. Her leg was dragging, failing to support her.

"Go on," she said, trying to hand Foloth to Elrabin while the cub spat and snapped at him. "Save my son—"

"Save him yourself," Elrabin said, putting his shoulder under her arm to support her and moving her forward. "You think I been through what I been through just to walk out on you now? What kind of stupid *nolo* you think I am?"

Tears stung her eyes, and she wanted to hug him in gratitude. But there was no time for that. Gritting her teeth against the agony, she struggled on as fast as she could while the computer continued relentlessly:

"Forty-nine seconds. Forty-eight seconds. Forty-seven seconds."

"Get out! Get out!" Elrabin yelled at the looters as they reached the reception section. But no one paid him much attention except to curse at him. Shrugging, Elrabin headed for the double air locks, urging Ampris on with every struggling step. He squinted against the snow blowing into their faces. "You do this?"

Ampris grinned with pride. "Yeah."

He patted her side. "Good going, Goldie. Make something of you yet, see?"

Ampris looked back in worry as the looters failed to follow them outside. "Your friends have to get out—"

"Ain't no friends of mine," Elrabin said grimly, panting as they stumbled outside into the deep snow. "Took all my charm and wit to get them here in the first place."

"But—"

"Drop it. I'll explain someday, but this ain't the time."

The cold air was a refreshing blast. Ampris gulped in air, her breath steaming around her face, and concentrated on forcing one more step, and then one more. The compound gates stood wide open ahead of them. She saw Toth guards lying sprawled on the ground.

"Out the gate," she said, gasping for air. "My friends . . . my other cub . . . keep going."

"You got that," Elrabin agreed, glancing back.

Ampris glanced back also and saw looters streaming forth in all directions, black silhouettes against the fire now raging through one side of the central building. An explosion rocked the facility, throwing looters in all directions.

A fireball whooshed upward into the night sky, and debris and ashes swirled through the falling snow. Then the blast's concussion reached Ampris and knocked her and

Elrabin sprawling. Curling her arms protectively around Foloth, Ampris rolled over and over until her back thudded against something hard and immovable.

For a moment she lay there senseless, Foloth wailing in her arms, then she came to and lifted herself on her elbows, shaking her head to clear it.

Elrabin lay beside her, groaning and rooting his face in the snow until with a snort he lifted his muzzle and shook himself. Blood dripped down his face.

"We alive?" he asked.

She tugged on one of his tall ears, still so glad to see him she couldn't find the words she wanted. "Think so."

He started coughing and dragged himself upright with another groan. "You okay?"

"Yes," she answered, although her leg felt like it was on fire. She'd overtaxed the weak muscles, but right now that hardly mattered. "Help me up. We have to find the others."

"Others?" he echoed in bewilderment while the fire roared across the roof of the building behind them. "What others?"

Worried about Nashmarl, Ampris was already on her feet, limping along and nearly falling. She could no longer put her weight on her left leg at all. Drawing it up, she hopped forward, struggling in the ankle-deep snow until Elrabin joined her and put his shoulder under her arm again.

"Okay, okay," he said. "We'll find them."

Outside the compound, the wind cut through Ampris's pelt mercilessly. She squinted her eyes and lowered her head against it, worried about Foloth, wishing she had a blanket to wrap him in.

"Elrabin, give me your coat please."

He shucked it off and she wrapped shivering little Foloth in its folds, tucking one end over his bare head. He was still crying, his tiny hands clutching her. She murmured to him, trying to soothe him, and knew she had to find Nashmarl before he froze in the snowstorm.

She looked around, trying to get her bearings. The snow swirled into her face, clinging to her ears and eyelashes, clumping on her shoulders. By the light of the fire sweeping through the buildings, she could see the mountain range, and that gave her the bearings she wanted.

"This way," she said.

They trudged in that direction, but before they'd struggled many steps, a shout caught their attention.

Looking back, Ampris saw a cluster of huddled figures surrounded by looters. Her heart clutched and she turned around. "There they are."

"Who?"

"My friends," Ampris said.

Elrabin muttered something under his breath. "Ain't mine."

The group met them halfway. A tall Reject held Niruo at his side, but when Ampris reached them, he shoved Niruo forward to join the others. They swarmed Ampris, all talking at once.

She smiled and nodded, paying no attention until she saw that Robuhl held Nashmarl safely in his arms. A little sigh of relief escaped her, and she gestured for Robuhl to come to her.

Grinning as broadly as possible, Robuhl stumped toward her on his bowed legs. "We got out, Ampris!" he said in triumph.

Paket's chest was puffed out, and Matiril was yipping to the night sky. No one seemed to care about the cold or the snow. They were too excited, too happy.

"Elrabin!" the Reject leader said sharply.

Elrabin flinched, but he stepped forward. "Yes?"

"Is that your famous Ampris, there with you?"

"Yeah, Sollusk. She's the one," Elrabin said.

The Reject pushed back his hood slightly and stared at her. "Ampris the Crimson Claw, the most famous gladiator in the empire," he said. His voice was flat, carrying little admiration.

Caution made the fur bristle around Ampris's neck. She noticed how carefully Elrabin held himself, and understood that this Sollusk was someone to be feared.

She met his gaze through the snow and shadows with her head high, looking fearless while she cradled Foloth in her arms. "I am Ampris," she said. "For your actions in helping to destroy Vess Vaas, I thank you."

Sollusk accepted the compliment with a tilt of his head. "And these pathetic creatures?" he asked, gesturing at the huddled band of escapees.

Ampris saw that they were starting to shiver, as was she. "My friends," she said. "We're going over the mountains, to seek the village of free abiru."

Sollusk's laughter was hoarse and mocking. "Long walk. Better off if you go to Lazmairehl, live in the Skugvo with us."

Elrabin's hand surreptitiously gripped hers in the darkness and squeezed hard, but Ampris needed no warning.

"No, thank you," she said clearly, understanding that Sollusk probably meant to turn them in for any reward the authorities might offer. "You are generous and kind, but we are set on the course we have chosen. Will you spare us blankets, or food? We can give you nothing in return but our gratitude."

Beside her, Elrabin rolled his eyes and muttered something, but Ampris went on meeting the Reject's gaze. She held her breath, not sure what he might do.

Sollusk pointed at Nashmarl, shivering in Robuhl's arms. "What spawned such an abhorrent creature?"

Ampris bared her teeth, but she managed to hold her anger in check. "The cub is mine."

The Reject flinched, and murmuring broke out among his band. Ampris held to her pride and reached out her free arm for her son. "Give him to me, Robuhl. Thank you for taking care of him."

The old Myal handed the shivering cub over. Nashmarl clung to her, burying his face against the warmth of her neck. She inhaled his scent, grateful he was safe.

"That cub is not Aaroun, and not Viis," Sollusk said harshly. "It is not anything. Who permitted it life?"

Ampris's anger boiled in her. Backing her ears, she said, "No matter how these cubs were created, they are mine. No one may say they cannot live. No one may say they should not be seen. We do not hide our cubs away. We do not reject them if they are not beautiful. The way of the Viis is not our way."

Sollusk flicked out his tongue, accepting her rebuke. "You speak boldly to me. Do you know that—"

"Yes, you are a Reject," she said fearlessly. "I know this. I think it is wrong of the Viis, to treat their own so harshly."

Again murmuring ran through the band of looters. Their leader lifted his hand to silence them. "Very well, Ampris. You show no fear. You speak like a warrior, and this I can respect."

"Shut up!" Niruo suddenly yelped. He shoved Matiril aside and stumbled away from the others, waving a side arm that made everyone come alert. "All of you, shut up!"

"Where did he get that?" Elrabin asked.

Ampris didn't take her gaze away from Niruo, who had trained the side arm on her. Holding her cubs tight, she glared at the Kelth and growled. Both Foloth and Nashmarl stopped crying instantly, instinctively knowing to stay quiet. "From Ehssk's office," she guessed.

Niruo yipped like one gone mad. "The Viis left me in charge. I will not let you get away with this. You—"

"Put it down," Ampris said to him. "You're guarding nothing. The lab is destroyed."

"No!" he yelled. "I have nowhere else to go. This is your fault, Ampris. I blame you for—"

Elrabin growled and tried to step in front of Ampris, but she half turned and handed her cubs to him. His ears swiveled back in protest, but he could do nothing about it—he was too busy juggling the squirming cubs, who spat and howled at him.

Ampris faced Niruo. "Put down the side arm," she said. "It's over, Niruo. Everything is over."

His eyes shifted and gleamed, catching reflections from the distant firelight. "They left me in charge," he whimpered.

Sollusk said something in disgust, but Ampris never took her gaze off Niruo. "Put it down," she said, limping one step toward him. "I know you hate me, but I am not your enemy."

Niruo's hand wavered, then another part of Vess Vaas exploded, making them all duck instinctively. Niruo fired, missing Ampris, who dodged with her old hair-trigger instincts. Elrabin yelped. Ampris whirled around in time to see him stagger and fall, his leg smoking from being hit. As he fell, he dropped the cubs, who bounced and tucked themselves instinctively so that they tumbled over and over in the snow.

Rage burst inside Ampris. She turned on Niruo with a roar that made his eyes widen. Staggering back, he lifted the side arm to fire again, but Ampris launched herself in the old Wind as Air move that had once made her famous in the arena. She leaped up and over the bright flash of deadly plasma fire and extended her right arm with her elbow locked. Niruo screamed, and Ampris hit him in the throat with her fist, bringing him down with her body.

His scream cut off abruptly, and his head snapped sideways. They hit the ground, but Niruo lay motionless beneath her. His neck was broken.

Ampris rolled off him, tried to stand, and staggered on her crippled leg. Pulling herself upright, she found herself facing Sollusk, who gestured to her in profound respect.

"Never have I seen such a move," he said. "You are more than a warrior, Ampris. It would not be wise to offend you. We will give you the assistance you ask."

Before she could answer, he turned away and snapped

out orders to his band to parcel out some of the loot, especially food rations and protective gear. The others stared at Ampris in awed silence. Matiril's mouth hung open, and Paket was nodding his head.

Ampris turned to check her cubs, scooping them out of the snow and licking their faces to reassure them before kneeling beside Elrabin.

He lay there, panting, his eyes squinted with pain. He had already packed snow on his leg wound, the best possible emergency treatment. "I think it's a graze," he said, wincing. "Didn't take my leg off."

Relieved, Ampris pressed her hand to his shoulder, letting the gesture convey what mere words could not. Kneeling there in the snow, while the lab burned steadily, shooting up smoke and ashes, she felt as though she had reached a distant place after a long, long journey.

Elrabin touched the Eye of Clarity swinging around her neck. "We did it," he said, trying to laugh and wincing again. "We're free, Goldie. Just got to climb a mountain with my busted leg and yours, and what's that? Hey, freedom. Sounds good, don't it?"

"It sounds very good."

He sighed, parting his jaws in a grin. "It's over at last."

Ampris straightened. "No, Elrabin," she said gently and lifted her gaze toward the mountains looming dark and massive beyond the flying snow. Her heart swelled with emotion. "Freedom means it's far from over. We are just beginning."